KILO CLASS

KILO CLASS

Patrick Robinson

C

CENTURY · LONDON

Published in the United Kingdom in 1998 by Century

1 3 5 7 9 10 8 6 4 2

First published in the United Kingdom in 1998 by Century
Random House UK Ltd
20 Vauxhall Bridge Road, London, SW1V 2SA

Random House Australia (Pty) Limited
20 Alfred Street, Milsons Point, Sydney, New South Wales 2061, Australia

Random House New Zealand Limited
18 Poland Road, Glenfield
Auckland 10, New Zealand

Random House South Africa (Pty) Limited
Endulini, 5a Jubilee Road, Parktown, 2193, South Africa

Random House UK Limited Reg. No. 954009

A CIP catalogue record for this book
is available from the British Library

Illustrations by ML Design

Papers used by Random House UK Limited
are natural, recyclable products made from wood grown in
sustainable forests. The manufacturing processes conform to
the environmental regulations of the country of origin

Phototypeset in Bembo by Intype London Ltd
Printed and bound in the United Kingdom by
Mackays of Chatham PLC, Chatham, Kent

ISBN 0 7126 7887 5 – Hardback
ISBN 0 7126 7966 9 – Paperback

This book is respectfully dedicated to the US Navy's Submarine Service – to the men who wear the dolphins, and who operate in the deepest waters.

ACKNOWLEDGEMENTS

My principal advisor for this second novel was Admiral Sir John 'Sandy' Woodward, the Battle Group Commander of the Royal Navy Task Force in the 1982 Falkland Islands War. After the battle in the South Atlantic, he was Flag Officer Submarines, and in later years he became Commander-in-Chief Naval Home Command. It would scarcely have been possible to work with a more knowledgeable and experienced officer, the only man to have fought a major sea battle in the last 40 years.

KILO CLASS is a thriller about submarines, which required months and months of planning. My office was permanently engulfed by charts, maps and reference books, in the middle of which stood Admiral Sandy, relishing the weaving of the various plots. I was actually quite surprised at his devious cunning, and careful attention to the smallest detail. Generally speaking I think the West should be profoundly glad he's not Chinese.

I also owe a debt of gratitude to Lesley Chamberlain, the English author of the most beautifully-written, scholarly book about Russia, VOLGA VOLGA. Lesley guided me and my Kilo-Class submarines all along the great river, and was more than generous recounting her memories of days spent as a lecturer in the tour ships of the Russian lakes.

In the USA I was assisted by a great many Naval officers, many of them still serving. I am deeply grateful for the many hours they all spent checking my work, correcting my errors, keeping me "real."

To them, I owe much. But to Admiral Sandy, I owe the book.

Patrick Robinson

AUTHOR'S NOTE

S HE WAS ONCE a familiar sight on all of the ocean waters which surround the European coastline: the 240-foot-long Soviet-built Kilo-Class patrol submarine, barreling along the surface, her ESM mast raised, usually with a few crew members huddled on the bridge beneath the old ensign of the USSR . . . she was a jet-black symbol of Soviet seapower.

Throughout the final 10 years of the Cold War, the Kilo was deployed in all Russian waters, and sometimes far beyond. She patrolled the Baltic, the North Atlantic, the White Sea, the Barents Sea, the Mediterranean, the Black Sea, and even the Pacific, the Bering Sea and the Sea of Japan, off the big Soviet base in Vladi-vostok.

At 3,000 tons dived, the Kilo is by no means a big submarine – the Soviet Typhoons are 21,000-tonners. But there is a menace about this robust little diesel-electric SSK because, carefully handled, she can be as quiet as the grave.

Stealth is the watchword of all submarines. And of all the under-water warriors, the Kilo is one of the most stealthy. Unlike a big nuclear boat, she has no reactor requiring the support of numerous mechanical subsystems, all potential noise-makers.

The Kilo can run, unseen, beneath the surface at speeds up to 17 knots, on electric motors, powered by her huge battery. At low speeds, the soft hum of her power-unit is almost indiscernible. In fact the only time the Russian Kilo is at any serious risk of detection – save by active sonar – is when she comes to periscope depth to recharge her battery.

When she executes this operation, she runs her diesel engines – a process known in the trade as 'snorkeling,' or, in the Royal Navy, 'snorting.' At this point she can be heard, she can be picked up on radar, the ions in the diesel exhaust can be 'sniffed,' she can even be seen, and there is little she can do about it.

Just as a car engine needs an intake of oxygen, so do the two internal combustion diesel generators in a submarine. She must have air. And she must come up to periscope depth at least in order to get it. That's when she is most vulnerable to detection, which is why a patrolling Kilo, in hostile waters, snorkels only when she must, to keep her giant battery charged. Even then she will only snorkel at night – to reduce the chance of being seen – and for the shortest possible time, to minimize the chance of being heard and pin-pointed for attack.

The battery gives the Kilo a range of some 400 miles, running slowly and silently, before she needs to recharge. She can travel 6,000 miles 'snorkeling' before refueling. It takes only 52 crew (13 officers) to run her as a front-line fighting unit. As well as a small battery of short range surface-to-air missiles (SAMs), she carries up to 24 torpedoes, two of which are routinely fitted with nuclear warheads.

Today, however, the Kilo is rarely seen on the world's oceans flying the Russian flag. Since the shocking demise of the Soviet Navy in the early 1990s, the Kilo has mostly been confined to moribund Russian Navy yards. There are only two Kilos in the Black Sea, two in the Baltic, six in the Northern Fleet and some fourteen in the Pacific Fleet.

And yet this sinister little submarine still serves her country. She is now being built almost entirely for export, and no warship in all the world is more in demand. The huge income derived from the sale of the 'new, improved, even quieter Kilo,' pays a lot of bills for a near-bankrupt Navy, and keeps a small section of the Russian Fleet mobile.

The Russians, however, have demonstrated a somewhat alarming tendency to sell the Kilo-Class to *anyone* with a large enough checkbook: they cost $300 million each.

And while no one minded particularly when Poland and Romania bought one each, nor indeed when Algeria bought a couple, secondhand, a few eyebrows were raised when India ordered eight of them. But India is not seen as a potential threat to the West.

It was Iran which caused deep worry. And despite a bold attempt at intervention by the Americans, the Ayatollahs managed to get hold of two Kilos, delivered somewhat mysteriously by the

Russians. They immediately ordered a third, which is scheduled soon to arrive in the Gulf port of Bandar Abbas.

All of this, however, paled into insignificance with the entry of a new and deadly serious player in the international navy build-up game. Because this was a nation which had built the world's third largest fleet of warships in less than 20 years; a nation with 250,000 personnel in her naval yards, and an unbridled ambition to join the superpowers.

And this is a nation with a known capacity to operate submarines, and a known capacity to produce a nuclear warhead of sufficient sophistication to fit into a torpedo.

A nation which suddenly, against the expressed wishes to the contrary of the United States of America, ordered 10 Russian-built Kilo-Class diesel-electric submarines.

China.

CAST OF PRINCIPAL CHARACTERS

Senior Command

The President of the United States (Commander-in-Chief US Armed Forces)

Vice-Admiral Arnold Morgan (National Security Advisor)

Admiral Scott F. Dunsmore (Chairman of the Joint Chiefs)

Harcourt Travis (Secretary of State)

Rear-Admiral George R. Morris (Director, National Security Agency)

US Navy Senior Command

Admiral Joseph Mulligan (Chief of Naval Operations)

Vice-Admiral John F. Dixon (Commander Atlantic Submarine Force)

Rear-Admiral John Bergstrom (Commander Special War Command [SPECWARCOM])

USS *Columbia*

Commander Cale 'Boomer' Dunning (Commanding Officer)

Lieutenant Commander Mike Krause (Executive Officer)

Lieutenant Commander Lee O'Brien (Marine Engineering Officer)

Chief Petty Officer Rick Ames (Lieutenant Commander O'Brien's Number Two)

Petty Officer Earl Connard (Chief Mechanic)

Lieutenant Commander Jerry Curran (Combat Systems Officer)

Lieutenant Bobby Ramsden (Sonar Officer)

Lieutenant David Wingate (Navigation Officer)

Lieutenant Abe Dickson (Officer of the Deck)

US Navy SEALs

Lieutenant Commander Rick Hunter (SEAL Team Leader and Mission Controller)

Lieutenant Junior Grade Ray Schaeffer
Chief Petty Officer Fred Cernic
Petty Officer Harry Starck
Seaman Jason Murray

US Air Force B–52H Bomber
Lieutenant Colonel Al Jaxtimer (Pilot, Fifth Bomb Wing, Minot
   Air Base, North Dakota)
Major Mike Parker (Co-pilot)
Lieutenant Chuck Ryder (Navigator)

Central Intelligence Agency
Frank Reidel (Head of Far Eastern Desk)
Carl Chimei (Field Agent, Taiwan Submarine Base)
Angela Rivera (Field Agent, Eastern Europe and Moscow)

Military High Command of China
The Paramount Ruler (Commander-in-Chief People's Liberation
   Army)
General Qiao Jiyun (Chief of General Staff)
Admiral Zhang Yushu (Commander-in-Chief People's Liberation
   Army–Navy [PLAN])
Vice-Admiral Sang Ye (Chief of Naval Staff)
Vice-Admiral Yibo Yunsheng (Commander, East Sea Fleet)
Vice-Admiral Zu Jicai (Commander, South Sea Fleet)
Vice-Admiral Yang Zhenying (Political Commissar)
Captain Kan Yu-fang (Senior Submarine Commanding Officer)

Russian Navy
Admiral Vitaly Rankov (Chief of the Main Staff)
Lieutenant Commander Levitsky
Lieutenant Commander Kazakov

Russian Seamen
Captain Igor Volkov (*Tolkach* master)
Ivan Volkov (his son and for'ard helmsman)
Colonel Karpov (Senior Officer on the *Mikhail Lermontov*)
Colonel Borsov (former KGB staff, Senior Officer on the *Yuri
   Andropov*)
Pieter (Wine Steward)
Torbin (Head Waiter)

Passengers on Russian Tour Ships
Jane Westenholz (from Greenwich, Connecticut)
Cathy Westenholz (her daughter)

Russian Diplomat
Nikolai Ryabinin (Ambassador to Washington)

Taiwan Nuclear Planning Group
The President of Taiwan
General Jin-chung Chow (Minister for National Defense)
Professor Liao Lee (National Taiwan University)
Chiang Yi (construction mogul, Taipei)

Crew of *Yonder*
Commander Cale 'Boomer' Dunning
Jo Dunning
Lieutenant Commander Bill Baldridge
Laura Anderson
Roger Mills
Gavin Bates
Jeff Hewitt
Thwaites Masters

Ship's Company *Cuttyhunk*
Captain Tug Mottram (Senior Commanding Officer, Woods Hole
    Oceanographic Institute)
Bob Lander (Second-in-Command)
Kit Berens (Navigator)
Dick Elkins (Radio Operator)

Scientists *Cuttyhunk*
Professor Henry Townsend (Team Leader)
Professor Roger Deakins (Senior Oceanographer)
Dr Kate Goodwin (MIT/Woods Hole)

Newspaper Reporter
Frederick J. Goodwin (*Cape Cod Times*)

PROLOGUE

September 7, 2003

THE FOUR-CAR MOTORCADE scarcely slowed as it turned into the West Executive Avenue entrance to number 1,600, Pennsylvania Avenue. Guards waved them straight through, and the four Secret Service agents in the leading automobile nodded curtly. Behind them followed two Pentagon staff limousines, with Navy guards in the front passenger seats. One more car-load of Secret Servicemen brought up the rear.

At the entrance to the West Wing, four more of the 35 White House duty agents were waiting. As the men from the Pentagon stepped from the cars, each of them was issued with a personal identity badge, except for the Chairman of the Joint Chiefs, Admiral Scott F. Dunsmore, who had a permanent pass.

From the same limousine stepped the towering figure of Admiral Joseph Mulligan, the former commanding officer of a Trident nuclear submarine and now the Chief of Naval Operations (CNO), the professional head of the US Navy.

The third man was Vice-Admiral Arnold Morgan, the brilliant, irascible Director of the super-secret National Security Agency in Fort Meade, Maryland.

The second staff car contained the two senior submarine Flag Officers in the US Navy: Vice-Admiral John F. Dixon, Commander Submarines Atlantic Fleet, and Rear-Admiral Johnny Barry, Commander Submarines Pacific Fleet. Both men had been summoned to Washington in the small hours of that morning. It was now 4.30 p.m., and there was a semblance of cool in the afternoon air.

It was rare to see five such senior military figures, fully uniformed, at the White House at one time. There was an underlying aura of authority about the Chairman, flanked on either side by senior commanders. In many countries it might have given the appearance of an impending military coup. Right here, in the home

I

of the US President, it merely caused much subservient nodding of heads by the Secret Servicemen.

The President may nominally carry the title of Commander-in-Chief, but these were the men who operated the front-line muscle of United States military power: the great carrier battle groups with their air-strike forces which patrol the world's oceans, and the nuclear submarine strike force.

These men also had much to do with the operation of the presidency. The Navy itself runs Camp David, and indeed is entrusted with the life of the President, controlling directly the private, bullet-proof presidential suite at the Bethesda Naval Hospital in the event of an emergency.

The 89th Airlift Wing, under the control of Air Mobility Command, runs the private presidential aircraft, the Boeing 747 Air Force One. The US Marines provide all presidential helicopters. The US Army provides all White House cars and drivers. The Defense Department provides all communications.

When the Chairman of the Joint Chiefs arrives, accompanied by his senior commanders, these are not mere visitors. These are the most trusted men in the United States of America, men whose standing and awesome authority will survive political upheaval, even a change of presidency. They are men who are not intimidated by civilian power; men to whom any President must accord due deference.

And on this sunlit late summer afternoon, the 43rd US President stood before the motionless flags of the Navy, the Marines and the Air Force to greet them as they entered the Oval Office.

He smiled and addressed each one of them by his first name, including the Pacific submarine commander whom he had not met. To him he extended his right hand and said, warmly, 'Johnny, I've heard a great deal about you. Delighted to meet you at last.'

They took their seats in five wooden 'captain's' chairs arrayed before the great desk of America's Chief Executive.

'Mr President,' said Admiral Dunsmore. 'We got a problem.'

'I guessed so, Scott.'

'It's one we've touched upon before, but never with any degree of urgency, because basically we thought it probably would not happen. But right now it's happening.'

'Go on.'

'The 10 Russian Kilo-Class submarines ordered by China.'

2

'Of which they have taken delivery of two in five years, right?'

'Yessir. We now think the rest will be delivered in the next nine months. Eight of them, all of which are well on their way to completion in various Russian shipyards.'

'Can we live with just the two already in place?'

'Yessir. Just. Because that means they are unlikely to have more than one operational at a time. But no more. If they take delivery of the final eight they will have the capability of blockading the Taiwan Strait, with a fleet of three or even five Kilos on permanent operational duty. That would shut everyone out, including us. They'd retake and occupy Taiwan militarily in a matter of months.'

'Jesus.'

'If those Kilos are there,' said Admiral Mulligan, 'we would not dare send a US carrier in. Because they'd be waiting. They could actually hit us – then plead we were invading Chinese waters with a battle group, that we had no right to be in there.'

'Hmmm. Do we have a solution?'

'Yessir. They must not be allowed to take delivery of the final eight Kilos.'

'You mean we persuade the Russians not to fulfill the order?'

'Nossir,' said Admiral Morgan. 'That is unlikely to work. We've been trying. It's like trying to persuade a goddamned drug addict he doesn't need money.'

'Then what do we do?'

'We use other methods of persuasion, sir. One at a time, until they abandon the idea of Russian submarines.'

'You mean . . .'

'Yessir.'

'But that will cause an international uproar.'

'It would, sir,' replied Admiral Morgan. 'If anyone knew who had done what to whom. But they're not going to know.'

'Will I know?'

'Not necessarily. We probably would not bother you about the mysterious disappearance of a few foreign diesel-electric submarines.'

'Gentlemen, I believe this is what you describe as a black operation?'

'Yessir. Non-attributable,' replied the CNO.

'Do you require my official permission?'

'We need you to be with us, on the leading edge of the intelli-

3

gence, sir,' said Admiral Dunsmore. 'But if you were to forbid such a course of action, we would of course respect that. In time, however, we will require something official. Right before we move.'

'Gentlemen, as always, I trust your judgment. Please proceed as you think fit. Scott, keep me posted.'

And with that, the President very deliberately terminated the conversation. He rose and shook hands with each of the five senior commanders. And he watched them stride from the Oval Office, feeling himself, as ever, like a little boy in the presence of such men. And he pondered again the terrible responsibilities which were visited upon him in this place.

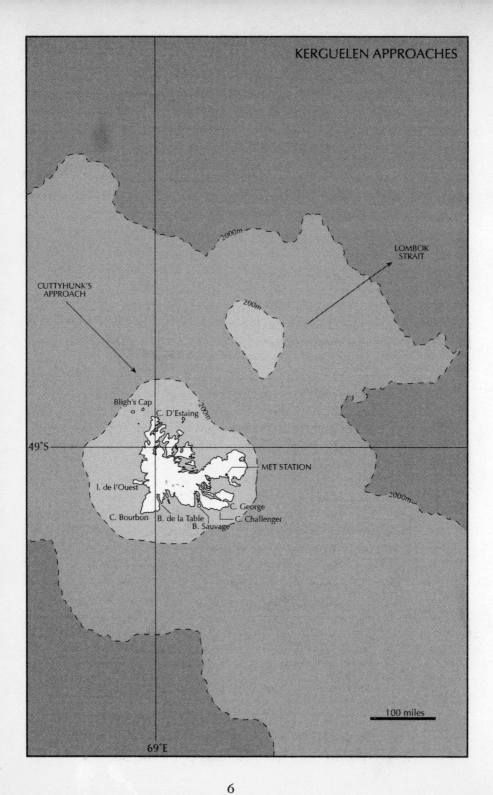

KERGUELEN APPROACHES

LOMBOK
STRAIT

2000m

200m

CUTTYHUNK'S
APPROACH

Bligh's Cap

C. D'Estaing

200m

49°S

MET STATION

I. de l'Ouest

C. George

C. Bourbon   B. de la Table   C. Challenger

B. Sauvage

2000m

100 miles

69°E

6

CHAPTER ONE

I

CAPTAIN TUG MOTTRAM could almost feel the barometric pressure rising. The wind, which had roared for two days out of the northwest at around 40 knots, was now, suddenly, increasing to 50 knots and more as it backed. The first snow flurries were already being blown across the heaving, rearing, lead-colored sea, and every 40 seconds gigantic ocean swells, a half-mile across, surged up behind them. The wind and the mountainous confused sea had moved from user-friendly to lethal in under 15 minutes . . . as it often does in the fickle atmospherics of the Southern Ocean, especially along the howling outer corridor of the Roaring Forties, before which *Cuttyhunk* now ran crosswind, gallantly, toward the southeast.

Tug Mottram had ordered the ship battened down two days ago. All watertight doors were closed and clipped. Fan intakes were shut off. No one was permitted on the upper deck aft of the bridge. And now the Captain gazed out ahead, through snow which suddenly became sleet, slashing sideways across his already small horizon. The wipers on the big wheelhouse windows could cope. Just. But astern the situation was deteriorating, as the huge seas from the northwest were made more menacing by the violent cross-seas from the beam, and now seemed intent on hunting down and engulfing the 279-foot steel-hulled research ship from Woods Hole, Massachusetts.

'Decrease speed to 12 knots,' he said. 'We don't wanna run even one knot faster than the sea. Not with the rear-end design of this bastard.'

'You ever broached, sir?' asked the young navigation officer, Kit Berens, his dark, handsome features set in a deep frown.

'Damn right. In a sea like this. Going just too fast.'

7

'Christ. Did the wave break right over you?'

'Sure did. Pooped her right out. About a billion tons of green water crashed over the stern, buried the rear gun deck *and* the flight deck, and then flooded down the starboard side. Swung us right around, with the rudders clear out of the water. Next wave hit us amidships. I thought we were gone.'

'Jesus. What kind of a ship was it?'

'US Navy destroyer. Spruance. Eight thousand tons. And yes, Kit, I was driving her. Matter of fact it makes me downright nervous even to think about it. Twelve years later.'

'Was it down here in the Antarctic, sir? Like us?'

'Uh-uh. We were in the Pacific. Far south. But not this far.'

'How the hell did she survive it?'

'Oh, those Navy warships are unbelievably stable. She heeled right over, plowed forward and came up again right way. Not like this baby. She'll go straight to the bottom if we fuck it up.'

'Jesus,' said Kit Berens, gazing with awe at the giant wall of water which now seemed to tower permanently above *Cuttyhunk*'s highly vulnerable, low-slung aft section. 'We're just like a cork compared to a destroyer. What d'we do?'

'We just keep running. A coupla knots slower than the sea. Stay in tight control of the rudders. Keep 'em under. Hold her course stern on to the bigger swells. Look for shelter in the lee of the islands.'

Outside the wind was gusting violently up to 70 knots as the deep low-pressure area, sweeping eastward around the Antarctic, continued to cause the day-long almost friendly northwester to back around, first to the west, and now, in the last five minutes, to the cold southwest.

The sea was at once huge and confused, the prevailing ocean swells from the northwest colliding with the rising storm conditions from the southwest. The area of these fiercely rough seas was relatively small given the vastness of the Southern Ocean, but that was little comfort to Tug Mottram and his men as they climbed 80-foot waves. Because *Cuttyhunk* was right in the middle of it, and she was taking a serious pounding.

The sleet changed back to snow, and within moments the gunwales on the starboard bow were gathering small white drifts. But they were only fleeting because the great sea kept hurling tons of frigid water onto the foredeck. In the split second it took for the ocean spray to fly against the for'ard bulkhead, it turned to ice, and Tug Mottram, peering through the window, could see the tiny bright particles ricochet off the portside winch. He guessed the still-air temperature on deck had dropped to about minus five degrees centigrade – with the wind-chill of a force-10 storm, the real temperature out there was probably 15 below zero.

Again, *Cuttyhunk* pitched slowly forward into the receding slope of a swell, and Tug could see Kit Berens in the doorway to the communications room, stating their precise position: 'Right now, 48 South, 67 East . . . heading southeast . . . just about 100 miles northwest Kerguelen Island . . .'

He watched his 23-year-old navigator, sensed his uneasiness, and muttered to no one in particular, 'This thing is built for a head sea. If we have a problem, it's right back there over the stern . . .' Then, louder and clearer now, 'Watch those new swells coming in from the beam, Bob. I'd hate to have one of them slew us around.'

'Aye, sir,' replied Bob Lander, who was, like Tug himself, a former US Navy lieutenant commander. The main difference between them was that the Captain had been coaxed out of the Navy at the age of 38 to become the senior commanding officer at the great Oceanographic Institute in Woods Hole. Whereas Bob, 10 years older, had merely run out his time in dark blue, retiring as a lieutenant commander, and was now second-in-command of *Cuttyhunk*.

They were both big, powerful men, natives of Cape Cod, life-long seamen, lifelong friends. *Cuttyhunk*, named after the most westerly of the Elizabeth Islands, was in safe hands, despite the terrifying claws of the gale which was currently howling out of the Antarctic.

'Kinda breezy out there now,' said Lander. 'You want me to nip down and offer a few encouraging words to the boffins?'

'Good call,' said Mottram. 'Tell 'em we're fine. *Cuttyhunk*'s made for this weather. Don't for Christ's sake tell 'em we could roll over any minute if we don't watch ourselves. This goddamned cross-sea is the worst I've seen in quite a while . . . there ain't a good course we can heave-to on. Tell 'em I expect to be behind the islands before long . . .'

Down below, the scientists had ceased work. The slightly built, bespectacled Professor Henry Townsend and his team were sitting together in the spacious guest lounge, which had been deliberately

9

constructed in the middle of the ship to minimize the rise-and-fall effect of a big sea. His senior oceanographer, Roger Deakins, was already feeling a bit queasy, which was hardly surprising for a man more accustomed to operating in a deep-diving research submarine.

But the sudden change in weather had taken them all by surprise. And now, Kate Goodwin, a tall, thoughtful, blonde scientist with a doctorate from the joint MIT/Woods Hole Oceanography Program, was belatedly dispensing seasick tablets for those in need.

'I'll take a half-pound of 'em,' said Deakins.

'You only need one,' said Kate, laughing.

'You don't know how I feel,' he replied.

'No. Thank God . . .' she said wryly. But their banter was interrupted by an icy blast through the aft door and the dramatic appearance of a snowman wearing Bob Lander's cheerful face.

'Nothing to worry about, guys,' he said, shaking snow all over the carpet. 'Just one of those sudden storms you get down here, but we should find shelter tonight. Best stay below right now, till the motion eases . . . and don't worry about the banging and thumping you can hear up front – that's just because we're in a very uneven sea, waves hitting us from different directions. Just remember this thing's an ice-breaker. She'll bust her way through anything.'

'Thanks, Bob,' said Kate. 'Want some coffee?'

'Christ, that's a good idea,' he said. 'Black with sugar, if it's no trouble. Can I take one up to the Captain, same way?'

'Yessir,' she said. 'Why don't I give you a pot of it? I'll clip it down. Save you throwing it all over the deck.'

Bob Lander chatted to Professor Townsend for a few minutes while he waited, but his mind was not locked into the words of the acknowledged American expert on the unstable southern ozone layer. It was preoccupied with the thumps against the bow, the dull, shuddering thud of big waves, which have a kind of rhythm, even in a grim Antarctic storm such as this.

Right now there were too many of them. And a couple of times Bob sensed a more hollow clang, although the sound was muffled in this part of the ship. It was, however, the pattern, not the noise, which bothered him. He excused himself quickly, told Kate he'd be right back, and stepped out once more into the gale, making his way up the companionway toward the bridge.

Out here he could really hear the shriek of the storm: the wind slicing through the upperworks, moaning across the great expanse of the water, then rising to a ghastly higher pitch with each thunderous gust. The sound of *Cuttyhunk* lurching forward into the waves held an eerie beat of its own, the big thump of the bow, followed by the slash of the spray across the ship: all of it broken only by the staccato clatter-clatter-clatter of a steel hawser from a topping lift whacking against the after mast. Bob Lander could see also ice forming along the tops of the rails and on the winch covers. If this had been winter it would soon have required men with axes to hack it off, before it became too heavy for the plunging foredeck. But at this time of year the temperature would rise when the storm passed.

'I guess you'd have to describe this as one heck of a summer day,' muttered Bob as he shoved his way through the bridge door, listening again for the offending noise he had observed below.

Inside, it was less obvious, because of the height above the deck. Nonetheless Tug Mottram had also heard something. He turned to face Bob Lander, and words were not required. He spoke in the terse language of the US Navy. 'Go and check that out will you, Bob? It's for'ard, I think. And for Christ's sake be careful. Take a coupla guys with you.'

Bob Lander made his way down to the rolling deck and rounded up a couple of seamen from the crew dormitory. All three of them changed into wet-suits and then pulled on special combination fur-lined Arctic oilskins, seaboots and safety harnesses. They clipped onto the steel safety lines and fought their way out, across the foredeck, where the now-louder noise was obvious. Every time the ship rode up, there was a mighty thump against the bow.

'FUCK IT!' roared Bob Lander above the wind. 'It's that FUCKING anchor again. Worked loose just like it did in that sea off Cape Town.' And now he yelled across to Billy Wrightson and Brad Arnold, 'WE'LL TIGHTEN UP ON THAT BOTTLE-SCREW STOPPER AGAIN. THEN LET'S GET DOWN INTO THE PAINT SHOP AND CHECK FOR DAMAGE.'

Just then a huge wave broke almost lazily over the bow. All three of the men were waist-deep in the freezing water, saved from going over the side only by the harnesses which held them to the safety lines. For the next five minutes they heaved and tugged at the crowbar tightening the stopper. Then they struggled back to

11

the bulkhead door, and bumped and lurched their way to the paint shop, Bob Lander secretly dreading what damage had been done by the swinging half-ton anchor crashing against the hull.

He needed only to open the door to the forepeak area. Tons of seawater surged out from the shop, knocking all three men flying as it rushed through the lower deck. Lander, back on his feet, ordered Wrightson back to the engineer's office to tell him to activate the pumps. Then he moved forward into the paint shop.

The gaping hole on the starboard side, two feet above the deck, told him all he needed to know. The huge anchor had worked its way loose and had bashed a jagged rip into the steel-plating of the hull. Worse yet, the seam between two plates had given way. God knows how far down that rip might travel in a sea like this.

Bob Lander knew two things had to be done. Fast. The hole had to be temporarily patched, and *Cuttyhunk* now had no choice but to run for cover, out of this dangerous weather to the nearest safe anchorage, and make a proper repair.

Meanwhile he told Brad Arnold to get together a group of six men, including the engineer, to go for'ard and shore up the bow inside the paint room, and shut it off securely. 'The anchor's secure for the moment, so get to it, Brad. I don't want that split to get one inch bigger, and I want the water confined to the one compartment. When you've done, set a watchkeeper at the bulkhead door.'

Bob Lander returned to the bridge and told Tug Mottram what he had already guessed. 'Bottle screw again, Bob?'

'Yessir. We have the anchor back tight on the screw and properly wired down. But we have to find some good shelter. There's a lot of water getting into the paint shop. You can see daylight through a big crack in the hull . . . Brad's shoring up around the hole, but we need to weld it, real soon, otherwise I'm afraid it'll run right down the seam. We can't do that kinda job out here.'

'Okay . . . KIT! How far to Kerguelen?'

'Just about 80 miles, sir. At this speed we ought to be in there sometime around 0400.'

'Okay, check the course.'

'Present course is okay . . . we'll come in past Rendezvous Rock, 12 miles north, then we can run down the leeward side into Choiseul Bay and hopefully get out of this goddamned weather.'

'This ain't gonna get any better for a day or two. I guess we'll have to cope with a beam sea, Kit, but if we stay to the east side of the Ridge, it should be a bit calmer. I don't suppose the boffins will be too happy altering course away from their precious research area.'

'Guess not, sir. But they'd probably be a lot less happy if the bow split and we went to the bottom.'

'This is not a life-threatening situation, Kit,' said Bob Lander quietly. 'Just a darn nuisance which we don't want to get any worse . . . Sir, I'll go below and check the patch-up operation in the paint shop.'

At 1957 Tug Mottram ordered a short satellite communication to the command center at Woods Hole: 'Position 48.25S, 67.25E. Intended movement 117 – 12 knots. Going inshore. Proceeding to inspect and repair minor bow damage caused by heavy weather.'

At 1958 he adjusted course for the northwestern headland of the island of Kerguelen, which sits, essentially, at the end of the earth, virtually uninhabited, its snow- and icebound terrain untrampled by the feet of man, save for a few Frenchmen at their weather station at Port-aux-Français way down in the southeast. No ships pass by this godforsaken rocky wasteland for months on end. No commercial airlines fly overhead. No known military power has even the remotest interest in checking the place out.

So far as anyone knows, no marauding submarine has passed this way in more than half a century. Not even the all-seeing American satellites bother to cast an eye upon this craggy wilderness, which measures 80 miles long from west to east, and 55 miles north–south. Save for the huge rookeries of king penguins, and an unreasonable plague of rabbits, Kerguelen might as well be on the moon. It is a huddle of frozen rocks rising out of the Southern Ocean, perhaps the loneliest place on this planet. It stands stark on the 69-degree easterly line of longitude, latitude 49.30S. Gale-swept almost nonstop for all 12 months of the year, Kerguelen is geographical proof that the Roaring Forties are really the Roaring Fifties.

It is, in fact, an archipelago of much smaller islands inset into a great uneven L-shaped mainland, and represents only the tip of a vast underwater range of mountains which stretches for 1,900 miles roughly due southeast from latitude 47.00S right down to the eastern end of the Shackleton Ice Shelf. To the west of this colossal ridge, the ocean is more than three miles deep. On the other side it falls away to more than four miles beneath the keel.

The whole concept of the place made Tug Mottram shudder. But he knew his job, and he knew also the importance the Woods Hole scientists with whom he traveled placed upon that unseen range of subsurface mountains – known formally as the Kerguelen–Gaussberg Ridge.

For, above those craggy underwater peaks, swim literally vast clouds of tiny shrimp-like creatures known as krill, a critical ingredient of the Antarctic food chain – so critical the entire ecosystem would collapse without them. For the krill are devoured by a large network of deep-sea creatures – fish, squid, seals and several species of whale, including the humpback. In turn the killer whale eats other whales and seals. Penguins feed on the small fish and squid which eat the krill. Flying birds also eat the krill, the fish and the squid.

And the Woods Hole scientific teams had discerned for several years a sharp reduction in the krill population. Professor Townsend had made himself world famous by announcing that as a result of a long research program he now believed that the krill were being wiped out by the ultraviolet rays streaming through the hole in the ozone layer which appears over the Antarctic in the September of the year. Furthermore, his studies suggested that the problem was worsening, and he now believed the ozone hole was growing steadily larger, much like the one in *Cuttyhunk*'s paint shop.

His pronouncement had lent a new urgency to this expedition. He planned to take samples of the krill off the Ridge for about six days, and then proceed on down to the US Antarctic Research Station on McMurdo Sound for another month. The questions were, are the phytoplankton, on which the krill feed, being harmed by the radiation, and is this in turn endangering entire species of sea creatures? Another sharp increase would signify to Professor Townsend that the ozone hole was increasing. The *New York Times* had run an entire section on this latest threat, and now the eyes of the world's environmental agencies were fixed firmly upon the *Cuttyhunk* scientists.

Tug Mottram's eyes were fixed on the raging sea now rolling in across his starboard beam, white foam being whipped off the wavetops by the gale, making grotesque lacy patterns in the troughs.

The anchor was secure enough right now, but the men in the forepeak were having a hell of a time trying to stop the sea coming in. They had two big mattresses jammed over the hole, and held in place by heavy timbers cut especially to length for such an emergency. Three young crewmen, almost waist-deep in the freezing water, were trying to wedge the beams into place with sledgehammers, but it was so cold they could manage only three minutes at a time. And when the ship pitched forward the water rose right over them. It would have taken 10 minutes in calm waters, but it ended up more than an hour before the ship was more or less watertight. Another 10 minutes to pump the water out. Two hours to thaw out the shivering seamen.

At midnight they changed the watch. Bob Lander came on the bridge, and the Captain, who had ridden out the worst of the storm, headed exhausted to his bunk. At 48 years old Tug was beginning to feel not quite so indestructible as he had been at 25. And he missed his stunningly pretty second wife Jane, who awaited him now in the Cape Cod seaport of Truro. In the small hours of an Antarctic morning he found it difficult to sleep, and often spent much time reflecting, guiltily, on his divorce from Annie, and the terrible, cruel half-truths he had stated in order to break free and marry a much younger woman. But when he thought of Jane he usually persuaded himself that it had, on reflection, probably been worth it.

Outside, the weather was brightening a little now, and although the wind still howled at around 50 knots, the snow had stopped falling, and there were occasional breaks in the cloud. The worst of the cold front was through.

On the bridge, Bob Lander sometimes caught a glimpse of the sun, a fireball on the horizon as *Cuttyhunk* shouldered her way forward, making 17 knots now on her southeasterly course one-three-five. Soon they would be in sight of the great rock of Îlot Rendezvous, which rises 230 feet out of the sea, a rounded granite centurion guarding the northwestern seaway to Kerguelen. It is sometimes known as Bligh's Cap, so named by Captain Cook in 1776 in honor of his sailing master in *Resolution* on his fourth and final voyage – William Bligh, later of the *Bounty*. But maritime law decrees the French somehow named it first, and the official charts reflect this.

Bob Lander spotted it first shortly before 0300, almost a half-mile off his patched-up starboard bow. He called through to Kit Berens, who had returned to the navigation office at 0200. 'Aye, sir,' he replied. 'I have a good radar picture. Stay on one-three-five and look for the point of Cap D'Estaing dead ahead 40 minutes from now. There's deep water right in close, we can get round a half-mile off the headland. No sweat.'

'Thanks, Kit. How 'bout some coffee?'

'Okay, sir. Lemme just finish plotting us into Choiseul. I'll be right there. But the chart is showing there's a few kelp-beds in the bay and I think we ought to give 'em a damned wide berth. I hate that stuff.'

'So do I, Kit. You better keep at it for a bit. Don't worry about me. I'll just stand here and die of thirst.'

Kit Berens chuckled. He was loving his first great ocean voyage, and was deeply grateful to Tug Mottram for giving him a chance. Tug reminded him of his own father. They were both around 6 ft 3 ins tall, both easy-going men with a lot of dark curly hair and deeply tanned outdoor faces. Tug's had been forged out on the world's oceans, Kit's dad's was the result of a lifetime in south Texas oil fields working as a driller. In Kit's opinion they were both guys you could really count on, just so long as they thought they could count on you. He liked that.

The young navigator pressed his dividers onto the chart against a steel ruler. 'There's a damn great flat-topped mountain on the headland,' he called to Bob. 'It's marked right here as the Bird Table. It's probably the first thing we'll see. We'll change course a few degrees southerly right there. That way we'll see straight up into Christmas Harbor. But I don't think it'll give us enough shelter from the wind. We'll have to run on a bit further.'

'What the hell's Christmas Harbor? I thought the whole place was French. Why isn't it called Baie Noël or something?'

'My notes say it was named by Captain Cook because he pulled in there on Christmas Day 1776. The French named it Baie de l'Oiseau around that same time. Shouldn't be surprised if no one's been there since. I'm telling you, this place is des-o-late.'

At 0337 Bob Lander steered *Cuttyhunk* around Cap D'Estaing. They were in daylight now, but the wind was still hooting out of the Antarctic and it swept around the great northwestern headland of Kerguelen. Fifteen minutes later Kit Berens was gazing up at the turmoil of white-capped ocean swirling through Christmas Harbor.

'Forget that,' he said. 'I'd say the wind was blowing right around D'Estaing but somehow it's also sweeping round that damn great mountain and into the harbor from the other direction. It's like a wind tunnel in there. The katabatics are gonna give us a problem. We're gonna have to run right up into one of the fjords.'

'Fjords?' said Bob. 'I thought they were more or a less a northern thing.'

'According to this chart, Kerguelen's got more fjords than Norway,' said Kit. 'I've been studying it for hours now. The whole place must have been a succession of glaciers once. The fjords here cut so deep back into the land I can't find one spot on the whole island more than about 11 miles from salt water. I bet if you measured every inch of the coastline it'd be about as long as Africa's!'

Lander laughed. He liked the adventurous young Texan. And he liked the way he always knew a lot about where they were. Not just the position, course, speed and distances. But it was typical of Kit to know that Captain James Cook and William Bligh had sailed through these waters a couple of hundred years ago.

Right then Tug Mottram returned to the bridge, bang on time as he always was. 'Morning, men,' he said. 'Is this goddamned wind ever gonna ease up?'

'Not yet, anyways,' said Lander. 'The cold front is still right here. I guess we should just be thankful the darned blizzard's gone through. Wind's still sou'westerly, and it's freezing out there.'

'Kit, you picked a spot for us?' asked the Captain.

The Texan stared at his chart. Without looking up, he said slowly, 'Kind of. About another eight miles southwest there's a deep inlet called Baie Blanche – a fjord really, 10 miles long. A mile wide and deep, up to 400 feet. At the end it forks left into Baie des Français, which I think will be sheltered. But it also turns right into another fjord, Baie du Repos. This one's about eight miles long, narrow but very deep. The mountain range on the western side should give some shelter. The swells shouldn't come in too bad, not that far up, and I don't see any kelp marked. I'm recommending we get in there.'

'Sounds good to me. Oh, Bob, on your way to your bunk, tell the engineers to be ready to start work on the hull at around 0800, will you?'

'Okay, sir. I'm just gonna catch an hour's sleep. Then I'll be right back for a bit of sightseeing.'

Kit Berens finally looked up and informed the Captain he was about to put a message on the satellite stating their position and describing the minor repairs, which would delay them for less than a day.

In the communications room, positioned on the port side of the wide bridge, the former Boston television repair man Dick Elkins was talking to a weather station when Kit Berens dropped his message on the desk: 'Intercontinental – direct to Woods Hole.'

And now, at last, they were getting a lee. The water was flatter, and *Cuttyhunk* steadied, sheltered now by the rising foothills on the starboard side as they ran down to Baie Blanche.

Kit Berens was back hunched over his charts, his steel ruler sweeping across the white, blue and yellow sheets. Finally he spoke. 'Sir, I wanna give you three facts . . .'

'Shoot,' said the Captain.

'Right. If you left this island and headed due north, you would not hit land for 8,500 miles and it would be the south coast of Pakistan. If you went due west you'd go another 8,500 miles to the southern coastline of Argentina. And if you went east, you'd go 6,000 miles, passing to the south of New Zealand and then 6,500 more to the coast of Chile. My assessment is therefore that right now we're at the ass-end of the goddamned earth.'

Tug Mottram laughed loudly. 'How about south?'

'That, sir, is a total fucking nightmare – 500 miles into the West Ice Shelf which guards the Astrid Coast. That's the true Antarctic coastline. Colder and more windswept even than here. But they do have something else in common, Kerguelen and the Antarctic.'

'They do? What's that?'

'No human being has ever been born in either place.'

'Jesus.'

At 0600 they swung into the first wide fjord, Baie Blanche, and immediately became almost unaware of the wind; the water was calm and seemed tideless. There were 400 feet below the keel. Tug Mottram cut the speed right back, because in these very cold, deep Antarctic bays, you could blunder into the most dangerous kind of small iceberg – the ones formed of transparent meltwater ice which float heavily below the surface, absorbing the somber, morose shades of the surrounding seas. To the eye they thus look bluish-black in color, and, unlike white glacier ice, are almost impossible to see.

After four miles, Bob Lander took the wheel while the skipper went outside into the freezing but clear air, and gazed up at the rugged sides of the waterway. Up ahead he could see the lowish headland of Pointe Bras where the fjord split. Beyond that, rising to a height of 1,000 feet, was the snow-covered peak of Mount Richards. Through his binoculars Tug could see gales of snow being whipped from the heights by the still blasting wind.

This lee would be fine for a while, but should a gale swing suddenly out of the north it would blast straight down Baie Blanche. That was why Kit Berens had advised running right down into the deeply sheltered Baie du Repos before they brought out the welding kit.

They turned into the long continuing fjord of Repos at 0655 and made their way over almost 70 fathoms of water around the long left-handed bend which led to the protected dead-end waters below Mount Richards.

Bob Landers slowed to below 4 knots while they searched for an anchorage, when Tug Mottram caught sight of two old, rusting, gray buoys spaced about 400 feet apart, some 50 yards off the rocky western lee shore. 'That'll do just fine,' he muttered, at once wondering if it had been Captain Cook who had left them there in the first place. But then, still looking through his glasses, he spotted something beyond both his imagination and his comprehension.

Speeding towards them, at about 14 knots, was the unmistakable shape of a US-made naval assault craft, one of the old 130 LCVPs, complete with two regulation 7.62 mm machine-guns mounted on the bow. In Tug's mind, none of that was good, but what was really disconcerting was the line of big red-and-white dragon's teeth artistically painted about two feet high across the shallow bow. Worse yet there were 10 occupants, each wearing white military-style helmets. Tug could see the sun glinting off the ones worn by the for'ard gunners.

'Where the hell did they come from?' asked Captain Mottram, standing stock-still on the deserted deck. He could only guess they were French, but he called out for Kit and Bob to take a look.

Lander was thoughtful. 'That's an old Type 272,' he said. 'Haven't seen one of them for a few years.'

But young Berens, sharper by nature, and a frontier Texan by heritage, took one look, grabbed for a set of keys and announced he was headed for the arms cupboard, '*Right now!*'

The Captain pulled his loaded sidearm from his drawer, and Bob Lander slowed the ship down to a halt. Moments later the assault craft pulled alongside, and the leader requested, in a slight American accent, permission to board. To Tug's eye he looked Japanese beneath his big helmet.

Eight of the armed military men on board the LCVP climbed over the rails. Captain Mottram offered his hand in greeting, but this gesture was ignored. Instead the visitors' guns were lowered. The Captain and Bob were ordered flat against the bulkhead, arms outstretched. Mottram did not reckon his pistol would be much of a match for the Kalashnikovs the raiders carried.

Bob Lander turned to ask by whose authority this action was being done, and was felled by a blow to the head from a machine-gun barrel. At which precise time Kit Berens swung around the corner with a loaded submachine-gun and opened fire.

Inside the communications room, Dick Elkins heard two bursts of machine-gun fire. He raced to the bridge window and tried to assess the situation. He knew there was little time, and he charged back into his office and slammed both locks home. A half-minute later, the first ax crashed through the top of the door.

Dick had only split seconds to operate. He opened up his satellite intercontinental link, punching out a desperate message: 'MAYDAY . . . MAYDAY . . . MAYDAY! . . . *Cuttyhunk* 49 South, 69 . . . UNDER ATTACK . . . Japanese . . .'

At which point the message to the Woods Hole command center was interrupted by an ax handle thudding into Dick Elkins' head.

And nothing, repeat nothing, was ever heard from the US Oceanographic Institute research ship again. No wreckage. No bodies. No communication. No apparent culprit. Not a sign.

And that was all 11 months ago.

II

Freddie Goodwin, at 41 years of age, was resigned to remaining a local newspaper reporter for the rest of his days. In his heart he had always wished to be either a marine engineer or a marine biologist, but a somewhat misspent youth on Cape Cod had caused him to fail most of his important academic exams. Then he failed to earn

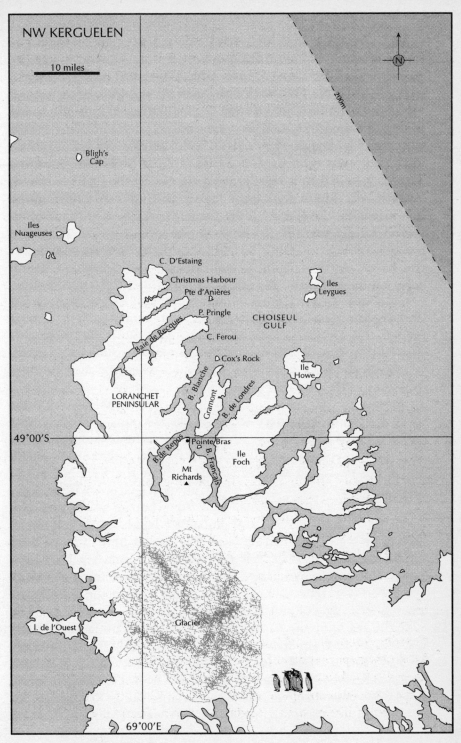

NW KERGUELEN

10 miles

200m

Bligh's
Cap

Iles
Nuageuses

C. D'Estaing

Christmas Harbour

Pte d'Anières

P. Pringle

Iles
Leygues

CHOISEUL
GULF

Baie de Recques

C. Ferou

Cox's Rock

Ile
Howe

LORANCHET
PENINSULAR

B. Blanche

Gramont

B. de Londres

49°00'S

B. de Repos

Pointe Bras

B. Français

Ile
Foch

Mt
Richards

Glacier

I. de l'Ouest

69°00'E

N

21

sufficient grades at Duke University to gain him a place in the MIT/ Woods Hole Oceanographic doctorate program.

Which more or less wrapped it up, deep-seawise, for Freddie. He decided that if he could not research the great oceans of the world, he would write about them instead. And he would leave the heavy academia to his much cleverer first cousin Kate Goodwin, with whom he had always been secretly and privately in love; since first he met her when she was just 19, after the death of her father, his uncle.

Freddie had thus set off into the rougher, more competitive paths of journalism, and was offered a place on his local newspaper, the *Cape Cod Times*, when he was 22 years old, after submitting a graphic and truly brilliant interview with a Greek sea captain who had been sufficiently thoughtless during a storm to dump a 20,000- ton sugar freighter onto Nauset Beach, near Freddie's family home.

He attracted the editor's attention because of his somewhat nifty turn of phrase, and his obdurate tenacity in running the captain to ground in the back room of a Cypriot restaurant in south Boston. The purple pen which had unhappily proved an insufficient weapon to impress the MIT professors, with their tyrannical insistence on *facts*, was just fine for the *Times*.

The news department in Hyannis also liked facts, but not with the self-effacing missionary fervor of the scientists. Within a very few years Freddie Goodwin became the leading feature writer on the paper, and could more or less pick his own assignments, unless something really big was happening over at the Kennedy compound in Hyannisport, where he was always a welcome visitor.

He was a bit of a hellraiser by nature, but he was a striking-looking man, and talented, and probably could have made it big in Boston or New York had he been able to tear himself away from Cape Cod. As it was, he felt contented enough when his better feature stories were syndicated to other papers, including the *Washington Post*. On reflection, he preferred to live on the humorous, unambitious edges of journalism.

And Cape Cod, the narrow land of his youth, his family's head-quarters for four generations, would forever be home to Freddie. He had never married — some said because no one quite measured up to his beloved, unobtainable Kate — but he had his boat, he even had a lobsterman's license, and he had a stream of girlfriends. In the summer he crewed in the hotshot local Wianno Senior racing class, and he watched the Cape Cod Baseball League, supporting the Hyannis Mets. In the winter, when the population of the Cape crashes by about 80 percent, he tended to drink too much.

On occasional assignments 'off-Cape' (as the locals put it), Freddie Goodwin quickly missed the sight of his homeland – not just Mulligan's Bar up in Dennisport, but also the great saltwater ponds, the marshes and the sweeping sandy coastline, the shallow, gentle waters of Nantucket Sound, the soft warm breezes of the Gulf Stream which wrap themselves around the western reaches of the Cape for six months of the year.

He missed them particularly right now, as he stood alone in the shadow of the great windswept icy cliffs which surround Christmas Harbor on the island of Kerguelen. And he wept helplessly again for his lost Kate, and in a sense for all of the 23 Cape Cod seamen and six scientists who had vanished off the face of the earth on that fateful December morning almost a year previously.

He had known so many of them, especially Bob Lander. Freddie's entire family had gone to the funeral of Bob's wife just two years ago. Her cancer had caused almost as much grief to the Goodwins as to her husband and three children. The Landers had all lived within a mile of Freddie's parents in Brewster for almost 50 years.

Through Kate, he knew big Tug Mottram, and Henry Townsend, and Roger Deakins, and Kate's two assistants Gail and Barbara. The Woods Hole oceanographic community, despite the vast size of the waterfront complex, the 1,400 employees and 500-strong student body, is as tight-knit as any law firm. Those who make long and perilous ocean voyages to the Arctic and the Antarctic in pursuit of deep scientific research are often bound together for all of their days.

Freddie Goodwin could not bring himself to believe the entire ship's company of *Cuttyhunk* was dead. And for months he had used the columns of the *Cape Cod Times* to rail against the Government Inquiry. He was emotionally and intellectually unable to deal with the words of the official report . . .

There is no evidence whatsoever to suggest that *Cuttyhunk* is still floating and it must be presumed that she has gone to the bottom of the Southern Ocean with all hands. The chance of survivors in those deserted waters, in those freezing temperatures, is plainly zero.

At various times Freddie had demanded to know in both his newspaper and in letters to different Washington government departments how anyone could explain away the last message: the assertion that the ship was under attack . . . and that the Japanese were probably responsible.

The Press Department in the Pentagon had patiently pointed out, over and over again, that *Cuttyhunk* had been the subject of an extensive US Navy sea-search over a period of three months. 'Mr Goodwin, sir, may I remind you that the President of the United States himself ordered a frigate from the Seventh Fleet into the area within hours of the last message from the research ship?'

Various other officials had written back in the self-interested, lethargic tones of the bureaucrat, explaining that 'exhaustive inquiries from the State Department to the highest levels of the Japanese Government, and indeed to their military High Command, have left everyone in a state of bewilderment.

'The Japanese, I am afraid,' wrote the official, 'have not the slightest idea what we are talking about.'

Freddie had replied by telephone after a couple of good-sized glasses of winter bourbon. 'Well, what about the goddamned Chinese, or the Vietnamese, or any of those other guys out there who look a bit the same to the American eye?'

But no one had been able to help. And he stood now beneath these dark, satanic-looking cliffs, staring at the gray, icy waters of Choiseul Bay, shivering despite his heavy foul-weather gear, and pondering the heart-breaking loss of Kate Goodwin.

Throughout the long ordeal of the past year, his editor, Frank Markham, had been his main supporter. It was the kindly and deeply sympathetic Frank who had suggested that it might be an idea for Freddie to get down to Kerguelen at the newspaper's expense and write a series of features about the island at the end of the world, all centered on the loss of *Cuttyhunk*.

'You find a way to get there, we'll pay and help you get organized, and then you can have a darned good snoop around and find out if anything shakes.'

Frank had put his arm around Freddie and told him that if he found even one thing, it would be a huge story, and that anyway it'd be a cathartic experience. 'Maybe help you lay your Kate to rest, at least in your own mind.'

And now the star feature writer from the *Cape Cod Times* stood alone on this blasted shoreline, trying to wipe the freezing tears from his face as he stared out forlornly to another research ship waiting with engines running 100 yards out, the one which had carried him from Miami to Kerguelen.

Their final destination was the McMurdo Station, from where Freddie would be airlifted out by helicopter and eventually flown back to Boston. Meanwhile Frank Markham had paid the ship's owners the sum of $4,000 to hang around for two or three days while the reporter gathered his material.

As it happened they would probably have done it for nothing. Everyone liked the writer from Cape Cod and he had regaled the crew throughout the long southern voyage with stories about *Cuttyhunk* and those who sailed in her. By the time they arrived off Christmas Harbor, no one aboard that research ship believed that the whole truth had yet come out. Freddie had convinced them all that his cousin might still be alive, though where, he knew not.

Today, with the sea calm for once, he had been permitted to go ashore alone in the rubber Zodiac. He had driven it onto the beach, raised the outboard and dragged it ashore – an exercise he had been carrying out in somewhat warmer waters since he was old enough to walk.

Alone now with his thoughts and precious memories, he stared in turn at the landscape and his chart of the island. A lifelong devotee of Agatha Christie's Belgian detective Hercule Poirot, Freddie kept telling himself the answers, if any, lay in the 'little gray cells.' He had jotted down the known final positions of *Cuttyhunk*, and he could see plainly they must have run down to Kerguelen's northwestern headland, right past Bligh's Cap.

He knew the bow of the ship had been damaged, and he knew they had been in heavy weather and were running for cover. The question was, where? Christmas Harbor? Not a chance in a big wind, they'd have gone farther down. Even in the light November breeze which now surrounded him, Freddie could feel the wind backing round in the cliffs. 'I bet this place is a goddamned disaster area in a big westerly,' he muttered. 'It'd come howling round that point out there . . . what's it called? . . . Yeah . . . here we are . . . D'Estaing. There's no way Tug would have put into here. He'da gone farther down the bay, looking for something a bit more sheltered. No doubt in my mind.'

High overhead he could identify the majestic flight of a big wandering albatross. And toward the east, in the more exposed area of the harbor, he could see a flight of storm petrels fluttering low over the water. So far as he could tell, nothing else stirred. It was the most silent place Freddie Goodwin had ever been. Large ice-floes, swollen and split by the searing cold, littered the long, rocky beach. Aside from the seabirds, it was a world of total lifelessness.

But standing around Christmas Harbor was not going to help anyone. He would have liked to walk to the end of the southern headland and take a look at the bays which lay beyond. But he was worried about the Zodiac, and the fact that the weather down here can change with such terrifying swiftness. So he walked down to the shore and shoved the boat out, jumping expertly onto the bow before even his seaboots got wet.

He lowered the engine, started it first time and chugged out to the harbor entrance where he swung right. He knew it was about two miles in reasonably flat water over to Pointe D'Anière, and during those two miles he would cross the mouths of two other bays, both of which he guessed would be even more exposed than Christmas Harbor. He was right. There was no possibility Tug Mottram would have gone in there.

The next bay, beyond the point, was a 13-mile-long fjord called Baie de Recques. His chart showed it narrow and deep, heading so far into the rockface it came within 3,000 yards of the *other* side of the island. Its sides were steep, sloping granite walls and Freddie, who fancied himself a bit of an expert on seabirds, could see through his binoculars a group of shearwaters wheeling 50 feet above the water. Basically, he did not consider this place would have been much of an idea for the stricken *Cuttyhunk* either, because Baie de Recques ran dead straight, due southwest, with nothing between its cold waters and the open ocean. 'Even with a westerly,' he murmured, 'I bet a gale finds a way into this great streak of a place . . . probably round that mountain at the far end. What do they call it? Yeah . . . Mount Lacroix, right on the west coast, 800 feet above the shore.'

He circled the Zodiac at the mouth of the bay for a few minutes, then pushed on around the corner where he was greeted by huge, black, forbidding cliffs set between a headland called Pointe Pringle and Cap Féron, a mile and a half distant.

Most high-ranging cliffs look grimly impressive from below, as does a great ship from a rowing boat. But to Freddie Goodwin's eye, this rockface looked nothing short of evil. And he thought of the awful consequences of *Cuttyhunk* running headlong into it and smashing herself to pieces in the dark, in the howling gale of that far-lost night. 'Katie . . .' he said, shaking his head, and feeling tears yet again well up in his eyes, as they had been doing for as long as he could now remember.

But he jolted himself together. Told himself sternly a) if *Cutty-hunk* had hit the cliffs there would certainly have been wreckage found, which there never had been, b) Tug Mottram would have given such a rockface a very wide berth even in these deep waters, and c) that Texan kid, Berens, was supposed to have been one of the best navigation officers Bob Lander had ever worked with.

Anyway, the Zodiac was getting a bit low on gas, and Freddie turned thankfully away from the black backdrop of Cap Féron, and roared back to his floating base at full throttle, to write up his notes before dinner. Even if he failed to find sight or sound of *Cuttyhunk*, he still had to write a series of feature articles. The next fjord, which lay beyond Féron, would have to wait till morning. Freddie stared at his chart. 'Here we are,' he thought. 'Christ! It runs down there for nearly 20 miles. What's it called? Right here . . . Baie Blanche.'

It was 7.40 p.m. by the time he finished his observations, about the seabirds, the seascape, the rising mountains above the fjords, and the unfathomable dark waters in which *Cuttyhunk* might sadly be resting. And yet he did not believe she was sunk.

He poured himself an heroic-sized glass of Kentucky bourbon, splashed in the same amount of tap water, and swigged deeply. Finally he kicked off his seaboots and sat in the warm cabin in slacks, shirt and light sweater. He felt the glow of the amber-colored spirit immediately and, as he did so, he saw again in his mind the face of the tall, willowy Kate Goodwin, her soft slow smile and her long blonde hair, her unusual, tranquil good looks.

For several months now, he had seen her face whenever he took his first drink of the day: perhaps in memory of the many evenings they had shared together on the Cape, but more likely because her disappearance seemed slowly to be draining away the entire purpose of his life . . . and yet he seemed unable to cast aside this secretive obsession, utterly unworldly, he knew, for a girl he could never have, and who might very well not be alive. The perfect daughter of his own father's long-dead brother.

There were times when Freddie seriously considered he might be losing his grip. But the sight of the frozen, loathsome place in which he now found himself had already stiffened the ramparts around his private labyrinth. He took another long mouthful of bourbon and announced to the deserted cabin, 'If you're alive, I'm gonna make sure someone finds you, even if it's not me.'

And he picked up his notebook and wrote in block capitals as he had done so many times, 'WHY WOULD THE *CUTTYHUNK* RADIO OPERATOR SAY HE WAS UNDER ATTACK IF HE WASN'T? AND IF THE SHIP WAS SUNK IN A FJORD WHY HAS NOTHING EVER FLOATED TO THE SURFACE?'

'Beats the shit out of me,' he added poetically. 'But I think *Cuttyhunk* is still floating. And I think someone knows where her crew and passengers are.'

That night, at the all-male dinner, Freddie planned his morning attack, persuading the Captain to take him for a run down Baie Blanche — 'Not all the way — just three or four miles, or maybe down to where the fjord splits. I don't think Captain Mottram would have gone farther than that point. If there's anything to be found, we'll find it. And if there's nothing I'll go take a shot at that sheltered anchorage on the Île Foch directly east. You move us on down Choiseul a bit in the afternoon, I'll just run the Zodiac through those narrows between the islands, if the weather's okay.'

No one had any objection to that, and they all settled back to a really classy dinner of *coq au vin*, prepared especially for the ship's officers by one of the French guest scientists on board. Considering Monsieur le Professeur had poured the entire contents of a bottle of Margaux Premier Reserve '86 into the pot, it tasted like chicken fit for the *Roi Soleil*. There was no objection from anyone when the Prof. also came up with three more bottles of the Margaux, and Freddie proposed a solemn toast to Kate Goodwin, in which they all joined, with much sadness.

'The thing about it is,' said Freddie, with the careful deliberation which invariably pervades that no-man's-land before serious drunkenness sets in, 'you can't sink ships without a lot of stuff coming to the surface. You take a big steel vessel like *Cuttyhunk* . . . you wanna put her on the floor of the ocean, you gotta blow a fucking hole in her, below the waterline. You need either a torpedo, in which case you need a submarine . . . or you need a fucking great hunk of TNT, which is noisy, messy and dangerous.

'Things break up when you scuttle a ship. The whole upper deck is full of stuff that can break away – rubber life-rafts, winch covers, life-buoys . . . stuff that *floats*. All through the interior of the ship there's clothes, wooden fittings and furniture, plastic bathroom fittings, suitcases. Not to mention about a billion gallons of oil and gasoline. *Something must have come up if she was sunk.*'

He twirled his wine around his glass. Then he looked up and added much more slowly, 'But nothing did. Not a trace was found . . . and we had the US Navy down here searching the waters with every possible modern device for locating stuff in the ocean. What did they find? FUCK ALL . . . that's what they found. Gentlemen, I'm going to bed now, thanks for indulging me . . .' And he wandered somewhat unsteadily back to his cabin, to sleep the deeply troubled but dreamless sleep of the unfulfilled detective.

He awoke early the following morning, regretting profoundly the last couple of glasses of Margaux. He understood that the skill of Kentucky's bourbon distillers very possibly equaled that of the Bordeaux wine-makers, but he was unsure that those two supreme but separate talents were ideally suited to share the same evening. At least not in abundance.

The ship was still on last night's fair-weather anchorage in shallow water behind Pointe Lucky, south of Cap Féron. But the Captain had taken the standard precaution of leaving two men on watch throughout the night, just in case another capricious Antarctic front should arrive and send the barometric pressure crashing.

Freddie took a couple of Alka-Seltzer tablets, declined breakfast, and prepared himself for Baie Blanche. Before seven they were under way, rounding the jutting ice-encrusted headland and turning hard right into the long waters of the fjord. The Captain killed the speed to 4 knots, and placed two lookouts on the starboard side, with one other seaman joining Freddie on the portside lower deck facing the coast of Gramont Island. All four men were carrying binoculars, which they used to scour every inch of the shoreline, hoping for the tell-tale piece of wreckage which would betray the former presence here of the American Antarctic ship *Cuttyhunk*.

They ran slowly south-southwest for six miles, and saw nothing solid that was not a rock or a hunk of ice. The sun cast light but no heat. The temperature was just below freezing, and the Baie Blanche yielded no secrets.

When they rounded the point at Saint Lanne on the left-hand side, they could see clearly the headland of Pointe Bras, and the Captain thought that was about as far as they needed to go, since he could not believe Tug Mottram would have required even more shelter for a simple welding job. This Captain had not yet, however, experienced his first raging Antarctic storm.

Freddie looked at his chart and noticed that there was a small bay inset into the Loranchet Peninsula, about two miles down into Baie du Repos on the right, bang on the 49th parallel. 'That's as far as Tug Mottram would ever have needed to go,' he said. 'I'd like to scoot down there in the Zodiac, just to take a quick look. Would you mind hanging around for an hour?'

The Captain had no problem with that, and Freddie set off alone, gazing around the still, silent waterway, and wondering inevitably if Kate too had looked at these frozen cliffs. He opened the throttle and flew up into the bay. Then he slowed right down and carefully searched the shoreline at the lowest possible speed. Only the soft beat of the engine and the light, gurgling bow wave broke the devastating silence. And Freddie gazed up at the four-mile-distant peak of Mount Richards, and irrationally wished that 'big white fucker could talk.' But essentially, there was nothing. Absolutely nothing.

Back at the ship, he suggested they might exit the fjords up through Baie de Londres on the far side of Gramont. They continued to travel at 4 knots, still searching. Still nothing. At the northeast tip of the island they were forced to swing wide to avoid a murderous kelp-bed two miles across.

And, as they went past in clear water, leaving the island to port and the jutting, eerie-looking Cox's Rock 50 yards to starboard, Freddie Goodwin, standing up on the bow, spotted it. They were almost by. He was late. But he saw it clearly. Something faded but red, modern Day-Glo red, jammed into the stones at the base of the Rock.

'WHAT'S THAT?' he yelled, pointing out over the gunwales and racing aft.

'WHERE? ... WHERE? ... FREDDIE ... WHERE-ABOUTS?' Everyone was anxious to help. And suddenly everyone could see the red on the rocks. The First Mate put the ship into reverse, they lowered the Zodiac, and Freddie Goodwin, now with three crewmates, sped across the short distance to Cox's. The water was deep, dangerous and freezing cold, and now they could all see the red crescent shape was a part of one of those hard styrene modern lifebelts. It was jammed pretty hard and might crumble if they went at it with a boathook. A couple of rocks might have to be prized apart. Their discovery had been there for a long time.

Forty yards farther on there was a flat, dry(ish) ledge and the helmsman maneuvered them in close, shoving the reinforced rubberized bow into a corner and holding it there on the engine. The other three clambered out and made their way back over the rocks to the red lifebelt. It took 10 minutes to wrest it free in one piece. And when they turned it over, the three big black letters were like a knife to Freddie Goodwin's already broken heart. C-U-T.

Worse yet, his seaman's instinct was telling him the prevailing west wind was no longer on his face. The broken lifebelt had been swept onto the windward side of the Rock, which meant it had not come in from the open sea. Rather it had been swept out from one of the 50-odd miles of fjords which surge around this small part of Kerguelen.

In a flash of logic, Freddie now knew that *Cuttyhunk* had almost certainly gone to the bottom in one of those deep, sinister waterways. He had been saying for so long that no wreckage meant she was still floating. But now there was wreckage, right from the Woods Hole ship's upper deck. He was holding it in his hand, for Christ's sake.

And he had no more tears to shed. Kate was gone. Of that he was now certain.

It would take him all of the next three days to find even a tiny chink of light in the progression of his thoughts. When it came to him, it came fleetingly, but hopefully. *Unless some really sharp member of the* Cuttyhunk *crew, during the attack, secretly heaved the lifebelt over the side, as one last futile signal to the outside world . . .*

The notion was so remote it took another week to germinate fully and settle into his mind as a logical deduction – as a potential truth, with which he could work.

It did so just before Freddie sat down in Hyannis to write the first of an outstanding series of syndicated articles, centered on the menacing, frozen island at the end of the world.

CHAPTER TWO

V ICE-ADMIRAL ARNOLD MORGAN, at the age of 58, was wryly
amused by the opulence of his new office in the White House.
For a man whose background was nuclear submarines, and latterly
a somewhat functional operations room as Director of the clandestine, hard-edged National Security Agency in Fort Meade,
Maryland, the controlled, carpeted hush of very senior quarters in
the home of the President was a culture shock. Also people were
apt to look a bit startled when he yelled at 'em.

After a lifetime in the US Navy, including several years commanding nuclear boats, the burly, 5 ft 8 in Texan had been
extremely circumspect about taking off the dark blue for the last
time – and accepting the exalted presidential post of National
Security Advisor.

But he really liked the southwestern Republican who currently
occupied the Oval Office. Where some Presidents seek, politically,
to dissociate themselves from the military, this highly educated, ex-
Harvard law professor from Oklahoma had always embraced the
United States Armed Forces, drawing admirals and generals right
into the heart of his administration.

Arnold Morgan and the President had worked closely together
during a particularly disagreeable 'black operation' the previous
year. And, less than three weeks after its conclusion, the President
had told his closest staff members that he really missed talking
regularly to Arnold: 'He's such a cantankerous old bastard. Doesn't
trust any foreign country except the UK, and them no further
than he can kick 'em; calls people up in the small hours of the
morning, and is mostly too bad-tempered even to say goodbye on
the phone. But a truly impressive mind. And a walking encyclo-
pedia on world naval power.'

The Secretary of Defense, Robert MacPherson, was also an
admirer of the Admiral, and, despite the few misgivings of the

32

rather more refined Harcourt Travis, the Secretary of State, it was agreed that Admiral Morgan should be brought into the White House. And even Travis raised no serious objection, stating drolly that he had to admit that Britain's Neville Chamberlain 'would have been considerably better off if he'd taken Admiral Morgan with him to meet Hitler in Munich in 1939.'

It took almost a year to disentangle the Admiral from the front line of the US Intelligence Service, but he now sat firmly in a deeply carpeted inner sanctum of the West Wing . . . pacing the floor and wondering 'what the hell we're gonna do about those fucking Chinese submarines.'

The Admiral did not, by instinct, trust the Beijing government one inch, and he trusted foreign submarines even less. The fact that they were being constructed in Russia, a nation he also bitterly mistrusted, had the effect of accelerating his irritation to the third power.

'Fuck 'em,' he growled. 'But we're not having it.'

He stood up and pulled on his new dark gray civilian suit jacket, which was well cut, especially for him, by a military tailor. He strode out of his office, his black lace-up shoes gleaming. Only the brisk, unmistakable gait of a senior naval officer betrayed his past. That and his severely cut gray hair, and his way of staring straight in front as he went forward. When Admiral Morgan set sail from his White House office he looked as if he was about to head into battle, and damn the torpedoes. On this particular day, he would not have found that too daunting a task.

'Goddamned Chinese,' he snapped as he passed a new portrait of President Eisenhower, whom he considered would probably have understood. And he continued muttering irritably, 'Napoleon said it, and he said it right . . . when the Chinese giant awakens, the world will tremble. I'm not sure who's going to be doing the trembling, but it's not going to be the US of A . . .'

At the West Wing entrance, his car and driver awaited him. 'Morning, Charlie,' he said. 'Pentagon. Usual spot. CNO's office. Gotta be there at 1030.'

Charlie, who had never before driven a senior military man until the Admiral's arrival, snapped back, 'SIR,' like a somewhat cowed midshipman. He had not yet recovered from their very first meeting, on Admiral Morgan's very first morning in office. Charlie had shown up two minutes late, and could hardly believe his ears when Arnold Morgan had growled, in soft but plainly menacing tones, 'You are adrift, late, AWOL, slack, and useless. If anything like this ever happens again, you are fired. Do you understand me, asshole? My name is Admiral Arnold Morgan, and I have a goddamned lot on my mind, and I will not abide this kind of bullshit from anyone, not even if he works in the fucking White House.'

Charlie Patterson nearly died of shock. And a month later, he was still genuinely afraid of the Admiral. From that first encounter onward, he was inclined to show up 20 minutes early for all of his assignments with the new National Security Advisor. The story of his confrontation with the tyrant from Fort Meade, and the verbatim recounting of Morgan's words to the chauffeur, had whipped around the White House like a prairie fire. Even the President knew about it; he thought it was just about the funniest thing he had heard all week.

Charlie Patterson gunned the big limousine through the streets of Washington, heading east along the waterfront and picking up I–395 at the Maine Avenue entrance. They crossed the Potomac out in the fast lane and made straight for the military headquarters of the United States Armed Forces.

Admiral Morgan was well used to these familiar routes, but for the past four years he had usually driven himself. The permanent driver was just one aspect of his new life with which he had to become accustomed. The others were the more stately office hours, and the more regular social occasions he was obliged to attend. If he missed anything badly, it was the time he used to spend prowling around his Fort Meade headquarters in the small hours of the morning, checking the signals from America's surveillance points all over the world, watching, listening, waiting to see if by any chance 'some foreign bastard was lying.'

He now believed it was entirely possible he might have to locate a new lady to run his life. The years in submarines and then in naval intelligence had wreaked havoc with both of his marriages. As far as he could tell neither of his two ex-wives, nor even his two grown-up children, were speaking to him at present, as a result of years of neglect when he was just too busy to concentrate on matters like family. Right now, with his highly salaried position alongside the President, he was becoming regarded as one of the most interesting middle-aged 'catches' on the Washington circuit.

Dangerous waters for an unarmed former commanding officer, who was having to re-learn any vestige of real charm he might once have had as a young lieutenant.

But that was all secondary. Especially now. Admiral Morgan, for years the Navy's most fearless, and feared, seeker after truth, was trying to string together a whole line of facts which seemed unconnected and indeed incompatible. But in the next few hours, he was going to sort them out, and almost certainly instigate silent, but nonetheless drastic, action against two of the world's most powerful nations.

Charlie slid the car down into the subterranean garage below the Pentagon. It came to a halt right outside the private elevator which runs up to the offices of the Chairman of the Joint Chiefs, Admiral Scott Dunsmore, the former Chief of Naval Operations. Admiral Morgan would spend 15 minutes having a cup of coffee there, and then head for the headquarters of the new CNO, Admiral Joseph Mulligan, the former Commander of the Atlantic Submarine Force.

Two US Marine guards were waiting to escort him to the offices of the CJC. But before the Admiral stepped into the elevator, he turned back to Charlie and said: 'I might pop out this door any time between now and 1630. Be here.'

One of the guards risked a slight smile. The Admiral fixed him with a gimlet eye. 'No bullshit, right?' he growled.

'Right, sir,' replied the guard, uncertain to what, precisely, the Admiral was referring.

Coffee with his old friend, the Chairman, was relaxed and informal, its purpose merely to brief Scott Dunsmore on the President's current state of mind regarding the China problem. There were no surprises. Admiral Dunsmore had guessed anyway. Admiral Morgan's briefing to Admiral Mulligan, and possibly another privately invited guest, would be a meeting of considerably greater detail. By nightfall Scott Dunsmore expected a clear resolution to have been made. It looked like they were heading for a black operation (nonattributable to anyone, even in the event of total failure). And, either way, the fewer people who knew about it the better.

Outside the CNO's office, a young Flag Lieutenant informed Admiral Morgan that the Chief would be about 10 minutes late. Problem in a carrier in Norfolk. Admiral Mulligan had cleared the

Navy yards in a helicopter a short while ago and was on his way here. 'I've just spoken to him, sir. He said to go right in, and he'll be as quick as he can.'

Arnold Morgan walked into the outer section of the CNO's quarters, and saw that a uniformed naval officer was already waiting, reading the *Washington Post*. He wore, directly above his line of medals, a small submarine insignia on which were set twin dolphins, the fabled attendants of the sea-god Poseidon. Admiral Morgan glanced immediately at the three golden stripes with the single star on the sleeve, offered his hand in greeting and said: 'Morning, Commander. Arnold Morgan.'

The big man in the armchair stood immediately, shook hands and said, 'Good morning, sir. Cale Dunning, *Columbia*.'

Admiral Morgan smiled. 'Ah yes, Boomer Dunning, of course. I'm delighted to meet you. You probably know I used to drive one of those things.'

'Yes, Admiral. I did know. You were commanding one of 'em when I first left Annapolis back in 1982. *Baltimore*, wasn't it?'

'Correct. She was brand-new then. Not so refined as your ship, but she was a damned good boat. There's a lot of days when I wouldn't mind commanding one again. They were great years for me. Make the most of yours, Boomer. There's nothing quite like it, you know, and you can never get 'em back, once they decide to move you onward and upward.'

The two submariners sat down in opposite armchairs, each one uncertain about bringing up the subject they both knew they were here to discuss. The Admiral had requested the meeting, and would essentially take charge of it. He had also suggested that Admiral Mulligan invite Commander Dunning. But the two men had never met.

Now he elected not to broach the critical topic until the CNO arrived, so he glanced at the open pages of the *Post* and asked Commander Dunning if there were any 'unusually hideous distortions in the newspaper today?'

'Not that I've hit on so far, sir,' grinned Boomer. 'Matter of fact, I've been reading a long article in here about that Woods Hole ship that vanished last year. I've read some stuff about it before by the same guy – he's called Frederick J. Goodwin. Seems to know a lot about it.'

'That'd make a change for a newspaper reporter,' growled the

Admiral. 'Normally they know just about enough to be a god-damned nuisance.'

Boomer chuckled. 'Well, sir, he's been down to that French island where the ship disappeared. Found the first bit of wreckage – a hunk from a bright red styrofoam lifebelt. Had the letters C-U-T on it. He's checked back at the base. *Cuttyhunk* was equipped with those.'

'Well, I guess that more or less proves she went to the bottom, eh?'

'This guy thinks not. He's saying that if she went down, there would have been stuff all over the place. And since the Navy sent a frigate in to search they *should* have found *something*. It was just a few days after the incident.'

'Yeah. That was kind of unusual. Our frigate was down there sniffing around for three months. Still found zilch. What does he say about the attack that was mentioned in the final message?'

'That's really his whole point, Admiral. He reckons they *were* attacked, and that a crew member made a desperate last-ditch attempt to alert the outside world by dropping a *Cuttyhunk* lifebelt over the side. He says there's no other explanation for the otherwise total lack of wreckage.'

'Yes there is.'

'What's that?'

'The guys who sunk her hung around for a couple of days and cleared everything up. By the time our frigate got there the place was empty.'

'Right. Except for one little bit of one lifebelt that got away.'

'That's it . . . Where did they find it, by the way?'

'That's another interesting bit of deduction by Mr Goodwin. He says it was trapped in the windward side of a large rock, not quite big enough to be called an island. He says the position of the lifebelt strongly suggests it did not come in from the open sea, but from the fjord itself.'

'Well, our frigate captain was of the opinion *Cuttyhunk* did not sink in the fjord. They found absolutely nothing, you know. I wonder how they missed the lifebelt?'

'Goodwin thinks the frigate captain would almost certainly have avoided that particular bit of water. It's apparently very close to a big kelp-bed, and the channel there is narrow and rocky. He doesn't think any Navy captain in his right mind would want to go through there in a warship.'

'Guess not, Boomer. Better to miss the odd lifebelt than get that stuff in your intakes and end up having to be towed out of there two weeks later.'

'Yessir. I'm with the Captain on that one.'

'So what's Mr Goodwin's conclusion? Does he think *Cuttyhunk* sank or not?'

'He thinks not, sir. He thinks she's still floating somewhere, but he doesn't offer much of an opinion about the crew or the scientists on board. He just thinks it unlikely that our frigate wouldn't have got some firm indication from somewhere that they were steaming right over the wreck of the Woods Hole ship.'

'Sounds like he's getting overexcited, hmmm? I hate mysteries, you know. But I read this report pretty thoroughly at the time. It is possible she sank out in the bay in 600 feet. Then you really might not find her.'

'That's true, Admiral. But Goodwin says the flow of the water, and the prevailing westerlies, make it a nautical impossibility for that lifebelt to have ended up where it did.'

'I doubt there's much accounting for which way the wind blows inshore there, whatever the hell it's doing out at sea. So I suppose we'll just have to let the matter rest. Pity.'

'Admiral, I don't think this character Goodwin is very anxious to let it rest. He's writing about the subject for the next three days. Tomorrow's piece is entitled: "The Menace of Kerguelen" . . .'

Just then the door flew open and Admiral Joe Mulligan came in, still wearing his big Navy greatcoat. 'Gentlemen, I am really sorry about this. Hi, Boomer . . . Admiral. Yet another problem with that new carrier. She's supposed to be commissioned in March, but God knows how that's ever gonna happen. She's supposed to be on station in the Indian Ocean by midsummer – I can't leave the *Washington* out there any longer. I guess I'll have to use *Lincoln* but she's due for refit. I wish to Christ we still had the *Jefferson* in service.'

'So do I, Joe,' said Admiral Morgan, slowly.

He smiled at the ex-submariner who now occupied the highest chair in the United States Navy. Arnold Morgan and Joe Mulligan had known each other a lot of years, since their days way back at the Academy, and to Arnold at least it had been very obvious for some time that the Boston Irishman was being groomed for the highest office.

Joe stood 6 ft 4 ins tall. He had a craggy face with a lot of laughter lines, since he did a lot of laughing. His wit was sharp, and both his hair and his eyes were battleship gray. His hair had been that way since he was 31 years old, which rightly foretold an extremely serious, contemplative nature, bordering on downright preoccupation with difficult naval warfare equations.

In his youth, Joe had been a real good football player, tight-end for the Midshipmen in the Army game of 1966. He was a submariner through and through, never wanted to operate in any other field. A former commanding officer of a Polaris boat up in Holy Loch, Scotland, Joe Mulligan had ended up in one of the most revered operational positions in the entire United States Navy – Captain of the 18,500-ton Trident submarine *Ohio* at the beginning of the 1980s, just when President Reagan was attempting to frighten the life out of the Russians.

The men who drove the Tridents were generally regarded as the élite commanders of the US Navy – in some ways even more important than the admirals in charge of the carrier battle groups. Each one of them had been blessed with that near-mystical ability not only to handle and run their giant underwater ships with chilling efficiency, but also to understand the greater picture of both the undersea world and the political world which surrounded them. They were men of stealth, ruthlessness and absolute certainty in their own abilities.

Captain Joseph Mulligan was widely considered to have been the best of them. But his promotional path to become a vice-admiral, and then swiftly on to the heady office of Commander Submarine Force, Atlantic Fleet and Allied Command (Atlantic), had taken many people by surprise. When Admiral Scott Dunsmore predictably moved up to become Chairman of the Joint Chiefs, there were three admirals in line to become the new Chief of Naval Operations. The outsider among them was Joe Mulligan, and when he was appointed over the other two more senior men, a lot of people were really surprised.

Arnold Morgan was not among them. He thought Admiral Mulligan was an outstanding naval strategist and administrator. He also knew him to be an expert on modern guided-missile systems, with a degree in nuclear physics. What Morgan really admired, however, was the new CNO's deeply cynical view of the motives of all other nations. The two men shared an unshakable view of the proper supremacy of the United States of America, and when push came to shove, in any international confrontation, their views coincided precisely: 'That's the way it's going to be, because that's the way America says it's going to be.'

Admiral Mulligan motioned for the President's new Security Advisor to join him in the inner office, leaving the Commander outside for a while. He issued strict instructions that they were not to be disturbed, short of an outbreak of war, mutiny or fire, and could someone please bring in some hot coffee, and a few cookies?

The desk of the professional head of the United States Navy did not seem too big for him. Admiral Mulligan looked like a man who had been born to occupy such a place, and Arnold Morgan smiled as the CNO growled, 'Right, Arnie. What are we gonna do about these Chinese pricks?'

He then pulled a classified file out of his locked desk drawer, thumbed through the pages, and said he thought he would like his old buddy first to brief him thoroughly on the complete political background to the problem. Then they could toss a few solutions around.

'Okay, Joe. And I want to go through this very carefully because I have a feeling there has been some kinda blockage in the flow of information. Either that, or things which I regard as critically important are not so regarded by others, which means we are dealing with a bunch of dumb-ass sonsabitches, right?'

'Right.'

'Now, this is going to take me a few minutes, Joe, so bear with me, will you? But I have two points of departure, the first when I was in Fort Meade, the second now that I have the ear of the President. Lemme see . . . I guess this all began back in 1993 when the Chinese Navy first placed an order with the dying Soviet Navy for one of those Kilo-Class submarines of theirs.

'Well, the Chinese Navy, even then, was in an expansionist mood, and no one got terribly excited. We were much more interested in the fact that the Iranians were in the process of ordering two or three of the same class.

'Then, in 1995, a few things began to happen which we did not like. In January, China took delivery of her first Kilo. It arrived

40

on some devious transport vessel registered in Cyprus. Took six weeks, but the important thing was, it arrived.

'Then, in mid-September, a second Kilo left the Baltic bound for China, and that too arrived. Then, at the beginning of 1996, the Chinese confirmed they had ordered a total of *eight* more of those Kilo-Class boats, not including the first two. Just a few weeks later they began a series of naval exercises in the Taiwan Strait which were obviously intended to unnerve the Taiwanese military. They started loosing off missiles very close to the Taiwan coastline, and right then we were obliged to sit up and take serious notice.

'I guess you remember we sent a CVBG in to remind them of our interest. It slowed them down a bit, and from then on we had to keep a very careful watch on the situation. You know how gravely we would view any action by the Chinese that threatened not only our own position in the Taiwan Strait, but that of the rest of the world's peaceable shipping trade along those Far Eastern routes.

'Well, for a few years after that things went somewhat quiet, I suspect because the Russians were plain unable to get further Kilos built. You know what a goddamned mess they're in. Since the breakup of the old Soviet Navy the shipyards have been just about moribund in many places, especially in the Baltic, and so far as we know there have been very few deliveries of any submarines.

'It is just possible that the Russians have taken note of our repeated warnings that they should not fulfill the Chinese order, but I doubt it. We stepped the pressure up this year when the Chinese again exercised their Eastern Fleet far too close to Taiwan – so close you'll remember it almost caused an international incident between a couple of our DDGs and a group of their aging frigates. Would have been a nightmare if we'd had to sink 'em, but at least they didn't have a submarine out there.

'Since then, we've called the Russian ambassador in a half-dozen times, explaining how seriously we would view the situation if China suddenly had a really efficient submarine flotilla patrolling the Strait of Taiwan. We know to our cost what damage a top-class commander in one of those boats can do. If China had a total of 10 of them she could probably deploy three or more in the Strait at all times. That would effectively shut us out.

'You know there is a strong feeling in the Navy that we ought not to place those big carriers in harm's way without real good reason. And the President is very aware that if the Chinese have an operational patrol of several Kilos in there, that argument would begin to sound very, very persuasive.'

'Yeah, it sure would, Arnie. It would be very bad for the Navy, and traditionally that means bad for the USA. And the President knows that better than anyone.'

'Right, Joe. You said it. Now lemme recap in some detail the events of September 5th – two days before our first meeting with the President. I was right in the thick of it; it started about 0100 our time. One of our guys in southern China reported in, unscheduled, something he had not seen before: the arrival in the morning of a big Russian military aircraft, landing, apparently empty, at the airport in Xiamen – you know, the naval base city in the very south of Fujian Province.

'They refueled it and within an hour, a Navy bus arrived with about 20 guys, obviously Chinese Navy personnel, with luggage, and they all boarded the aircraft, which took off right away, heading north.

'Then we get another report into Fort Meade about two hours later. The Russian has landed at Hongqiao Aiport, Shanghai. Another of our guys sees two large Navy buses arrive, 'bout 1300 their time, and this time 60 to 70 guys get out and board the aircraft.

'Then, at 0500 our time, we get another call which says the Russian military aircraft has showed up in Beijing. Came in direct from Shanghai. And 15 more guys joined it. But these were fairly senior officers. In uniform. Right after that it went quiet. Until midday when a CIA guy from the embassy got a message through to Fort Meade that a Russian military aircraft with about 100 Chinese naval personnel on board had landed at the Sheremetyevo II airport in Moscow shortly after 1900. That's unusual for a military plane, but the embassy guy says there was quite a serious welcoming group of Russians at the airport.

'Anyhow, I ran the routine checks, aircraft numbers, time of journey etc. It was obviously the same aircraft – and, equally obviously, crew for the two Kilos which we have known for some months were nearing completion at Severodvinsk.

'Now, Joe, I took this matter very, very seriously. I made a report detailing how important I thought this was. But I think my predecessor as National Security Advisor was a bit more of a dove.

And I believe he did not recommend any of my concern to the President. Not even when we confirmed the 100 Chinese crew had in fact arrived in Severodvinsk and were beginning to work on the two submarines.'

'Jesus, *my* predecessor left me nothing on this.'

'Joe, I actually find the whole fucking thing unbelievable. I have been going on about this crap for months, and my reports are getting shelved by some goddamned political shithead who doesn't know his ass from his fucking elbow. Nor does he know how dangerous these Chinese motherfuckers actually are.

'Anyhow, mid-October, the two Kilos remained alongside, probably doing harbor exercises and trials we think, and the next thing I'm hearing is the overheads have picked 'em up heading out of the White Sea, apparently going home. However, we tracked 'em up toward Murmansk, 500 miles to the northwest. They were obviously getting the hell out of the White Sea before it froze and locked 'em in there for almost five months.

'Well, then I really blew the whistle. I actually called the President, the hell with fucking protocol, and told him these bastards were on the move, and if we were not damned careful, by my count the Chinese would have *four* Kilos bang in the Taiwan Strait in the very foreseeable future. He was extremely concerned and told me to keep him personally appraised of the situation.

'And this did not take long. The two Kilos headed right into the Russian submarine base at Pol'yarni – that's the one close to the head of the bay, before you get farther down to Severomorsk and Murmansk.

'And that's where they've been ever since. Just doing harbor exercises. They've never dived, and never been out for more than about 48 hours, which suggests to me they're probably going home, sometime in the near future, on the surface. I have suggested to the President that we may have to arrange for them *not* to arrive home. NOT EVER. Devious Chinese pricks.'

Admiral Joe Mulligan did not smile. 'Now I know why you recommended Commander Boomer Dunning join us this morning. I'd like to bring him in now, if it's okay with you?'

'Absolutely. Get him in here. Because today there's been another development, which I think all three of us should discuss.'

Joe Mulligan picked up a telephone and summoned Boomer

into the inner sanctum. The nuclear commanding officer entered and awaited permission to be seated.

Admiral Morgan was succinct. 'Boomer,' he said, 'you may know that China has taken delivery of two of those Russian Kilo submarines. They have ordered eight more. Two of these are right now being worked-up in the Barents Sea near Murmansk. And are expected to leave for China quite soon. We are fairly relaxed about this because neither boat has ever dived, and they seem to be preparing to make the journey on the surface, which is good, because we can watch the bastards. And then act when we're good and ready.

'However, today, December 4th, a new situation emerged, which we are now watching with considerable interest. The overhead just picked up, in the last 24 hours, a damned suspicious-looking freighter making her way through the Malacca Strait. We apparently spotted her before, off the west coast of Africa, heading south. So we kept an eye on her . . . couldn't quite work out her cargo or destination. We have now established she's Dutch, and under that big cover on her main deck is what looks like a submarine. Her course on clearing Singapore looks like she's bound for China.'

'Christ,' said Mulligan. 'Are you going to tell me how you found out about all this?'

'Too fucking late is how we found out. You wouldn't believe this, Joe, but I hadn't vacated my chair at Fort Meade for more than an hour and a half when some brain-dead asshole gets ahold of a report from the satellite which suggests a Kilo-Class submarine is on the move, on a freighter, from St Petersburg. They alert the Defense Secretary, and the office of the Secretary of State, and presumably someone here or hereabouts.'

'Not me,' said Admiral Mulligan.

'Anyway, they have a very high-level conference and decide the Kilo is probably going to the Middle East or Indonesia, especially as they seemed to think the freighter carrying it might be Dutch. Decided there was not much we could do about it anyway, and let the matter rest.

'*Do you guys know what they shoulda done? They shoulda said "CHINA" – and gone out and sunk the motherfucker. That's what they shoulda done.*'

'Yeah. Good idea, Arnie,' said Admiral Mulligan. 'That is what they shoulda done.'

'Delivery of these bastards is a goddamned absolute. The Chinese either get 'em, or they don't get 'em, right?' The Admiral was not pleased, but he continued. 'Without telling you the whole story, we then had to track the damned thing right across the Indian Ocean. We watched her enter the Malacca Strait, which as you know is a darned long bit of water – divides the entire 1,000-mile-long coast of Sumatra from the Malaysian Peninsula. It's really the gateway to the East, and we have a kinda sentry right in there. You don't need to know exactly who, or how, but we have friends . . . well, employees anyway. Guys who specialize in this type of stuff.'

'Couldn't be anything to do with the requirement for pilotage past Singapore, could it?' asked Admiral Mulligan, an eyebrow slightly raised.

'In this case, the least said, Joe . . . Anyway, once she gets through there and steers northeast, she's into the waters of the South China Sea. It's 1,500 miles – around four and a half days for a big freighter making 15 knots – and she's right off the first Chinese naval base – that's Haikou on their southern island of Hainan. We're guessing that's the freighter's first stop, and it's too damn late for us to do anything about it. We can't just take the fucker out, not in front of the whole goddamned world, right on China's front doorstep. I told Fort Meade this morning they should expect some kind of a Chinese escort from the Southern Fleet to come out and meet her, and then accompany her right into Haikou. Devious Chinese bastards.'

'Glad to see you're mellowing some, Arnold,' observed the CNO with a grin.

'I cannot see one thing to *be* mellow about,' said Admiral Morgan. 'Neither can I see how the hell this one got through the net. But I'm going to find out – and there's gonna be big fallout in my old department by next week. Christ! This'll be China's third Kilo . . . and it better be their goddamned *last*.'

Joe Mulligan shifted in his chair. 'You know, Arnold,' he said, 'I just wonder whether you're not getting overexcited about these Kilos. I mean, are they really so important? It's a medium-sized, kinda slow, kinda basic ex-Soviet design with a limited endurance. If I knew where they were, I could probably wipe out three of 'em in as many minutes.'

'CNO,' said Admiral Morgan formally, '*you* could probably wipe

45

out 10 of them, *if* you knew precisely where they were. But remember, they are diesel-electrics, not nuclears, and at under 5 knots they are silent. And we expect them to be working close to their base, in what are extremely difficult, shallow waters, where our antisubmarine capability is least.'

'Well, Boomer here had a successful run-in with one of 'em, didn't he?'

The Captain of *Columbia* looked up. 'Only once with a Kilo, and I'd have to say that boat was dead quiet at less than 7 knots. We only picked him up originally because he was snorkeling in deep open water. So at least we had an accurate position and fire-control solution on him. But when he stopped his diesels, and went silent on his electric motor, he was impossible to hold except on active.

'We had picked up fairly clear engine lines passive at about 12 miles, but once he stopped running his diesels the real problem started. Fortunately we were ready for that. But if he is not going to be decent enough to run those engines, the problem never even begins. And we are in all kinds of trouble.'

'Exactly,' growled Admiral Morgan. 'They're bastards to find if they're going slowly, and out there in the China seas, they can go as slowly as they like. They'll only need to recharge their batteries every couple of days, and we'll never get a handle on them.

'All the way up that Chinese coast – South China Sea, Taiwan Strait, East China Sea, right up to the Yellow Sea, the place is nothing but naval bases. They have 'em everywhere. From Haikou and Zhanjiang in the south right up through Canton and Shantou. Then we got the East Sea Fleet with an expanding base at Xiamen – dead opposite Taiwan – and another one at Ping Tan, which is less than 100 miles across the Strait from Taipei. And then they got bases at all stops north to Shanghai, and the big submarine shipyards at Huludao, which is damn nearly in Manchuria.'

Admiral Morgan paused, gathering his thoughts, assuming as always that everyone else knew as much as he did about the world's navies. Then he spoke again.

'If the Chinese get those Kilos in place, they will cause havoc if they want to. It will be impossible to protect our interests in Taiwan, because we'll be living in fear of losing another big carrier. And I don't think anyone would be able to deal with that.'

'She does pack a bit of a punch too. We know that,' mused Admiral Mulligan.

'Well, we know she can deliver a torpedo sophisticated enough to carry a nuclear warhead. And that's pretty damn dangerous,' answered Morgan. 'Chinese technology can actually provide that. I don't know if they'd use such weapons, but could we ever be sure? Their other, conventional-headed torpedoes are quite bad enough to send our carriers home. I guess we could hit two or three of them in retribution if they did hit us, but Jesus! That'd be a bit fucking late in my view. The fact remains the Kilo can literally vanish if it's being handled by a top man. And as we know, it can pack a *terrific* wallop.'

'And the Russians have been improving them all the time, I guess,' said Mulligan.

'Yes. Even for export. This sonofabitch is their big chance to keep making big bucks, and they want to please their clients. What's more, just to make your day, I also read somewhere they have a couple of improvement programs in place. The new Type 877EKM has significantly better weapons systems – *two* tubes which can now fire wire-guided torpedoes, and advanced, new torpedoes, which the goddamned Russians are quite likely to supply.

'And I guess I told you the new Type 636 Kilo has an automated combat-information system. Allows them to place simultaneous fire on two targets. They have *never* been able to do that before. And the fucking thing is even quieter now, if that were possible.'

'Beautiful. Just what we need in the Strait of Taiwan. But maybe it's not really such a surprise, Arnie. That's what they've worked on for all of their submarines these past few years. Somehow they've found the money and they now have a good few nuclear boats which are supposed to be quieter than ours. I expect they developed the Kilo improvements at the same time. Basically, the clients of Moscow are tin-pot nations who either hate us, or don't much like us. Or, in the case of the Chinese, want to be as powerful as we are.

'Whatever the Russians say, they've built the Kilo to please those clients, like Iran, Libya and a variety of none-too-competent operators. The Chinese order represents a major change in policy by the Russians and gives us a serious problem. It seems we are not going to be able to persuade them *not* to fulfill the China order. Nor are we going to persuade the Chinese to back off.

Those last seven diesel-electrics will get to Shanghai, and then to Xiamen, right on the Taiwan Strait. Whether we like it or not.'

The room was very still for all of a half-minute. Then Vice-Admiral Arnold Morgan spoke. Slowly.

'No, Joe. No they are not,' he said.

And the tone was not menacing. It was uttered as a simple statement of opinion. Boomer Dunning felt a chill run right through him. Now he knew for certain precisely why he was in this particular room. He betrayed no emotion, but he glanced up at the CNO, who also remained expressionless. Boomer thought he noticed the smallest hint of a nod.

'I speak in this way because I believe, politically, we are never going to persuade the Russians to give up that order. They've got too much riding on it. Not just cash.'

'How d'you mean exactly?' asked Admiral Mulligan.

'Well, right here we have another development, Joe. You remember that Russian aircraft carrier the *Admiral Kuznetzov*?'

'Sure. It's their main surface ship in the north, isn't it? Not so big as a Nimitz, nor even a JFK or an Enterprise-Class of ours. But still big, close to 1,000 feet long I thought?'

'You thought right. She's big, she's dangerous and the Russians had decided to build a whole class of them. However, when the entire house of cards caved in round about 1993, and they simply could not afford to continue such grandiose plans, they found themselves stuck with a couple of fucking great carriers, both half finished, in a shipyard in the Ukraine they no longer even owned. By this time they were just about bust. Terrible things happened – like the town threatened to cut off the power supply to the shipyard. No one was getting paid and naturally the new carriers were more or less abandoned.'

'Jesus. Yeah, I remember. Remind me, what were they called?'

'There was the *Varyag*, which I think they got rid of locally, and there was the *Admiral Gudenko*. And she's still sat right there at the Chernomorsky Shipyard in Nikolayev while the governments of Russia and the new Ukraine argue about who owns her, and who's going to pay for her completion. The answers to both questions are the same: no one. Which has been a major blow to the local shipbuilding industry. People ended up almost starving in that town.'

'And?'

'Not much happened for a long time. The *Admiral Gudenko* had been launched but she was covered in scaffolding, and they eventually moved her out to one of the unused piers in the south of the yard, where no one much goes. Then someone had a brainstorm: let's sell her to some other country which will pay for her completion. Who was the first name on the list?'

'As we know, China.'

'Right. They wanted her, but they could not really afford her, thank Christ. And again things went a bit quiet. But we just learned yesterday that terms have finally been agreed and China will buy the *Admiral Gudenko* for around two billion US dollars. Which you can guess is sensational news all over Nikolayev, and effectively puts the yard right back in business . . . We learn, however, that there is one condition on which this huge order depends.'

'Oh no,' groaned Joe Mulligan. 'They gotta deliver the last seven Kilos?'

'You gottit.'

Admiral Mulligan shook his head. 'I guess the State Department is pulling all of its strings?'

'Sure are. Travis had the Russian ambassador and two naval attachés in there early this morning. Read 'em a kind of velvet-coated riot act. Then I understand he was planning to try all kinds of persuasion, trade agreements and God knows what else. I also understand that none of it worked.'

'Bob MacPherson was talking to someone in Moscow round about the time I was leaving for Norfolk,' said Admiral Mulligan.

'I had a talk myself to an old sparring partner in the Russian Navy at 0400 this morning,' added Morgan. 'Admiral Vitaly Rankov. Used to be their head of intelligence – he's pretty high up in the Kremlin now, and he knew all about the problem. Even said if it was left up to him, he would not risk alienating the United States by fulfilling that order for the Kilos. Unhappily it is not left up to him.'

'Like so many things in Russia, the problem is political,' said the CNO. 'But this kind of crap ends up having huge military significance. Arnold, what do you think the chances are of dissuading the Russians?'

'I think we might have a shot at stalling them for a very short time, while we talk about it some more. But in the end no Russian

49

President is going to risk the wrath of the entire Ukrainian nation by scuttling the Chinese order for the big carrier. I'd say the completion of the *Admiral Gudenko* represents a kind of Slavic "mission critical."

'They are not going to endanger that. Which means they gotta build the fucking Kilos. Whatever we might say. Also, I hear the Chinese are paying 300 million US dollars each for those boats. That's a hell of a lot of dough for an impoverished Russian shipping industry. We *know* at least two of them are almost ready for delivery – the ones up near Murmansk – and five more are under construction, in two different yards.'

Joe Mulligan frowned. 'I don't suppose the situation is helped any by the endless bullshit over the remnants of the Black Sea Fleet between Russia and Ukraine. It's been going on for 10 years and in my view will keep on going until the ships rust to bits. I can't think of a single thing they ever managed to agree on except that Russia will somehow lease the big base at Sevastopol, and the Ukrainians will build some kind of a headquarters up in Balaclava Bay.'

'You're right, Joe. Ever since Ukraine decided to put together a Navy of her own, we hear every few months about a major agreement between the two navies, and then it gets blown out of the water by the politicians. Moscow and Kiev, deadlocked again. Right here we have two near-penniless countries arguing like hell over warships neither of 'em can afford to run.'

'That's correct, Arnie. But the one thing they all know they have to preserve is a spirit of goodwill and cooperation, and so I agree with you: that aircraft carrier project for the Chinese in Nikolayev will go ahead. The only way either of their navies can survive, with their shipbuilding industries, is to export ships for cash.'

'Right. And the most commercial property is the Kilo-Class submarine. Every Third World despot currently in power wants one. Or three.'

'Or ten.'

'Yeah. And that's the richest Third World country.'

Just then the telephone rang. The call was for Admiral Morgan. He picked it up, and both Admiral Mulligan and Commander Dunning suppressed chuckles as the new NSA rasped, 'Yeah, right, George. Forget the geography. I know where the fucking place is . . .' Then he regained his natural patience, and snapped, 'Give it to me straight and quick, George. No bullshit. We are dealing right here with the topic of the week, if not the year.

'Yeah . . . Right . . . Fuck it.' At which point Admiral Morgan replaced the receiver, and turning to the CNO reported, 'That was about that damned freighter we spotted in the Malacca Strait.

'She's running northeast now, about 400 miles into the South China Sea, already under escort. We got some decent measurements on her. Whatever's under the cover on the deck is exactly 240 feet long – which just happens to be the precise dimension of a Kilo-Class submarine.

'They put one over on us this time. Still, we could never have done much about it, save for instigating a deliberate act of war. You wanna nail a submarine, you gotta get the sonofabitch *under* the water. That way no one knows what the hell's going on.'

'Anyhow,' said Joe Mulligan. 'The Chinese now have, effectively, three Kilos. And there's not a whole lot we can do about that. I suspect our new preoccupation will be the other seven. And since we are almost certainly looking at a potential black operation, I suggest we give 'em a name. The two at Pol'yarni . . . right now I guess they gotta be K-4 and K-5.'

It now occurred to Boomer Dunning that *Columbia* was being designated the black ops submarine for the US Navy – the one no one knew about, where it was, or where it was headed. That way, if it disappeared, it would be a long time before its demise became common knowledge. Maybe never, since most of the time no one knew its whereabouts anyway. His thoughts began to wander, as ever, out to the deep dark waters in which he and his team must operate on behalf of their nation. And the sudden voice of Arnold Morgan took him by surprise.

'I'd say we've just about reached the point where we're gonna need a plan,' he was saying. 'Since Boomer here is the man we want to carry out the operation, I guess he might as well start work on it.'

'Right, sir,' said Boomer. 'As far as I can see there are three quite definitive possibilities. 1) The submarines have never dived, therefore the Chinese crews, in company with a few Russian advisors, are planning to head home on the surface, which makes life very simple for us.

'Possibility 2) is that they plan to dive the boats in the not-too-distant future, then spend about three weeks training for basic safety and operational procedures, then head home probably dived some of the way. Not much of a problem there for us either.

'Possibility 3) is a lot more awkward: the Chinese plan to wait out the winter working up in the Barents Sea, which does not freeze, and then head home as a fully operational, combat-ready unit, prepared to fight and defend against any enemy. Don't like 3) nearly so much.'

'You gottit, Boomer,' said Admiral Morgan. 'You gottit right there. If it's number 1), we don't have a problem. We can catch 'em anywhere down the Atlantic. If it's 2) we'll have to keep our eyes open and have *Columbia* on station ready to strike. If it's 3), that'll just be 2) to the power of 10. Meantime, if it's okay with you, Joe, I'd like Boomer to work on that – the trap for K-4 and K-5. I just don't want *another* one of those damn things to reach Chinese waters. Three's plenty. Three's all they're getting.'

'Right. Boomer will stay here, make a preliminary plan, and bring it back when he's done,' said Mulligan. 'You probably want to get back to the White House and inform the President we will now need his formal approval.'

'He's more anxious than anyone. That's not going to be difficult. We'll talk later.'

Arnold Morgan headed out the door onto corridor seven, then swung left onto E-Ring, the great circular outer-throughway of the Pentagon, where the senior commands of all three services operate, the Army on the third floor, the Navy and Air Force on the fourth. The President's National Security Advisor knew this mighty labyrinth as he knew the inside of a Los Angeles-Class submarine. He made straight for the office of the Chairman of the Joint Chiefs, and asked the Flag Lieutenant if anyone minded if he used the private elevator in which he had entered the building.

The young officer practically fell over himself organizing a guard to escort the legendary intelligence Admiral to the garage, where 'Charlie's waiting for me – if he values his life, career and pension, that is.'

Charlie valued all three, and was precisely where the Admiral wanted him to be. They drove out of the dark gloomy garage into an equally dark gloomy December Washington. The driver sensed his passenger was in a greater hurry now than he had been earlier, and he drove as fast as he could back across the Potomac and into the city traffic. It was raining hard now, and the highway was swept by spray from a lot of tires all flying along above the speed limit, but not as fast as Charlie.

He gunned the White House automobile straight down the fast lane, encouraged by the Admiral who told him: 'Keep going. I'm used to deeper water than this.'

Back at his office in the West Wing, the Admiral found an immediate communication requesting his presence in the Oval Office. He picked up the phone and checked the President's availability and was told to 'Get along here right away.' There were a lot of problems to deal with this winter, but this particular President knew the exact difference between a problem and a deadly serious, potentially life-threatening international situation.

He was staring out at the rainswept south lawn when Admiral Morgan arrived. His expression was extremely preoccupied, but he smiled and said, 'Hi, Arnold. I'm glad to see you. Anything new in the Malacca Strait?'

'Yessir. It's the third Kilo all right. Steaming northeast about 400 miles into the South China Sea. Under Chinese escort. Heading for Haikou, I'd guess.'

'*Damn* . . .' The President of the United States whispered the word, hesitated, then looked up at his National Security Advisor. 'Nothing much we can do, right?'

'Not without a fucking uproar,' said the Admiral. 'But there's one thing we *must* do . . .'

'Uh-huh?'

'We must make certain that goddamned Kilo, on that god-damned Dutch freighter, is the last goddamned Kilo they ever get.'

'No doubt about that, Admiral. What do I need to do?'

'You have to inform me, as your NSA, Admiral Mulligan as the professional head of the United States Navy, and your CJC, that you and your most senior political colleagues, Bob and Harcourt, authorize the Navy to ensure that not one of the seven remaining Kilos on the China–Russia contract ever arrives in a Chinese port. You must further authorize Joe Mulligan that he has presidential permission to use any means at his disposal in order to ensure this instruction is carried out. Save, of course, for either declaring or causing a world war. It will of course be a black operation.'

'Right. Do you have any feeling about the diplomatic route?'

'I'd say nothing at the moment, sir. I do not want too many people to realize how worried we are.'

'Yes . . . of course. I'm seeing the Defense Secretary and the Secretary of State in the next hour. There'll be a highly classified memorandum to both you and Admiral Mulligan by the end of the afternoon.'

'Yessir.'

'Oh, Arnold . . . I do have two questions. First, how much of a grip do we have on the other five Kilos?'

'Sir, there are two other hulls under construction in Severodvinsk, not nearly so far advanced as the two we're worried about. And there are three others at Nizhny Novgorod on the Volga. All of these are fairly close to completion. If we're right, we will have located all of the final seven for China, and you may assume they will all be on the move by the end of next summer . . . And your last question, sir?'

'Oh yes . . . Arnold, how much risk is there to our own submarines?'

'Some, sir. But every possible advantage is with us. I do not anticipate a major problem.'

'Thank you. Will you and Joe dine with me when it's over?'

'Honored, sir.'

Eight days passed, and then on the morning of December 12 Arnold Morgan received a phone call from Fort Meade, suggesting he might like to drive out there and see some newly arrived satellite pictures. There was only one subject that commanded this kind of urgency, and the Admiral yelled through his open door for someone to get Charlie 'on parade real quick.'

Including four minutes to cancel a lunch-date, it took only 41 minutes to reach the Fort Meade exit on the Baltimore–Washington Parkway, which was about five minutes off the Admiral's own all-time record for the White House–Fort Meade dash. He was a bit disgruntled at how long it had taken them, but probably not so badly as he might have been if Charlie had broken that record.

At the entrance to his old domain, Admiral Morgan told Charlie to go get himself some lunch. 'I'll be at least one hour, maybe three. Be here.' And he strode through the door, beyond which at least four members of staff stood rigidly to attention at the mere sight of their former boss.

The Director's office at Fort Meade, which represents the front line of America's world military surveillance network, has housed some hard-nosed chiefs in its history, but none quite so pitiless in the pursuit of truth as Arnold Morgan.

The new man in the big chair had been hand-picked by Morgan himself before he went to the White House. He was a New Yorker, Rear-Admiral George R. Morris, who had previously been on patrol in the Far East, in command of a carrier battle group, flying his flag on board the *John C. Stennis*, a 100,000-ton Nimitz-Class ship commissioned in December 1995.

Admiral Morris, always a serious, concerned kind of an individual, was a bit jowly in appearance, and was known for his rather lugubrious sense of delivery. Right now, as Arnold Morgan was shown into his office, the new Fort Meade Director had taken on the appearance of a lovesick bloodhound.

'Things aren't looking too clever up in the Barents Sea,' he said. 'Take a look at this sequence of pictures. They're in order.'

Admiral Morgan stared down. Pushed them closer together. Checked the times. 'Jesus!' he said. 'That's the Kilos. They've dived. How old are these?'

'A few hours, picked 'em up on Big Bird. About five minutes before you arrived, I got a message saying they had surfaced about 20 miles offshore, and were headed back towards harbor.'

'At least they haven't left for good.'

'No. Guess not. Looks like they're continuing to check out the boats work okay and to train up the Chinese crew.'

'That set of training exercises has been our "critical path" ever since they got there. I don't know how good the Chinese submariners were when they arrived, but if they want to drive those things home safely they have a lot to master. Just to operate the Kilos safely underwater is at least a three-week program. And by the time they start diving they ought to be competent with the hydroplanes, the diesels, the electric motors, and the sensors, the sonar, radar and the ESM. No one in his right mind would dive a submarine without understanding how it works and what to do in all conceivable emergencies.

'After just three months, I'm not certain they will have had time to tackle all of the combat systems, but I do think that by the first or second week in January they'll know enough certainly to go home underwater, without yet being a fully trained front-line fighting unit.'

'I suppose, Arnold, the longer they stay in Russia, the more competent and dangerous they become.'

'Correct, George. It's in our interest that they leave as soon as possible. And since they have been in no hurry to get those Kilos underwater, my guess is they will clear Pol'yarni in the next three weeks. At least that's what we should work to.'

'I assume we do not plan for the Kilos to reach China?'

'Correct, George. But this is black. *You* plainly have to know, but inform no one else.'

'Nossir.'

Admiral Morgan picked up one of his old telephones, the safe line to the Pentagon, direct to the office of the CNO; he requested Admiral Joe Mulligan to expect him within the hour, on a matter of high priority, and that if Commander Dunning was close, he should be there too.

Then he left Fort Meade, as swiftly as he had arrived, and told Charlie to step on it.

Back at the Pentagon, Joe Mulligan was waiting. Admiral Morgan came through the inner door without knocking. 'This might be it, Joe,' he said. 'K-4 and K-5 both dived today for the first time. Worked offshore for a while, then headed back in. They may be there for the entire winter, but my instincts tell me they're gonna be on their way home under their own power in three weeks. Straight out of harbor, sharp left, and on down the Atlantic. With six Russian submariners on board each boat to assist them. Six weeks from their departure date they'll be in Canton. That'll mean exactly one half of the 10-Kilo contract will have been fulfilled.

'Right now Fort Meade is watching the situation almost on an hourly basis. We have to move real quick. I'm assuming our plans are in order.'

'Yeah. As well as they can be with no real start date,' replied Admiral Mulligan. 'I suppose there's no earthly point trying to put the arm on Beijing, is there?'

'Well, we might just be able to blackmail them somehow over trade, but that's not the problem really. What holds us back is we don't want to let 'em know how much we care. That way they might get even more cunning than nature has already made 'em.'

The CNO laughed at the irritated turn of phrase. But by this time Admiral Morgan was pacing the office. 'I just hope,' he was growling to anyone who happened to be listening, 'that we do not have to take out all seven of them . . . however, the Chinese may be a lot of things but they're not stupid. I think they'll get the message early in the proceedings. They'll buy the *Admiral Gudenko*, which is not terrifically good news. But if we nail K-4 and K-5, they'll almost certainly bag the order for the last five Kilos.'

'I wouldn't be absolutely certain of that, Arnold.'

'I'm not absolutely certain, for Christ's sake. That's just my best guess. Meanwhile I better tell Harcourt to get the Russian ambassador in there right away and warn him what the subject is gonna be, so's he brings the right aide.'

The Admiral picked up a telephone, got through to the office of the US Secretary of State immediately, and Admiral Mulligan heard him end by saying, 'Okay . . . I'm on my way.'

Forty minutes later Admiral Morgan was in political mode, talking to the Secretary, who was voicing a very real fear, 'that the Russians might in turn put the Chinese in the picture. Tell 'em precisely how anxious we are. Which we do not want.'

'No chance of that, Harcourt. Because it would not be in their best interest to do so. What would happen if the Chinese, amazingly, said, "Oh, okay then, we won't go ahead"? I'll tell you the answer to that, right now. The aircraft carrier order would go straight down the gurgler, which would probably cause a military trade war with the Ukraine; and Moscow would lose the biggest submarine order it has ever had, worth in total around $3 billion, not including the *Admiral Gudenko*.'

'Hmmm. Then I suppose we better give old Nikolai some kind of a time limit, two days maybe, to make sure the submarines do not go to China. I don't hold out a lot of hope though, how 'bout you?'

'None. But that's the way we have to proceed. And when he refuses?'

'You know the President's views, Arnold. He would just like the plan carried out in the most discreet way possible.'

'Right. Where we gonna meet the ambassador?'

'I think in this instance your office. There's a kind of naturally hostile, quasi-military atmosphere in there. And we might just have a better chance of frightening him.'

'Okay, see you there at 1700, right? He ought to make it by then.'

'Correct. And by the way, you wouldn't be civilized enough to produce a cup of decent coffee, would you?'

'Very possibly, but don't count on it,' the Admiral called back. He was already thundering down the corridor, back to his lair, in which he intended to unnerve the senior Washington representative of the Russian Government. He was good at that type of bare-knuckle diplomacy.

Harcourt Travis showed up on time, asked how his coffee was coming on, and confirmed that Nikolai Ryabinin, the Russian ambassador, was on his way over to the White House, as all ambassadors surely must when summoned by the most senior representatives of the President of the United States.

Mr Ryabinin was a short, stockily built, white-haired career diplomat of some 66 summers, or, in his case, winters. He was a native of Leningrad, now St Petersburg, and had survived an early setback to his career when he was expelled from the Soviet Embassy in London as a spy, after working as a junior cultural attaché for only three months. That happened during Sir Alec Douglas-Home's sudden purge in the mid-1960s, along with about 90 of Nikolai's more senior colleagues, who were also suspected of skulduggery.

But Nikolai had survived. He had represented the Kremlin in various posts in the Middle East including Cairo, and served as the Russian ambassador in Paris, Tokyo and then Washington. He was wily, evasive and extremely sharp. Deceptively so.

And now he entered the West Wing, in company with his naval attaché, Rear-Admiral Victor Scuratov, a big heavily built serving naval officer who had until very recently been in charge of combat training programs in the Baltic.

The two men looked extremely uncomfortable as they were shown into the new grandeur of Admiral Morgan's office. Nikolai himself had been so concerned about meeting the former lion of Fort Meade that he had taken the trouble to call Admiral Vitaly Rankov, now ensconced in the Kremlin as the Chief of the Main Navy Staff, for a quick brief on what he might expect from the Americans.

Since it was now after midnight in Moscow, the Russian Admiral had been in bear-like mood, but he liked Mr Ryabinin, and had stayed with him at the embassy in Washington two years previously. He was gruff, and to the point. 'Arnold Morgan will not hesitate to have you removed from the United States if he feels you are not playing straight. He's a ruthless bastard and I'm glad I'm not in your shoes. Just remember one thing, if he makes a threat he will carry it out. So don't even think of calling his bluff. Be honest with him, as honest as you can. His bark's bad, but his bite's worse.'

Mr Ryabinin was not terribly encouraged. And now he stood in the lion's den, shaking hands with the lion himself, and being told to 'Siddown, and I'll give you a cup of coffee.'

The four men sat around a large polished table at the end of the room not occupied by the Admiral's great naval desk. Harcourt Travis came to the plate, and said he presumed the ambassador and his attaché knew why they were here.

They confirmed that they did, but were very afraid that progress might prove extremely difficult. The Ukraine problem was not easily solvable, and if the Chinese did not get their submarines, there would be no completion of the aircraft carrier. This could cost the current Russian Leader his presidency, such would be the unrest in the Ukraine, not to mention the despondency in the great Russian shipyard cities. And in Mr Ryabinin's view, the present Leader would rather have an angry America than no job.

'Do you have any idea how angry, Mr Ambassador?'

'Yes, I do. And to make matters rather worse, I also understand why. My own view is that we should think very carefully about this. But in the end, the President of Russia will have to decide between a peaceful solution with yourselves, which would involve not selling the ships, and losing the next election. It would also involve seriously upsetting our biggest customer.'

'But if you do not do as we request, relations between East and West may deteriorate into the dark ages of the Cold War, which in the end would be far more damaging for Russia than losing an order for a half-dozen smallish submarines.'

'I understand entirely, Mr Travis. But it must be my unhappy task to hand this over to my President, and, shall we say that most men who have attained very high office have, somewhere, a self-interested streak?'

'Well, Ambassador, I think you must understand we feel very

strongly about this, and if you do proceed with the Chinese order there will be a few hard financial truths for you to face in your future dealings with us. You realize we are able to make things difficult for any Russian president, including this one. On the other hand, we can be, and are, extremely good friends to you.'

'So, I am afraid, are the Chinese.'

Admiral Morgan, who had been silent until now, decided it was probably time to fire a shot or two across the Russian bows. 'How would it be, Ambassador,' he said, 'if we went out and blew the two Kilos out of the water, and then told the Chinese you knew all along what was going to happen, but deliberately failed to warn them, in the interest of keeping your hot little hands on that huge bundle of Chinese yuan and your President's job?'

Nikolai Ryabinin was shocked at the frontal assault. So indeed was Harcourt Travis, who dropped his expensive gold pen on the table with a clatter.

Again in flawless English, the veteran Russian diplomat, mindful of the warning of Admiral Rankov, said quietly, 'That would be widely construed by the international community as an unwarranted act of war. Unworthy of the United States of America. A large number of dead sailors, whatever their nationality, does not . . . shall we say, play terribly well in front of a large world television audience?'

'How about if we did it in secret, and then somehow alerted the Chinese Navy that *your* submarine had sunk the Kilos, as a way of holding on to the export order, *and* keeping us happy at the same time. Such treachery.'

Harcourt Travis went white. The ambassador made no reply. And the Navy attaché just shook his head.

Finally, the ambassador said, 'Admiral Morgan, I do not think even you would try to pull off something like that.'

'Don't you?' growled the Admiral.

And now it was clear that this meeting was going absolutely nowhere. The ambassador was not going to change his President's mind on account of Harcourt Travis's firmly reasoned statements. And whether Arnold Morgan's bludgeoning threat had worked was anyone's guess.

But the US Secretary of State now called the meeting to a close, by informing the Russian ambassador that he had in his possession an official communiqué from the President of the United States,

'Who formally presents his compliments to the President of Russia, and requests that he gives very serious consideration to NOT fulfilling the Chinese order for the submarines.

'We are sending this formally, through your diplomatic offices, and would like your assurances that it will be with your President within a half-hour.'

'You do have those assurances, Mr Travis, despite the disagreeable hour of the morning in Moscow. It's about 2 a.m. there now.'

'Thank you, Ambassador. You will see when you read it that we are giving your President exactly 48 hours to inform us that he has canceled the order, otherwise we shall be obliged to consider different options.'

'I understand, Mr Travis. And hope, most respectfully, that this does not affect our own personal relationship in the future.'

He held out his hand to receive the white envelope. And Admiral Morgan added, 'A whole lot of things are going to be affected, most respectfully, if those goddamned Chinese make even one move towards shutting us out of the Taiwan Strait. Especially if Russian-built submarines are deemed, by us, to be the culprit. And that you guys, knowingly and willfully, let it happen.'

The time was 1810 when the ambassador left. 'I guess we just have to wait it out,' said Harcourt. 'Want some dinner?'

'No, thanks. I wanna get back down to Fort Meade to see what's going on in the world. I'll get a beef sandwich there. Since the die is now cast and time is running out, the whole drift is now towards the CNO. The President does not wish to be informed farther, and as you know, the communiqué asks that the Russian reply go direct to the Navy office.'

'No, I realize that, Arnold. It's a pretty weak attempt to lower the profile. But it's better than nothing. Anyway, I don't think there's going to be a reply. Let's have a chat sometime tomorrow. In private.'

'Sure, Harcourt. Anything big happens, I'll let you know later.'

Two days later, on December 14, the digital clock on the wall of the CNO's office showed 1830. No message had been received from the Russian Government. Admiral Morgan was checking with the White House and the State Department. There was nothing. Admiral Mulligan was walking back and forth the length of his office. Commander Dunning sat quietly in an armchair. Like the Russian President, he too was saying nothing. He had a great deal on his mind.

As the clock went to 1836, the CNO said: 'Okay. Let's go down and see the Chairman.' And they left, walking briskly out of the office, onto the eerily deserted E-Ring. Their steps were right in time, militarily precise as they made their way down to the second floor.

The guards in front of the Chairman's office immediately escorted them into the inner office where Admiral Scott Dunsmore awaited them.

'Good evening, gentlemen,' he said. 'Any news?'

'No, sir,' replied Admiral Joe Mulligan. 'We have received no reply to the President's communiqué.'

'Very well, I believe we are all clear as to the wishes of the President,' said Admiral Dunsmore. 'I would like you to set those plans in motion immediately. Needless to say, the operation is black. No one will discuss this with anyone who does not already know – just the President, Harcourt, Bob and the Director at Fort Meade.'

All three men nodded. No further words were spoken. The ruthless near-silent efficiency of the US Navy was on display for their military leader. Admiral Mulligan led the way out, followed by Admiral Morgan. Commander Dunning brought up the rear.

And as he made his exit, he heard the Chairman say, almost imperceptibly, 'Boomer . . . good luck.'

CHAPTER THREE

Jo DUNNING, VALIANTLY attempting to back the family Boston
Whaler into the garage for the winter, was not having that
much luck. Thus far she had run over and probably ruined an
expensive deep-sea fishing rod, and somehow succeeded in
jamming the white 40 h.p. Johnson outboard motor that hung off
the stern of the boat firmly into the right-hand wall of the wooden
garage. She was not anxious to drive the jeep forward, in case she
went over the fishing rod again, and anyway she was half-afraid
the entire building might cave in.

However, the phone was ringing in the house, and with huge
relief she opened the door and fled the hideous scene, hoping
against hope that the call would be from Boomer. Even harassed
and angry, even dressed in old jeans and a white Irish-knit fisher-
man's sweater, Jo Dunning was a spectacular sight. Her dark-red
hair, long slim legs, and what Hollywood describes as 'drop-dead
good looks' somehow betrayed her. It was impossible to believe
she was merely a naval officer's wife; here, surely, was a lady from
show business.

Half right. Jo was very definitely the wife of the nuclear submarine commanding officer, Boomer Dunning. But she had retired
from her career as a television actress on the day she had met him,
15 years previously. This was not, as it happened, an incident which
had threatened to bring CBS to its knees, since at the time Jo had
been 'resting' for several months, and, in the less than original
words of her own mother, was wondering if, indeed, her 'career
was down the toilet.'

And now, as she ran to the telephone in the big house which
would one day be theirs, she hoped her wretched luck on this day
was about to turn, that it would be Boomer, *and* he would be
confirming that he had been granted three days off at Christmas

so they could spend it together with the children in this waterfront house on the western Cape.

But Jo's luck had not turned, except for the worse. The voice on the line was that of a young Lieutenant Junior Grade from the SUBLANT headquarters in Norfolk, Virginia, where she knew Boomer now was.

'Mrs Dunning?'

'Speaking.'

'Mrs Dunning, this is Lt. Davis down here at SUBLANT. Just to let you know that Commander Dunning has been assigned to a special operation, beginning almost immediately, and, as you know, it's difficult for him to speak with anyone outside the base. You may of course call here any time and we'll do our best to let you know how long he's going to be. But for the moment, he's terribly busy – he'll try to call you tonight.'

Jo Dunning had had a few conversations like this before, and she knew better than to probe. However, she was so anxious about Christmas, which would be their first together for three years, that she asked the question directly. 'Will he be home in a few days?'

'No, ma'am.'

Her heart fell. 'How long, Lieutenant?'

'Right now, he's expected to return towards the end of January. We're looking at a five-week window.'

'A five-week widow,' she murmured. And then, 'Thank you, Lieutenant. Please tell my husband I'll be thinking of him.'

'I certainly will, ma'am.'

'Oh, Lieutenant, are you going with him?'

'Yes, ma'am.'

'Tell him to drive carefully, won't you?'

'I sure will, ma'am.'

At which point Jo Dunning put the phone down and wept. Just as she had wept last summer when all of their plans were ruined because of another operation at the end of the world down in the South Atlantic. Except she had not known at the time *where* he was.

And as she sat now in her father-in-law's wooden rocking chair, staring out at the sunlit waters of Cotuit Bay, she could think only of the terrible, deep waters in which she knew her husband worked, and the monstrous, black 7,000-ton nuclear killing machine of which Boomer Dunning was the acknowledged master. No one, in all of military history, had ever hated anything quite so badly as the lovely Jo Dunning loathed the United States Navy at this particular moment. Her tears were tears of desolation. And fear. No one ever said it, but everyone remotely connected with the submarine service knew the dangers, and the anxiety pervaded every family whose father, son or brother helped to operate America's large underwater strike force.

It was not that she couldn't cope with it. Jo thought she could cope with anything, even, if it came to it, the death of her husband in the service of their country. It was only the hateful unfairness of it all. Why Boomer, why her wonderful sailor-husband, and not someone else? But she already knew the answer to that. She'd been told often enough. Because he was the best. And one day he was going to be a captain, and then an admiral, and then, who knows, she said aloud, 'President of the Universe for all I care.'

It took her a little over an hour to compose herself. At 38 years of age, she still looked perfect, and she was still dewy-eyed over her husband. She adored even the sight of him in uniform, this handsome, commanding man, about a half-inch taller than six feet, blond hair, massive arms and tree-trunk legs. Boomer looked what he was, an ocean-racing yachtsman when he had the chance, a man who was an America's Cup-class sailor, a true son of the sea. His father had been very much the same, but had left the Navy after World War II as a lieutenant commander and proceeded to make a great deal of money with a Boston stockbroking firm.

Right now, since he was close to 80 years of age, Jefferson Dunning was busily spending some of it wintering on a Caribbean island. Though he had made the house on the Cape over to Boomer years previously, in order to skate around heavy Massachusetts death duties, the family still thought of the house as Jefferson's. Boomer was a better sailor than his father had been – just – but not so financially astute. However, he would have no need to be so. He would inherit a reasonable amount of money, and Jo herself would one day share with her two sisters the legacy of the family boatyard up in New Hampshire.

She was a curious dichotomy, Mrs Boomer Dunning. A lifelong dinghy sailor, she was an ace racing the local Cotuit skiffs, and she could handle any power-boat around. She'd been doing that all of her life. Jo could also, however, to quote her Irish mother again, 'frighten the bejesus out of you behind the wheel of a car.' Which was, essentially, why the Boston Whaler was at this moment jammed into the side of the Dunning garage. Jo judged water-distance better than land-distance.

She had never really fitted into the glitz of the acting trade, although her looks might have carried her far. She had quite enjoyed living in New York and attending acting classes. But her first television soap-opera part had been, well, a bit wooden. The Hollywood producer who had once written of Fred Astaire, 'Can't act, can't sing, can dance a bit,' would probably have remained unimpressed had he studied the young Jo Donaghue in screen action.

She had a couple more chances, including another soap which ran for eight weeks, after which things went quiet. At 23, she was going nowhere, except that in the spring of 1988 she was intro-duced at a yacht club dance in Maine, of all places, to a young Navy lieutenant who had just crewed on a big ketch up from the Chesapeake. Cale Dunning was his name, from Cape Cod. They were married within five months, just before he decided to spend his career in the submarine service.

Even now, on this sunny but now depressing Monday morning, Jo would not have traded one day of her life as Mrs Dunning for the leading role in any movie. All she wanted was for him to come home for Christmas. And that was not going to happen.

Their own house was in Groton, Connecticut, near the big US submarine base, New London. But she and their two daughters, Kathy, 13, and Jane, 11, often came up to the kids' grandparents' Cape Cod house during the winter when it was empty.

The whole family had been together here during the Thanks-giving holiday a month ago, and this particular weekend had been arranged for Jo to put the house in shape for Christmas next week: ordering heating oil, and log supplies, as well as reconnecting the cable TV for the month, organizing a couple of special garbage pick-ups, setting the thermostats on 60 degrees.

Now none of that would be necessary. Jo and the girls might as well stay in Groton, where they had school friends, and where there were other naval families close by, old friends who would invite them to parties, at which no one would mention the absence of Commander Dunning. Special ops were like that. They cast an unspoken cloak of secrecy over their participants and all of those on the fringes. Jo knew she could be talking to a colleague of

Boomer's who had at least some vague idea of where Boomer was on Christmas Day, but that nothing would ever be mentioned between them. That was how it was, and she was not some skittish television actress any more. She was the wife of a US Navy nuclear submarine commander, and she might one day be the wife of an admiral. So she had better shape up.

Jo wandered outside to retrieve the stupid fishing rod, and to work out a way to remove the Boston Whaler from the right-side garage wall without driving the jeep into the other side. Stepping once more out in the cool bright December morning, she gazed along the water, up the narrows and into North Bay. There was still some foliage left on the trees which lined the opposite shore of Oyster Harbors, since it had been a warm and late Fall. But the reds and golds on the Cotuit side were brighter in the midmorning sunlight, and the flat, calm, empty channel out beyond the open harbor made her think, as she had many times before, that this place was indeed paradise.

The sailing and fishing boats were almost all put away for the winter now, except for those which belonged to the Cotuit Oyster Company, and the only sign of marine movement was the big Gillmore Marine tugboat *Eileen*, now chugging quietly out of the Seapuit River beneath the steady grip of the master dockbuilder and waterman George Gillmore himself.

Soon the winter would set in here; North Bay might freeze right over, and docks could move in the ice, and George Gillmore would be working overtime to protect the waterfront bulkheads and piers all around these bays. The high winds would swing in from the Canadian northwest, and snow would cover the summer gardens, and the spring would be cold, and wet, and late coming. But the weather neither inspired nor depressed Jo Dunning. She considered this place to be paradise in wind, rain or shine. And rarely a day went by without her thinking of it, and the years she and Boomer would have here together when, finally, he retired from the Navy.

There were times, when he was on duty heaven knew where and the house was empty, when she would just make the two-hour drive up here for the day, while the children were at school, to sit and read in this rambling Cape clapboard house in which Boomer had grown up. When he was far away, she felt closer to him here than in any other place, certainly closer than in their own home at Groton, which she knew was only transient, while *Columbia* was based at New London. She knew too she might yet have to move to Virginia, or California, as so many officer's families did, but she could deal with that. Just so long as she knew that one day they would all return here.

Sometimes she would walk down to the water and imagine Boomer as he had been as a little boy, learning to sail, right out there in the harbor. There were people in Cotuit who still talked about his awesome junior sailing record, and even now, out of practice in these tricky waters, Boomer Dunning could still angle a 48-foot sailboat tight-hauled through the unmarked narrow gap in the two-and-a-half-mile-long Succonnesset Shoal, the shallow offshore sandbank which guards the southwestern approaches to the Cotuit Anchorage.

Jo stared out to the horizon, across Deadneck Island to the waters of Nantucket Sound, beyond which her husband might well be driving *Columbia* in the near future, out into what he cheerfully called his 'beat,' the vastness of the North Atlantic and the terrible depths of an ocean which had petulantly swallowed the *Titanic* and a thousand others, not so very far from these tranquil bays.

The awful part was not knowing *where* he was, nor, precisely, when he would return. And the only comfort she had ever found was in this house, in this seaward, tree-lined Cape Cod village, where everyone it seemed had known Boomer for all of his life. She looked back out across the harbor and waved as the tugboat went by. George replied with a resounding short double-blast on the horn, which scattered the cormorants along the docks. Basically, George Gillmore did not require that much of an excuse to make *Eileen* sound like his own fighting ship. Boomer always said the tall, bearded Gillmore might have made a pretty good captain of a naval warship.

As Jo reflected, Boomer himself was in private conference in a specially fitted and closely guarded Operations Room, euphemistically called a 'Limited Access Cell,' at SUBLANT HQ, which would serve as the command center for all the US dealings with the Chinese submarines.

In here, the US Navy Black Ops Team would finalize everything: their various positions on the ocean; their patrol areas; their cycle of operations; their dates; their orders; their rules of engagement; their overall targeting; their charts. Everything required for the efficient management of a small force of submarines with a special tasking.

Even the signals left this room carefully encrypted. If you took papers in – any papers – you couldn't take them out again without special signatures and meticulous logging. Armed guards stood before the doors. No one was allowed access without a special pass. And these were issued only to the few who 'Needed to Know.' Even executive officers and navigation officers were not permitted inside, except for pre-patrol and post-patrol briefings. Four communications staff kept watch behind those doors at all times.

The successor to Admiral Mulligan, and now the new Commander of the Atlantic Submarine Force, was Admiral John F. Dixon, an austere and rather forbidding man with a narrow, serious face, renowned for his meticulous preparation for any situation. This severe appearance, however, shielded from his subordinates a reckless, youthful past which had almost had him removed from the US Naval Academy: something about a large bronze statue of a departed Admiral, which had been mysteriously filled with water by an unknown expert with a small drill . . . The statue peed for three days from a tiny hole in the front of its dress trousers.

Admiral Mulligan always called Admiral Dixon 'Johnny.' The statue incident was rarely, if ever, recalled, but there were those who felt that its distant, hysterical memory among those senior officers who were there might yet prevent the superefficient submarine chief from making it to CNO.

Before the small meeting today began, Commander Dunning was requesting that despite the long mission he was about to undertake, he still be guaranteed the one-month sabbatical he had been granted throughout the month of February.

Admiral Dixon had no problem with that. *Columbia* was due in for maintenance that month anyway, and he knew that the Cape Cod commander would be away for four weeks. Should there be a foul-up in the North Atlantic it was unlikely that *Columbia* would be required to pursue its quarry around the world, and anyway Admiral Dixon did not anticipate a foul-up.

'You going away with Jo?' he asked.

'Yessir. I'm sailing a 65-foot ketch from Cape Town to Tasmania. We'll probably have another couple of friends with us, and there's a couple of deckhands, and a cook to make it all bearable. But we're really looking forward to it. I've never been through those southern waters. And we haven't had a good vacation for years.'

'Blows a bit down there.'

'It'd better. I don't have that long!'

Admiral Dixon smiled, and the two submariners walked over to the chart desk, a big, sloping, high, polished table which had belonged to the Admiral's grandfather. On the ledge below were sets of dividers, steel rulers and a calculator. Spread upon the surface beneath the desk-light was a detailed map of the north-eastern Atlantic, placed on top of a large map of the world.

Admiral Dixon spoke as a man who has given the subject a lot of thought. 'Okay, gentlemen. To bring us all up to date: until a few days ago we expected the two Kilos to make their journey home to China on the surface. But we now have reason to think that may no longer be so, and for the purpose of this exercise we should assume the submarines will dive close outside their work-up base, then proceed west out of the Barents Sea along the Russian coastline. We expect them to run on down past the North Cape, off Norway, and straight down the northeast Atlantic.

'From there a few different things could happen. They might swing through the Gibraltar Strait where we will see them, but be unable to do much about it. Then they will transit the Mediter-ranean, the Suez Canal and the Red Sea, which are also areas somewhat difficult for our purposes.

'They may of course head on south, and skip Gibraltar. Though it's longer, it's a more straightforward route. And they would then head around the Cape of Good Hope, across the Indian Ocean and through either the Malacca Strait or the Sunda Strait. By then they may have acquired a close surface escort. So we will concen-trate on taking them out good and early, somewhere before they get through the GIUK Gap. Because, if they choose to make a covert dived passage all the way to China, and we lose them, the search area rapidly gets hopelessly large. We want them as they approach the GIUK Gap.'

The Admiral was now referring to one of the most important choke points on this planet: the great narrowing of the waters in the northern reaches of the Atlantic where Greenland, Iceland and the UK's northern coast form a direct northwest/southeast line only 1,300 miles across – the tightest point in the entire ocean. But situated directly on this line is the 500-mile-wide island of

Iceland, which cuts the navigable waters considerably. This was the great hunting ground of the US and UK submarine strike forces, the deep, icy waters where commanding officers have been trained for generations.

Throughout the Cold War this was the route for all Russian submarines heading for the Atlantic. And they passed through the GIUK Gap under the watchful attention of their US and UK adversaries, deep beneath the surface. Night and day, month after month, year after year, the two great naval allies watched and waited. Few Soviet submarines ever made their way through the GIUK undetected.

There are three main routes through the Narrows: 1) closest to the UK, east of the Faeroe Islands, which stand 400 miles northwest of Scotland's Cape Wrath; 2) west of the Faeroes across the Aegir Ridge; 3) the Denmark Strait, which runs between Iceland and Greenland's Grunnbjorn ice mountain. These are the lonely, haunted waters in which only four men survived when the giant 42,000-ton British battle-cruiser HMS *Hood* was sunk by the *Bismarck* in May 1941.

Admiral Dixon had placed his steel ruler across the gap, and he muttered, 'Somewhere in here, Boomer. We'll take 'em out just before they head into the Gap.'

'Yessir. And the sooner the better. Actually, I *had* been considering the possibility of the Barents Sea, as soon as they clear the Murmansk area.'

'I don't think so. It's a bit too close to their starting point. Ideally, it would be perfect if we could catch them right off the North Cape . . . right here. It's deep water, and it's off Norway rather than Russia, and they could scarcely avoid it if the buggers are on their way home to China.

'Trouble is we don't have the time. They'll be off the North Cape two days from their time of departure, which will almost certainly be a Monday morning. It might take us till Friday before we realize they're not coming back. By which time they'll be well down toward the UK. For our first contact we'll have to rely on SOSUS.'

The Admiral was referring to the ultrasecret American underwater network of acoustic surveillance, which covers most of the world's oceans, but especially sensitive areas like the GIUK Gap.

'Once we get a SOSUS fix on 'em, we can use maritime patrol

71

aircraft, MPA, to localize. This is going to take time and a bit of luck, but it's all we've got. I think we should first look at a holding area, where you will await your prey. I was thinking of here . . .' The Admiral pointed to an area in a 300-foot depth of water south of the Shetland Isles, 59.70N, right on the two-degree line West, 180 miles due north of Scotland's granite city of Aberdeen.

'This will put you about 4,000 miles from New London, Boomer,' said Admiral Dixon. 'If you run at about 25 knots across the Atlantic, it'll take about six and a half days. Right now we think the Kilos will leave in the first week in January. You should be on station southwest of the Shetlands by December 31st.'

'Yessir. Hell of a way to spend New Year's Eve. But before we begin a detailed plan, I should like to ask one question –'

But as he spoke, the door was unlocked. It swung open and the guard let in the pugnacious figure of Admiral Morgan. 'Hey, Johnny . . . Boomer . . . how we comin'?'

'Just started,' said Dixon. 'I've selected a holding pattern for *Columbia*, but Boomer has a question. Commander?'

'Sir, do we expect the Kilos to be armed? Or are they just a couple of freighters transporting a bunch of Chinamen around the globe?'

Admiral Morgan answered: 'You have to assume they will be armed, Boomer. Fully armed. You may expect each one of them to be equipped with its full complement of torpedoes – that'll be 24 each. These two hulls we're looking at are older than the remaining five, but I think we should assume they've been fitted with the newest Russian system. Which means they probably have wire-guided torpedoes, which can be fired in pairs, and engage two targets simultaneously.'

'Yessir. Got that, Admiral. Seems they're catching us up all the time. I guess I need to plan for the worst case – like they're both dived when we meet up? D'you think they'll be on the surface, or will they make the whole journey dived?'

'We can't be absolutely sure about that. Of the three Kilos the Chinese now have, they all went by freighter. Brand-new submarines are normally delivered on the surface, because it's much more fuel-efficient, less wearing on machinery, and plainly safer. But this is a bit different: we have two Chinese crews in training in Russia for several months, and as we speak they are working the boats dived, out in the Barents Sea . . . I got a hunch they might be planning to make this journey underwater.'

Boomer nodded. And Morgan continued thoughtfully: 'Either way we have no options. I just spoke to the President again. He is very clear. We cannot allow ourselves to be shut out of the Taiwan Strait and permit another power to dominate the sea in that part of the world. Right here I'm thinking not only of Taiwan, where we have billions of dollars invested, but of our friends in South Korea, and our trading partners in Japan. They're more worried than we are. That Chinese Navy is a world fucking nuisance. They got 250,000 people in it.

'The President thinks this issue is about the balance of power in those waters. If China gets a working submarine fleet, they'll call the shots on every level. We would be impotent in the Taiwan Strait, because the risk to our ships and people would be too great. They may *not* have those submarines. Because we're not gonna let 'em.

'*Columbia* will be lying in wait. It's your ambush. You must strike hard and fast. Take 'em out, and right there 14 percent of a bitch of a problem will be over. There'll be five left. And not all of them will be your problem. Maybe none.'

'Nossir. I guess the only real difficulty could be getting 'em both at once. Can't loose off one weapon active too quick, or it'll alert the other Kilo, which will then have time to go silent and fire back. Maybe even get away long enough to tell his base what's happening. Still, my team is well trained, and unless the Chinese have the Kilos more than four or five miles apart, or less than 500 yards apart, we should be okay. Just need to wait till they're close enough to separate on the screen.'

'I'm assessing they'll make their passage in loose company, Boomer, about 2,000 yards apart, which they'll know is good for low-power underwater telephone, but not so close they have to worry about running into each other. I just can't see 'em having time to get one off themselves.'

'But I can't count on that, sir. They got one off in the South Atlantic. Damn quick.'

'Yeah,' Admiral Dixon interjected. 'But didn't they have that Iraqi commander on board?'

'Not according to Baldridge. He says the Russian Captain got it away.'

'Hmmm. We'll have to trust you to get it right, Boomer. I do not want *Columbia* fired on,' said Admiral Dixon. 'I do not want anyone even to know she's there. We're looking for a silent, sudden, deadly trap, from which there is no escape. Meantime I think we ought to run through the broad outlines of the search phase now, because we have Admiral Morgan right here, and I've a feeling we could use his help.

'Just for a start, we want one of our special-fit fishing trawlers in place, as near as they can get, without being arrested, to the entrance to the bay. You know, the one which leads right down to Pol'yarni, just in case the Kilos do, after all, stay on the surface. We also want the regular Barents Sea SSN on standby – though I don't want to sink 'em right there. Too many ears in the water, right in the Russian backyard.

'The MPA boys will work out their own plan. But they can't start too far east, or the Russians will see what they're up to. Equally, we don't want to start too far west and south, or we might use up two years' worth of sonobuoys in a week and still not get 'em. I guess we're agreed, the GIUK Gap is the last resort.'

Arnold Morgan stared at the chart. 'No alternative to those thoughts,' he said. 'We have to get these guys as early as we can without being caught. If they stay on the surface the Gap is the sensible place. If they dive, we want them as soon as we can after they round the North Cape. The MPA boys can work there without being obvious, if, as I suspect it will, the Barents Sea SSN either misses or loses them.

'And Johnny . . . they're gonna need a mass of support close to the op. area. You have any idea yet where we're gonna work from?'

'Well, it'll be from the UK. I've penciled in my choice, a perfect spot, but we'll need some clearance in Whitehall.'

'Don't sweat it, Johnny. I'll fix.'

'Excellent. I'm looking at Machrihanish, an old disused former NATO air base stuck right down on the southwestern Atlantic corner of the Mull of Kintyre, opposite Campbeltown Loch – that's an old submarine haunt on the west coast of Scotland. But it's a quiet place.

'I'm working on the theory that we'll probably want six MPA for two weeks. More would be suspicious, and less couldn't hack it. They've gotta operate passive, without their radars – keep Ivan in the dark, right?

'We'll fly the aircraft in – Orion P-3Cs; they've got a pretty good long endurance: about 15 hours. Then we'll need Galaxy transporters to bring in possibly 8,000 sonobuoys, and all the support equipment. We'll need a ton of fuel for the aircraft. But there are NATO stocks on the field. We ought to be able to rely on that, so long as we pay. The problem is, what do we tell the Brits? And what do we tell NATO?'

'NATO, nothing. We don't have to tell them anything. The Brits probably know too much already. But they might help us out on fuel.'

'Okay, Arnold. How do you suggest we move things forward?'

'I'll get on to our London Embassy and tell 'em to assign a naval attaché to this and go directly to the Ministry of Defence. Meantime I'll do some groundwork as high up as I dare to make sure it goes through quickly.'

'What's our cover story?'

'Oh, that. Something on the lines of we're running a big exercise to show how we can still deploy MPA anywhere in the world, to vestigial support airfields, and operate for at least two weeks. It's something we don't do very often, but we're conducting this training in Europe, deliberately in midwinter thousands of miles from a home base.'

'Hey, that's good. Will the Brits believe it?

'Anyone would. Except the Brits. Cynical bastards. They'll suspect the worst, and they'll be right. But they'll cooperate anyway.'

At 1600 the meeting adjourned while Arnold Morgan telephoned London, attempting to contact an old friend he usually found at his London club – the UK's Deputy Chief of Defence (Intelligence), Rear-Admiral Jack Burnby, a man who had had the dubious experience of watching his ship burn and sink in the battle for the Falkland Islands 20 years previously.

He had just dined, and was in amiable mood on the telephone, as Arnold Morgan knew he would be. Admiral Burnby was delighted to hear from his old American ally, whom he had come to know while Arnold had been at Fort Meade. He listened carefully to the short request which essentially required him to do nothing except not get terribly excited when six big American patrol planes, plus a cloud of C5A Galaxys, came lumbering out of the night sky to land on the Mull of Kintyre two weeks from now.

Eventually, the Royal Navy Admiral said, 'I don't see any difficulties with that. I'll speak to a couple of people tomorrow and you'll have clearance in 48 hours, direct from the MOD to your naval attaché in Grosvenor Square. Need any positive help from us, Arnie?'

'No thanks, Jack. Just your goodwill. Like always.'

'Feel free to call if you do need anything.'

'Appreciate it, Jack.'

'By the way, old man, you don't happen to feel like telling me why you *really* want that disused base in Kintyre, do you?'

Admiral Morgan's eyes rolled heavenwards, 3,500 miles away. But he just said, quietly, 'You don't need to know, Jack.'

'Very well. I'll do my best not even to make an educated guess, if that's the case. I might get it right, hmmm?'

'Bound to, I guess. You normally do.'

'Well, goodnight, old chap, hope to see you in the summer. By the way, your boys ought to know we've gone metric over here since we joined Europe; everything's measured in meters and . . . *kilos* now.'

The tiny emphasis was not lost on Arnold. 'Is that right, Jack? Well, damn me. Anyway, 'bye . . . and thanks.'

Just then the door was unlocked for the second time, and the Navy guard announced crisply that the CNO's helicopter had just landed and he was on his way here. Four minutes later, Admiral Joe Mulligan came through the door. 'Hi, gentlemen,' he said. 'Johnny . . . Arnold . . . Boomer. How do we look?'

'Not too bad,' said Admiral Dixon. 'But I'm glad you're here, sir. We were just getting into the detail of how to catch Kilos. And I'd really appreciate your input right here.'

'Okay. Lemme take a look at that chart. Any coffee? I missed lunch and to the best of my knowledge there is no one in the United States Navy who gives one thin dime whether I starve to death or not.'

Everyone laughed and Commander Dunning's navigation officer, the junior man among the exalted company in the room, picked up the telephone and ordered coffee, then, remembering the CNO's preference, of which his wife Diana Mulligan did not approve, he added jauntily, 'And cookies for the CNO.'

Meanwhile they all gathered around the big North Atlantic chart and Joe Mulligan familiarized himself with the projected route of the two Kilos, and the preliminary plan Johnny Dixon had mapped out for entrapping them, on the assumption they would travel beneath the surface.

The Admiral anticipated the Kilos would make between 7 and 9 knots through the water, dived, and that it might very well take five days for the US surveillance to know for sure that they had indeed sailed, and were on their way home to China.

'First contact is almost bound to be SOSUS, sir,' he said. 'When we get an approximation of their position, we'll vector the MPA, and they'll begin to localize, using passive sonobuoys only.

'The main trouble is those Kilos need only to snorkel for a couple of hours or so at most, every two days. And it's only while they snorkel we have any real chance of catching them. One hour is very tight for decent localization . . . well, it is if the MPA can't use radar to pick up their masts.'

'We're just gonna have to get used to it,' interjected the CNO. 'To the fact that it's gonna take several days before we know the rough speed of their advance, and their approximate course. But with luck, we'll get a pattern, which will speed things up, and nail 'em down. That ocean's a fucking big place, right?'

'Sure is. But by the sixth night, we should have enough data to clear *Columbia* to proceed to the next battery-charging area.'

What Admiral Dixon meant was clear to everyone: that this time when the Kilos came up to snorkel, they would unknowingly betray their position on the sonar screen of a modern-day warlord – Commander Boomer Dunning from Cape Cod, waiting in his fast nuclear boat in the dark depths somewhere north of the Faeroe Isles. Waiting to execute the wishes of his President and Commander-in-Chief.

Joe Mulligan liked what he was hearing. 'That's it, Johnny,' he said. 'Once SOSUS comes up we'll find 'em. So far as I can see the only problem we might get is to assume they will come up to snorkel every night at around the same time. What happens if they don't establish a pattern? Say they snorkel only every other night at different times?'

'Then, sir,' replied Admiral Dixon, 'we will have to think again. But I daren't use active sonar. This way is the only shot we have, without showing our hand. Otherwise they'll go all quiet and clever, maybe even make a run for it, perhaps down the Denmark Strait, or inshore, or even straight back to the Barents.'

'Yeah. That could be a bitch. *Columbia* in the wrong place. No overheads. Shifting the MPA to Iceland, or Norway, and back. Dealing with poor quality SOSUS right inshore. We'd be just sitting here, guessing.'

'Yessir,' said Admiral Dixon. 'If it starts to go that way, we're gonna need a whole raft more of assets brought in. On the double.'

'Forget about that, Johnny. If we have to tell the President we lost the Kilos, and need more units, he's gonna have a fit, because it will be almost impossible to keep it black. I'd probably have a fit myself. This thing has to work according to our present plan. So think positive, guys . . . the goddamned Chinese don't even know we're coming, and they won't get clever unless we do something careless. Just remember, this operation has to work first time. Otherwise we're in deep shit. The deepest possible shit.'

By December 23, the command team from *Columbia*, the men Commander Dunning judged to be crucial to the mission, were assembled at the SUBLANT HQ, each one of them having flown down from the New London base. Working now in the Limited Access Cell, cut off from the rest of the world, they added a few delicate touches to the critical path they had plotted for the destruction of Beijing's submarines.

The combat systems officer, Lt. Commander Jerry Curran, a tall, bespectacled man who many believed was the best bridge player in the Navy, was there. Boomer's executive officer, Lt. Commander Mike Krause from Vermont, had made the journey to Virginia in company with the navigation officer, 29-year-old Lt. David Wingate, whose work would be vital during the long, dark days deep in the GIUK Gap.

Lt. Bobby Ramsden, the 29-year-old Marylander in charge of the sonar room, was there on the basis that he, of all people, had better know precisely what he was looking for. In this cocooned US Navy intelligence cell, the only people in attendance were those who must know the complete purpose of the mission. Each one of them was sworn to secrecy. Each one of them was forbidden contact with the outside world.

Admiral Morgan flew down for the final briefing, sharing a helicopter with Admiral Mulligan. Everyone watched the incredible plan of action evolve. That evening, Commander Dunning, in company with Mike Krause, Jerry Curran, David Wingate, and Bobby Ramsden, was flown back to Connecticut in a Navy helicopter, where the great black hull of *Columbia* awaited them.

She was still moored alongside, ready for sea. During the previous few days her engineers had worked her over, checking every working part, every mounting, replacing anything suspect. The slightest rattle on a prowling nuclear boat will betray her position. Every man knew that this mission, whatever it was, could be shot to pieces by one careless test.

The electronic combat systems were checked, re-checked and then checked again. *Columbia* would carry to the GIUK Gap 14 Gould Mk 48 wire-guided ADCAP torpedoes. She was also loaded with eight Tomahawk missiles, with a 1400-mile range, plus four Harpoon missiles with active radar-homing warheads. Boomer hoped these would not be necessary: they wouldn't, unless the entire Russian Northern Fleet intervened on behalf of China's Paramount Ruler.

What might very well be necessary, however, was the small arsenal of decoys *Columbia* would carry. These were the systems designed to seduce an incoming torpedo away from the American submarine. Boomer thought it was entirely possible that one of the Chinese Kilos would open fire on his vessel, probably at the moment *Columbia* sent her own torpedoes active. In Boomer's view he should expect instant retaliation, a desperate last-second shot, from a doomed ship. Boomer's men knew where the big, lethal Russian torpedo would come from: straight back down the American torpedo's own track. Straight at the hull of *Columbia*. Classic operational procedure in submarine warfare. That was where the decoys came in. And they better come in real quick, was Boomer's view.

Columbia carried Emerson Electric Mk 2s, and a MOSS-based Mk 48 with a noise-maker. Her IBM sonars were the BQQ 5D/E type, passive/active search and attack. On station *Columbia* would use a low-frequency, passive towed-array, designed to pick up the heartbeat of the oncoming Kilos.

The 7,000-tonner operated on two nuclear-powered turbines which generated 35,000 h.p. driving a single shaft. If necessary, she could work 1,000 feet below the surface. Right now she was scheduled to clear the New London Base at 2030 on December 24.

There had been some work carried out on one of the turbines, and on December 21 they had taken the nuclear reactor critical and driven *Columbia* for a short sea-trial, just out of sight of the shoreline. When Lt. Commander Lee O'Brien, the marine engineering officer, and his team were satisfied, the submarine returned to her mooring and the nuclear plant was shut down. She would not move again before December 24.

And so Christmas approached without any participation from the principal *Columbia* officers, sealed off from any contact beyond their own number. Most of them were wondering about wives and families, but they were promised an excellent dinner which would be prepared especially for them. It was probably as bad for Boomer as for anyone. He guessed correctly that Jo would not take the girls up to the Cape house, but would remain in Groton throughout the long holiday. Thus while he spent Christmas Eve with his senior staff, he knew that his beloved Jo and the children were a mere three miles away, and he could not even buy any one of them a present.

And then, in the gathering gloom of the afternoon, Lt. Commander O'Brien and his team began to pull the rods, the slow and careful procedure of bringing the nuclear power plant up to temperature and pressure, to provide the required energy for all of *Columbia*'s needs. You could run a small town off the nuclear reactor in a Los Angeles-Class submarine.

By 1850 they were almost ready. The last of the crew had long been aboard, and down below they were finalizing the next-of-kin list, which detailed every single member of the ship's company, and whom the Navy should contact should *Columbia* be hit, and fail to return to the surface. The name of Mrs Jo Dunning was at the top of the list, accompanied by her telephone number, and the address of the ranch-style home on a hillside which looked out to sea, even though it was two miles inland.

Some of the younger members of the crew were carefully completing letters home which would serve as their final wills should *Columbia* not make it.

And now it was snowing lightly along the Connecticut shore, and by 1930, the base seemed nearly deserted, barring the few line-handlers, their duty officer, and Boomer's squadron commander. The snow seemed to muffle all sound, and everyone could see it billowing high around the dock-lights which surrounded the great hull.

The order to 'attend bells' was issued. By 2010 Commander Dunning and Lt. Wingate were on the bridge, at which precise time Boomer ordered the engineers, 'Answer bells.'

His executive officer ordered all lines cast off, and the engines of the tugs began to pull the big hull off the pier. And Boomer announced the ship formally under way in the cold northwest wind on this cold Christmas Eve. Commander Dunning called to let go the tugs, waiting for them to clear before ordering, 'Ahead, one-third.'

And now *Columbia* began to move forward, slowly at first through the harbor, covering the first few yards of her deadly mission to the GIUK Gap. Just the sight of her cruising out into the darkness seemed to cause the night to simmer with peril. For someone.

Boomer, warmly wrapped in a greatcoat, stayed up on the bridge with his navigator as they ran fair down the channel and out into the waters of Gardiner's Bay. Their initial course would take them out through the gap between Block Island to the north and Montauk Point to the south. Big, almost weightless snowflakes were now falling upon these waters, which annually serve as the playground of vacationing New York and are also the submarine freeway in and out of the New London base. There was already a layer of pulverized white frost out on the casing of *Columbia* as she cut her way effortlessly into the short winter chop.

Boomer would stay on the surface while the water was relatively shallow, but he would go to periscope depth somewhere southeast of Martha's Vineyard. They would not go deep until they reached the edge of the continental shelf and turned marginally north, away from their initial easterly course.

By dawn on Christmas Day, Columbia had covered 300 miles of her journey. Coming to periscope depth, Boomer accessed the satellite, briefly, for routine traffic. Then he ordered the submarine deep for the 3,500-mile northeasterly run up to the Shetland Isles. They steamed along at a steady 25 knots, knocking off the miles, usually 600 a day, 500 feet below the surface. They crossed the

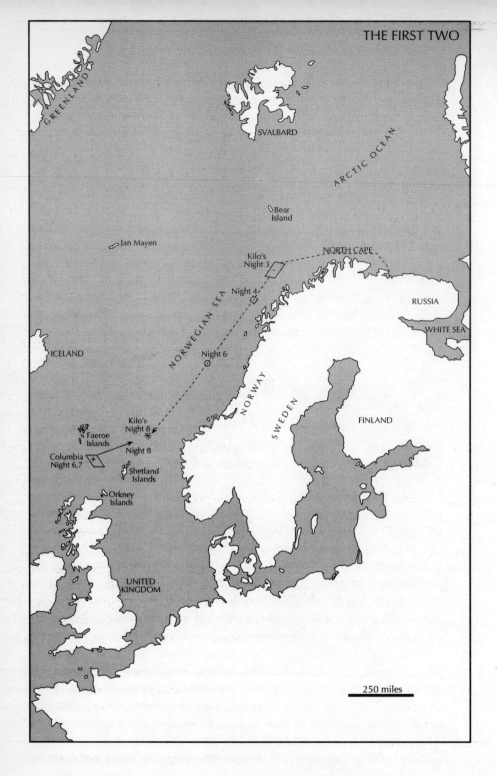

GREENLAND

SVALBARD

ARCTIC OCEAN

Bear
Island

Jan Mayen

Kilo's
Night 3

NORTH CAPE

Night 4

RUSSIA

WHITE SEA

NORWEGIAN SEA

ICELAND

Night 6

NORWAY

SWEDEN

FINLAND

Kilo's
Night 8

Faeroe
Islands

Night 8

Columbia
Night 6,7

Shetland
Islands

Orkney
Islands

UNITED
KINGDOM

250 miles

Great Atlantic Ridge right above the fracture zone on the 50th parallel, but mostly they ran through ocean water which was two and a half miles deep.

The six Orion P-3Cs passed *Columbia* high over the Atlantic two nights before Boomer and his men reached the Shetlands. The maritime patrol aircraft then curled away on a more easterly course, lumbered north over the Irish County of Donegal, and followed the rugged northern coastline, before heading in to the Mull of Kintyre: a long area of land which, on the charts, hangs like an old shillelagh from the west coast of Scotland.

The US aircraft came roaring out of the darkness into Machri-hanish shortly after dawn, which was as well since the landing lights at the disused air base were unserviceable, and would have to be put right in the next three days. The first giant Galaxy C5A was already in and parked, having made the journey over the previous night and landed in broad daylight. The Americans who would man the airfield were hard at work in shifts organizing electricity, heat and water supply. They brought all their own food, spares, weapons and a couple of military jeeps with them.

Boomer and his men continued straight on, past the Rockall Rise, and headed, slower now, for the waters off the southern side of the Shetlands. The Captain reached his holding area, and cut the engines back, as he accessed once more the American communications satellite. It was 1600 on January 1, and there was a message awaiting him, beamed down from the overhead, inside five seconds.

The Kilos had cleared Pol'yarni at 0500 that day and not returned. They had traveled north into the Barents Sea, in line ahead, making 7 knots, unaccompanied, on the surface. But they had dived before they reached a special-fit trawler waiting 15 miles offshore. This was a pity, because inside that trawler was more American tracking expertise per square foot than they had in Fort Meade. The 'fishing boat' immediately lost contact when the Kilos slid under the surface. And the regular patrolling American SSN was not yet in a position to *make* contact.

In layman's terms, the fishermen had lost the Kilos before the SSN could find them. And now no one knew precisely where they were. For the moment, *Columbia* could only wait, until SOSUS provided some kind of a solution.

Back in Virginia, Admirals Mulligan, Morgan and Dixon had said '*Fuck it!*' just about in unison when the grim signal had arrived late afternoon at SUBLANT. But they gritted their teeth and sent the news on to *Columbia* by satellite. 'Well, both Kilos will be forced to snorkel two nights from now,' said Admiral Morgan, who was back in his natural element, tracking foreigners at all hours of the day and night. 'I still think we'll pick them up.'

And so the Americans waited, and on the third night of the journey along the Barents Sea, January 3, the Kilos came to periscope depth to snorkel, and SOSUS picked them up. Contact was fleeting, right at the end of their charging cycle. The patrol SSN was too far away to pick them up before they went silent. But at least SUBLANT had a rough fix, and they were able to make a first estimate on the Chinese SOA (speed of advance) of 7 knots, which was a whole lot better than nothing.

Admiral Dixon ordered *Columbia* to a new holding area close to the Faeroe Islands. Neither he nor Admiral Mulligan believed the Chinese were alerted, but both men thought it possible they might suddenly go for the western side of the Faeroes.

And now Boomer just had to wait patiently for SOSUS to start the hunt, hopefully in the next 24 hours.

And it worked. The Kilos came up snorkeling bang on time at 2300 the following night, January 4. SOSUS alerted the P-3C operators roughly where to start looking with the sonobuoys. But the weather was bad, and the sea was rough, and sonar conditions were consequently poor. The MPA men were able only to narrow down the Kilos' position to about 2,000 square miles, with an SOA of not more than 7 knots, and not less than 5.

Admiral Dixon ordered the patrol aircraft into the air on the fifth night of January, standing by to follow up *any* SOSUS contact either side of the Faeroes. But this was fruitless. The Kilos never showed. Everyone missed them.

Night six was better. Again SOSUS gave the 'heads up' at 2315. The patrol aircraft picked the two submarines up shortly after midnight, still snorkeling. There was now time to localize, and they established the Kilos were on the offshore eastern route, closest to the UK – the route Admiral Dixon had expected and hoped for. SUBLANT's satellite message to *Columbia* was succinct. It gave the Kilos' position, course and speed at 0100 on January 6, and ended with, '*Plan to intercept two nights from now.*'

The seventh night was spent in comfortless ignorance. No one heard anything.

And night eight saw Boomer Dunning out in his attack area, moving up from the Faeroes toward the Kilos' 7 knot farthest on circle from the night six position, knowing nothing had been heard from the Kilos for almost 48 hours. Back in SUBLANT, Admiral Morgan believed they would come up early to recharge the batteries. 'They have to be low,' he said, banging his fist on the desk. 'These guys must come up to snorkel.'

But the hour of 2100 came and went. So did 2200. At 2300, irritation was beginning to set in, not only at SUBLANT, but also in the operations room of USS *Columbia*, where Commander Dunning was trying to get his thoughts in order. 'They *must* snorkel soon, otherwise their batteries will be completely flattened. They *can't* have crept by me, but they may have deliberately slowed down. Anyway, they are obviously still up ahead, so I'm going forward. They *can't* stay on batteries much after 0400, of that I *am* certain.'

By 0100, there had been no contact. Nothing by 0300. Boomer was beginning to think they might have reversed course and returned to the Barents with engine trouble.

And at 0400 everything was still quiet.

0410. 'Captain, sir. Comms. From SUBLANT. SOSUS reports dynamic start. Initial classification, multi Kilo-Class engines – probability area large. MPA called in.'

'Sonar – Captain . . . the Kilos are snorkeling. What do you have?'

'Nothing, sir. Looking.'

Boomer's mind raced. He reckoned he was on the line of their approach. He knew they had not snorkeled for 52 hours and that they were late starting their battery-charge. He concluded that the Chinese must have dropped their SOA to something less than 7 knots. The question was, how much less? At 6 knots he would be more than 50 miles south of the Kilos' 0400 farthest on circle now. He knew they had not snorkeled for 52 hours. They had to start soon. But if he moved only at good sonar search speed back up the route, he would not get there until 0630. Too late. Daylight. They would have finished their battery charge and would be deep and quiet again. If he was to catch them he had to sprint and drift towards them, increase to high speed with his sonar virtually deaf for a short period, then slow down and listen; then sprint and drift again if nothing was heard the first time. And so on until the 50 miles were covered.

He quickly realized he could temporarily forget about any

reduction in the Kilo's SOA below 6 knots since they would have stopped snorkeling long before he reached them, even by sprinting and drifting. He'd have to start all over, possibly in two day's time, somewhere down in the GIUK Gap. That hardly bore thinking about and certainly not at this moment.

Meanwhile he also had to remember the downside of this tactic was the danger that the Kilos might hear him while he sprinted. But at least it allowed him to cover any SOA between 6 and 7 knots.

Boomer decided to sprint anyway, calculating that if they were snorkeling now, overheard by SOSUS, but not by him, they must be a good 12 miles away at this very moment – if they'd kept their speed up to about 6.75 knots – and he'd be safe if he restricted his sprint to 15 minutes. He'd risk 20 to increase his coverage. Boomer issued his orders instantly:

'*Left standard rudder. Down all masts. Twenty down. Eight hundred feet. Speed 30 knots. Steer course zero-three-zero.*'

He then addressed his team. 'Now listen up. I'm reasonably certain these guys are between 12 and 50 miles back up the track and still coming towards us, snorkeling until at least 0600. We should pick them up next time we slow down. But we may have to sprint again, and a close pass and a short-range detection, while we're sprinting, is a possibility. Get four Mk 48s and the decoys on top line all of the time. I hope it won't turn out that way, but we have to face facts. They may open fire on us first. The advantage only swings back to us when we slow down.

'But if we have to, we'll do it the hard way, in a short-range shoot-out, using active sonar. No holds barred. Thank you, gentlemen.'

0431. 'Twenty up. Make your speed 5 knots. Right standard rudder. Steer 100. Make your depth 62 feet. Radio, stand by for satcoms. Sonar, slowing down and continuing to PD. Be ready with active for snap shot.'

'Sonar, aye.'

'Radio, aye.'

0437. 'Captain – sonar . . . new contact, bow arrays only. TA not established yet. Bearing red 83. Analyzing. Very faint aural. Not close. Track 2307. Tracking.'

'Captain, aye. Stand down snap attack. Left standard rudder. Steer zero-one-seven. Set guess range on computer 20,000 yards. Sonar – Captain, I am assuming this is a direct-path contact, course two-one-zero, speed 6.5 knots.'

'Captain – sonar . . . Analysis in. Kilo-Class engines. No cavitation, weak signals, but steady. Bearing moving slowly left, zero-one-five.'

Boomer then turned to his navigator, ordered a contact report to SUBLANT: 'Kilo-Class, snorkeling, bearing 017, range 10 miles north of us. Course 210, speed 6.5. Closing to investigate/attack.'

Columbia now slid forward, making 8 knots for the quietest, quickest approach. But the Captain's attention was caught by another message from sonar, reporting a garbled underwater telephone on the bearing. 'Not Russian, interpreter thinks it could be Chinese.'

'Well,' thought Boomer, 'if they're on the UWT there's gotta be two of 'em, and they can't be very worried about being detected. I doubt they heard me either, though I suppose they could just be warning each other.'

But right now was not a time for speculation. Boomer changed course to help the fire-control solution. The news from sonar was good – firm contact, direct path, good bearings, no change in characteristics. 'Feels a bit closer than 20,000 yards.'

'Captain, aye. Stand by one and two tubes. I'm holding course for another three minutes for the tracking solution.'

0456. 'Captain. Computer has a good solution. Track 2307, course two-one-two, speed 6.4, range 12,500 yards. You're 2,200 yards off track.'

For Boomer this was the moment of which he had reminded his superiors back in the Pentagon. The two submarines are close together. And right now sonar can't separate them. 'I don't want to warn one by shooting the other,' he murmured, 'because if the sonofabitch gets loose he'll announce something to the whole world.'

He spoke his thoughts to himself. They were clear in his racing mind. 'I want them both at once, or within 30 seconds of each other. So I'll let 'em come by a bit until I get sonar separation. But I'm a bit too close off-track, and I can't tell how long I've got before they stop snorkeling and go silent. I give them till 0600 though.'

Boomer ordered right standard rudder again. 'Steer zero-eight-zero. Lemme know the instant you can separate the contacts for simultaneous attack with two Mk 48s.'

'Sonar, aye.'

0508. 'Captain – sonar . . . I have two contacts. Tracks 2307 and 2310 now bearing 011 and 014.'

'Captain, aye. Take 2307 with number one weapon, and 2310 with number two. I want passive approach, slow speed, until reaching 1,000 yards, then go shallow and active on both. I'm gonna turn and point before firing.'

'Weapons, aye.'

'Computer – Captain . . . set same course and speed for 2310. I think they're roughly in line ahead. Put them 2,000 yards apart.'

'Computer, aye . . . *Set.*'

Boomer Dunning, tightly controlled, told himself to stay cool. 'I've got a ton of time,' he muttered. 'Get comfortable off-track before you turn back in. Wait till we get in toward their stern arcs – less chance they'll hear the launch transients. Maybe I should speed it all up a bit by turning back along their track nine minutes from now. That'll give me another 1,500 yards clear to the east, and into their stern arcs quicker.'

0517. 'Captain – sonar . . . 2307 bearing 341, 2310 bearing 352. Both in high frequency. Good aural. Good bearings. No change.'

'Left standard rudder. Steer zero-three-zero. I shall turn toward 11 minutes from now, to fire.'

0527. 'Captain – sonar . . . 2307 bearing 265, 2310 bearing 281. No change.'

'Captain, computer tracking right on, sir.'

0528. 'Left standard rudder, steer two-seven-zero. STAND BY ONE AND TWO TUBES.'

0530. 'Steady on two-seven-zero, sir.'

'FIRE ONE!'

'Number one tube fired.'

'FIRE TWO!'

'Number two tube fired.'

Columbia, for the second time in her life, shuddered as her big Mk 48 ADCAPs arrowed out into the ocean in search of a Russian-built submarine.

'Both weapons under guidance, Captain.'

0536. 'First weapon 1,000 yards from 2307 . . . SWITCHING TO ACTIVE HOMING . . . SHALLOW DEPTH . . . HIGH SPEED.'

Boomer heard the same report called for weapon two, then the warning he had expected. 'Weapons masking target . . . still holding . . . no change.'

'Captain, aye.'

88

'First weapon contact active, sir.'

'Release first weapon on 2307.'

'Second weapon contact active, sir.'

'RELEASE!'

Columbia's two torpedoes smashed home into the Chinese Kilos within seconds of each other at 0537, shortly before first light on the morning of January 9, east of the Faeroe Islands. A gaping hole was blown into each submarine, and the onrushing water of the icy Atlantic Ocean flooded and then dragged the new hulls two miles to the bottom. Echoes, lonely, terrible echoes from the explosions rang back into the American submarine's sonars for almost a minute. The Chinese weapons operators had not been sufficiently swift of thought to fire back.

Death came suddenly to the 100 crew members, both Chinese and Russian. Neither their ships nor their bodies would ever be seen again. The Kilos were invisible when they were hit, and would remain so for all of time. It would take another day and a half before their masters in China realized there might have been an accident.

Commander Dunning would scarcely have been recognized by his wife as he stood stern and hard-eyed in the attack center. To him, there was nothing personal about it. He was ice-cool in the face of so much death; a man who had done it before and would do it again if necessary. He was a man who recognized the needs of his country, and would execute them to the letter. If required he was perfectly prepared to die in the attempt. The United States Navy breeds such men for such tasks.

Boomer took Columbia to the surface to search for any trace of the Kilos. He went up to the bridge for the short journey, and he waited for the sun to rise from out of the eastern Atlantic. Then he could see with his own eyes that there was nothing other than a small oil slick. And he ordered Columbia back into the deep, and to New London.

He could, perhaps, have thought about it more deeply. But he was not paid to have philosophical thoughts. He was a loyal servant to the government of the United States. He was trained to carry out the bidding of his superiors. And that was what he had done.

Boomer accessed the satellite, sent his 'mission completed' signal to SUBLANT, and hoped someone would contact Jo, just to tell her he was safe. And that he was coming home.

Two down. Five to go.

CHAPTER FOUR

A BITING NORTHWESTER was sweeping through the Gate of Supreme Harmony in the freezing small hours of January 12. It brought with it the first snow of winter, directly from the high plateau of Inner Mongolia; the snow gleamed white on the great roof-tops of the Forbidden City, guardian for centuries of the Dragon Throne. The broad moat of the Golden Water Stream beyond the huge gate was hard frozen. Tiananmen Square was silent under a four-inch carpet of snow. It was almost two o'clock in the morning. The City of Beijing slept. Nearly.

To the west of the Square, deep inside the colossal Great Hall of the People, one medium-sized, second-floor government conference room remained operational. It was filled with cigarette smoke from the endless chain-smoking of the tall, stooped figure of the Paramount Ruler of China, on whose behalf eight armed personal guards patrolled the outside corridors.

Before him, at the long table which took up most of the room, sat the most powerful men in the country, including the General Secretary of the Communist Party, whose great office also entitled him to chair the Military Affairs Commission, paymasters to the People's Liberation Army – and Navy. The Chief of General Staff, Qiao Jiyun, was seated next to him.

At the far end of the table sat the High Command of the Chinese Navy, including its Political Commissar Vice-Admiral Yang Zhenying. The three Deputy Commanders-in-Chief, Vice-Admirals Xue Qing, Pheng Lu Dong, and Zhi-Heng Tan, spoke quietly together. The Chief of the Naval Staff, Vice-Admiral Sang Ye, had arrived in the last hour from Shanghai. The East Sea Fleet Commander, Vice-Admiral Yibo Yunsheng, had been there all day, as had the Commander of the South Sea Fleet, Vice-Admiral Zu Jicai, from Fleet Headquarters, Zhanjiang. The mood was somber and deeply reflective, save for one man.

Admiral Zhang Yushu, the uniformed Commander-in-Chief of the People's Liberation Army—Navy (PLAN), a turbulent man at best, was seething. He could not quite bring himself to sit down, but instead paced up and down the thin stretch of blue carpet not blockaded by the mighty polished table.

He seemed to be fighting for control, enunciating his words carefully and politely. Too politely, as if trying to teach algebra to a bloodthirsty Emperor's demonically stupid son. 'It is beyond credibility . . .' he was saying. 'Quite beyond any form of credibility. They have been out of communication for three days. That is impossible. One day is suspicious. Two is unheard-of. Three is trouble . . . That would, gentlemen, be the case for just one, but we are dealing with two. Is anyone suggesting that a simultaneous disaster could have been an accident . . . ?'

'Ah, Admiral Zhang,' ventured Zu Jicai. 'Perhaps they collided under the water.'

'BUT THEY WERE BOTH GOING IN THE SAME DIRECTION,' roared Zhang, all further attempts at control slipping from him. 'ONE OF THEM MUST HAVE SURVIVED AT LEAST LONG ENOUGH TO GET A MESSAGE AWAY . . . CAN'T ANYONE SEE THAT?' And then, to the head of the table, a discreet bow. 'Forgive me, sir . . . I do myself no honor, nor to the exalted leaders in this room.' And, almost in tears of rage and frustration, he finally sat down and held his head in his hands.

No one spoke for several moments. And then Admiral Zhang looked up and said quietly, 'If we assume that there could not have been catastrophic but separate, identical, mechanical failures at exactly the same time, we must, I suppose, examine the case of collision. But with two submarines going in precisely the same direction, and at precisely the same speed, it would be most unlikely and a scientific impossibility to arrange for an impact of such force, that *both* submarines were so badly damaged they sank to the bottom of the ocean with their entire crews, leaving no trace whatsoever.

'I suppose the leader *could* have reversed course 180 degrees, possibly to regain telephone contact, and then crashed into his consort. But I calculate those chances at several million to one.

'My professional judgment is, therefore, that whatever has befallen our two ships, it was most certainly not an accident. I am obliged to remind everyone of an old saying: When you have eliminated the impossible, whatever remains *however improbable*, must be the truth. This was no accident.'

He waited, as if for the inevitable argument from men who have no wish to confront a highly unpleasant truth. But there was none. The Admiral rose once more to his feet, and stared around the room. 'My friends and colleagues,' he said, 'the question I believe we must ask is, who could have done this terrible thing? And the answers are very few. To hit and destroy two submarines without being seen, you need a faster, bigger submarine with very sophisticated weaponry and tracking ability. Almost certainly a nuclear boat, with unlimited range, to hunt and find its targets in that huge area of water.

'That means our enemy is either Russia, France, Great Britain or the United States. Because no other nation has that capacity. I dismiss Great Britain and France, as having insufficient motive. I consider most seriously the case of Russia, which we know was under pressure from the United States not to provide us with the Kilo-Class submarines. But I am drawn to the conclusion that we are such close business partners in naval matters that Russia simply would not have wanted to perpetrate such an outrage. Especially with several of their own very best submarine officers on board.

'No, gentlemen, of the possibilities before us, I find, with much regret, that action by the Americans is by far the most likely. AND I AM SAYING WE HAVE GOT TO DO SOMETHING ABOUT IT.'

The Paramount Ruler looked up, drew deeply on his cigarette, smiled, and said, 'Thank you, Zhang. You are as my own son, and I admire your unflinching loyalty and your great care in this matter. But I wonder if perhaps my good friend Yibo Yunsheng from the Eastern Fleet would honor an old man, whose fighting days are over, and explain to me the mystery of vanishing submarines, and why such events apparently have no bearing on vanishing anything else?'

Admiral Yibo, a former commanding officer of China's 8,000-ton strategic-missile nuclear submarine *Xia*, the old Type-092, rose to his feet, and bowed formally. 'You do me honor, sir,' he said. 'And I may not be able to add to your great wisdom, but the problem with submarines always arises from the simple fact that you cannot easily communicate with them when they are under-water. You cannot see them and you cannot talk to them.

'Therefore everyone is entirely dependent upon their communicating, and in this case they were in touch with us through the Russian Northern Fleet Comms Center, which set up a satellite link back to our Southern Fleet Command Center. The arrangement was that they would access the satellite every 48 hours, when they came up to periscope depth to recharge their batteries.

'Let us assume the most likely scenario. They came to periscope depth at 0405 and passed us their message, time, position, speed and course *etc. etc.* The Americans were waiting and sunk both Kilos with two simultaneously controlled torpedoes a half-hour later when the submarines were both still running their diesel engines, and could be tracked.

'The following night, we naturally receive no communication. And if the Kilos were running at, say, 8 knots, we naturally assume they are now perhaps 180 miles southwest of their last known position, and are having a radio mast problem, or something's gone wrong. The following day we are plotting them 360 miles beyond the point where they were hit . . . but we do not know their precise course, and this means there is now an area of some 65,000 square miles in which they could be.

'But the ocean is two miles deep. And now another day has passed and our search area is even bigger, and even if someone were to tell us exactly where the boats were, what could we do? Send down a diver. Of course not. And for what? Everyone is dead. The submarine is not only wrecked, it's beyond the grasp of our Navy. Not even the mighty USA could do that much about it.

'Sir, it is my most depressing duty to tell you there is *nothing* we can do about a lost submarine that far from home. Which is why we may not wish to admit losing one. We are dealing here, sir, with the most brutal, underhand form of warfare. No one admits what they did. No one admits what has happened to them. In submarines that has always been the way. You will know, sir, in your great learning, that we cannot ever announce that our two new Kilo-Class boats were hit and destroyed by the imperial forces of the United States.'

'Thank you, Admiral Yibo. I am indebted to you for your wise counsel . . . but, comrades, the hour grows late, and I am tired, and must retire for the night. I think we should have a talk to the

Russians tomorrow. I am sure they are as concerned as we are. Perhaps they may know even more. Let me leave that to you, and perhaps we should reconvene here later in the morning, say at 11 o'clock, and decide what, if anything, we ought to do.'

He rose wearily to his feet and was escorted out into the corridor by two secretaries. The Political Commissar followed them out, and the Party General Secretary, and then the Chief of Staff. The naval officers made no move to leave; Admiral Zhang picked up the telephone yet again and called the Southern Fleet Headquarters, hoping against all hope that something had been heard from the missing submarines. But the answer was as it been for three days now. An unvarying nothing.

At the age of 56, Admiral Zhang Yushu was probably the best Navy C-in-C China had ever had. He was a big man in stature, six feet tall, with a swarthy, rounded, but somewhat Western-looking face. He wore his thick dark hair longer than is customary in the Chinese political and military establishment, and glared at the world from behind heavy, horn-rimmed glasses. He was the son of a freighter captain from the great southeastern seaport of Xiamen. In fact he had been born on the freighter, during times of terrible poverty just after World War II. At the age of 12, he could have stripped down the ship's engine and put it back together. He knew how to navigate the South China Sea, and at 15 had been capable of commanding any one of the medium-sized freighters which plied that busy coastline to the west of the Formosa Strait.

He won a place at Xiamen University and gained the best possible marine engineering degree. He took two further courses in the study of nuclear physics, and then, at 22, joined the Navy, where his rise to prominence, was, by Chinese standards, swift and sure. At the age of 39 he was Commanding Officer of the new Shanghai-built Luda-Class guided-missile destroyer *Nanjing*. At 44, he was appointed Commander of the East Sea Fleet, and four years later became Chief of the Naval Staff. The Great Reformer, the late Deng Xiaoping, who at that time was still holding on to his last active chairmanship, that of the Military Affairs Commission, promoted him to Commander-in-Chief of the People's Liberation Army–Navy, because he believed that Admiral Zhang was the man to mastermind the modernization of the Chinese Navy.

Deng made the appointment because of one conversation he

had with the young Admiral, who had told him, 'When I was a very little boy, my father was the best freighter captain in Xiamen. He worked harder than anyone, and he was cleverer than anyone, but our ship was old and it continually went wrong. My father was probably the only man on the whole waterfront who could have kept it going . . . but the struggle was impossible, because we were poor, and people with better, faster and more reliable freighters took the best of the trade, especially in transporting fruit and vegetables. In maritime matters, sir, there is no substitute for the best equipment. I would rather have 10 top-class modern submarines than 100 out-of-date ones. Give me 10 brand-new guided-missile destroyers, 50 modern frigates, and a new aircraft carrier, and I'll keep this country safe from attack from the sea for half a century.'

Deng liked it. Deng actually loved it. Here was a modern man, who could see beyond the horizon. He knew the elderly High Command of the People's Liberation Army would not like what they heard, since most of them still believed that huge numbers of half-trained men – 2.2 million soldiers – and a vast, near-obsolete fleet of aging warships was preferable. But Deng instinctively knew that Admiral Zhang was his man.

The decision to equip the Chinese Navy with the 10 Russian-built Kilos had in the end been Zhang's, and it was he who urged the Navy paymasters to buy the 67,000-ton aircraft carrier, *Admiral Gudenko*, still unfinished in the Ukraine yard of Nikolayev. And now his plans were in ruins, his strategies for the 21st century in chaos, and he faced the reproving stares of the elderly Vice-Admirals Pheng Lu Dong, 71, and Zhi-Heng Tan, 68, with a mixture of anger and inhibition.

In his soul, he knew that he was being blamed personally for all of this. The older generation believed that China had no further need to expand its borders, save for some future opportunity to bring Taiwan back into the fold. They had all the territory they would ever need, they basically had no natural enemy since the demise of the Soviet Empire, and the worst that could ever happen would be border skirmishes, of little significance, in the north. And now the totally unnecessary purchase of US$3 billion worth of submarines from Moscow was sucking them into a war with the United States of America. At least that's how it looked to Pheng Lu Dong and Zhi-Heng Tan.

Admiral Zhang, and his friends the Chief of Naval Staff, Vice-Admiral Sang Ye, and the South Sea Fleet Commander, Vice-Admiral Zu Jicai, viewed the matter rather differently. All three of them felt that this was a terrible affront to the honor of China, and a momentous loss of face in front of the world community. China owns the largest Army in the world, and the third largest Navy – in numbers, not in capability. And all three men believed they should carry out some ferocious retribution against the USA.

Admiral Sang Ye was prepared to finance and organize a terrorist attack on the American mainland, similar to the Oklahoma bombing in 1995. As he said, 'There are 1.6 million Chinese people living in the United States. I am sure we could arrange for 20 of them to carry out a bombing in New York or Washington, and when it was done we could send a one-word message somehow – "KILOS" – so they would know. And better yet, *we* would know that our honor had been saved.'

None of the three suggested having a shot at a US Navy warship. But Admiral Zhang said, as he had said so many times before, 'We must get the rest of the Kilos. Only by doing so can we ever hope to dominate the Taiwan Strait. Those submarines could allow us to carry out a naval blockade of Taiwan.' And then he added, 'I am just afraid our political masters will not have the will for this, and that the entire order will be canceled, and we will be forever powerless. It is the Kilo submarine which really bothers the USA, and they know we can send their big aircraft carriers away for good, if we can just get 10 Kilos in service.'

'Well, we do have three in our possession right now,' said Admiral Pheng. 'Would it not be possible for us to build the rest ourselves, perhaps under license from Russia? It happens quite often in the West.'

'It happens, Admiral,' replied Zhang. 'But it does not often work. Submarines are capricious creatures unless they are perfectly constructed. They have millions of working parts. And if one of them in a critical place is not correctly fitted the whole is flawed, and you end up with a boat that is not right, cannot be properly fixed, and never will be right. Almost every Third-World nation which has made submarines under license has had trouble from them. The Middle East is a scrapyard of ambitious nations who thought they could run a submarine force, and never got to sea, never mind underwater. I am afraid that to own and run super-

96

efficient inshore submarines, you have to get them from Great Britain, Russia, France, Holland, Sweden or Germany. The USA does not make them any more.'

'Then perhaps we should not bother with them, and build destroyers and frigates instead,' ventured Admiral Pheng. 'They are very much less expensive and can be very effective.'

'Admiral, you have been a friend to me, for all of my time in the Navy, and I have been honored to be taught by you in many ways,' replied Zhang. 'But I have made a study for years of the American capability, and you must believe me when I tell you that if the United States Navy turned a couple of carrier battle groups loose on us in the South China Sea, they could annihilate our entire available Southern Navy in less than a day. The only way to combat them would be to hit and destroy their carrier, and the only way to do that is with a submarine capable of deploying a torpedo containing a nuclear warhead. All other subjects are irrelevant.'

His voice softened a little when he added, 'In the end, we are talking about Taiwan, and repossession of the island. Just by having a Kilo fleet, we are deterring anyone, including America, from interfering. In the end you will find we are merely, as they say in the US, upping the ante. If we can get those Kilos, there will be no war. Because no one else will like their chances.'

'I must bow, then, to the great wisdom of the Navy's young master,' said Admiral Pheng, smiling. 'As ever you have my loyal support.'

Admiral Zhang also smiled. But he found it difficult. He rose to his feet and announced that he too was retiring for the night, and perhaps they should all go now to bed. 'Walk with me, Jicai,' he said to the South Sea Fleet Commander. 'I'm staying in naval quarters tonight, and we'll take my car. We need to be back here in six hours, and in my view the entire future of the Navy is in the balance.'

Five Navy staff cars awaited them at the side entrance in Chang'an Avenue. It was 4 a.m., and the snow had stopped, but the ground was covered, the temperature was 12 degrees below freezing, and the wind was raw. Admiral Zhang and Vice-Admiral Zu boarded the first Mercedes-Benz saloon. The others bowed as they left. And the wide tires of the German-built limousine made a soft, creaking sound on the fresh snow as they drove carefully away from the white, crystal plateau of Tiananmen Square.

★

At 11 o'clock sharp the following morning, the Paramount Ruler, smoking fiercely, walked unsteadily into the conference room on the second floor of the Great Hall of the People. Parliament had been temporarily suspended for the day while he and the General Secretary of the Party were attending to an 'important military matter.' No other members of the ruling Politburo had any idea what had happened. And they never would. Each man in the private conference room had been sworn to absolute secrecy.

And now they deferred to the Paramount Ruler, who wished them all good morning, and trusted they were all well, and then said that first he would like to hear the clear recommendations of his Commander-in-Chief Admiral Zhang Yushu, who rose to his feet and confirmed that he would be honored to offer them.

'I do not think there should be anyone in doubt that our submarines were hit and destroyed by the United States Navy,' he began. 'There is no point speaking to them about this because they will simply deny all knowledge of it, and act as if they are shocked that such an outrage should have occurred.

'I have been in contact personally with the Russians this morning who have arrived at an identical conclusion. Apparently they were given an ultimatum by the United States less than a month ago that our order for the Kilos ought not to be fulfilled. They did not, however, think that even as barbarous and self-interested a country as the USA would dare to pull off something like this. Nonetheless, to our cost, we now know differently.

'The Russians are as upset and angry as we are, and later today we will be working out an escort plan to ensure the safe arrival of the remaining five Kilos —'

'If,' interrupted Vice-Admiral Yang Zhenying, the Political Commissar of the Navy, 'we decide to proceed with the remainder of the order. I believe we did have to pay for the two missing Kilos before they were allowed to clear the Murman coast . . .'

'Yes, that is partially so,' said Admiral Zhang. 'I am afraid no one gets any credit in Russia. Not even us.'

'Well, we may think that US$600 million is a very high price to pay for nothing. Though not as bad as US$1.5 billion would be if you managed to lose the other five in the same way,' replied Admiral Yang.

'With respect, Admiral,' replied Zhang. 'We have paid only $400 million. And it is hard for me to assume responsibility for an unwarranted and unprecedented act of war by the United States of America.'

'Then you have much still to learn, Admiral. In military matters, as in the boxing ring, the rule is, Defend Yourself at All Times. Those who have forgotten this basic discipline have, traditionally, had the error of their ways thrust upon them. I am very much afraid that as the Commander-in-Chief of the People's Liberation Army–Navy, you are entirely responsible for the safe passage of *all* Chinese warships, and I am obliged to mention, with the greatest respect for your high authority, that you did a singularly unpleasing job of protecting our substantial investment in the Russian-built submarines.'

Admiral Zhang stayed calm. 'And what would you recommend I should have done?' he asked coldly.

'I am afraid that I cannot be expected to solve your problems as well as my own,' replied Admiral Yang. 'I would, however, prefer we had a man in the job who was, shall we say, big enough for it, and might have shown foresight in the light of known hostility from the USA.'

'It would do me no honor to remind you that you were never once considered sufficiently competent to command even a regional fleet,' rasped Zhang. 'You were a fourth-rate captain of an aging frigate which would have fallen in half if you had ever fired one of its guns. And you consider you have a right to sit in judgment on me . . . You are a political commissar because you married well, and had already failed abjectly as a commanding officer –'

The Paramount Ruler banged his frail fist softly on the table. 'Gentlemen, this is unseemly and unproductive. Admiral Yang, you are now a member of a greatly revered naval family and I forbid you to cast doubts on the ability of my Commander-in-Chief. It does you no honor, and is of no value to this meeting. I am looking to the future and if you cannot be constructive perhaps you should not be here – but I admire you, and would like you to think more deeply before you speak. Please continue, Zhang.'

'Of course, sir . . . and I think we should concentrate on two areas: whether we consider taking a serious retribution against the USA, which I am in favor of doing, and how to ensure the safe delivery of the final five Kilos.'

'Yes, yes, I do understand the anxiety of the Navy in this matter, but you know, Zhang, there is a broader picture here and we should not ignore it. Let me just say that we have already agreed we are a "satisfied" state – and do not really have any territorial claims. We enjoy a permanent seat and a veto on the United Nations Security Council. We also enjoy Most Favored Nation status with the United States – not an annually reviewed situation, but permanent.

'Let me remind you of the words of Deng Xiaoping when discussing our foreign policy. He said we should hide our capacities, bide our time, remain free of ambitions and never claim leadership. He meant, Zhang, that we should avoid adventures. And I am drawn to the conclusion that this is an adventure, you know . . . but I would like to hear you say more.'

'Sir,' said Zhang, 'I am wondering if I should just clarify for myself, and with the wisdom of your guidance . . . was it not decreed in all of our greatest councils for the past 40 years that we must work carefully towards the reintroduction of Taiwan to the mainland government? And have we not stated endlessly that we would like to remove the formal American influence in the area, just as we removed the British from Hong Kong?'

'Yes, Zhang, you are correct in those assumptions.'

'Then, with respect, if I may speak as a military man, I would like to put forward the idea that unless we can frighten the American carriers out of our waters we can *never achieve those aims*. As we now know, more clearly today than we did last month, the United States is utterly ruthless in the pursuit of her own aims. She wishes to dominate the sea-trade routes which surround our eastern seaward border, and with every passing year she drives a bigger and bigger wedge between us and Taiwan.

'Even when we show any sign of naval muscle in our own Taiwan Strait, the next thing is the appearance of a giant American aircraft carrier, which, let's face it, could very nearly take our Eastern Provinces off the map if it felt so inclined. And who could do anything about it? No one. We have one chance, sir – the Kilos, and I implore you, in your unfathomable wisdom, to permit the program to go forward, with, of course, the additional security Admiral Yang would like me to organize. And in which he is, of course, entirely unqualified to play a part.'

The Paramount Ruler smiled and shook his head. 'You are not a good man with whom to pick a fight, Zhang,' he said. 'But I am indebted to you for your clarity of vision . . . and there is one further thought I would like to offer. You know of course that we did sign the Nuclear Non-Proliferation Treaty in 1991. Well, I do not want to provoke the West into believing that the acquisition of the Russian Kilos is merely to provide us with a vehicle to deliver an underwater nuclear warhead.

'Zhang, we are not at war with anyone, and I do not want that situation to change. I want this nation of ours to join the world, to be a part of the great interchanges and relationships that go with world trade. There is nothing for China in having a major military disagreement with the United States. Might we not be better off forgetting the whole thing and letting the Americans prowl around in the Taiwan Strait for as long as they wish? They are, Zhang, our biggest customers, and we are growing rich on the proceeds. The distant joy of reuniting Taiwan with Beijing is a very long-range hope, and I wonder if it could be worth it.'

Admiral Zhang smiled. 'I am always awed by your discernment and learning, sir. And as usual your erudition is beyond reproach. But might I ask you for a few moments to consider the question of Taiwan from another angle – perhaps from *her* angle. As that Chinese island grows ever closer to America, we must face the fact that it is just a matter of time before she acquires her own nuclear deterrent. Every country in this world which has grown rich enough, and felt threatened enough, has always tried to have an independent nuclear capacity.'

The Paramount Ruler spoke again. 'You know, Zhang,' he said, 'we should not perhaps forget that Taiwan is not a country alone. It remains a part of China. It was not so long ago they stopped threatening to "retake the mainland." '

'No, sir. I am very aware of the situation. But I would also remind everyone that it was not so long ago that the United States sent in warships from the Seventh Fleet when they thought the forces of Communist China might attempt to retake Taiwan. The lines of self-interest are finely drawn.'

'They are, Zhang, they are,' replied the old man. 'And we should attend to the unmistakable truth that all of our efforts to prevent major arms sales to Taiwan have in the end come to nothing. The island grows ever richer, and I agree will soon wish to own a nuclear deterrent.'

'Taiwan, in my view,' said Zhang, 'has already reached that stage, and I am certain has given the matter serious consideration. The only way we can discourage having a rich, possibly hostile, nuclear power right in our own backyard is to return them to our own fold. They will not come voluntarily. And we can only achieve that by ensuring that the big American carrier battle groups cannot roam at will through our trading waters, 200 miles out from the mainland, encompassing the whole of Taiwan.

'The Kilos from Russia will give us that capacity, and subsequently that freedom. But time is not on our side. The Taiwanese, as we all know, are very clever. I regard them as a time-bomb which we cannot defuse, not for as long as they remain under close American protection.'

The Paramount Ruler nodded. 'Then you are saying, Zhang, that in your judgment we are not dealing with a problem which places us in an unwanted aggressive mode, you are saying that in the end, the Kilos represent the heart of a possible Chinese defense policy?'

'That is precisely what I am saying, sir. This is a turbulent world, and for a country of our size and potential wealth, a nation which represents one-fifth of the population of the earth, we surely must have a capability to keep our own seas free from enemy warships. And our huge Navy cannot do that at present. The 10 Kilos will alter that equation absolutely in our favor.'

The second of the elderly Deputy C-in-Cs, Vice-Admiral Zhi-Heng Tan, now spoke for the first time. He was respectful but in disagreement. 'I understand your desire to own the Kilos, Admiral Zhang,' he said. 'And I also understand a certain youthful desire to exact a revenge on the USA. But there is a saying among Western lawyers which has a significance here: they say *never* go to the law for revenge, only for money.

'I believe it should also be applied to acts of war. *Never* attack anything or anyone for revenge. Only for money or control. And there is neither money nor control in such a move against the USA for us. I see only heartache, problems, and possibly bloodshed, and damage to our trade. The United States wears a large and friendly smile, but she has very sharp, white teeth. The men of the Pentagon are as vicious as Genghis Khan. They are 10 times as strong as we are, and are likely to remain so for another half-century. If we try anything against them, they will strike back at us. There will be loss of life – and perhaps even worse, the most horrible loss of face.

'I am as much of a patriot as you are, Admiral Zhang, and I offer my wholehearted support for whatever this Council decides. But I would like to implore all of you not to sanction some kind of direct action against the USA. Because that's a fight we are destined to lose, to no sensible purpose.'

'I understand your concerns, Admiral,' replied Zhang. 'And I hear great wisdom in your words as I hear that same wisdom in the words of our Paramount Ruler. And they have been words which have removed much of the venom from my mind. But I would like to request, with all humility, that we do continue to build our little fleet of Kilos. Because that way lies security, and ultimately our mastery of the South China Sea, and the waters which surround Taiwan.'

'That is, unless the US Navy decides to eliminate the entire Kilo fleet before we start,' interjected Admiral Pheng.

'May I remind you, sir, they have to find them first, and that's not easy.'

'It was apparently easy four days ago – they got them two at a time,' snapped Admiral Yang.

'But I accept your rebuke, Admiral,' replied Zhang. 'And you have my word, such a thing will never happen again.'

'I remain unsure about your word, Admiral,' said Yang.

'For the moment I am unsure about your motives,' growled Zhang. 'But I do know you speak not in the interests of China . . .' At this point the crisp veneer of the Fleet Admiral slipped away temporarily, and the haughty, supercilious Admiral Yang found himself face to face with a man who had been brought up on the rough waterfront of Xiamen. A hard, seasoned street-fighter whose brain had carried him far, and who remained afraid of no one. Zhang snarled across the political table: '*Yang, you are either a fool or a coward.*'

Like a panther, the old man who ruled China was on his feet, tipping his chair over backwards. 'STOP,' he shouted. But his anger was directed at the Commissar. 'I warned you, Admiral Yang, that I would not permit you to cast doubts on the abilities and integrity of my Commander-in-Chief. You have chosen to ignore me, which is unwise of you, because I happen to believe in what he is saying. Your insults to him are thus insults to me, and to the great and exalted Navy commanders in this room, who also agree with him, and who have illustrious careers behind them, perhaps even greater than your own.

'It is my judgment that we do not require a political commissar in this room who challenges the sincerely held views of our High Command. We already have here the General Secretary of the Party, and the matter is, in any event, military. We are dealing with a possible strike against a proven enemy, and/or the buildup of our submarine fleet. I would be honored if you would leave us.'

Admiral Yang, a slight man of perhaps 50 years, with a rather upright way of walking, stood up without another word, bowed to the head of the table, and left in silence. Only one man in the entire country could have orchestrated his public demise in such a way. It was not much credit to Yang that he had chosen to defy that particular man, elderly though he might be, in these particular, most sensitive, circumstances. He left with a bland but arrogant expression upon his clean-shaven face – another mistake, perhaps, for an officer whose career was drawing to an inevitable close. The Paramount Ruler was unused to disobedience. In another age he would have been an Emperor.

Admiral Zhang stood while the Ruler was seated again. And then he offered his most humble apologies for any part he might have played in incurring the great man's displeasure. But the Ruler merely looked up and said gravely, 'You, my son, have elected to shoulder all of these terrible burdens yourself. You are, as ever, treating China's woes as if they were yours alone. I see in you much of myself when I was a younger man. How can I be displeased with a loyal and distinguished officer, whom I know will torture himself unto the grave over the loss of those submarines? The difference between you and most people, Zhang Yushu, is that I would gladly trust you with my own life.'

Several of the men seated around the table nodded in assent. And Admiral Zhang replied, 'I can only thank you for your kindness, sir, and hope that you always understand that I have no motives of a personal nature, only those which I judge to be correct for our nation.'

The East Sea Fleet Commander, Admiral Yibo Yunsheng, spoke on behalf of his colleagues when he said that he knew of no one who was unhappy with the leadership of Admiral Zhang, nor anyone who seriously disagreed with his policy.

The Paramount Ruler at that moment asked for some tea to be served, and then he made his judgment. 'There will be no strike against the USA. We will act as if nothing has befallen us. I entrust Admiral Zhang to do everything in his power to ensure the safe delivery of the last five Kilos . . . and my thoughts will be with him and all of his commanders.'

They sipped their tea as the meeting broke up, and again it was the South Sea Fleet Commander, Admiral Zu Jicai, who walked with Admiral Zhang along the endless corridors of the Great Hall of the People, which is probably the biggest city-center government building on earth, comprising 562,000 square feet.

'Well done, sir,' said Zu. 'I thought he was going to cancel the last five.'

'You did? What do you think I thought? I thought I might have to remind him of the words of Mao Zedong: "Real power comes from the barrel of a gun." '

'If he was still alive, he'd have to admit that in the 21st century, real power lies with the Navy, and its capacity to own and operate the most modern warships.'

'You're right, Jicai. And I'll tell you something else. Nothing, absolutely nothing, would give me greater pleasure than to sink one of those American aircraft carriers, and then say in amazement, "Us? Don't be ridiculous. You are our friends. We would not dream of doing such a thing. How could you think that of us?" '

'Sometimes, Zhang, I have thought your hatred of the American military was unreasonable. But I no longer think that. I only think: "Who do they think they are?" '

'That's the trouble, Jicai. They know who they are. The world's policemen, and they're too big, too tough and too damned clever to be challenged. But if we get our hands on enough of those Kilos to have a permanent force in the South China Sea, I'll challenge them. I'll wait it out, and I'll sink one of their carriers. I live for the day when I sink one of them.'

'Tread carefully though, my honored friend Yushu. And remember the Gulf War in 1990. Our finest weapons helped to arm the Iraqis, and the Americans made them look like children in a grown-up world. They are very, very dangerous.'

'So am I, Jicai.'

The two men walked out into the snow, which was now scuffed and downtrodden by a million walking feet and a million skidding bicycles. The Forbidden City towered in the background, and the northwest wind still blew raw across Tiananmen Square. It was no warmer and more snow was forecast. Both men pulled their Navy greatcoats around them, and the black staff car drew up alongside in slushy splendor.

'I'll ride out to the airport with you,' said Admiral Zhang. 'We'll talk more about the deployment of the next submarines, and the escort plan we must make with the Russians. And I'll try not to allow my anger to rise whenever I think of the US Navy. But if I could have one wish, it would be to blow up the Pentagon, and everyone who works in it. I simply cannot believe they wiped out two brand-new submarines and a hundred crew, without warning, and without reasonable motive. That is piracy, and no one is ever going to know.'

'We know, Yushu,' said Admiral Zu. 'And perhaps that will be enough for our purposes.'

The snow began to fall again as the People's Liberation Army staff car bearing the two admirals turned northeast out along Jichang Lu on the 13-mile journey to Beijing airport. The time was 1 p.m. On the other side of the world, 10,000 easterly miles away, it was nine o'clock on the previous evening, and the weather was not much better on the cattle-rearing prairies of central Kansas.

Great herds roamed through the snow, and cowboys fought their way through blizzards getting feed to the more remote areas. It had been a long day, and everyone was tired at the big ranch which lies between the Pawnee River and Buckner Creek, way out in Hodgeman County.

Beyond the wide wrought-iron gates, which bore the distinctive B/B brand of the immense Baldridge spread, the lights still burned in the main house. But only one man was still awake, the new president of the family business, the 40-year-old Bill Baldridge, a former United States Navy lieutenant commander.

He sat alone in front of a log fire, debating whether to buy another half-mile of land along the southern bank of the Pawnee. It was expensive, too expensive, but the river gave it added value, and Bill was thinking of expanding one of the Hereford herds in the summer. He was staring at the prospectus, mentally working out what he could reasonably bid for the 600 acres at auction next week, when the phone rang in the far corner of the room.

He walked over and answered. 'Baldridge.'

'Bill? Hi, this is Boomer Dunning.'

'Boomer! Old buddy. How ya been?'

'Pretty good. Busy, nothing too serious. How 'bout yourself? Enjoying retirement?'

'Yeah, right,' said Bill. 'Never worked so hard in my life. The weather's been hell out here for three weeks: snow, wind and ice. Me and my brother have been out all day every day. My manager's got the goddamned 'flu, my good horse Freddie's lame, and it's a goddamned miracle I haven't got frostbite. If this is retirement, lead me to a nuclear boat.'

Boomer laughed. 'Then my call is fortuitous. Because I am on this line to take you away from all that.'

'Christ, you're not offering me a job, are you?'

'Hell no. Better than that. I'm offering a vacation.'

'Yeah? What kind of a vacation?'

'A bit unusual. But it might be fun. A friend of my dad's – some Australian banker – has asked me to deliver a boat for him. I've only seen pictures, but she's brand-new – 67-foot sloop, Bermuda-rigged, teak decks, power winches, big Perkins Sabre engine, the whole shebang. Looks very comfortable. All-teak interior. Carries two foresails, and I guess she'll go like the bejesus. She's called *Yonder.*'

'Yeah? Where is she?'

'Right now she's lying in Port Elizabeth, South Africa. The banker sailed her down there himself from the Hamble in England where she was built. Took him six weeks, with four guests, three serious crew, and a cook. I got a letter from him, says she handled the Bay of Biscay no trouble, in bad weather.'

'Where we gonna take her?'

'Hobart, Tasmania. Southeast corner of Australia. This guy's building a hotel there, right on Storm Bay. That's the huge yachting area out in front of the town.'

'Christ, Boomer. That's a hell of a way from Port Elizabeth, isn't it? It's gotta be 10,000 miles.'

'No. Less than six. He says 5,793. We'll take the Great Circle route, but we'll stay away from the Antarctic. And right from the start we'll be in the prevailing westerlies, dead astern almost all the way. The guy says she can make 20 knots on a run. It's her best point of sailing, if you don't lose your nerve.

'Anyway, we've no need to push it, and we won't have the crew to race the boat all the way. You'd need a dozen pros for that. But we should average a good 9 knots for a couple of weeks. That'd leave us two weeks to cover the last 3,000 miles. We'd only need to average 9 knots to make the journey in 28 days. He says it gets done regularly in lesser boats in 26 days.'

'Roaring Forties, right?'

'Yup. Hobart stands on longitude 42.53 South. And of course it's midsummer down there.'

'Hell, you make it sound very attractive. When you thinking of going?'

'February. I got a month's sabbatical while *Columbia* goes in for maintenance. I'm aiming to clear Port Elizabeth on February 1st. I gotta be back in New London March 4th. Jo's coming with me. Her mom's coming down from New Hampshire to look after the girls while we're away. C'mon, Bill, how about it?'

The former Lt. Commander Baldridge, still holding the land prospectus, demurred. Three thousand bucks an acre was a lot of cash for grazing land. 'What's it going to cost us?'

'Nothing. The boat's completely equipped with all food and drink. She's fueled up. The crew are paid for, three of 'em plus the cook. Aside from their quarters, there are three big double berths, two bathrooms. It looks really great.'

'Yeah, but we gotta get there, by air. And back.'

'You ready for the good news?'

'Hit me.'

'Still nothing. The guy's flying us out to Port Elizabeth from wherever we are in the States, and home from Tasmania via Melbourne, Australia. He's flying us up there in his own plane. It's only about 400 miles.'

'Jeez, this is getting better by the minute.'

'I told him this was a very serious journey. And that I would be happy to skipper the boat. But I would not do it unless I had another American sailor with me who I knew was a good navigator. I told him that would probably cost him four round-trip air fares. He never blinked. Said that since he was trying to get a $750,000 yacht safely across the world, he was not much bothered by 5,000 bucks' worth of air fares.'

'Sounds a bit too much fun, and a bit too good for me to pass up,' said Bill. 'I have to bring Laura with me.'

'Good. Jo's coming too. It's gonna be great. Hey, who's Laura?'

'Laura is the lady to whom I will be married when her divorce comes through in May.'

'Not the one you told me you were going to marry a year and a half ago – the one you'd only met twice for a total of about an hour and a half?'

Bill chuckled. 'You gottit.'

'The Scottish Admiral's daughter, right?'

'That's it.'

'Jesus. You're a man of your word. Where is she now?'

'Asleep.'

'Yeah, where?'

'Right here. The yellow bedroom, on the right, down at the far end of the top landing, view down to the creek. Need more detail?'

'Yeah. Where's your room?'

'Not that far to the south. Next door actually. As far away from my mother's room as I can manage. She won't move out till we're married.'

Boomer yelled with laughter. 'Now I know why you're coming south. Free at last, you rascal!'

The two men chatted on for another 10 minutes about the Navy and mutual friends, and agreed to travel from New York to Johannesburg on January 29, arriving in South Africa on the morning of the 30th. That would give them a couple of days to get the yacht sharpened up for the voyage.

News of their impending arrival was faxed from New London to Tasmania immediately Boomer put down the phone. Another fax was sent on, from Hobart to Port Elizabeth, which had the effect of making the English crew instantly nervous.

The first mate, Roger Mills, read the news out glumly. 'One of 'em is supposed to be a nuclear submarine commanding officer, the other's a millionaire rancher from Kansas who was a submarine weapons expert for about 15 years. Both outstanding sailors . . . Shouldn't think either of them will stand for a lot of bullshit.'

The following morning in Kansas was clear, bright and cold. Bill was out at 7 a.m., and back for breakfast at 8.30. His mother was out, and the slim, beautiful Laura Anderson was pouring coffee as he kicked the snow off his boots, took off his sheepskin coat and headed for the great log fire which burned in the entrance hall throughout the winter in the home of the master of the Baldridge Ranch.

Bill stood 6 ft 2 ins tall. As a teenager he had honed his body while wielding a sledgehammer mending fenceposts for his father.

He had never lost that hard edge of fitness, even in the Navy where he served for months on end in submarines. But out here in Kansas, back on the historic family ranch, riding horses all day, he still had the build of a Navy wide-receiver, which he could have been, had he been prepared to take football seriously. He actually looked like a slender Robert Mitchum. But he had unnaturally broad shoulders, and in uniform he had looked like a god with his piercing bright blue eyes. The fact that he had never lost the rolling gait of the cowboy had caused certain girls almost to faint with admiration as he strode over the horizon.

Laura had not reacted precisely like that when first they had met, but right now she brought him a mug of coffee anyway as he stood by the fire, thawing out. He took it 'black with buckshot,' which was a throwback to his Navy days working in Fort Meade with Admiral Arnold Morgan, who thus referred to the tiny saccharin pills he fired into the brew from a blue container with a clicker.

Laura kissed him lightly on the cheek, and told him – as she told him every morning – that she loved him beyond redemption. And that she regretted nothing.

Bill smiled and put his arm around her. 'You've been very brave,' he said. 'And it'll all work out in the end . . . but right now, I have a surprise for you.'

Laura's green eyes widened. 'You have?'

'I have. We're going on a vacation. At the end of this month. We'll be gone for four and a half weeks. And you'll probably die when I tell you what we're doing.'

'I will?'

'We're going to South Africa, and then we're going to sail a big 67-foot sloop to the southeastern tip of Australia. We're going with an old friend of mine, a Navy commander, Boomer Dunning, and his wife – and it's a brand-new boat, beautiful interiors, big engine and a crew of three, plus a cook.'

'Well, it sounds wonderful, my darling. But are you sure I'm ready for the Southern Ocean? That's the Roaring Forties, isn't it? Dad says it can be the most fearsome place in the world.'

'Yes, it can. But not so bad in the high summer. Which February is down there. All it really means is that we sail almost the whole way with a stiff, gusting westerly astern which should get us there real quick. Two of the crew are very experienced hands, and

Boomer is a world-class ocean-racing skipper. I sailed with him last August in Newport while you were in Scotland, remember?'

'Oh, I do. He's the nuclear submarine CO, isn't he? Weren't you both in that short Maxi race round Block Island in the big Greek boat?'

'Whaddya mean, in it? We won it,' chuckled Bill.

He kissed her on the cheek, and noticed, as he had done for several days, the tiredness in her face, the kind of tiredness that comes when a person is taking an endless mental beating, as Laura now was. As they had both known she would, when first they had embarked on their long adventure together.

They had known it would be bad. But not this bad. The divorce had been a nightmare, but the custody battle had been worse. Much worse. Bill did not know how much more Laura could take of it, and whether she might, in the end, leave him and return to Scotland. Although she had said from the very start that she would never do that.

Boomer's offer of a voyage had come as some kind of a godsend to Bill Baldridge. For it provided an opportunity to take Laura right away from the endless lawyers' letters, the government forms, and the court proceedings half a world away. Each one of the cold, emotionless documents seemed to confirm in her mind that in the eyes of the law she had abandoned her two daughters, and was an unfit person to raise children.

Both she and Bill knew that to be spurious lawyers' rubbish. But it made no difference. No one in the Scottish legal world, or in the media, agreed with them, and the wheels of justice ground ever onward. The letter that had arrived only this week suggested there was no chance she would even be permitted to see the girls before July at the earliest.

But they had entered this relationship with their eyes open. After only three meetings with her American naval officer, Laura had left her children at home, with their nanny and their father, and flown to New York to meet Bill. He was, she knew, the only man she had ever truly loved, and the only man she ever would love. They had stayed at the Pierre Hotel on Fifth Avenue opposite Central Park, gone to bed together before dinner and stayed there for the night. In the morning Bill Baldridge had told her flatly he was going to marry her. She did not know it, but that was the only time in a somewhat rakish bachelor life he had ever uttered those particular words to anyone.

Bill then took her to the opera on successive nights, before flying her out to Kansas to meet his family. She and Bill's mother Emily instantly became soul-mates, and after one week Laura flew back to Edinburgh and told her husband, Douglas Anderson, a landowner and banker, that she wanted a divorce, and that nothing would change her mind.

Douglas Anderson was stunned. His parents, the inordinately wealthy border farmers Sir Hamish and Lady Barbara Anderson – he a senior magistrate, she a power on the main board of the Edinburgh Festival – were equally shocked. As for Laura's parents, Admiral Sir Iain and Lady MacLean, they could scarcely believe it, though they had received some warning that Laura had made the journey to Kansas.

The problem was going to be the children. Except that the problem had turned out to be a bit more than that. It had turned into a public battleground. Douglas Anderson, the deputy chairman of the Scottish National Bank, had consulted the revered Edinburgh law firm of MacPherson, Roberts and Gould, who had made one thing very clear. If his two daughters, Mary, four, and Flora, six, were not to be whisked off to the American Midwest and never seen again, he had but one course of action. He must file for divorce immediately, citing his wife's adultery with this naval officer from the United States. They must then make every effort to paint Laura as a totally unstable, wanton woman, prone to affairs, and utterly unsuited to raise the children.

No one really believed any of this, but that is what the divorce papers claimed. The tabloid press got ahold of the story when it appeared on the court lists and gleefully charged ahead under the headline: 'ADMIRAL MACLEAN'S DAUGHTER ELOPES WITH KANSAS COWBOY – Edinburgh Bank Director Stunned by Wife's Treachery.'

From then on the situation worsened. MacPherson, Roberts and Gould moved to have the girls placed under the supervision of the Scottish Court, which would preclude their leaving the country at all until they were 18 years old. The Anderson estate was under siege by photographers hoping for a glimpse of the children. The great MacLean mansion on the shore of Loch Fyne was besieged by another group of photographers hoping for a glimpse of the 'scarlet woman,' Laura Anderson.

The custody hearing was brutal. With the separation order under way, Bill Baldridge flew from Kansas to be with Laura while a lawyer pleaded her case. They sat on the defendant's side of the Court of Sessions in Edinburgh's Parliament Square, while the Admiral and Lady MacLean sat with the Andersons, lifelong friends.

No one would help Laura except for Bill. Ostracized by Scottish friends, relations and society alike, she faced the music alone with the man she loved. And she wept while Urquhart MacPherson, a man she had known for many years, described her as little better than a cheap slut, who had brought disgrace upon her own family, disgrace upon the Anderson family, and heartbreak to her husband and children.

'And now this . . . this . . . lady . . . seeks to make off with the children to some shack at the back end of beyond in the Wild West. I would remind you, with the granddaughters of the most eminent Scottish Admiral, and one of Scotland's most eminent landowners. There are questions of inheritance, of the natural rights of these children – but perhaps, above all, there are questions of morality . . . and I refer now to the environment to which Mrs Anderson intends to remove these two innocent daughters of Scotland.'

'Say what you like about ole Urquhart,' whispered Bill. 'Th'ole bastard gives it everything.'

Laura's own solicitor, citing a loveless, mistaken marriage, emphasizing the eminence of the Baldridge family in Kansas, imploring the Court to use its powers to give her custody, or at least access during the long school holidays, was irredeemably ignored.

The assessment of the judge, who sat imperturbably in his wig and flowing scarlet gown, was plain. If Laura Anderson chose to continue her adulterous relationship with the man named in her divorce, and indeed to leave for the United States, it would be a very long time before she saw Mary and Flora again. Custody would unquestionably be given to their father, with formidable assurances from the entire Anderson family, and also from the MacLeans, that the children's needs would be perfectly attended to for the rest of their lives. Until they were 18 the girls would be, formally, wards of the court, permitted to leave the country only at the judge's discretion. It was a devastating brick wall for Laura to have hit. But hit it she did.

And she walked out of the courtroom, rejected by both families, clutching the arm of Lt. Commander Bill Baldridge. She had no more tears to weep, and she never looked back.

They left for New York that evening, and waited at Kennedy Airport all night for the first flight to Kansas City. Bill's mother sent a private, twin-engined Beechcraft out to bring them home.

And that had seemed to be the end of it. Until one evening last September, when there was a knock on the front door of the Baldridge Ranch. Bill answered it and found himself face to face with Admiral Sir Iain MacLean, who said quietly, 'Hello, Bill. I've brought you a bottle of decent whisky. Wondered if we might not have a talk. I won't take up much of your time. I've got a driver.'

As it happened, the Admiral had stayed for four days, charmed Emily Baldridge almost to distraction, and on the third day made his confession – that he had come to see them because he knew he would never have forgiven himself for having sat in that courtroom and turned his hand against the daughter he loved. 'Besides,' he told her, 'I am very fond of your . . . er . . . fiancé. Matter of fact, I like him much better than I ever liked young Douglas . . . and I've been trying to mend a few fences.'

The Admiral had come with some fresh legal advice – a course of action which would never have stood a chance against the combined Anderson–MacLean battalions, but would most certainly stand a chance if Sir Iain now stood alongside Bill and Laura.

He proposed they file a new appeal against the decision of the court that the girls not be allowed to leave Scotland, and their father enjoy sole custody. 'Thing is, you know, I found out that Douglas has got a new girlfriend, a girl with a bit of a past, actress up from London for the Festival. Totally unsuitable, of course. But I think we might have a chance now . . . I mean, my daughter did run off with a highly regarded United States naval officer who owns a degree in nuclear physics from MIT, and counts the President among his friends. But Douglas Anderson is cavorting around with some actress from Notting Hill Gate in London. Quite frankly, my dear, I'd prefer my granddaughters to live here. And if the Court won't grant that, they'll grant something, I'm sure.'

In the weeks that followed their appeal was heard twice with lawyers only, plus a private appearance by the Admiral. It was then put back until March, pending a suitable defense from Douglas Anderson. But, in Sir Iain's opinion, he had done the damage. And no one thought the court order would remain in place after July of this year.

And now Laura Anderson was looking forward to her divorce decree coming through. She and Bill were to be married on May 20, and the awful strains of the past year would soon be behind them. But it had all taken a toll on the dark-haired daughter of Sir Iain. She looked every one of her 35 years, she had lost weight and often seemed preoccupied. The rift with her own mother was also a source of grave worry to her.

Bill had known he had to take her away somewhere interesting, warm and relaxing. He wasn't exactly sure that a voyage down the Roaring Forties was absolutely ideal – but it was a lot better than a ranch out on the frozen Great Plains at this time of year. And he regarded with profound gratitude the summons to the lonely Southern Ocean from the Commanding Officer of USS *Columbia*.

CHAPTER FIVE

Boomer Dunning took the helm of *Yonder* shortly after first light on the morning of February 1. The sky was cloudless, and the waters of Algoa Bay were deep and clear blue. There was a large scattering of yachts moored in the harbor of Port Elizabeth and the Captain of *Columbia* ordered his first mate, Roger Mills, 'to heat up the old iron spinnaker,' American sailor's jargon for 'start the engine,' which brought a frown of confusion to the young Englishman's face, who'd heard only of 'the iron stays'l.'

But he caught on quickly and hit the button which would bring the big Perkins Sabre to life, and Boomer steered expertly through the anchorage and out into the open waters of the big South African bay.

From just below him, in the chart, radio and radar area at the foot of the companionway, Bill Baldridge called up: 'Steer course zero-nine-zero for 25 miles, then one-three-five to Great Fish Point . . . which will come up to starboard. We'll give that sonofabitch plenty of sea room. The chart marks a light up there flashing every 10 seconds. Right after that we sail into the open ocean, upon which I expect to be served a superb lunch.'

Everyone who was awake laughed at the mock-serious tone of the Kansan cattle rancher. Mills and his two cohorts, Gavin Bates and Jeff Hewitt, began to think this trip might not be such a pain after all — despite the fact that Commander Dunning had made it clear that on no account were the three men to touch alcohol under any circumstances whatsoever between Port Elizabeth and Hobart.

His warning was delivered with the authority of the biggest, most powerful man on the boat, who was not used to being questioned at sea. None of the three uttered one word of protest, mainly because, in the words of Gavin Bates, 'He looks like he could throw all three of us overboard with one hand.'

Boomer's own words had been both strict and forbidding. 'The weather down here is extremely fickle. It can change faster than anything you've ever seen . . . and I mean from a stiff breeze to a howling gale in less than 20 minutes. If we were ever to find ourselves in a big and dangerous sea, and I detected one shred of evidence that any one of the three of you was even slightly drunk, I should without hesitation slam you straight between the eyes for endangering the lives of us all, especially the lives of my own wife and Laura.

'So if any of you have a couple of bottles in your quarters, go and get 'em and give them to me. I will return them to you in Hobart. But if I find them myself, I will empty them over the side. It goes without saying that neither I nor Lt. Commander Baldridge will drink on the voyage either.'

Roger, Gavin and Jeff took no offense. They had a half-dozen bottles of rum and Scotch with them, and they handed them over. None of them had ever sailed with a really severe captain before, and while this was not altogether much fun, all three of them were more than happy to be sailing with a man who knew absolutely what he was doing – an experience quite rare for professional crew working for boat owners who are only part-time sailors.

It also brought home to everyone that the Roaring Forties were not to be taken lightly.

At 6.30 a.m., well clear now of the anchorage, Boomer ordered, 'Okay, guys, hoist the mainsail, then lemme have the cruising spinnaker. We got a light nor'wester off the land . . . looks as if it'll hold, so we'll want the pole out to port, then we'll cut the motor . . . Haul in that jib on the starboard main-winch . . . Come on, Masta, get into it.'

Whether Gavin Bates took exception to his new nickname, he made no indication. But it was a nickname which had been used periodically in his life, and usually the instigator grew tired of it, once the pure joy of invention had subsided.

Anyway, he got into it, and Boomer eased the mainsail and settled *Yonder* onto an easy broad reach with the wind steady force-three on their quarter. He noticed the big white sloop was making 9 knots through the calm water, and he thought then, as he had thought from the photographs, 'I'll bet this baby flies downwind.'

He handed over the wheel to Roger at 7.30, while he and Bill had some breakfast together, served in the state room by the beaming West Indian cook, Thwaites Masters from Antigua, aged 24. 'The most ambitious black man I ever met,' said Bill. 'He could end up owning Antigua . . . either that or the Zealand Bank.'

By 11 a.m., they were within sight of the headland of Great Fish Point. Jo and Laura were both sitting in the cockpit with Boomer, drinking coffee, while Bill sailed the boat. Lifelong friendships get made at sea – in the case of Bill and Boomer, under the sea – but the laughter between Jo Dunning and the future Laura Baldridge was conspicuous. And already, after just a couple of days in the warm south, the care lines were vanishing from Laura's face, and she had gained three or four pounds.

Even Jo, who was apt to cling on to the physical self-preoccupation of all actresses, was obliged to admit that Laura was a stunning brunette by anyone's standards: quiet, understated, under-made-up, but, from certain angles, quite demonstrably beautiful. And, thank God, good-humored.

On the eve of the voyage, they had stayed up half the night drinking ice-cold West Peak Chardonnay, from the historic Rustenberg Estate in the Stellenbosch Valley. Jo found the story of the runaway romance between Laura and Bill as good as a novel. 'But when did you think you first loved him?' she persisted. 'Was it before or after you played the operas together?'

'I think about that time.' Laura smiled.

'How 'bout you, Billy . . . how long before you thought you loved Laura, before or after the operas?'

'A bit before that. And I didn't fool with preliminaries like "thought" – I *knew.*'

'My God, this is wonderful,' sighed Jo. 'It was just like that with me and Boomer. Anyone got any opera CDs?'

'I have,' said Laura. 'I took the CDs of *La Bohème* and *Rigoletto* from my parents' house the next day, and I've never gone anywhere without them since. They're in my bag.'

'You mean the actual CDs that you both heard those nights in Inverary?'

'The very ones.'

'Oh, my God . . . I can't stand it,' said Jo, theatrically. 'Play the music someone, before my trembling heart breaks.'

At this point Boomer Dunning shot South African Chardonnay from the great Rustenberg Estate clean down his nose, since he always fell apart laughing at his zany wife, who should have been a comedienne instead of a serious actress. But he made the state-of-the-art music system work, and before long the divine voice of Mirelli Freni was drifting out over the southern Indian Ocean. Even Boomer, whose taste in music had ceased to develop once he heard Bob Dylan and then Eric Clapton in action, sat silently as she sung the most poignant aria.

'I just wish I could understand the words,' said the skipper.

'She's in a cold, unheated garret in Paris, and she has consumption, and she's singing "My tiny hand is frozen," ' said Bill.

'You'll know how she feels when we get a bit farther to the south,' said Boomer boisterously. 'You'll be singing "My tiny rear-end is frozen." '

The spell had thus been broken by the submarine CO, but the curiosity of his wife was not. And for the next hour she made Laura tell the entire bitter-sweet story of her romance with Bill, the fight over the children, the bruising war with her husband's divorce lawyers, the public humiliation back in Scotland, a place she never wanted to see again as long as she lived. And how she would have probably committed suicide but for Bill.

'Course, if it hadn't been for him, none of it would have happened in the first place,' Boomer had remarked cheerfully but unhelpfully. 'Still, I guess he proved himself to be what we all know he definitely ain't: steadfast, reliable, sound of judgment, loyal . . .'

'Will you guys gimme a break?' yelled Bill, laughing. And Jo had joined in, 'Yes, shut up, Boomer. Bill's gone through a terrible time.'

'As the Captain of the ship, I just wanna announce I'm ready to marry 'em,' said Commander Dunning, 'by the powers invested in me. Right here, I'm talking holy matrimony. No bullshit.'

'Jesus, this is unbelievable,' said Bill. 'I'm sailing to the end of the earth with a goddamned heathen skipper. Laura's still married.'

'Well, sir,' replied Boomer formally, standing to attention and raising his glass, 'if that's the case I'd have to say you are regarding the 10 Commandments . . . er . . . opportunistically.'

'Try to ignore him, Billy,' said Jo. 'He's drunk with power.'

'This is probably the nearest to drunk anyone's going to be for the next four weeks,' added the skipper. 'So I guess I'll have another scoop of that good wine before I turn in. We're underway early . . .'

But that had all been the night before, and now they had set sail, and the sun was high up behind them, over the mast, and the temperature was in the low nineties. All four of them were experienced sailors and they all wore large, peaked caps and layers of zinc sun cream, the cooling breeze disguising, as it does, the fierce rays of the blistering sun.

Thwaites served lunch in the state room at 1 p.m., and received a round of applause for perfectly cooked Spanish omelets, with french fries and salad. The crew ate ham sandwiches in the cockpit, where Roger Mills had the helm. Bill Baldridge kept them on a southeasterly course, one-three-five, and as the wind increased they were making 12 knots through a quartering sea. Down here they were way out of range south of the Trades, but were still slightly too far north for the big westerlies.

At 4 p.m. they saw their first whale, a 50-footer, with a massive square head, blowing not 30 feet off the port beam, the vaporized jet of oily water aimed unmistakably forward in a fan shape. 'That's a sperm whale,' said Boomer. 'Biggish male, migrating north from the Antarctic.'

'How the hell do you know that?' asked Bill.

'Because he's obviously a sperm whale by the shape of his head – no other whale this big looks anything like that. And because he blows at a forward angle, out in front of him. I also know that only the male sperm whale migrates. The females stay in the tropics. This guy's been feeding in the Antarctic all summer and now he's on his way home. I know about whales like you know about cattle . . . coupla friends of mine run one of the whale-watching boats back home on the Cape.'

As he spoke the big whale moved forward with the ship, staying close in a kind of camaraderie. It was a huge demonstration of might and majesty. And there was something touching about this docile giant. Bill and the women stood watching him transfixed. 'Christ,' said the Kansan. 'Can you imagine going after him with a harpoon in a tiny whaling boat with two guys rowing? Can you just imagine what it musta been like when the harpoon hit and that sucker charged forward?'

'A bit more tricky than it is today,' growled Boomer. 'Those Japanese butchers never give him a chance – they blow him apart from the main ship before he even has time to dive. That used to be the big danger to the guys from the old whaling ships – a big sperm whale like this guy can dive 2,000 meters – and stay there for about an hour and quarter.'

As if on cue, the whale suddenly arched forward, and they all heard his great sigh; it sounded like a long drawn out SAAAAARRH – and then he was gone, his massive tail-fin rising 15 feet out of the water and then sliding slowly beneath the waves, almost without a ripple. And the ocean seemed strangely bereft without him.

They all scanned the water for a long time afterward, and 10 minutes later he blew again. And they saw him four more times, until he was on the horizon, edging his way north, one of the last of a badly endangered species . . . the largest of all the creatures on this planet, being slowly hunted to extinction.

'I once debated the propriety of banging an ADCAP torpedo straight into a big Japanese whaling ship out in the Atlantic,' said Boomer. 'To me, they're just death ships . . . slaughtering the whales, for no good reason whatsoever, except their own greed. But I decided not to do it in the end. Woulda looked pretty colorful on my résumé, wouldn't it?'

'Oh, outstanding,' said Bill. 'Probably coulda kept it quiet. Called it a black operation – unaccountable.'

But Boomer still looked thoughtful. 'I hope they don't get him though. I sure hope they don't get him.'

They sailed on without the whale for the whole of the evening, taking turns on watch until midnight and then handing over the wheel to Roger and Jeff, who would work 1 a.m. to 4 a.m. and then 4 a.m. to 8 a.m. 'Call me instantly if the wind gets up,' was Boomer's last instruction.

By eight o'clock the following morning they had made 280 miles from Port Elizabeth and were holding their southeasterly course. There was an ocean swell now as the water grew deeper, but there was little chop and the only difference in the weather was the wind backing round to the west, and increasing to just less than 20 knots.

Boomer ordered them to 'hoist a reaching spinnaker, and see if we can make some serious headway this morning,' but shortly after nine the barometer began to fall. And Bill, staring at his *Antarctic Pilot*, thought this might herald a whole series of depressions, in which the wind might swing northwest again, and they could look for some torrential squalls of rain. He was right about that, and the weather began to cloud over very quickly.

They put up the number three jib in place of the 'chute, which they shoved back into the 'sewer' under the foredeck; Boomer ordered all hatches battened. Bill Baldridge came on deck in his foul-weather gear and suggested everyone go below, except for Roger and Jeff, who were to reef the mains'l. Gavin was still asleep.

Bill told them to trim the main out a bit, and fit a preventer for heavy weather. 'Be ready to take down the main if the wind goes above 35 knots.' They were ready for anything except, perhaps, for the speed of the weather change. The wind gusted and increased, then it howled in from the northwest at 30 knots, gusting to 40 in driving rain, and *Yonder* raced forward, making 14 knots in huge swells. There were no high waves yet, none with the really big breaking crests, which can be so dangerous. And Bill rather enjoyed sliding through these mountains of water, all alone at the helm, in a top-class sailing yacht he judged could handle just about anything.

As he expected, the squall died as quickly as it had arrived. The skies cleared after less than 90 minutes, and the wind drifted back around to the west. They jibed without incident, and the sea slowly became less heavy. Glancing over his left shoulder he sensed another buildup of cloud to the northwest which he judged might approach inside another couple of hours. But in general terms, their first serious squall had not been too difficult. He ordered the spinnaker to be hoisted again in the much lighter 15-knot breeze which now blew over their stern. But the real difference was the temperature. It was just that much cooler, about 70 degrees, although the sun was high.

Boomer and Laura came on deck together, since Jo had fallen asleep again. And Bill was glad of the chance to hand over the helm, take off his jacket, and have the coffee and French toast which Thwaites had brought up to him.

Boomer had his foul-weather gear with him since he too judged they might end up in another squall before long. Bill, who wanted more coffee, went below, announcing he was going to 'siddown and read for a while, let the commander move us forward some.'

Bill was an inveterate reader of newspapers and magazines, and he had brought a whole pile of them with him from Kennedy Airport. He had the Kansas paper, his local paper, the *Garden City Telegram*, the *New York Times*, *Washington Post*, *Time Magazine*,

Sports Illustrated, and a couple of Midwestern farming papers. But it was an article in the *Washington Post* that caught his attention.

It was long, and he read it right through. Then he yelled up to Boomer, 'Hey, you read anything lately about that research ship which vanished down in the Antarctic 'bout a year ago – *Cuttyhunk*?'

'Not lately, but I know about it. Find something new?'

'Not really, just a pretty good article in the *Post*. Guy seems to think she's still floating somewhere, and he makes out an interesting case.'

'Yeah, I read some stuff by someone coupla months ago. Is he called Goodyear or something?'

'You're thinking of the blimp, dingbrains. He's called Goodwin.'

'Yeah, that's him. Goodwin. He wrote a whole bunch of syndicated features on *Cuttyhunk*. I read 'em all. He was saying that if the research ship had really gone to the bottom in its last known position in some bay down there, there must have been more wreckage come to the surface than a small piece of a deck lifebelt.'

'Right. He's still saying it. And he's also saying that if the ship really was under attack, and thus far there have been no survivors reported, then that must have been mass murder, and in this modern world it's almost unthinkable that no one has found out anything. Not a whisper. He thinks there's more to it than meets the eye.'

'I thought the same when I read the stuff last time. But Admiral Morgan did not agree. He thinks she went down with all hands. Anyway, save it for me, Bill, will you? I'd like to read what he's saying now.'

'I'll do better than that. I'll bring it up now, and hold the wheel while you read it. It's a real good mystery.'

Bill headed back up to the cockpit with the *Washington Post* and handed it over to Boomer, who sat for 15 minutes reading the long feature article. At the end of it, he said, 'Yeah. This is definitely the same guy. He's a staffer on the *Cape Cod Times* – this stuff is syndicated. As I remember he's actually been down to Kerguelen.'

'Well, he sounds like he's done a lot of research. And he does make a point. It's kinda difficult these days to wipe out 29 people in complete secrecy, and nothing be heard about them, or their ship, ever again. Specially when everyone knows exactly who they all were, and exactly where it happened.'

'Yeah, and they signaled they were under attack from the Japanese, who have since denied everything.'

'Like their goddamned whalers,' muttered Boomer.

'He makes that island sound pretty damned creepy, don't you think?' said Bill.

'Sure does. Says it's the end of the earth. Nowhere.'

'Well, Boomer, it might be the end of the earth to a guy in Hyannis, but it's not the end of the earth to us. We pass close to it, coupla hundred miles to the north of us.'

Laura, who had thus far listened in silence, suddenly said, 'Why don't we call in, find the ship, rescue the people, and return home to universal acclaim? Jo can go on the *Today* show and explain to a grateful nation about the two Navy heroes she sailed with.'

Boomer chuckled and wondered what he was required to do in order to get a cup of coffee around here. Then he said, 'You know, I wouldn't mind having a look at Kerguelen. Would we have time, Bill?'

'I'm not sure. But I'll hop below and check out the chart, then I'll bring the coffee pot and the *Antarctic Pilot* back up with me, and we can find out for ourselves.'

'Thanks, Laura,' laughed Jo. 'You've just talked these two nitwits into a nice little holiday on the most barren, desolate, freezing coastline in the southern hemisphere – there's nothing there except penguins. I read that stuff about Kerguelen in the *Cape Cod Times*. And there was one fact I remembered: there is a gale-force wind there every single day. The guy said it comes out of the southwest, across the high mountains, and then literally roars down the fjords.'

'Yeah, well, we probably won't be going anywhere near the fjords,' said Boomer. 'Matter of fact we might not even go inshore if the weather's bad, except for shelter in the leeward side.'

At this point Bill handed the coffee and the southern navigator's bible up through the hatchway and then emerged himself. 'It's a couple of thousand miles from here,' he said, 'Which at our present rate of progress is only about eight days at most. It's not that far out of our way. Right now we're heading for the south end of Tasmania, latitude 43.5 South, on the Great Circle route, the shortest way. The northern approach to Kerguelen is on 48.85 South . . . that would be about a couple of hundred miles north of us. If we alter course a few degrees right here, we'd hardly notice it. I guess it would be fun just to see it.'

'Okay, guys, this is a democracy,' said Boomer. 'Anyone hate the idea of going there?'

'Yeah, me,' said Jo. 'But I can't wait. Change course, Captain, and let's go find that *Cuttyhunk.*'

They all raised their coffee mugs, Boomer made an elaborate show of altering course two degrees to the north, and Laura snuggled up to Bill in the corner of the cockpit while he studied the *Pilot.*

They sailed on in silence for a while until the former Lt. Commander Baldridge spoke up from the depths of his studies. 'This place is unbelievable,' he said. 'Let me tell you something: our course will take us well north of the Prince Edward Islands, which are quite big and warrant just less than two pages in the *Pilot.* Then we may pass within sight of the Îles Crozet, a coupla fair-sized groups of islands 50 miles apart on latitude forty-six South – they get about three pages.

'Kerguelen has more than 300 islands and about a zillion bays and fjords. The *Pilot* names and advises on all landmarks, dangers, bays, potential anchorages, cautions – and it takes up 19 big pages, 15 of 'em just naming and describing the places. Can you imagine trying to find a sunk ship in there? It'd take about a thousand years.'

'Yeah,' said Boomer. 'Guess so. But I wouldn't take this yacht in there. First of all it's not ours, and if we hit a rock or something, it would probably rank somewhere near me sinking the Japanese whaler on my résumé. But most of all, they are plainly very lonely, dangerous waters. Any traffic down there at all, Bill? Anything military likely to be around?'

'I can't see any traffic routes at all. It simply doesn't lead anywhere. It's not on the way to anywhere. Unless there's a specialist penguin feeder or something, I cannot see one reason why anyone should ever go there, except for scientific researchers like the Woods Hole guys.

'Militarily? Jesus, there's no one to shoot! I think the place is uninhabited. You couldn't get an army down there, and there's no place for an aircraft to land. The only thing that could get there is a warship, but I'd be amazed if there's been a warship in those waters for 60 years.

'According to this, there was a big old whaling station down there in the last century, but I think Ahab and his harpooner Queequeg pulled out a while ago. Militarily there were three German warships down there, Commerce Raiders in World War II: *Pinguin*, *Atlantis* and *Komet*. The Brits chased 'em out and then mined the place in case they went back. The *Pilot* has mine warnings all over the place, though not for floating mines. They've all been cut and exploded, but the hydrographers seem to think there's quite a few left rolling about on the bottom.'

'Yeah, well, that settles it,' said Boomer. 'We're staying offshore. Definitely. I don't like loud bangs. Hey! You don't think that's what happened to *Cuttyhunk*, do you?'

'No chance. I believe Goodwin on that one. He says those guys must have been under attack, otherwise they wouldn't have sent a satellite message to say they were. Also, if they'd hit a mine there would have been wreckage all over the place.'

'Right. There would have. One of those damned things can blow a ship to smithereens. When I was a kid in a frigate we once found four of 'em right under the surface in a bay in the Azores. The Royal Navy sent down a couple of minesweepers to clear them, and after they cut the wires we had a contest with rifles to see who could hit and explode one. I nailed one of those suckers from about 100 yards, and I can still remember the spray from the blast raining down on the ship.'

'Yeah. We're definitely not going inshore,' confirmed Bill. 'I don't like big bangs either.'

'Well,' said Jo, 'if you two wimps are afraid of a few underwater explosions, I guess Laura and I'll just have to settle for a long offshore view of this romantic place. We'll turn the CD up loud and hit the king penguins with a burst of Pavarotti.'

'Don't count on anything down there,' said Boomer. 'We may not even see it. You get huge banks of fog, low cloud over the water, and sometimes even snow. I'm glad we all brought warm clothes. It can drop to freezing very quickly.'

'What about icebergs?' said Laura.

'We're running well north of the Antarctic convergence,' said Bill, confusingly. 'And we're out of the northern range of the icebergs. You don't see 'em much at this time of year, and I'd be surprised if we met any on our route. Might be a bit different if this was July.'

By now the weather was closing in again. The spinnaker was taken down and stowed while Boomer was still pulling on his foul-weather gear, and the wind was rising out of the northwest as they jibed yet again. He yelled for Roger and the boys to 'fit the trysail in place of the main.' Then he instructed them to get the mains'l below, but 'Don't hoist the trysail – just have it well lashed in case we need it. Get the larger storm jib up and set. Then we'll roll the jib away. Batten everything down, and get a couple of long warps ready in the cockpit for trailing astern . . . hold us steady and slow us down a touch, right? From now on it's full harness, clipped on, for *anyone* on deck.

'The rest of you might as well go below and close the hatch. No sense anyone else getting soaked. I'll take her for the next couple of hours myself.'

He spoke to Roger Mills, told him to stand by in case the weather got worse. But he could feel the wind coming up and he judged this next squall might be a bit worse than the one earlier that morning. He was right, the wind and rain came lashing in on big, breaking seas with great swells 30 feet high between trough and crest. *Yonder* rode them out easily enough, but Boomer kept the trys'l down, making less sail area to catch the 40 knots blowing fiercely over the stern.

He held the southeast course, with Roger Mills standing next to him in the cockpit. Forty-five minutes later he saw the crest of a big wave break right astern of them, with a great roll of steep, white water. 'I want to stay before the wind if we can,' he said. 'I had a look at that jib before we sailed . . . she looks good and she's brand-new. Should hold okay.'

The wind continued to increase, and was soon blowing steadily at 50 knots. The sea was up too, big waves now cresting and breaking high above them astern. But *Yonder* kept rolling forward, staying out ahead, and Boomer sailed her with a lifelong expertise that made it look too easy. Roger and Gavin stayed with him in the cockpit, still in driving rain, all three of them admiring the brilliant way this big new yacht sliced her way onward, shouldering off the water which occasionally slid over the bow.

Just before dark, Boomer felt the wind shifting. 'Oh, Christ,' he said. 'It's backing round to the southwest, that's not good.'

At this point Bill Baldridge came on deck, battened down in his foul-weather gear. 'This wind's changing,' he said. 'I'll take her for a while, Boomer, but I'm afraid she's going southwest. I can feel it . . . and according to my navigation stuff, that means she'll blow hard and colder, and we might get some confused seas that'll bump us around a bit.'

'Yup. I was just thinking the same. Everyone okay down below?'

'Fine. They're both reading. No seasickness yet. Laura says she's never been seasick, but then some people don't. But she's only sailed a Scottish loch!'

Boomer laughed. 'Okay, Bill. I'll go below, and you wanna arrange a watch change? Thwaites has early dinner for Roger and Gavin, who are then going to turn in. Jeff can come up here now, give me a hand, and take the wheel while we have dinner about eight. And the boys can take over at midnight . . . Unless this gets a lot worse, then we better get back here right after dinner.'

Bill took over the helm, and as he did so, the wind seemed to come up fractionally, and there was a sudden chill in the air. 'It's backing around, right now. STAND BY, JEFF!' he shouted. 'I'm gonna jibe onto starboard – get down on that winch and haul the jib sheets across, under control all the way. Then when she swings over, ease the starboard sheet to port . . . and stand by to let her go some more when I yell.'

Bill turned *Yonder* a couple of ticks to starboard. The wind eased momentarily, then blasted around the trailing edge of the storm jib with a tremendous bang. Bill barked, 'Right . . . now tighten it some . . . Yeah, that's good, right there, Jeff . . . Ease it a little . . . Better . . . That's real good. Hey, we just hit 16 knots. Shit, this baby flies, doesn't she? Even on a storm jib.'

Throughout the night, the wind rose and fell back, twice shifting to northwest, bringing more rain, but each time returning to blow from the cold southwest. Boomer and Bill were in the cockpit intermittently all night, and when it gusted above force-nine for a few minutes they debated whether to heave to, and ride it out with bare poles. But Boomer thought the big, sturdily built *Yonder*, with her every modern refinement, was doing so well, they could safely charge on. Her storm jib, made of the newest liquid crystal sailcloth from Hood's of Rhode Island, gave him huge confidence even in winds like this. In the 16 hours between 4 p.m. and 8 a.m. the following morning, Boomer calculated on the GPS they had covered over 200 miles.

'How long will it take to Kerguelen?' asked Jo.

'At this rate we might be there before lunch,' chuckled Boomer. 'Right now we've been going for two days and we've knocked off close to 500 miles. Not bad. I don't suppose this wind will last quite like this. Matter of fact, that last gust didn't seem to have real conviction, did it? And it's shifting round to the west. Still, I don't suppose anyone will mind a nice day, which is what I think we're gonna get. Bill thinks we'll be into the Roaring Forties late tomorrow, so we better make the most of it – summer's very erratic down here. The weather never settles, but at least it never stays awful for more than a day or two, without some kind of a break.'

And so they fought their way through the capricious Southern Ocean, in varying hard westerly breezes. Sometimes it blew a gale, sometimes more, sometimes not so bad. Sometimes the sun came out, sometimes it stayed cloudy. But they never once hove-to and it was a sharp bright February 8, shortly after lunch, when Bill Baldridge announced, 'I think we might see Kerguelen at around first light tomorrow. Right now we're about 150 miles out, the wind's steady and west and we're making around 10 knots. According to the GPS we're on meridian 66.50 East, and from what I can tell, there's no seriously bad weather around, although you never quite know down here.'

'The boys are taking the helm tonight, so I think we might risk a glass of that good South African Chardonnay,' said Boomer. 'Splice the mainbrace, right? And let the boys have a glass each. We all deserve it. This has been a hell of a sail. And I hope you've all enjoyed it – I have. I needed it to take my mind off a few things.'

'So did I,' said Laura. 'And you've all been wonderful. I feel very American, and for the first time for months, I feel really well. I can't wait to see this bloody island we've been talking about all week.'

'Well, it's not gonna be that long now,' said Boomer, pulling the cork out of a bottle of Rustenberg's finest. 'Here guys, lemme give you a splash of this.' He poured generous mugs for all four of them, so generous there was only about a drop left. At which point he went right back into the fridge and opened up another. 'In the unlikely event anyone should want a bit more,' he chuckled.

'By the way, if your divorce is through, Laura,' he added, 'I'm a man of my word. I'm still ready to marry you and Bill . . . although

I am drawn to the conclusion that you might be a bit too good for him.'

Bill shook his head and smiled. 'You coming to the wedding on May 20th?' he asked. 'It's going to be in Kansas, obviously, since Laura and I are not acceptable in Scotland, and her mother's not speaking to us, and the Anderson clan would like us in some Highland dungeon for the rest of our lives.'

'Course we're coming. How about your dad, Laura, is he?'

'He told me he was,' said Bill. 'And I hope he does. You'll really enjoy meeting him, Boomer. He's without doubt the most knowledgeable submariner I ever met. Funny, the President asked me a few weeks ago if Sir Iain was coming. He likes to talk to the Admiral. He says he's coming himself, and that if it hadn't been for him, Laura and I would never have met – and he's right!'

And so the night drew in. They finished their coffee, and retired gratefully to their quarters. The sheer purity of the southern air tends to make sailors very tired, and all those off watch crashed before eleven, warm in the bunks below, with the dark, freezing hell of the South Atlantic rushing by beyond the hull.

Boomer and Bill were awake by six, dressed and up on deck five minutes later. And their disappointment was total. There was thick fog along the choppy water, and Roger was still holding their course, but no one could see anything. Bill noted from the GPS they were about 22 miles east-northeast of Rendezvous Island, the big rock which Cook had named Bligh's Cap.

'We passed that a coupla hours ago,' said Bill. 'I'm putting us about 23 miles due north of Cap d'Estaing. That's the northern tip of the entire island, the place Goodwin went past, and where he says *Cuttyhunk* headed for shelter 15 months ago. We should steer south now if we want to have a look . . . just hope the fog clears in the next two hours. The wind's out of the northwest now. How about getting the main back up, and reaching down on starboard?'

'You heard what the man said,' Boomer told Roger. 'We'll come round to one-eight-zero. I'll take over as soon as you have the main up. Then you better go get some sleep.'

Two hours later, the GPS put them three miles north of Cap d'Estaing, but the weather was still very murky, and Boomer reckoned Kerguelen was under a blanket of fog from one end to the other. Without their radar they could have gone no closer.

'Steer course one-three-zero,' said Bill. 'There's no sense going straight for the headland: we may as well sail down into Choiseul Bay, then if the wind gets up from the west or southwest and blows this crap away, we'll have a bit of shelter and we'll be able to see the island. If we haven't found *Cuttyhunk* by lunchtime, we're outta here.'

'Our frigate didn't find her in three months,' said Boomer. 'So we'd better tell the girls not to hold their breath,'

By ten-thirty, *Yonder* was a mile off the entrance to Baie Blanche, and a northwester was rising. Bill held her on the starboard tack, but he could have sailed either side since the wind was dead astern, and still only force-three. The fog was beginning to thin now, and the sun was not far away. But the temperature was only 38 degrees and it felt very damp and cold on deck.

When the clag finally cleared, it happened swiftly. One moment they were peering through a thinning shroud of tallow-colored mist; the next moment they could see the shoreline of Kerguelen across 2,000 yards of bright blue but freezing water. From their vantage point the island looked dramatic. The 500-foot rise of Gramont, between Baie Blanche and Baie Londres, was still snow-capped, and a mile off the port bow they could see the more gentle rise of Howe Island. 'We're not going anywhere near that,' said Bill. 'It's kelp city in there.'

In the distance, in this light, the mainland of Kerguelen looked nothing less than spectacular, with its great craggy mountains, desolate shoreline, and high remnants of the winter snows. Bill pointed out a jutting rock due north of Gramont Island. 'According to my chart, that's Cox's Rock,' he said. 'That's where Goodwin found the lifebelt from *Cuttyhunk*.'

While Jo and Laura peered through binoculars, Boomer ordered the sails down, and started the engine, 'So we can chug around for a bit. I don't want to leave much sail up – the katabatics round here are supposed to be horrendous, and apparently you don't see them before they hit you. For Christ's sake, watch the chart and the depth for me, will you, Bill? It would not be perfect if we put this baby on a rock.'

'That's never been part of my master-plan either,' replied the man from the High Plains. 'We're staying in deep water, don't worry. If I even see a rock within 200 yards I'm setting a course for Hobart.'

Laura went below to fetch coffee. Jo wanted to drive. Boomer said, 'Fine, so long as there's no speeding, and you listen to Bill, and do exactly what he says.'

'Not sure about that,' said Jo. 'Not the way he's been going on with Mrs Anderson!'

There was an atmosphere of some levity as Jo made a great, lazy circle in the bay and headed slowly north. 'There's kelp-beds all the way to starboard,' said Bill. 'Stay close to the mainland where it's deep and clear.'

Jo slurped her coffee and kept chugging. Laura miraculously produced a plate of hot buttered toast, and the four of them munched contentedly while Roger and Gavin continued to furl the big mainsail, and Jeff sorted out the sail wardrobe under the foredeck.

At 11.40 Boomer went for'ard to give Jeff a hand, and to make sure the storm jib was right on top of the pile, should it be required in a hurry, since everything happened in a hurry down here.

At 11.41 Bill Baldridge saw it. And he could not believe his eyes. Two hundred yards off their starboard bow, slicing through the water, leaving a V-shaped feather on the flat surface was . . . No, it couldn't be . . . a shark's fin maybe?

'BOOMER!' Bill yelled at the top of his lungs. The Captain of *Columbia* thought he'd gone over the side. He swung around to face the cockpit to see his shipmate pointing out in front of him, still bellowing, '*BOOMER! BOOMER!*'

Commander Dunning followed the direction of Bill's right arm, and what he saw almost took his cold breath away. 'JESUS CHRIST!' he shouted, as they both stared at an utterly unmistakable sight, cutting across Choiseul Bay at about 5 knots, heading southwest.

It was the raised periscope of a submarine, about three feet of it, pushing through the water.

It was there for only about 20 seconds before it vanished beneath the surface as swiftly as it had arrived. Neither Jo nor Laura saw anything. But then, of course, neither of them were submariners.

March 4. The White House. West Wing. Office of the National Security Advisor. Admiral Arnold Morgan was beaming with good spirits. 'Well, well,' he was saying. 'So you're the fabled daughter of Admiral MacLean, the lady who captured this rascal's heart . . . and also did us a thousand favors a year and a half ago?'

Laura smiled. 'That's me, Admiral. And I believe I have to thank you for the very mixed blessing of being instrumental in throwing Bill and me together.'

'Yes ma'am,' replied the Admiral. 'This office is actually just a front for my nationally known dating service.'

Bill could hardly believe his ears. Arnold Morgan making small talk? Chatting to a lady? Being witty? 'Jeez,' thought Bill. 'Politics is turning him human. The President better watch that. He might lose his edge.'

But the former Lion of Fort Meade was warming to his task. 'Laura, I'm delighted to meet you at last. I'm a great admirer of your father's, have been for a lot of years. And between the three of us in this room, your insights into the life of a former Israeli commanding officer were invaluable.

'Also I often wondered what you might look like. You have, after all, captivated two thoroughly outstanding naval officers, and now I know I'd trust their judgment . . . not just on submarine warfare.'

Laura laughed. 'You're too kind to me, Admiral. I'm actually very ordinary. At least, I was until you sent your inquisitor across the Atlantic: now I'm just very lucky.'

'So's he,' chuckled the Admiral, nodding his head in Bill's direction. 'And I'm very glad you called me. We're staying here for lunch in one of the private dining rooms. The President and Bob MacPherson both intend to stick their heads around the door to say hello. And after that my driver's gonna run you both out to the airport. Can't wait to hear about your sailing trip with Boomer. Musta been great.'

Bill smiled at him. 'I'll tell you about the journey during lunch. But meanwhile there is something I want to inform you about, and, in my view, it might be quite significant.'

'You do? What is it?'

'Arnold, we took a little side trip down to Kerguelen, just to see the island at the back end of nowhere, because Boomer is really interested in that Woods Hole ship that vanished, *Cuttyhunk*.'

'Yeah. I've talked to him about that. He *is* interested – I guess everyone from the Cape is. You didn't find it, did you?'

They all laughed. 'No, we didn't find it. But something happened on the morning of February 9th, just before midday.'

The Admiral nodded at the precision of Bill's words, the way he stated only what he knew to be absolutely correct, the dead giveaway of a former intelligence officer.

'I looked over the starboard bow and I saw, making about 5 knots, southwest, the periscope of a submarine. It was a couple of hundred yards away. Boomer saw it as well.'

Admiral Morgan looked up sharply. 'Are you certain about that?'

'One hundred percent.'

'But there can't be a submarine down there. There's nothing to be down there for. Not even aircraft fly over the place. It's a military desert for thousands of miles in all directions. They don't even have shipping lanes, never mind ships. Except for a few dingbat researchers from Woods Hole.'

Bill said calmly, 'It was a submarine, Admiral. No ifs, ands or buts. I saw it first and there was no doubt in my mind.'

'Did Boomer see it at the same time, or did you tell him it was there?'

'No, I did not. I just shouted his name three times. And pointed.'

'What did he say?'

'He actually yelled, "JESUS CHRIST!" '

'Then what?'

'Boomer shouted, "That's a goddamned submarine, or am I dreaming?" I told him I knew it was a submarine. There was not, and is not, one shred of doubt. And you have to believe us. We both saw it, clearly and definitely.'

'Did you see it, Laura?'

'No. I was looking the other way. But I heard Bill shout, and I heard Boomer say it was "a goddamned submarine." It's very quiet down there. I should think about three billion penguins heard him as well.'

The Admiral wrote down a few words on a small notepad on his desk. Then he picked up the telephone and issued the command he had issued so many times before: 'Get me Fort Meade. Director's office. I'll hold. Hurry.'

'Yeah . . . Is Admiral Morris there? . . . Morgan, Arnold Morgan . . . Hey, George, how ya been? . . . Yup, fine . . . I wonder if you could do a thorough, but basically routine check-out for me . . . yeah, now . . . Okay, can you find out for me if, around midday on the morning of February 9th, there was any submarine in all of the world which could possibly have been on patrol around the island of Kerguelen in the Southern Ocean? . . . Yeah, I realize it's the ass-end of the earth, George, that's why I wanna know. Run the checks on everyone. Lemme know every submarine unaccounted for on that morning, including all the friendly nets, then gimme a call back . . . yeah . . . I'm in my office, but the switchboard knows where I am all the time. Thanks, George.'

He turned back to Bill, and said carefully, 'Lieutenant Commander, as well as I know you, and as much as I trust you, if you had come in here alone with no corroboration for this story, I would not, *could* not have believed you. And precisely the same thing applies to Commander Dunning, whom I happen to think is the best submarine commanding officer in the US Navy. I would not and *could* not have believed him either.

'But I also know you would not both have got it wrong. Of that I am very certain. I now know there was a submarine down there, but what in the name of Christ it could have been doing, I have no idea. There's nothing to do down there, except feed the penguins and count the ice-floes. But someone's down there, or at least someone's *been* down there, and in the next couple of hours I'm hoping Fort Meade will enlighten us. C'mon guys, let's go find some lunch.'

The small private dining room was elegantly laid for three. But before the first course of smoked salmon had been dealt with, the President of the United States stopped by to visit Bill. He just opened the door and walked straight in, smiling. 'Don't get up . . . Bill, good to see you . . . Arnold, holding back the enemy, right? And you must be Laura . . . I am a particular admirer of both your father and your future husband, both of whom I count as friends – but I'm not quite so sure about one of your ex-boyfriends!'

Everyone laughed at that, and the President sat down next to Laura and poured himself a glass of fizzy water, which everyone was drinking. Bill marveled, as he always did, at this President's way of being smooth, yet not at all smooth, presidential yet unfailingly able to say precisely the right thing to put everyone at ease.

Laura, let's face it, should have been paralyzed with nerves in the presence of the most powerful man in the world. But she was not. She reacted to him like everyone else meeting him socially for the first time. And they immediately began to chat about the long yacht voyage in the south, and what fun it had been.

'You know,' he said, 'I would love to do something like that. Just clear off with a few good friends and vanish from civilization for a month. No phones, no faxes, no staff, no harassment and no bullshit. Wouldn't that be great? But it ain't gonna happen . . . and I gotta go back to work. Bill, Laura, I wish I could stay longer – but I'm coming to the wedding. May 20th, right? Tell your dad, Laura, I hope to see him . . .'

And with that, he gulped his fizzy water, and was gone. 'Wow,' said Laura, shaking her head. 'What a man. I adore Americans.'

Thirty minutes later, mid-roast beef, the telephone rang in the corner. 'Hey, hey, hey,' said Arnold Morgan. 'This could be George.'

He was right. Fort Meade on the line. 'Hold it, hold it, George, lemme just get a pen and a pad.' The conversation was long, all of 15 minutes, and in the White House dining room Bill and Laura could only hear snatches like. 'What about the Soviets?' . . . 'China?' . . . 'No, that about wraps up the big players.'

But at the conclusion of the call, Admiral Morgan returned to the table looking very serious. 'They did a fast, thorough job,' he said. 'Checked out all of the computerized lists, all the latest overhead pictures and drew some very sound conclusions. Mainly that every submarine in the United States, Russian, and Chinese navies was accounted for. So was every one in the Middle East, which was easy since they're nearly all moored alongside with some technical defect. All the small European fleets were accounted for too.

'Except for three boats. The Brits have a Trafalgar-Class nuclear boat, *Triumph*, missing for a month, but we are nearly certain it's patrolling off the Falkland Islands, looking at the Argentine mainland. They're just not telling us for the moment, so it's probably doing something it ought not to be doing. We can confirm very quickly if we have to, but the Royal Navy often has a submarine down there since the Falklands War, so we're not in any way surprised or suspicious.

'The French have a big 12,500-ton strategic missile submarine missing. She's called, coincidentally, *Le Triomphant*, number S616, based at Brest. Last detected in the Bay of Biscay, but not seen for 10 days prior to February 9th. She'll still be on the French deterrent patrol in the Bay somewhere. But from there to Kerguelen is around 12,000 miles – even running at 30 knots, dived, all the way from Biscay, there's no way she could have got there in 10 days or even 12, or 14. I dismiss both of them.'

'Anyone else?' asked Bill.

'Just one other. Almost too bizarre to think about. But we are showing a missing submarine in the Taiwan Navy: a small *Hai Lung*-Class diesel-electric. She's called *Hai-Hu*.'

'As in Silver,' said Bill, deadpan.

Admiral Morgan chuckled. 'No. As in *Sea Tiger*. That's what it means in Chinese. *Hai Lung* means *Sea Dragon*. Anyway, this is a Dutch-built boat, 18 years old, that's been missing, according to our sources, for a month and a half. She's got a range of 10,000 miles and could conceivably have got down there. Kerguelen's 7,000 miles from Taiwan. But I can't imagine what she was doing, if it was her you and Boomer saw.'

'And even if it was,' said Bill, 'what's it gotta do with us?'

'Plenty,' said Arnold Morgan. 'If someone's sneaking around the world's oceans in a goddamned submarine that I don't know about, then that someone is up to something devious; and when it's devious, I don't like it. And when I don't like something on behalf of this government, then someone's gonna need to come up with a few answers. Or I might get downright awkward, instead of just curious.'

'How do you feel now, Admiral?' asked Laura.

'I'm curious. And I want to know where the Taiwan submarine is, and I wanna know exactly when it returns home. I don't expect to be told where it's been, but I'll be watching them all, very carefully.'

Lunch ended at three, and Bill and Laura were driven out to the airport for their flight home to Kansas; direct to Kansas City, then a local flight down to Wichita, and a private Beechcraft from there up to Burdett. Bill's brother Ray would meet them with a truck out at the airstrip.

Meanwhile, back at the White House, Arnold Morgan was talking to the CIA, trying to get some kind of a pattern involving the comings and goings of Taiwan's two *Hai Lung*-Class Dutch-built submarines. Their numbers, 793 and 794, were painted high, white and distinctive up on the side of the sail. They were easy to identify. The officer on the Far Eastern desk promised to get someone on the case within the hour.

He did in fact achieve this. But it took five weeks for any serious intelligence to emerge. And around the second week in April, a few facts started to fall into place and there did appear to be a pattern. A somewhat mysterious pattern, but nonetheless a pattern.

Only one of the *Hai Lung*s went out at a time. And when it left, it did not return for 11 weeks. Each time it returned, there was a 10-day period when both the submarines were moored alongside, and then the other would leave, again for 11 weeks. There was no evidence as to where they went. But they always dived 30 miles outside the harbor, and were not seen again until they reappeared off the base.

Arnold Morgan pondered. 'That little *Hai Lung* couldn't make more than 8 or 9 knots on a long journey, 200 to 220 miles a day, which means it could cover 7,000 to 7,500 in five weeks. Sounds like five weeks out, five weeks back, one on station. No doubt, the *Hai-Hu* could have been the submarine they saw off Kerguelen. But was it? That diesel could have gone anywhere in five weeks.' He walked over to his computer and pulled up his world mapping program. He measured out 7,000 miles and described a large arc covering the area in which the submarine could have traveled.

It was pretty depressing, simply because of its size. The *Hai Lung* could have gone almost anywhere from the Bering Strait to the Cape of Good Hope – by way of the coasts of Mozambique, Australia, New Zealand, Japan or just about any of the islands in the South Pacific. It could have gone to the Antarctic. 'Just about anywhere,' growled Morgan. 'But all of my logic tells me it went to Kerguelen. Because that's where my boys saw it.'

Admiral Morgan then put in a call to the Baldridge Ranch, and spoke to one of the maids. 'Mr Bill and Miss Laura are both out riding now,' she told him. 'We lost some cattle in a storm out in the western end of the ranch last night. They both rode out of here right after lunch. I guess they'll be back all depending on whether they find 'em real quick or not.'

The Admiral smiled. 'Okay,' he said. 'Please leave word I called, and I'll try again this evening.'

They finally connected at 9 p.m. It had been a day of searches, for both cattle and submarines, and Arnold Morgan still had no real fix on where the Taiwanese were going. But he recounted to Bill the pattern which had emerged and concluded the conversation by saying, 'I know you've been there and I haven't, Bill. You think there's something going on down there, don't you?'

'Well, I'm not sure what's going on, if anything. But I do know for sure we have two major mysteries: one missing research vessel which apparently came under attack; and one prowling submarine from Taiwan. And they may be connected.'

'Two outlandish happenings in precisely the same spot are, historically, likely to be connected,' said the Admiral. 'I'd send a boat down there if I had even a remote idea what we were looking for. But I haven't, and I can't really make out a very good case for taking any action.

'But I think I'm going to thicken up our surveillance in Taiwan – my gut instinct tells me something's afoot. We're in the dark. And I need light. Lasers, preferably.'

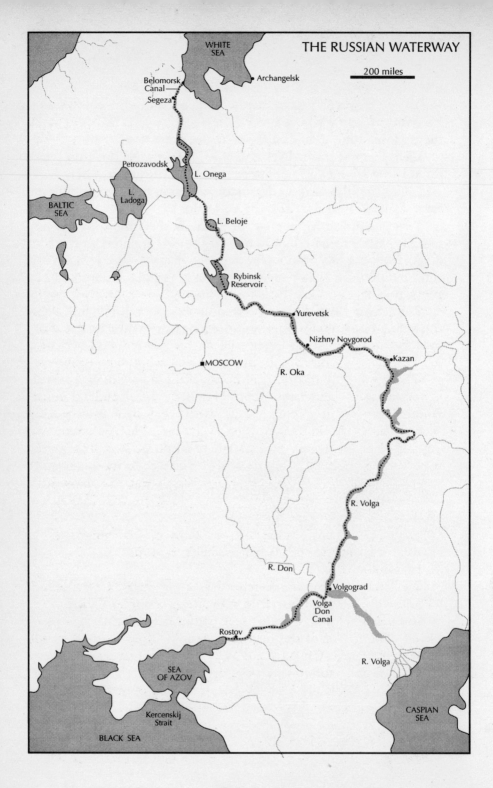

THE RUSSIAN WATERWAY

200 miles

WHITE SEA

Archangelsk

Belomorsk Canal

Segeza

Petrozavodsk

L. Onega

BALTIC SEA

L. Ladoga

L. Beloje

Rybinsk Reservoir

Yurevetsk

Nizhny Novgorod

MOSCOW

R. Oka

Kazan

R. Volga

R. Don

Volgograd

Volga Don Canal

Rostov

R. Volga

SEA OF AZOV

CASPIAN SEA

Kercenskij Strait

BLACK SEA

CHAPTER SIX

Admiral George Morris was not normally light on his feet. He was a big, heavy character, with a superior brain, and a slow ponderous way of moving. A widower, he also had a slow ponderous way of sleeping, flat on his back, snoring like the old Chicago Superchief running late. He slumbered only just above the level of unconsciousness traditionally associated with the dead. Telephones by night he neither heard nor answered. Hibernating grizzlies have occasionally been recognized as more receptive.

Which was why in the small hours of the morning of April 21, a young naval lieutenant, John Harrison, was standing in the Admiral's bedroom at Fort Meade, with every light switched on, shaking him, and imploring him to awaken. He was about two steps from a small glass of cold water to be poured strategically upon the forehead of the Director of National Security — a mutually agreed tactic if all else should fail — when George Morris woke.

'What in the name of Christ is going on?' he said, blinking in the lights. 'Someone declared war?'

'Nossir. But there is something we think may be important.'

'Jeez. It had better be. What the hell's the time?'

'Er, 0300, sir.'

'Well, what's going on, Lieutenant? Speak up for Christ's sake.'

'Something about those Kilo submarines going to China.'

Admiral Morris was on his feet before the sentence was completed. The image of the ferocious Arnold Morgan stood starkly in his mind's eye. 'Christ, man! Why didn't you say so?'

'I was waiting for you to wake up, sir.'

'Wake up! Wake up! I am awake, aren't I? Gimme three minutes and we're outta here. Got a car outside?'

'Yessir.'

'Get in it. I'm right with you.'

Inside the Director's office, a set of satellite pictures was already spread out on his desk. Two night-duty officers were comparing details, staring through a magnifier into a lightbox.

'There's not much doubt about it, sir,' one of them said as Admiral Morris approached. 'The three Kilos in the shipyard at Nizhny Novgorod are almost ready to leave. And judging by these pictures, it's not gonna be that long.' He stood up. 'Take a look, sir. See that scaffold all over the sail on boats one and two a week ago? Look at it on the pictures we got last night. It's reduced by at least two-thirds . . . and you can see here that the third boat now has less stuff all over it than it did two weeks ago. These things, as you know, sir, tend to finish quickly. The submariners don't have to do much in the way of trials until they get to the coast. They're gonna be gone very soon.'

Admiral Morris stared at the evidence before him, the evidence which dramatically highlighted the critical path of the President's National Security Advisor's personal project. It was clear that if the work progressed at this rate, the submarines could be moved onto a transport barge within two weeks. And then they might start their long journey north more or less immediately. It looked as if the three hulls would travel together, possibly on barges and probably with an escort.

The CIA had intercepted several Beijing–Moscow signals, and two of them suggested there would be hugely heightened security in the light of the unfortunate accident which befell the last two Kilos on their way home to the Orient. It was not, however, clear whether that security would stretch to the inland part of the journey.

The director did not need to study the pictures for long. Then Lt. Harrison handed him three other photographs, also taken from the satellites, showing views of the Volga River several hundred miles south, along the stretch which passes the sprawling industrial city of Volgograd (formerly Stalingrad), to which the German army laid siege for 200 days in the appalling winter of 1942–3. Today, risen again from the ruins of the battle, Volgograd stretches for almost 60 miles along the bank of the Volga, right where it changes course on the great southeastern bend which leads down to the Caspian Sea.

Exactly here, on the long gentle curve of the river, the overheads had picked up a shot of a giant two-part, articulated transporter barge making its way slowly upstream. A *Tolkach*, such as this, has a load capacity of 10,000 tons, and while there are many big freight barges plying their way along Russia's greatest river, these monster 900-footers, powered from the stern, are comparatively rare. The name *Tolkach* means, literally, pusher, and these barges utilize a large rising wheelhouse on the bow deck to operate a massive for'ard rudder, without which they'd never get around a sharp bend.

In line astern, this particular one was followed by another *Tolkach*, not so long, but all of 600 feet. Both were of the Class of the XXIII S'ezd (KPSS, The 23rd Congress of the Communist Party), both were making approximately 5 knots through the water on this busy industrial reach. Both were of the precise type used by the Russians to transport submarines.

Of course, in the West, it is traditional to build submarines, indeed any ships, in yards close to the sea, or at least a major estuary. The Russians, however, have a mammoth shipbuilding industry in the old city of Gorky, now named Nizhny Novgorod, which is situated bang in the middle of the old Soviet Union, almost 1,000 miles south of Murmansk on the Barents Sea, and almost 1,000 miles north of the former Black Sea naval base of Sevastopol. Thus generations of Soviet warships would have been, to the Western eye, stranded at birth, like so many Atlantic salmon born up an often-shallow river. Or, more graphically, as if Trident submarines were being built in central Kansas, or Bedfordshire.

But the frozen heartland of Russia possesses one major natural asset missing from both central Kansas and indeed England: the 2,290-mile-long Volga, the fifteenth-longest river in the world, which forms the very soul of the Communist Dream to construct a great waterway interconnecting the entire Soviet Empire.

The Dream was not of course fully realized, and in the process the Communists murdered almost all living creatures of the Volga, but they did build a series of stupendous canals, which have made it possible for the Russians to transport big submarines and other warships between the Black Sea in the south to the White Sea in the north. The route begins at the Kercenskij Strait, east of the Crimean peninsula, and crosses the Sea of Azov going northeast. Entering the Volga–Don Canal, it continues northeast, up through the lakes and along a further canal joining the Volga just south of Volgograd.

From that point, heading north, the great river widens into long breathtaking river-lakes, up to 200 miles long, before swinging westerly past the city of Kazan, and on up to Nizhny. Here the River Oka, flowing in from the southwest, converges with the Volga, and forms a great wedge of land called the Strelka (the arrow) upon which are situated the 150-year-old shipyards of Red Sormovo. The Russian word Strelka is painted in massive red letters on the concrete bank.

In recent years this yard has built a succession of merchant and low-draft passenger ships, but it has a long tradition of building submarines which can be transported by barge south to the Black Sea and also to the Northern Fleet. They constructed the Charlie II nuclear boats here, and the old Julietts. The 7,200-ton Barracudas of the Sierra II-Class were built here, and the nuclear-powered Victors, and a whole line of Tango-Class diesel-electrics. The yard also has an acknowledged capacity to construct the most modern Kilos.

Because of the landlocked geographics of the Black Sea, and with the Mediterranean another virtual dead-end ocean, most of the submarines built at Nizhny tend to go north through a colossal waterway masterminded by Joseph Stalin. It begins on the Volga as the great river winds its way north along silted-up shallows, all along the timber-growing west bank, with its bargeloads of sweet-smelling birch logs.

Right off the town of Yurevets, 75 miles upstream from Nizhny, the river swings left, zig-zagging its way on a lazy westerly course to the huge Rybinsk Reservoir. Right here the Volga swerves hard south, eventually to join Stalin's astonishing creation, the Moscow Canal.

But at that point, the Russian Mother, as the Volga is known, turns its back on the frozen north, and the submarines must continue their journey toward the Arctic Circle in colder waters. The great *Tolkach* barges keep heading north, up the 70-mile-long reservoir, through the wide waterways and canals which skirt Lake Beloje, journeying a total of 150 miles before entering the tranquil northern waters of Lake Onega, 120 miles long and the second largest lake in Europe.

This is the most beautiful part of the journey, for the lake is wild, and spotted with picturesque islands and quite exquisite wooden churches, many of them standing beneath carved onion-domes. On the island of Kizhi, the Church of the Transfiguration is decorated by 22 domes, all perfectly shaped and carved by local eighteenth-century craftsmen. Not one nail was used in the construction of this building.

Along these near-silent waters the *Tolkach* barges shoulder their huge underwater warships, and they make a malevolent sight, moving across the surface, against the backdrop of some of the most lovely waterscapes in all of Russia.

At the end of the lake, the idyllic and peaceful waters cease to flow, and the submarines enter the black shadows of the Belomorski Canal, perhaps the embodiment of the cruelest of Stalin's ambitions. Thousands of slave laborers perished in the frozen hell of its making, while the commissars forced them beyond all limits of human endurance.

The result was a masterpiece of engineering: a straight 140-mile-long waterway joining the lake to the White Sea, and also on to the Baltic; a military throughway to echo all of the remorseless ambitions of the old Communist dictator. But the endless deaths among the political prisoners and thinkers who formed that terrible army of forced labor scarred the name Belomorski. The Russian writer Maxim Gorky, who was judged to have approved the canal because he joined 120 writers on a 1933 press trip, was attacked for it years later by Alexander Solzhenitsyn.

Today the tourist boats do not enter here. And the military keeps a watchful eye on the efficiency and the running of the canal. But as the submarines looked so alien, so outlandish on the lovely waters of the lake, so their jet-black hulls seem at home in the waters of the Belomorski. Because they are ultimately instruments of death, and the canal is a place of remembered death. The shades of sadness will never leave there.

The slow 800-mile journey from Volgograd to Nizhny, through often congested industrial waters, would be a long one for the empty *Tolkach* barges. And Admiral George Morris gazed first at the pictures taken off the Volgograd waterfront, and then at those of the three Kilos. There was little doubt in his mind. The Russian diesel-electrics were nearing completion, and those two gigantic transporters were on their way to pick them up. Including stops, and various hold-ups, locks and freight traffic, the Admiral assessed they would probably average 60 miles each day, which would put them off the Red Sormovo yard in about two weeks.

He went to a big computerized screen and pulled up a map of

central Russia, zeroing in on the Volga River and the reaches upstream from Nizhny Novgorod. It was hard to assess the possible speed of the *Tolkach*s when loaded, but they'd probably average 5 knots and make a steady 120 miles a day, which would put them on the waters at Belomorsk about a week after their departure. George Morris thought the loading time in Red Sormovo might take anything between two and four weeks, given last-minute corrections and repairs. He guessed, correctly, that the Chinese would have their top technicians at the shipyard, signing off on everything, before China would pay the next installments of the US$900 million total the three Kilos were costing.

On reflection he decided four weeks' loading time might be closer to the mark than two, and in his mind he began to assume those submarines would be out of Nizhny, and on their way north, some time around the first week in June. The ex-carrier battle group commander frowned, and wondered whether indeed the Chinese and the Russians had yet decided the loss of K-4 and K-5 was no accident, and that the culprits were probably operating under the flag of the United States.

He noted the distance of almost 750 miles between Nizhny and the White Sea, and he deliberated in his mind the strength of the escort the Chinese would demand of the Russians when, finally, the Kilos pulled out and began their transworld journey to the South China Sea. He wondered also whether they would travel under their own power as the last Kilos from the Baltic had done, or whether they would make the journey on freighters like China's first three. One thing, however, was immutable in the mind of the Fort Meade Director: there was no way the USA was going to allow the submarines to arrive in China.

But George Morris was uncertain as to the best course of action for the USA. So far as he could guess, if the Kilos were to make the transit under their own power, they would probably be given a strong Russian escort force. They would all be fully armed, and there was no way a covert US operation could remove all three of them. Not that he could see. Not without a sizable support force. And George Morris knew SUBLANT would be highly reluctant to employ its LA-Class boats in any other capacity than that of the lone hunter-killer.

To achieve the guaranteed destruction of the three Kilos, under heavy Russian escort . . . well, so far as George could see, you'd be talking about a US Navy Task Group stalking three brand-new Russian submarines, plus another couple of ex-Soviet hunter-killers, not to mention several frigates. It all struck him as a mind-blowing scenario. 'Jesus Christ!' he muttered. 'This is beginning to sound like the Battle of Midway. We obviously can't do anything like that. I guess it's Arnold's problem.'

The Admiral walked over to his desk. It was 1715. But his duty was clear. Admiral Morgan had insisted he be informed the instant there was any kind of development with any of the Kilos currently under advanced construction. Morris thus picked up the telephone and dialed the home number in Montpelier of the ex-intelligence chief. Arnold Morgan, who had been awake for 15 minutes, picked it up immediately, in the refined manner which had endeared him in the past to so many high-ranking politicians and serving officers. 'Morgan. Speak.'

'Hi, Admiral. George Morris. Sorry about the time.'

'If I was, or ever had been, worried about the goddamned time, George,' growled Morgan, 'the world would doubtless be a more dangerous place. Shoot.'

'Your three friends, Admiral. I have some pictures I know you'll want to see right away. Your place or mine?'

'I'll be with you in 15,' snapped Morgan, and slammed down the phone, leaving Admiral Morris standing somewhat awkwardly in a roomful of people with the phone still at his ear, yet connected to no one.

He did what many other people had done in similar situations with his irascible predecessor, who rarely if ever hung around for telephonic etiquette once he had heard what he wanted to hear.

'Yes, okay then, Admiral,' he said, pretending Morgan was still on the line. 'See you then. 'Bye.'

By which time Arnold Morgan was burning rubber, driving himself from his former marital home close to the base, directly to Fort Meade. His automobile could probably have made the journey on its own. Though not as fast.

He came through the door of the National Security Agency at high speed. As ever his steely presence galvanized the night staff into activity, and a two-man escort accompanied him down to Admiral Morris's office, where the resident Director had already ordered coffee for them both; 'black with buckshot,' for the Big Man, which at least alerted the entire building as to the imminent arrival of their former boss.

George Morris vacated his desk for Arnold Morgan who now sat quietly studying the pictures taken from space. 'Yup,' he said. 'Yup, George. You gottit. These babies are on their way, real soon.'

Admiral Morris explained his fears about a serious confrontation in the Atlantic, with a small flotilla of American ships effectively doing battle with the Russians.

Morgan waited, unusually quiet and patient for him. He did not wish to betray the fact that his plans had been in place for several weeks. Nor did he wish to tell anyone about them, unless there was a copper-bottomed reason for that person's 'need to know.'

'Don't worry about the details, George,' said Morgan grimly. 'I've had this in hand since the day we found out the Russians had put the Chinese right at the front of the Kilo build-stream.' He turned and stared at the Fort Meade Director. 'I wanna thank you and your team for your vigilance in this matter. But right now there's no need for you to know more. Just keep me posted every inch of the way.'

Then he lightened, just a shade. 'George, old buddy, as you well know, we each have to sit in our own chairs in this game. You in yours and I in mine.' The fact that Arnold Morgan was actually sitting in George's chair at George's desk, at that precise moment, was regarded by both men as an irrelevance.

The bells of the watch tolled for 0800 on the Director's maritime clock as the Admiral left Fort Meade. He decided not to stop at home, but to press on for the White House, at which, in heavy traffic, he arrived at 0930. He turned the engine off and told someone to take care of his car, and also to tell Charlie the chauffeur to call him on the telephone.

He arrived at his office in the West Wing just as the chauffeur was put through from the garage. 'Charlie,' he said. 'Go get my car from wherever the hell it's parked, and get it back to my home in Montpelier. Then come right back here with the office car, and be on parade by 1230. I could be moving in a lot of directions.'

'Yessir. But sir, how do I get back here from your house in Montpelier?'

'Charlie,' Admiral Morgan spoke kindly and patiently, 'right now I'm tackling two or three very minor matters at once: I'm trying to ensure the northwestern area of the Pacific stays safe and secure for world shipping; I'm trying to retain our dominance over the Taiwan Strait; I may have to kick a few Chinese butts . . . Charlie, dear Charlie, I know your problems are many . . . but would you just get my fucking car to Montpelier? AND THEN GET YOUR ASS BACK HERE ON THE DOUBLE, BEARING IN MIND THAT I DO NOT GIVE A FLYING FUCK IF YOU NEED TO HIRE THE SPACE-SHUTTLE IN ORDER TO ACHIEVE IT!'

Charlie was about to drop the phone in terror when the Admiral softened again. 'Do try your best, Charlie,' he said. 'It is only because of these immense problems that men such as yourself are hired.'

He replaced the phone, grinning at a new degree of wit which he found himself increasingly utilizing. Life at the White House was smoothing away the rougher edges of his choleric personality. Almost.

He picked up the phone once more, and told the operator to connect him to the Director's office at Fort Meade. But the reception there was only marginally better than that in the garage. Admiral Morris had left for the Pentagon and would not be back before lunch. He might, however, be located with Admiral Joe Mulligan.

Arnold Morgan, not wanting to alert the entire Navy as to the urgency with which he now considered the Kilo situation, elected not to interrupt the meeting in the office of the CNO. This was unusual since the Admiral would not have hesitated to interrupt a conversation between God and the Pope had he considered it fell within the military interests of his beloved United States of America.

He glanced at his watch. 0945. 0645 in California. No good. Admiral John Bergstrom would not yet be at his desk. 'Lazy prick,' snarled Morgan impatiently. 'Have to give him another hour.'

Meanwhile he hit a button on his space-age telephone and requested some coffee. The voice which answered was male and quick. As he crashed down the phone, the Admiral actually considered the possibility that he might have given a 'black with buckshot' order to the President of the United States. And he suddenly cracked up with laughter, the laughter of a man who knew that in the Chief Executive he had a friend for life.

He gazed at his map, absent-mindedly picking up a jade-handled magnifying glass, and looking closely at the waters of the giant

Russian Lake Onega, the 120-mile north–south stretch through which those Kilos *must* travel on their way to the Belomorski Canal. He had asked Fort Meade to run back through their records, and through all of their photographic evidence, to try to find a pattern to these outlandish inland waterway journeys of the Russian submarines.

'There must be something,' he murmured. 'Some place where they stop, or refuel, or change guard or something . . . someplace where they might be vulnerable.' He stared at the map, noted the position of the island of Kizhi, and considered the largest port on the lake, Petrozavodsk. Arnold knew the name means, literally, Peter's Factory. He also knew that Peter the Great had converted the entire place into a cannon foundry, ransacking the town and nearby areas of all of their metal in order to melt it down for artillery hardware in the opening years of the eighteenth century. The result was, of course, that Peter had forced the Swedes into submission in the Great Northern War of 1700–12. 'If I can just get this situation in order, I'll give 'em some more scrap metal to fuck around with,' he growled. 'I just need someone to get me some kind of pattern on those submarine internal delivery voyages.'

It was hard to work out with whom he was most irritated: Admiral Morris, Admiral Bergstrom, or 'the goddamned Soviets.' On reflection he decided it was probably a dead heat. With Charlie the chauffeur right in there behind 'em.

He also informed a secretary that he was deeply depressed by the continued absence of coffee. He did so in a voice rather louder than was considered normal in the West Wing. And when it finally arrived, he slurped it in solitude, leaning back from his desk, trying to ensure his own thoughts about the immediate future of the Kilos conformed with solid, well reasoned military logic. He had gone over it so many times in his mind, in a personal process of elimination. And now he went over it one more time.

'You have to start with one fact,' he declared to himself. 'These three little bastards ain't never gonna get to the South China Sea. Not to that ocean, nor to any other.

'And that gives us three military options, and only three. Option 1): we arrange an air strike and blow them to pieces, right there in the shipyard where the satellites have been watching their progress for almost two years. This would of course instantly start World War III.

'Or we could go to Option 2). Wait for the Russians to load them, and then obliterate the barges and their cargo with a missile strike. This would also detonate World War III.

'Option 3) is even simpler. Another air strike to blow up a section of the 25-mile-long Belomorski Canal, which would end the northern journey of the submarines, and for that matter the northern journeys of everyone else. You might need a nuclear device for this, but you might not, if you could launch a big enough bomb or missile. Either way, here comes World War III.

'Which essentially renders options 1), 2), and 3) out of the question. Therefore, it remains as I have thought from Day One of this problem. It's gotta be special forces. And it's not gonna be easy. But neither is it impossible. Just so long as we stay very quiet.'

He returned once more to the big table, and looked again at the canal. 'The trick is,' he pondered, 'to confuse the life out of the goddamned Russians. Maybe get 'em to blame someone else. Which means we are going to have to get very stealthy. Our big problem is technology and organization. I just wonder what the hell time Bergstrom elects to get out of the sack. And what time Morris intends to terminate his banquet at the Pentagon.'

His preoccupation with the bachelor Admiral Bergstrom was justified. The head of SPECWARCOM had endured a late night, and would not be at his desk before 0800 – 1100 Morgan-time. Admiral Morris? The President's NSA had underestimated him.

Immediately upon arrival in the CNO's outer office George Morris had called Fort Meade and told them to give Admiral Morgan the latest update on the research with regard to a 'pattern' in the submarine journeys. And now John Harrison was on the line to the White House, being put through to the office of the National Security Advisor.

'Morgan. Speak.'

'Er, Admiral . . . Lt. Harrison, Fort Meade. The line's secure. I'm calling for Admiral Morris, who thought you would like to hear an update right now on our search for a journey pattern regarding the north-going Russian boats.'

'He was right. Shoot.'

'Sir. Well, as you know, we've gone back about 25 years studying all of the submarine journeys out of Gorky up to the White Sea. Naturally we do not have data on them all, but we have a lot, about 50 – and there is just one thing we think stands out. They all seem to stop at a certain point on Lake Onega, right up in the north, on the left, beyond Petrozavodsk. It was difficult to find a reason, but in the end we thought it was something very simple. At the time they stopped, there was always a buildup of traffic astern of the barges. We think they just pulled over to free up the north-going waterway, take a break and get some sleep. Our notes suggest they stopped in the summer at around 2100, then set off again at around 0500.'

'Interesting. And very helpful, Lieutenant. I'm grateful. Have you finished writing it up?'

'Almost, sir. Say one hour from now.'

'Okay, Lieutenant. I'll send an officer down to collect it. Usual high security: manacled briefcase, mark the envelope for very limited distribution, Top Secret . . . US Eyes Only.

'My own White House chauffeur will drive him. Charlie. Tall, gray-haired guy, about 50. He ain't that swift of thought, so call him by name or he might get bewildered.'

The Lieutenant laughed. But he had no time to start wondering why such an apparently minor point should have earned the dreaded Admiral Morgan's gratitude, because the phone was dropped back on its hook with a resounding clunk, leaving young John Harrison still holding the phone to his ear, connected to no one, just as his boss had been earlier in the day.

Arnold Morgan poured himself some more coffee and instructed a secretary to locate for him a detailed map of Lake Onega. It was almost 1100. He also told her to connect him to SPECWARCOM in San Diego, then to get Admiral Bergstrom on the line, and if he was not in to get him to call as soon as he was. As it happened, he wasn't, but the call came bouncing back from the headquarters of the US Navy SEALs by 0815 Pacific Daylight Time.

By then, the Admiral had commandeered from the library a very finely detailed map of the lake, and he gruffly asked the SEALs' ultimate boss if he wanted him to do all of his work while he slumbered in the West Coast sun, or whether he was proposing to pull his act together.

Admiral Bergstrom told him, 'If you had been on the receiving end of my luck last night, Arnie, you would not begrudge me my few moments of pleasure.'

Admiral Morgan chuckled. 'How are you, John?' he said. 'Sorry

I've been a bit out of touch, but I wanted to wait until I had something definite to tell you, and now I have.'

'Are we looking at a basic plan similar to what we discussed?'

'Exactly that. We should meet soonest.'

'Okay, you want me to come to Washington, or will you come out here?'

'The latter. Two days from now. As you know, the Chief's coming to LA for the day. I can get a ride. They'll drop me off in San Diego.'

'Jesus. You sure you can use that aircraft like a taxi?'

'No problem. I'll be in San Diego about 0900. Get someone to meet me, willya, John? I'll wanna lift back to the airport around 1600. We wanna be home by midnight if possible.'

'Right. I'll start to get this revved up. What's our priority?'

'Timing and recce.'

'Okay. You want me to alert the guys. You know they're all in place?'

'Yeah. We better get three of 'em moving within three days. Right after you and I finish.'

'Okay, Arnie. I'll start it up. Look forward to seeing you before 1000 day after tomorrow.'

Air Force One touched down at San Diego's Lindbergh Field at 0900 precisely and headed for the seclusion of an outer runway. The airway steps were down for exactly 45 seconds, and Admiral Morgan was out and gone, ensconced in the back seat of a US Navy staff car. By the time it reached the freeway exit to the airport, Air Force One was off the ground and heading north for LA.

The Navy driver swung down onto the Pacific Highway heading south, before the road began to climb up onto the spectacular curved bridge which crosses San Diego Bay on towering concrete stilts, like a mammoth centipede, 140 feet above the water. From its highest point it curves steeply down to the island of Coronado, where the headquarters of the SEALs is located right behind the beach, surrounded by heavy-duty wire, and patrolled by armed devils disguised as men. It is not a place which invites intruders. At least not the type of intruder who may have plans to continue taking up space on this planet.

SPECWARCOM is the jargon for US Navy Special Warfare Command. Rear-Admiral John Bergstrom, its Commander, was the latest in a line of outstanding officers who had also served in its ranks, learning the ropes as Navy SEALs themselves, working often undercover, usually in life-or-death situations. SEALs are the equivalent of the British SAS or the Royal Navy's Special Boat Service – highly trained killers, experts with explosives, and possessing thorough knowledge of dozens of weapons, systems and demolition techniques. They operate behind enemy lines, anyplace where the bravest angels might fear to tread. SEALs do not, normally, expect to die. In the words of General Patton they expect 'the other poor dumb bastard' to take care of that part.

It's harder to become a SEAL than to get through Harvard Law School. Even when the goal is almost reached, there remains the brutal indoctrination course, BUD/S (Basic Underwater Demolition/SEAL), known colloquially as 'The Grinder.' To enter here a man must be a paragon of physical, intellectual and emotional strength. Aside from his speed, his professional fighter's devastating reactions, and his natural agility in the water, he needs also a first-class memory if he wants to stay alive.

The BUD/S course is designed to eliminate anyone who may be suspect either mentally or physically. It comprises days of running in the heat of the day, all along the great five-mile-long Pacific beaches which guard San Diego Bay. Periodically recruits are driven into the freezing ocean by instructors, then made to roll in the sand, and then keep running up and down the dunes, ignoring the agonizing pain of the sand clinging inside wet shorts . . . 'Keep moving, son, I'm probably saving your life.'

As the courses move on, and exhausted men drop out, the instructors drive them harder. 'Hell Week' is when the pressure really goes on, and men on the verge of collapse are driven one more time through the underwater tunnel, one more time out onto the dunes, into the ocean, and one more mile home. Half of the men who enter 'Hell Week' never make it through. The instructors seek only those who are shattered, but still defiant, those who think they have nothing more to give, but still, in desperation, find more. That's a US Navy SEAL.

And the USA runs six teams of them: Three at Little Creek, Virginia, numbered Two, Four, and Eight. Three from Coronado, numbered One, Three, and Five. Admiral John Bergstrom, a veteran of Team Two, was the overlord of all the SEALs. From his office in Coronado he oversaw every SEAL operation worldwide, and there were a lot of men under his command.

Each team comprises 225 men, of which only 160 are active members of the Attack Platoons. Twenty-five people, several of them technicians and electronics experts, work in support and logistics. Forty more are directly involved in training, command and control. The SEAL strike squadrons require enormous back-up, for these are valuable men, with a code of their own. In all of their comparatively short but valiant history they have never left a colleague on the battlefield. Neither wounded nor dead, not even in Vietnam.

Admiral Arnold Morgan was shown into the office of Admiral John Bergstrom shortly before 1000. The two men greeted each other with warmth. They were old friends, each with a huge respect for the other. They were both tough and ruthless in the execution of their duties, both fiercely protective of the men who served them. But whereas Arnold Morgan had allowed his career to destroy his two marriages, John Bergstrom had suffered the agonies of watching his wife of 30 years die of cancer only 24 months ago.

Alone now in his official on-base residence, Admiral Bergstrom was considered a major asset by innumerable West Coast hostesses. Like all SEALs, he carried a mystique about him. He stood 6 ft 2 ins tall, and still had the hard athletic look of a Platoon commander. His sleek, dark hair had not yet grayed even though he was 57 years old. In tennis clothes, you noticed his forearms, which seemed to belong to a much more beefy body. He had big hands, and gray, sad eyes. It would not be true to say he laughed a lot, but he chuckled a great deal. It was the deep, amused chuckle of a man who had operated in the face of terrible danger, and who now regarded all the rest of it as essentially kids' stuff.

Arnold Morgan not only liked him, he trusted him, and there were not many who fell into that category in the eyes of the President's NSA. 'Good to see you, John,' he said. 'It's been a while. But I got a few goodies here to show you . . . and I think we're about to get this show on the road.'

Admiral Bergstrom grinned and shook his head. 'I'm telling you, Arnie, this is not as goddamned simple as it looks. Quite frankly I've never worked on a special ops project deep inside Russia. It's a minefield of problems, and if the guys get caught it would be the biggest embarrassment to the United States since the U2 pilot back in the '60s.'

'You want me to tell you a bigger embarrassment?' said Morgan. 'If the goddamned Chinese get ahold of 10 of those fucking Kilos and shut us out of the Strait of Taiwan. Right then we'd damned nearly have to go to war to restore the peaceful trading rights of all Western nations in those Eastern waters.'

'Yeah. I know. I haven't taken my eye off the ball,' said Bergstrom. 'I just hope we have enough data to make it happen.'

Admiral Morgan patted his slim-line briefcase. 'I have some good stuff in here,' he said. 'Pour me a cup of coffee and I'll show you. By the way, the President asked me to pass on to you his kindest regards.'

'That's very thoughtful of him,' said John Bergstrom. 'I've only met him two or three times.'

'This President just happens to like military men a lot more than he likes politicians. He makes it his business to befriend all of his senior commanders. He actually takes pride in the fact that he knows the first name of his SEAL C-in-C. As I left the plane he just said, "My best regards to John." '

'Hope he's still saying that a couple of months from now,' replied the SEAL Chief.

Arnold Morgan opened the briefcase and took out the manila Fort Meade envelope which had been perfectly delivered to him two days previously by the much-abused Charlie. He walked over to the detailed map of the European North of Russia which was laid out on a wide sloping desk with a green shaded light curved over it.

He traced his finger up the left-hand side of Lake Onega, past Petrozavodsk, beyond which the lake is cut in half by two large peninsulas, forcing through-traffic to the eastern side of the waterway. He ran his finger past the lakeside town of Kuzaranda, and then 25 miles farther on through the narrow gap between two other jutting peninsulas.

'About another 25 miles farther on,' he said, 'along here on the left, we come to one of the loneliest spots on the whole journey. See this town, Unica, which looks like it might be on the lake? . . . Well, it's not . . . it's about eight miles west. All the way up here there's just nothing but a few small farms run by dirt-poor peasants.

'And right here' – he pointed with the sharp end of a pair of dividers – 'is where these submarine barges stop. If you draw a line due northeast from Unica right across the lake to Provenec where the canal comes in, top right-hand corner, that's where the barges stop, on that line about a mile offshore.

'Follow the western shoreline of the lake for about a mile due north of where that line first reaches the water . . . right here . . . and we have something even more interesting. Along here, right on this desolate coastline, is where the big tourist boats pull over. They call it a "Green Stop." The boats ease right over to the port-side and park alongside the tall grasses along this shore. Then they let down a long 50-foot gangway, like you get on a car ferry, and everyone can get off and take a look at the virgin Russian countryside.'

'Jesus, Arnie. You might be a genius. Did I ever tell you that?'

'Well, I can't claim credit for arranging the Green Stop, but I sure as hell claim credit for finding out about it.'

'Was it difficult?'

'Murder. I had someone call the Odessa–American Line right here in the States, and tell 'em he was a bird watcher and would he get a chance to go ashore for a while at the northern end of Lake Onega. I was so careful I actually booked him on the ship before he made the call . . . now the sonofabitch thinks he's going on a 10-day paid vacation.'

'Whatever it costs, it's cheap,' said Admiral Bergstrom. 'That's some kind of a break, right?'

'Generally, you make your own breaks in this game.'

'Which I guess brings us to problem number one: how, Arnie, are we gonna get the guys onto the precise tourist ship which will be parked up there when the barges stop off for the night? And anyway, where the hell do the tour boats start from?'

'They mostly run out of St Petersburg.'

'St Petersburg? Remind me, what's the route up to the lake from there?'

'Through Lake Ladoga, then the River Svir' and into the canals that join Lake Onega. The route of the tour boat kinda converges with the barges in the southern half of the lake. I expect our tour boat to pass the barges somewhere in the northern half. Then I think they'll both make an overnight stop within a mile and a half of each other.'

'Right. But how do we get our guys on the right boat? How often do they run?'

'Matter of fact that's the least of the problems. There are a lot of tour boats operational now, since Russia opened up. There's one leaving just about every day. Sometimes three or four on weekends. And basically they all seem to end up at the north end of Lake Onega for their various Green Stops sometime in the early part of the evening. Remember it never gets dark up there in summer . . . you know, the White Nights and everything.'

'Right. But I still can't see how we get the guys on precisely the right boat.'

'Well, if you can't, maybe the Russkies won't figure it out either. The tour boats run about four times quicker than the barges, which tend to make a steady 5 knots from Nizhny right up into the lake. And they don't stop. Which means we can get a very accurate fix on what time they're going to reach the shoreline near Unica. We watch the barges on the overheads all the way, then the guys get on the precise tour boat we *know* will come sliding past the submarines around 1700, up in the north of Lake Onega. That Green Stop represents the end of the line for the tourists. The ship turns round then, and heads back to St Petersburg the next day.'

'Yeah, but you can't just get on a tour lasting several days. You have to book cabins and Christ knows what,' said Admiral Bergstrom.

'Yup. No sweat, John. We take a coupla suites on the upper deck on all of the probable boats, day after day. We book 'em right here in the USA.'

'Yeah. But there'll be a lot of suspicion when we keep canceling.'

'What d'you mean, canceling? We're not canceling anything. We'll get people in to take up the reservations. Secretaries, boyfriends from embassies and American corporations all over Europe. Give 'em a free vacation for a few days. The boats are packed with Americans. I got a survey in here . . . Of 300 passengers on the last three Odessa–American Line boats, an average of 284 were Americans. The worst thing that can happen is we have to change four or five names when we put our own team in. But we'll be giving them several days' notice, because we'll know the precise time they're gonna reach the northern end of the lake . . . we'll know it the moment the satellites spot the barges leaving Nizhny.'

'Jesus, Arnie. We're really gonna do this, aren't we?'

'No doubt. Anyway, we have no choice.'

The two admirals sat in silence for a few moments, each one of them momentarily stunned by the enormity of the mayhem they were about to unleash.

'Your guys must have had a real headache with the kit and packing it,' commented Arnold Morgan.

'Plenty,' replied John Bergstrom, not bothering to mention the complicated details of such a mission: preparing the men's requirements; the four Draegers, their helmets, masks, flippers and wetsuits; the four attack boards. The light machine-guns, well balanced, effective Soviet-designed RPDs with their characteristic sound, which might confuse a Russian guard should it come to a fight. Their sidearms, Sig Sauer 9 mm pistols. The piles of ammunition clips. The Kaybar combat knives. The medical kit with codeine and morphine and battle dressings. Water purification tablets, radios, plus batteries, plus a GPS. And five ponchos with liners and groundsheets, just in case the SEALs might be forced to shoot their way out and then take to the countryside until they could be rescued.

'I've made just one change to our original plan, Admiral. We're sending in a kind of back-up SEAL caretaker to nanny them. CIA agent, worked behind the Iron Curtain in the 1980s. Very tough character, Angela Rivera.'

'ANGELA!' yelled Admiral Morgan. 'Is this a girl? On a mission like this?'

'This is a girl. Make-up and disguise *expert*. Finished first in the CIA Tradecraft Class at Camp Peary. Highly trained and unobtrusive.'

'What if she gets hurt, or can't cope with a getaway?'

'Arnie, remember when that bastard Aldrich Ames was in the process of shopping 25 top US agents working in East Germany, Russia and Romania?'

'Do I ever.'

'Well, he blew the cover on the slim and clever Miss Angela Rivera in some Berlin hotel. And the KGB sent a couple of spooks to her room. They apparently decided that one should go in after her and one should keep watch. When the first one seemed a bit delayed, the second one went in himself, stupid bastard. He just had time to find his mate dead on the floor. It was the last thing he ever saw. She garroted 'em both. And got away, back to Langley, Virginia. She's up to it.'

'Jesus,' said Arnold Morgan. 'Guess we're gonna need a lot of explosive?'

'According to my calculations, each of the four swimmers is going to need eight small shaped charges, which weigh five pounds each. These things make a fairly small bang, but blow a biggish hole, with a kind of cylindrical shape to the explosion, forcing it just one way, rather than a regular outward/inward blast. Each charge has its own timer . . . very, very accurate. That's 40 pounds of explosive for each man, and I don't think they want to carry more.'

'Not with a mile, or even a little more to swim . . . Anyone looked at the water depth yet?'

'Since I only found out seven minutes ago *where* the operation was taking place, hardly.'

'Jesus, you guys are getting slack,' said Morgan in mock seriousness.

'Well, on that note, lemme announce to you what I believe is a bit of a road block right here,' replied Admiral Bergstrom. 'And let me also tell you that I'm not at all sure how to solve it . . . How the hell are we gonna get all the stuff into Russia, and then transport it somehow up to that northern wasteland? I'd say we're going to end up with around 750 pounds of gear – that's a third of a ton. We're talking fork-lift truck, minimum.'

'Christ, so we are . . . I'd kinda assumed we could somehow run it over the border from Finland, up in the Laani area.'

'Arnold, there are no roads which cross the old Soviet border up in that area. There's a long border road running north–south but it doesn't cross into Russia. And a couple of roads just come to a dead-end. There's a railroad, but even today the Russians keep a careful eye on it. We can't start running cargoes of fucking Semtex all over the place.

'Of course, there is a regular freeway that runs straight up from St Petersburg to Petrozavodsk. But it would be just about impossible for us to bring in a cargo of this size under the eyes of the Russian customs and port authority guards. And if they found it, there would be an unbelievable uproar.'

'You're right there . . . How about an airlift from some remote spot in eastern Finland, straight over the border and right into the area we need it?'

'We can't chance that, Arnie. The Russians are still pretty hot about any air transport crossing their borders. Specially after that Chechen bullshit.'

'Well, how about by the waterways?'

'Too risky. The canal traffic is subject to checks at various points all along the routes. The truth is we *cannot* get caught.'

'What do you consider the best chance of success?'

'I suppose a helicopter over the border . . . flying very low, right under the radar. But if one of their military listening stations picked it up, they'd shoot it down. If push comes to shove we might just have to accept that risk and go for it.'

'Christ . . . If that happened, there'd be all hell to pay.'

'I know it. But it's hard to find a way round the problem.'

By this time, both men were pacing the room, deep in thought. Neither of them spoke for several minutes. Then John Bergstrom said, 'Arnie . . . there is something in the back of my mind . . . You read about that new HALO development? It's not perfected, but my guys in the industry say it's gonna work.'

'HALO,' replied Morgan. 'That's High Altitude, Low Opening, right? A free-fall situation from above 20,000 feet. You're thinking of dropping a coupla guys out of an aircraft high over Russia hanging on to all that kit? Jesus. I'm not sure about that, John.'

'No, Arnie. I'm not talking about that. I'm talking capsules. Big metal canisters that operate on the same system as laser-guided bombs. We're gonna pitch 'em out of a military aircraft high over Russia — maybe as high as 35,000 feet — and get 'em to home in on a beam.'

'Home in on what?'

'A beam. We get our guys in there — on the ground, somewhere out in the wilds near the lake — and they turn on their device and wait for the aircraft. The beam locks on and the air crew dump the canisters out. Then the computerized steering activates a small power unit in the canisters, and steers 'em right in.'

'Christ. That's pretty smart. But I got a few questions.'

'Hit me.'

'Do these things just crash into the ground like a bomb?'

'No. They fall like stones for 34,000 feet. Then the 'chutes open, and they float in the last 800 feet at around 12 m.p.h. From the moment the 'chute opens it's only about 45 seconds before they hit the ground. And barring a gale, they come in within 30 yards of the beam. The guys will not only see them floating down, they'll hear them thud into the ground.'

'How about radar?'

'Well, with those things hurtling through the air, straight down from 35,000 feet, the chances of the Russians getting a good fix before they disappear are pretty remote. And even if they did, it'd be a bit late to do much about it. On a screen I guess they'd look like meteorites or something.'

'What would they weigh?'

'I guess three of 'em at about 250 pounds each . . . specially fitted with handles, of course, to make 'em easy for two guys to carry.'

'Then what? Bury 'em somewhere near the edge of the woods?'

'Exactly. As soon as the SEALs open 'em up, the first thing they take out are a couple of spades. Then they lock 'em up again and bury 'em, all ready for the night when they'll be back for 'em.'

'I got another problem, John. How are we going to send a military aircraft over Russian airspace without them asking all kinds of questions?'

'That's pretty simple. With sensible care, there's nothing to identify a military aircraft from a commercial one, unless they just happen to put up an interceptor for a visual ident. And that's most unlikely.'

The SEAL Commander walked over to a large globe in the corner of his office, and ran a length of tape measure across the top, edging it into position. 'There you are,' he said. 'The polar route from Los Angeles to the Emirates, right on the Gulf, passes directly down the right-hand side of the lake. We bring in the chief executive of whichever American airline flies that route, and have him file a commercial flight plan with the Russians for that night. No one would think of questioning it. And the only difference is, it'll be a high-altitude echo-enhanced military aircraft making the journey, five miles up there, instead of a regular Boeing.'

'Did I ever mention the fact that you might be a genius?' said Arnold Morgan.

'Not lately,' said Admiral Bergstrom.

'And they have actually tested this system?' said Morgan. 'In the desert, and it happened just as you are saying?'

'I have no hard report, but a couple of my guys were out there, and they said it was a goddamned miracle. Those things just came floating in from 35,000 feet and landed right there, just a few yards from the beam.'

'John, old buddy, we got ourselves a real plan. That's the way we'll go. Where are the guys right now?'

'They're in a hotel in the middle of Helsinki, waiting for the word to move into one of the tour ships across the bay in St Petersburg. They have excellent papers and passports as we agreed before.'

'Sounds good. Now, I'll get the CIA to take care of all of those tour ship bookings. I think we better start those for four days after the *Tolkach* barges actually arrive off the Red Sormovo yards. Because, in theory, they could load and depart right away. Although that probably won't happen.'

'Right. I think I'll send a veteran chief petty officer into Helsinki, and he can go with two SEALs up the lakes on a ship right away.

'We need to move fast. They'd better get the canisters made and trucked down here right away, in a couple of days. We'll load them, and have 'em ready to go that same day. I'll get the chief on a flight to Helsinki tomorrow morning. In the end we'll almost certainly have a couple of weeks to spare, but we wanna be ready.'

'One thing, John, are we going to need good timing to get the recce team away from the tour ship, and out to the drop zone?'

'Not really. You see, we'll *know* the exact time they're scheduled to arrive at the Green Stop before the ship departs. We just need to get the dropper overhead, say two hours later. That way the guys can just appear to take a walk and set up their beam, and we'll make sure the aircraft is up there right on time. If he's late, it just means the guys will have to hang around for an hour. Which doesn't matter. The thing is, he mustn't be early, because he can't slow down much during his approach through Russian airspace. But I'm not seeing a problem there.'

'No, John, neither am I. But the key to this lies in our ability to organize it without a hitch. And then it's in the hands of the SEALs . . . By the way, how do we get 'em out? They're not going back on the ship, are they?'

'The recce team will — the ship makes very fast time back, running non-stop at around 20 to 25 knots all the way to St Pete's. Of course, the strike squad won't return to the ship. We'll have them out in a small truck, but there will be nothing incriminating in it. Just a small group of tourists trundling around in the land of their forefathers. No problem to anyone. It's very rural up there. Nothing much for anyone to be sensitive about.'

'Until the charges go off bang. That might change things a bit.'

'So it might, Arnie, but we'll be long gone by then.'

'How about afterwards? There's gotta be a fucking uproar, whatever happens.'

'Now that's your problem. Not mine. I'm here to bang out three little Russian diesel-electrics. And I think I can do it. The uproar will be political. And that's your beat. We better get the guys at the CIA to work on it.'

'Yeah. Guess so. Somehow we want to be indignant . . . get some complaint or other going, try to sow the seed of doubt in the Russian mind that the whole thing might have been done by those Chechens, or a fundamentalist group. We're not the only country which is not always very pleased with the Moscow government.'

'No, Arnie. We're not. But we are the only country which has made it absolutely clear we're not having those Kilos going to China. And I have a feeling that's the clue which will dominate the minds of the Russians.'

'I don't suppose the Chinese Navy will be throwing a party in honor of the US Embassy staff in Beijing, either.'

CHAPTER SEVEN

THE LAKE WAS 50 miles wide here, and the *Mikhail Lermontov* was cutting through the short seas at a steady 25 knots, straight up the middle, heading north. It was midafternoon on May 1, and the spring sky was overcast, deep, dark gray clouds drifting northeast before a steady breeze, the sure harbinger of rain, sweeping in off the cold Baltic, where it had already slashed through the city streets of Helsinki and St Petersburg.

'This weather,' said Lt. Commander Rick Hunter, 'could turn out to be a serious pain in the ass.' He sat huddled with his two companions in the corner of the small bar on deck three, right at the stern of the 300-foot-long blue-and-white tour ship. 'Matter of fact, if it rains like I think it's gonna rain, this little holiday could turn out to be a royal fuck-up. Still, we can't turn back now.'

His words were carefully chosen and hard-edged, betraying nothing to possible eavesdroppers. They were US Navy SEAL words. Factual, substantive, unaffected, without incongruity. SEALs on missions don't really do euphemism. To them, danger is there to be faced down, and dealt with, sometimes brutally, just short of the point of overkill. Their creed was simple: take no chances, nor prisoners, not if one of us might die.

Rick Hunter was a rare man. He was a SEAL Team Leader, selected from a pack of equally rare men, because in him the instructors and commanders had spotted something different. There was a coldness there behind his bright blue eyes and aw-shucks Kentucky hardboot manner. They had judged this rugged, country lieutenant commander from the Bluegrass as a man that other men would follow, and who in turn would treat his team's problems as if they were his alone.

Back at Coronado, and at his home base in Little Creek, Virginia, most everyone had a hell of a soft spot for Rick Hunter. Perhaps not least because of his unwavering eye for a thoroughbred racehorse, and finely tuned ear to the Kentucky gossip. Three times in the last four years he'd correctly forecast the winner of the Kentucky Derby: two of them had been favorites, but one had gone in at 20–1. There were young SEALs who believed that Lt. Commander Hunter was some kind of a god.

His father, old Bart Hunter, who bred his own thoroughbreds on an immaculate horse farm out along the Versailles Pike, near Lexington, was not among this particular fan club. He found it a profound mystery that his eldest boy had not the slightest interest in coming home to raise horses just like he did, and like his daddy before him. There was no way he could understand the 35-year-old Rick when he told him, as he had told him every year since he was about 15, 'Dad, it's too passive. I just can't spend all year wandering around in a daze looking at baby racehorses, waiting for the Keeneland Yearling Sales to see if we're gonna go on eating. I need action. In the horse business I would have considered becoming a jockey. But that's not possible.'

It sure wasn't. The 6 ft 3 in Rick Hunter tipped the scales at 215 lb and he carried not one ounce of fat. He actually weighed the equivalent of two jockeys, and he had quarters on him like the racehorse Man O'War. Rick Hunter had been a swimmer all of his life; a collegiate champion from Vanderbilt University, he had very nearly made the Olympic Trials for the 1988 Games – but had dropped out of college suddenly, and been accepted a year later at the US Naval Academy, Annapolis.

His immense third-generation farmer's strength, allied to his coordination and dexterity in the water, made him a natural candidate for the SEALs. The fact that he was a deadly accurate marksman, and a man used to exercising authority from a very young age on the 2,000-acre farm in the Bluegrass, made him, right from the start, a potential team leader. Rick Hunter disappointed no one. Except Bart.

And now he sat, frowning, staring through the big stern windows at the lowering sky. 'Fuck it,' he thought to himself as the *Mikhail Lermontov* ran smoothly onwards beneath thick gray cloud. 'Not much light tonight. Even with the full moon that cloud cover will just about kill it. Another pain in the ass.'

It was not perhaps quite the phraseology of the young intellect for whom the ship was named, but the nineteenth-century romantic author of Russia's first major psychological novel, *A Hero of Our Time*, did deal principally with the twin demons of frustration and isolation . . . and Rick Hunter sure did understand all about that shit. 'Specially right now.'

He and his two colleagues had spent a while in the little ship's museum which was devoted to the short life of Mikhail Lermontov – all Russian tour ships these days are like cultural theme parks built around the person the ship is named for. The three SEALs had watched the illustrated account of Lermontov's demise, killed in a duel at the age of only 26. 'Shoulda rolled off to the right when he'd fired his one shot,' thought Chief Petty Officer Fred Cernic. 'Then come right back at him with his knife, low off the ground, leading off his right leg . . . blade forward, one movement . . .' Then, aloud, the Chief observed, 'He'd probably still be around if he'd been properly taught.'

'Yeah, right,' said Rick, 'He'da been about 200 years old.'

The third SEAL was Lieutenant Junior Grade Ray Schaeffer, a lean, dark-haired 28-year-old native of the Massachusetts seaport of Marblehead, where his family traced their lineage back to the time of the Revolutionary War. There was a Schaeffer pulling one of the oars when the Marbleheaders rowed General Washington to safety from the lost Battle of Long Island to Manhattan. Ray was proud of his heritage. His father was a fishing-boat captain, and the family home was a medium-sized, white-painted Colonial down near the docks. The Schaeffers were a deeply religious Catholic family, and they had lived there for generations.

Ray had gone straight from High School to Annapolis. A lifelong seaman, expert navigator, swimmer, and Platoon middleweight boxing champion, he had SEAL written all over him from a very young age. Both he and Rick Hunter were considered destined for high office in this unorthodox branch of the US fighting forces.

All three men were traveling along the Russian waterways on false passports and false identities. They kept their correct first names, to avoid foolish errors, but their last names were completely different. Not a vestige of the military was apparent. They stayed fairly clear of other passengers, but not obviously so. In fact, the slim, dark-haired divorcee Mrs Jane Westenholz, and her doe-eyed 19-year-old daughter Cathy, from Greenwich, Connecticut – each of them a separate pastel symphony devoted to Caroline Herrera and Hermès – had taken rather a shine to Rick and his friends. Mrs Westenholz was apt to call them Ricky, Freddie and Ray

Darling, as if they were three hairdressers, which would probably have amused Admiral Bergstrom.

Lt Commander Hunter looked at his watch. They were still four hours away from the Green Stop, and, because the tour boats were not yet on their full summer schedules, they were due to arrive at 7.30 p.m. Tonight they would dock in a grim, damp northern twilight. The springtime plan of the Russian boats was to secure alongside the jetty overnight and then allow the passengers the morning to look around, with the possibility of a barbecue lunch ashore, weather permitting, before returning south to St Petersburg.

Right now Rick could feel the boat altering course to the west for the programed swing around the island of Kizhi, which has become a national treasure, a kind of museum of wooden architecture. Some boats make a long, four-hour stop here to see the three carved eighteenth-century churches and to visit other historic wooden buildings, in a place where time has essentially stood still for three centuries. The *Mikhail Lermontov* was not stopping at Kizhi and its detour would be swift, but the island is a unique place, and its onion-domes adorn every guidebook of the great lake.

The three SEALs pulled on their parkas and baseball caps, paid and tipped the young Russian waiter, and went outside to see the island. Fred brought a camera with him, and they all leaned over the portside rail on the upper deck while the Chief Petty Officer shot pictures. Ray said he didn't think there was a snowball's chance in hell that any of 'em would come out, because of the light. Mrs Westenholz, who turned up in a fluorescent scarlet raincoat with bright yellow boots, told all three 'boys' they ought not to be out in the rain as they 'could catch severe chills in this awful Russian weather.'

Ray was kind to her. 'Ma'am,' he said, 'I been walking around big fields in the pouring rain all of my life back home in Kentucky. Doesn't affect me now – 'cept I sometimes get a little rust creeping up under my eyelids.'

Mrs Westenholz squeaked with laughter, and opened her own dark eyes wide. 'But this isn't proper American rain,' she said. 'This is Russian rain, and it's colder, comes from the Arctic. It'll freeze you right through.'

'Don't worry about him, ma'am,' said Ray Darling. 'He's insensitive. That chill couldn't get through to him.'

'Ooh,' said Jane Westenholz. 'I think Ricky could be very sensitive . . . and I think you should all come inside now and I'll get us some coffee and a glass of brandy to warm us up.'

Chief Cernic actually considered that to be an appealing idea. He also considered, very privately, that Mrs Westenholz might be a bit of an athlete in the sack. Trouble was she plainly had eyes for only the big, straw-haired Team Leader from Kentucky. And at 44, Fred realized too that he was 'out of the game with the good-looking daughter.' His wife and three sons back home in San Diego would probably have been pleased about that.

Rick grinned at Jane Westenholz. 'Okay – you go ahead. We'll see you in the stern bar in five minutes, but hold the brandy . . . I forgot to tell you, Fred here is a recently reformed alcoholic. He gets really difficult after even one drink . . . we always try to go along with his program, just to help him through it. So Ray and I never drink when he's around.'

Chief Cernic raised his eyebrows at the enormity of the lie. Mrs Westenholz said, 'Oh, darling Freddie, we mustn't allow you to slip back, must we? One day at a time – and no drinkie-poohs for anyone in the afternoon.'

Ray Shaeffer shook his head. 'Jesus,' he muttered. 'This old broad could be a real fucking nuisance. We may end up heaving the bodies of her and her daughter over the side before long.'

The identical thought had occurred to Rick Hunter, but in general terms he thought it would probably be better if they could get through this without taking anyone out. 'We're going to have to make ourselves a bit remote this evening,' he said quietly.

The 10,000-ton *Mikhail Lermontov* turned back to the southeast, towards the narrow strait which divides the headland of Bojascina from the island of Kurgenicy, beyond which was the main 50-mile north–south channel up to the Belomorski Canal.

The rain stopped as they turned away from Kizhi, and a watery sunlight lit the surface of the lake intermittently. But the high rolling cloudbanks out to the southwest remained in place. The dying afternoon breeze had slowed down the low pressure system as it moved northeast, but Lt. Commander Hunter had baleful forebodings of the night's weather, and he was already shuddering at the thought of the forthcoming conditions in which he and his team would almost certainly have to work.

To Rick, this strange and foreign place was merely an operational zone, and he tried to view it dispassionately. But the sight of the hills climbing away in a misty purple shroud on the eastern shore of the glistening silver lake was almost overwhelming to anyone who had not previously witnessed its desolate beauty. Lt. Commander Hunter, no stranger himself to breathtaking rural landscapes, shook his head at the thought of three Soviet-designed submarines moving innocently, yet somehow obscenely, like huge black stranded slugs, across these waterways of God.

The light began to fade again now, and the air seemed suddenly colder. The three SEALs left the deck and wandered down to the stern bar, where Jane Westenholz and Cathy were ensconced with two large pots of coffee and a plate of small pastries. Rick and Fred, nerves beginning to tighten now as the Green Stop grew closer, managed only to sip coffee. Ray, full of confidence in his own ability to survive anything, ate seven pastries with deceptive speed.

By 6.00 p.m., the bar had become quite full, and very smoky, and filled with the aromatic smells of coffee and alcohol. Many of the 140 Americans on board were coming in now for a drink before dinner, which was served early, in one sitting, during these springtime weeks before the tour ships became really crowded to their 300-passenger summer capacity. It was even busier in the big horseshoe bar in the bow of the ship, where there would later be Russian folk dancing and then a disco for the younger passengers, of which there were only about 16 in the entire ship.

Outside it was raining lightly again, slanting in from the southwest, glistening in the bright lights of the three upper decks. Through the rain, Rick Hunter could see the warning lights were on now on the big channel markers, as the ship headed north into the drop zone. He was dreading the condition of the fields, worried about the mud and the mess they must surely find themselves in. Worried more about the return to the ship, when they would be trying to look normal. It would be long after midnight.

Jane Westenholz chattered on, and invited the three Americans to join her and her daughter at dinner in the big dining room. Trapped, unable to use Fred's 'alcoholism' as a way out, Rick found himself agreeing to meet at 7.30 p.m., just about the time the ship was scheduled to pull up. The worst part was that he knew they could not possibly get to the dining room at the correct time, since he wanted to get a GPS 'fix' on the anchorage location . . . and, assuming they were in the right place, a damned hard look at the surrounding country.

Once out there in the dark, they would have only the little numbers to go by, the ones written in his brain, *62.38N, 34.47E.* That's where the *Mikhail Lermontov* must be when she came to a halt, the precise spot Fort Meade had designated the Green Stop. Those were the numbers Rick must see when he switched on the Global Positioning System. Four hours later, less than five miles northwest of those numbers, the three SEALs must 'light up' their electronic beacon in the middle of some godforsaken Russian field, and pray the laser homing device on the canisters would find it. Find it at 2330 exactly. Five hours from now.

Meanwhile, as the tour boat ran on up the lake, leaving the town of Sunga to her port side, a 220-ton United States Air Force B-52H long-range bomber was thundering at 440 m.p.h. through the ice-cold skies 45,000 feet above the Arctic circle.

Lt. Colonel Al Jaxtimer, a seasoned front-line pilot out of the Fifth Bomb Wing, Minot Air Force Base, North Dakota, was at the controls, concentrating on maintaining precise speed over the ground in the northwesterly jet-stream up there beyond the cockpit. It had been a long day for him and his crew, co-pilot Major Mike Parker, electronics warfare officer Captain Charlie Ullman, and the two navigators, Lt. Chuck Ryder and Lt. Sam Segal (radar).

They had first flown the B-52H up from Minot to Edwards Air Base, north of Los Angeles. They had taken off again at 1000 (Moscow time) that morning, except that it was 2300 the previous evening for them in California. The big Edwards tanker aircraft had waited high above in the dark as they roared upwards to their climb-out refueling point. And then they headed north with full tanks, a 10,000-mile range and a very light cargo load of only 750 lb, plus 180 lb for the parachutes. Deep inside the bomb-bay were just the three 250-lb computerized bomb-shaped canisters, attached to furled black parachute containers. Each one had been personally packed by the senior petty officers at Coronado; the kit was detailed right down to a couple of shovels, and the SEALs' twin godsends of a flashlight and a plastic-sealed three-pack of towels.

Since the climb-out refuel, they had been arrowing up over the Northern ice cap, through the time zones en route to the drop-point over the western shore of Lake Onega. No one was bored or tired, because the adrenalin would not allow that. All five men understood that even a minor foul-up could cause the most embarrassing international crisis for the USA, and each of them was determined no foul-ups were going to happen. Not in their bomber. Not in MT058.

The time was 1830 now in Moscow, and the B-52H Stratofortress was skirting the north coast of Greenland. The giant, 160-foot-long, gun-gray aircraft, with its distinctive shark's-head nose and 185-foot wingspan, was rumbling on south of east now, toward Russia.

Colonel Jaxtimer kept the aircraft's speed up as he headed out toward the Barents Sea. According to their computer they were bang on schedule, although they were deliberately flying at 10,000 feet too high an altitude, to conserve fuel. ETA over the drop-zone if they maintained this speed: 2336, six minutes late. Not bad. Four hours and six minutes from now the B-52H would enter Russian airspace.

Major Mike Parker had their official flight plan stowed in his flight bag. It had been filed formally by American Airlines the previous day. Basically it described a routine commercial flight, number AA294, Los Angeles International to Bahrain, on the polar route. A Boeing 747 leaving LA at 2300, and flying over Norway's North Cape. Estimated arrival in Russian airspace from Finnish airspace, 400 miles west of Murmansk: 2230, Moscow time. The flight plan then described briefly the journey across Russia, passing just east of Moscow, down the center of the Caucasus, and on over Iran to the Gulf.

As they approached Northern Europe, Major Parker would report in to each new air-control zone. First Norway. Then Finland. Then Russia. The B-52H would have no military radar switched on. At the lower altitude of 35,000 feet they would be regarded as any other big passenger jet, with an officially cleared flight plan, heading south. At least, with reasonable luck, they would. Routine commercial flights are not normally identified visually over Russia, certainly not at night.

Jane Westenholz poured more coffee for each of the three SEALs. Then she stood up gracefully, and announced that she and Cathy were leaving now to change for dinner, and that she looked forward to seeing them all at 7.30 p.m. Rick stood up gallantly and said he was sure they all looked forward to it, and should he inform the dining room of the table change . . . since one of such severity might send the *Lermontov*'s rigidly trained Russian head waiter into a state of near collapse.

Jane smiled and said no, she had already taken care of that. The SEALs watched her walk away, Fred Cernic more appreciatively than the other two. 'How the hell are we gonna get out of this bullshit?' wondered Lt. Schaeffer.

But not a word was spoken between them. All SEALs are trained, indoctrinated to understand that there may always be a hidden microphone. The words of their instructors at Coronado would be with them always: 'If any of you guys are ever standing in a group of three in the middle of a prairie, where you can see every movement in every direction for five fucking miles, YOU WILL ASSUME THERE IS A SHIT-ASS LITTLE RUSSIAN SPY HOLDING A MICROPHONE IN A FUCKING HOLE SIX FEET FROM WHERE YOU ARE STANDING . . . DO YOU UNDERSTAND ME?'

And now, on this Russian ship, the need for professional silence was uppermost in their minds. Without one sentence uttered, they each knew, instinctively, they must be unobtrusive and normal; that this well meaning, irritating lady must never say one word about them to anyone, except how nice they were.

She might be a bit of a pain in the ass, the circumstances being what they were, but it would be a *real* pain in the ass if she drew *any* attention to them by telling *anyone* they were rude or strange or suspicious. All three SEALs had noticed the boat contained a few officers who were plainly ex-Soviet military.

This applied specifically to the obvious senior official on the ship, whose manner suggested he was an executive of the shipping company, superior in rank even to the Captain. He actually went by the title of *Colonel* Karpov, and to Rick's eye he was very probably ex-KGB. The man was lean, smooth and bright-eyed, with clear skin. He was immaculately turned out in a civilian suit, and grotesquely polite to everyone. He was a fit-looking 'new Russian man,' the diametric opposite of the old pale-faced lumpen officials who gave the place a bad name for the best part of 60 years.

Colonel Karpov, at the age of about 45, might easily have been a ladies' man, but there was something missing. He *almost* flirted with the best-looking of the female passengers, including Mrs

Westenholz. But it was not quite flirtation. It was as if the true personality had been drained out of him. Cathy Westenholz, who was going to Yale in the Fall to study psychology, had informed her mother, memorably, that she regarded Colonel Karpov as 'sexually obscure.'

Rick Hunter thought he was 'fucking dangerous,' watchful, wary, and smart. The SEAL lieutenant commmander always greeted him if they passed each other by, but he preferred to watch the Colonel from a distance. He decided that the man essentially missed nothing which took place on the *Mikhail Lermontov.*

He also knew that they could not even consider taking him out, not even if the man elected not to mind his own business. Because such an assassination would quickly cause the place to become stiff with KGB men. The SEALs would never get out. No, they would just have to be meticulously careful, as always. The Colonel must neither see, hear nor smell anything suspicious. And Lt. Commander Rick Hunter would continue to walk around in a slumped, sloppy civilian way, trying to keep away from the Colonel. He would also try to keep Jane Westenholz cheerful, even hopeful, and, above all, unsceptical.

At 1914 Fred Cernic sensed the change in the beat of the engines. The tour ship was slowing down. Through the big square windows they could see little in the gloom outside, but Ray Schaeffer guessed the land was not far off to port. The deck-lights were still highlighting the slanting but light rain, and the three SEALs zipped up their parkas and replaced their baseball caps – Rick's was emblazoned with the big 'C' of the Cincinnati Reds, Fred's was Dodger Blue, and Ray's carried the distinctive red-and-white 'B' on dark blue of the Boston Red Sox.

Out on the second of the upper decks there was a sheltered walkway along each side, but the seating area at the stern of the ship was exposed to the weather. As far as Fred could see there was no one else in sight. They leaned over the rail, apparently watching the white foamy lake water slash along the side of the ship, but actually straining their eyes to become used to the dark, trying to see the shoreline.

Ray Schaeffer was sure it was no farther than a couple of hundred yards away, and they all heard the engines drop in tone as the ship eased to port toward its Green Stop. It was unsurprising the shore was so difficult to see. The land up here on the northern reaches of Lake Onega was flat, growing and grazing land for cereals and small herds of cattle. Quite apart from the drizzle, the hard black line where the water ended was partially obscured by very tall grasses and bulrushes.

They all looked up as the Captain suddenly switched on a couple of big lights up near the bow, and, craning forward, Ray could see a low gray jetty, not more than three feet high, set deep into the rainswept water's edge. 'This is it,' he muttered. 'He's gonna bring her right in against the jetty. Guess he'll lower the gangway down onto the grass, so's it reaches firm ground. That way everyone can just walk right off.'

'I hope he lowers it tonight, whatever the weather,' said Rick. 'They did say the gangway would come down as soon as the ship docked, and stay down, so everyone can walk about.'

The *Mikhail Lermontov* was almost stationary now. As she moved through the shallows at less than 1 knot, Lt. Schaeffer felt her lurch gently against the jetty. Then he heard the starboard engine reverse, rev quickly, and die as the 10,000-tonner came to a complete halt. 'This bastard's done it before,' murmured the lieutenant from Marblehead.

They moved quickly into a deserted part of the deck. Rick Hunter pulled the little black GPS from his pocket and switched it on. The green light on its square face glowed dimly in the dark. Rick held it out in the rain, as its beam sought the satellite 22,000 miles above. A minute went by, then another 30 seconds. Then the numbers flicked on: '*62.38N, 34.47E.*'

'We're right on the money,' said Rick, turning the GPS off and stuffing it quickly back in his jacket pocket. 'Now, what can we see out there? Anything hopeful?'

'Not much. But there is a light close to the shore, just about 50 yards left of dead center where the gangway is supposed to go down. See it? Right there . . .' Ray pointed out over the long lake grass, and now they could all see the glow of a light, coming and going, probably behind the swaying branches of a tree,

'Guess it's a house,' said Chief Cernic. 'Or maybe a shop. I don't think there's much out here. They said it was a kind of nature place, wild birds and lonely farmland . . . give everyone a real feel for rural Russia.'

'Yes,' said Rick. 'But there's supposed to be a few people around selling things, carvings and stuff to the tourists; possibly a little café selling coffee, brandy and sausage late at night to the passengers.'

'Not in this weather there won't be,' said Ray. 'I wouldn't be that surprised if no one left the ship except us.'

'Jesus. I hope you're wrong,' said Fred, and just then they heard the metallic bang as the gangway went down. Moving back to the port side, they could see the lights shining out from the interior of the ship, over the grass, where a brown dirt road lay beyond. There seemed to be people out there, probably the rope-handlers and a few locals out for a quick buck from the tourists. They could hear members of the crew calling out greetings in Russian.

'I hope the rain stops, that's all I hope,' said Rick, turning away. 'And how the hell are we gonna get in to dinner with Jane, and out by nine o'clock? She'll never buy we're going for a walk . . . I'll just have to come up with something.'

'Well, you've told her I'm an alcoholic, why not tell her I've got blackwater fever, or something exotic, and I have to be in bed early?' said Fred. 'You guys are my nurses.'

'How about AIDS?' asked Ray helpfully.

'Gimme a break, willya? A drunk, okay. A drunk and a fag, forget it. I can't take the humiliation. My wife would have a fit.'

'All right,' said Rick, grinning. 'Leave it to me. I'll come up with something reasonable.'

The SEALs headed for the dining room. It was 7.45 p.m., and they apologized to Jane and her daughter. Dinner was like all meals on the ship, plain and plentiful, light years better than the old Soviet Union of the '70s and '80s, but still no better than an American diner. The waitress was young, and Russian, and eager to please. Mrs Westenholz had ordered a bottle of dark red Bulgarian wine, but Rick shook his head and leaned over to her conspiratorially. 'Not for us . . . not while Fred's here. Perhaps later. He's not feeling too good this evening.'

Lt. Schaeffer fought to stop himself laughing. Fred told him almost inaudibly to shut up. And the Connecticut divorcee whispered back to the SEALs Team Leader, 'Of course, Ricky.' She touched his hand fleetingly, and added, 'Perhaps later.'

They ordered some fizzy water from the Ukraine, and the food arrived with conveyor-belt speed: large, well roasted portions of chicken, with mashed potatoes and cabbage. Jane and Cathy picked at theirs, but the SEALs ate steadily, each of them aware of the long cold night which lay before them, and the need of their bodies for fuel, especially carbohydrate. They all requested second servings of potato with gravy. Ray had another breast of chicken as well.

Between them they also demolished almost a loaf of heavy Russian black bread. No one else in the entire dining room was eating anything except white bread, since the popular perception was that black bread was for the peasants. However, they had been briefed direct from the White House. Admiral Morgan himself had passed a message through Admiral Bergstrom to the departing SEALs. It had read starkly: 'On ops nights tell 'em to eat a lot of Russian black bread – it's pure wheat and highly nutritious. That white crap they make is like eating the *Washington Post* and just as fucking worthless.'

'They don't seem like low-life,' whispered Jane to Cathy, 'and they all look fit . . . but I can't imagine how they can be, eating like that.'

All five of them declined dessert, which was very sugary pastry and ice cream, but the two SEAL lieutenants both asked for cheese, and 'a bit more of that black bread with butter.'

'If I ate like that I'd weigh 220 pounds,' said Jane Westenholz.

'That's right, ma'am. That's about what I do weigh. Gotta keep my strength up.'

The clock ticked on to 8.40 p.m. Jane and Cathy sipped the wine. Rick Hunter had to get his team out of this dining room, back to their cabins, pick up the few things they needed, and out of that lower deck exit, on to the shore. Nothing could stand in the way of that, but he wanted to do it smoothly. Leaving no trace of suspicion.

'Jane,' he said suddenly. 'I'm afraid I have to take these two reprobates away for a while. Every week they gamble too much on the American baseball scores . . . it's a terrible weakness, and one I've never had myself. But here's the thing – we can only get the results on one of the American Forces in Europe radio wavebands, and I have to get it going up on the deck before nine o'clock – that's one in the afternoon in New York.'

'But Ricky, darling, it's pouring out there! You'll all get soaked.'

'No, we'll get under the shelter on the second upper deck. The radio works fine in there. We do it often – these two clowns have $300 apiece riding on this. Which is very bad news for Fred, who thinks the Reds are going to lose to the Dodgers, which is plainly impossible.'

'I'll just go and get the pen and writing pad,' said Ray. 'See you up there in five.'

Jane said, 'Well, hurry back and let's meet in the stern bar a bit later.'

'You gottit,' said Lt. Commander Hunter. 'We'll try to get Fred to bed . . . then we can jump into some of that Armenian brandy.'

Jane Westenholz laughed, a quizzical look in her eyes. He really was a mystery to her, that Ricky. He was like a big country boy, but sometimes his eyes seemed so knowing, so hard. And they were so blue, and he had such a physique. Yet he ate like a longshoreman in total contradiction to his graceful southern manners. 'I wonder who and what he could be?' pondered the lady from Greenwich.

In cabin number 289, Lt. Commander Hunter gave himself 10 minutes. He strapped onto his belt the big hunting knife he had bought in a back street in St Petersburg. He took out the laser-beam target-marker which had been especially designed to resemble a small transistor radio, and fitted the batteries into their slots. He crammed the high-tech device into the big, zipped parka side-pocket along with the GPS, snug in its padded leather case. He put a pair of Russian-made sneakers into the inside pockets of the jacket, and two full-sized black garbage bags, folded dead flat, into his other side pocket. He put his hat back on, and made his way down to the gangway.

He could see Ray and Fred chatting right under the light in the doorway, which was fine. What was not fine was they were talking to Cathy Westenholz. Ray could see the rain had just about stopped, and Cathy was dressed to go outside. He could not turn away. They had all seen him, and he walked boldly up to them. 'Hiya, Cathy,' he said. 'There's some kind of electrical stuff on this ship that's playing hell with the radio, we gotta get out on shore. Get some distance between us and the ship's generators.'

Cathy laughed. 'I'm going to the little café and shop. I just wanted a walk. It's over there by those trees . . . Wanna come?'

'Well, not really,' said Rick, whose mind was racing as he blurted out the first reasonable sentence he could think of. 'But, Cathy, I don't want you to leave your mother alone in that bar. I just came by and there were some Russians getting kinda rowdy. The Colonel was in there, but they weren't slowing down any.'

'Oh, Mom'll be fine,' said Cathy brightly. 'Come on, let's walk outside for a bit. The rain's stopped.'

Rick put his arm around her shoulders and moved her to the side. 'Cathy,' he said. 'I want you to do me a favor . . . Go up and get your ma out of that bar. I know I should have stopped myself, but then we'd miss the scores, and I thought you were with her . . . Please, Cathy, go up and make sure everything's okay . . . please?'

'Okay. Will you guys be right out here when I get back? Maybe I'll take Mom over to the café.'

'Sure,' said Rick. 'See you a bit later . . . and thanks.'

Cathy headed back to the upper decks, and the three SEALs walked across to the dirt road and swung right, breaking into an easy loping run as soon as they were out of the artificial light. The time was 2114 and Rick kept going for about 1,500 yards before leading the way quite suddenly into the woodland, away from the lake. All along the left side of the road there had been tall, soaking wet foliage, and he knew, from endless study of the satellite photographs, the trees went back deeply for a long way. And he whispered to his companions they must keep going for one mile, to the open field beyond the pines, in which the canisters could safely land.

After 50 yards they came to a stop in a place where the trees seemed less dense, and Rick signaled a halt. Each of the SEALs changed into sneakers and zipped their street shoes into their parka pockets. They then took out their tightly wrapped Goretex lightweight waterproof trousers and pulled them on over their regular pants.

While the SEAL Leader checked the GPS, Chief Cernic pulled out his tiny compass and set it for a walking bearing, three-two-zero. They would endeavor to hold that line as they went, knowing the way back would be course one-four-zero. But a mile in a dense wood is very different from a mile along a road. It's almost impossible to walk dead straight through a wood in broad daylight. In pitch dark it is impossible.

The 'alcoholic' led the way, trying to avoid thick brush, and correcting the course when he could. They pressed forward for 15 minutes, making somewhat slow progress. Rick thought they had gone no more than a half-mile, and it was beginning to rain again.

There was not a sliver of clear moonlight through the invisible clouds, and the skies were without stars. Nonetheless, the full moon was back there somewhere, and it did provide a muted, diffused light, good enough for Fred's visibility to stretch to around three or four yards. He walked with his left arm out in front of him to avoid thin overhanging branches. Their footsteps made only a soft padding sound, broken by the occasional noise of a snapping twig.

Above them they heard three times the unmistakable call of a night owl, and once Fred cried, 'Jesus, what the hell's that?' in response to a quick scuffling of footsteps in front of him. 'Probably a fucking grizzly,' said Lt. Schaeffer, walking right behind him. 'Don't worry, I'll tell Rick . . . He'll kill it with his bare hands.'

But the wood seemed endless, and Rick thought they must have gone almost a mile when the trees suddenly began to thin out. They could tell this was so because they could now feel the rain driving at them sideways from the left. The trouble was the dark. Visibility was so limited they could just have been in a clearing. Only a whispered cry of '*Fuck it!*' from Fred clarified the situation. The Chief had hit a brick wall. Actually it was a low, dry-stone wall, and he had hissed in fury rather than pain. It was fury with himself, really, that he had slightly misjudged its position, when the satellites had identified it so clearly for them.

They gathered by the wall; they could feel the wind rising, and the rain slashing down. Exposed now, without any cover, the SEALs' waterproof jackets and trousers were becoming priceless.

Ray placed one of his dim chemical light markers, glowing red, on the wall, and they proceeded forward, still warm in their 'double trousers' and shirts and sweaters under waterproof parkas. The baseball caps were too wet to matter, but at least helped to keep their heads warm.

As the weather worsened and the clock ticked on, it became clear they had reached the wide flat grazing pasture the satellite pictures had shown. Most of the other neighboring fields were growing cereals or vegetables, presently sprouting green but sparse shoots. The mud was pretty terrible right here on the firmer grazing land, but on the winter wheat it would have been impossible. Tiresome clods of mud were already forming on the SEALs' sneakers.

This heavy rain was the one single factor for which the backup team in Coronado had not been able to plan. The satellites had photographed these fields over and over, and they knew there was only limited grazing land right here . . . land over which the SEALs must heave their heavy burdens.

Thus the drop-zone effectively selected itself. It had to be pasture, and the Coronado executive had decided to take a chance on the weather, hoping there would not be long consistent rains as the SEALs headed north on the waterways. Those hopes had been dashed during a filthy, wet week. And now it was as bad as anyone could have imagined. Rick Hunter knew he had the option to abort the mission, and that everyone would understand. But he, with his great strength, believed they could get the job done whatever the conditions.

And now they stood in seriously soft going. They were in open country, with about 300 yards between themselves and the wood, the chemical light barely visible against its blackness. The time was 2236; almost 500 miles to the north, Lt. Colonel Jaxtimer was flying over Finland, towards Russia, 400 miles west of the old port of Murmansk.

The entry into Russian airspace went without a hitch. Major Parker called down their identifying numbers and the Russian controllers cleared them instantly, scarcely checking that the numbers did in fact coincide exactly with the flight plan filed by American Airlines. Thus, with the blessing of the authorities, the B-52H pressed on southward toward Lake Onega, toward global position 62.38N, 34.46E.

Colonel Jaxtimer knew they had to drop their three-part cargo into a four-mile-radius circle, if the canisters were to lock on and land close to the beam from the SEALs' high-tech target-marker down on the ground.

Both the aircraft and the SEALs were working to the five-yard accuracy of the GPS. If the SEALs were down there, Colonel Jaxtimer would find them. The big laser sensor in the nose of the B-52H would pick up the beacon from 20 miles, about two and a half minutes' flying time. The canisters would be released when the special bombsight signaled. Once the marker had been picked up, it was, in US Air Force parlance, a 'hands-off' routine.

Behind the Colonel, in the control cockpit, Lt. Chuck Ryder was calling out their 'distance to go' every 15 miles, and Lt. Segal had located no threatening indications of a military radar sweep yet, from the ground or the air. To Russian eyes, the United States Air Force B-52H was just another long-haul commercial passenger jet headed south for the Middle East.

In fact, just about every aspect of the flight plan was a total fabrication. The aircraft was not headed for Bahrain, but for the gigantic US Air Force base outside of Dahran on the east coast of Saudi Arabia. There was also a chance the B-52H's fuel would not last out the journey, if they met serious headwinds, and the Air Force was sending another tanker out to meet them high over the northern end of the Gulf.

By 2310, the SEALs were becoming very cold, and the rain had not abated. They stood shivering in the field, jogging up and down trying to get the chill out of their limbs. Water streamed down their Goretex legs into their sneakers, which were now full and squelching. They were still dry under their parkas, but the cold rain on their faces was numbing, and Rick Hunter prayed the aircraft would not be late, and that the rain would stop. But it didn't. The SEALs waited in soaking, windswept silence. None of them uttered one word of complaint.

And while they waited the B-52H raced southward, high above and out to the west of the coastal city of Belomorsk at the southwest corner of the White Sea. Its route would take it above the canal, maintaining its speed, but flying slightly to the west of the shoreline of the lake. Lt. Chuck Ryder had them steady on the required approach course, the GPS mechanically counting down the range and bearing to the unseen waypoint high above the tour ship's Green Stop.

As they flew, the Air Force lieutenant kept his eyes glued to the GPS, watching the numbers change as the satellites gave an update of their position every one and a half seconds. Right now they were crossing 65.30N. At 63.42N they would be slightly to the west of the city of Segeza, just 60 miles from the northern point of the lake, less than 11 minutes from the drop-zone. There were only two rules for Colonel Jaxtimer: Don't be early; and maintain a steady course and speed, because any change would be like a red rag to a Russian bear in a control tower.

The first part was easy because they were already six minutes late, the favorable jet-stream having eased off. The second part required no great effort because everyone was right on top of their game. This was the US Air Force at its very best. Major Parker's radio crackled. Ground control again, and once more he called out the identification numbers that would give him clear commercial airline passage across the old Soviet Union.

Back on the ground Lt. Commander Rick Hunter strained to hear the sound of an approaching aircraft, although he knew full well that the B-52H would be far too high for that, and anyway there would be no sound whatsoever until it had passed overhead and downwind. But it might just give him a few seconds' warning of the arrival of the canisters, so he still listened, and wondered how long they would have to wait. The rain was, if anything, harder, and he struggled to control the trembling such remorseless, cold, wet conditions can bring about.

By 2325, he had placed the laser marker-unit on the ground, and activated it, with the aerial pointing up and northward. The three SEALs then spread out around it, in a triangle, 20 yards apart. Such a formation would give them the best possible chance of seeing or hearing the airborne canisters as they came in. The marker-unit made no sound as its beam lanced upwards into the dark Russian sky. The silence in the field was total, save for the splashing of the rain in the mud, and for a moment Rick Hunter thought he might be going mad. How could anyone or anything ever find him in this freezing wasteland? What could he possibly be doing here?

The trouble was he knew exactly what he was doing here, and he tried to imagine the big long-range bomber heading south towards him. He glanced at his watch, as he did every 30 seconds. It was 2334. He did not know it, but Colonel Jaxtimer was out over the northern end of the lake. And Chuck Ryder was counting. The laser marker had just started 'painting' on the aircraft's receiver, the final seconds ticking now automatically.

Lt. Ryder, quietly and professionally helping to keep his Colonel right on track, confirmed, 'Red light, sir. Bomb doors open . . .

'Looking good, sir . . . on track . . . left . . . left . . . on track . . . on track . . . six-two-three-eight, sir . . . that's it . . . bombs gone.' No elation. No emphasis. Just quiet information.

Beneath the great bulk of the US Stratofortress, the doors of the weapons bay, located in the central fuselage section between the fore and aft sets of wheels, began to close behind the falling canisters, which were already hurtling through the darkness, straight down the laser beam.

The eight mighty Pratt and Whitney TF33 turbofan jets, powering the B-52H on towards Moscow, left behind a deafening, throaty growl, but it was still not quite audible to the SEALs waiting in the mud below.

Lt. Commander Hunter and his men, hunched away from the driving rain, stared at the sky to the north, alert for any warning they might get of the arrival of the canisters. It was almost impossible to see more than about 20 feet above them, and right now there was only blackness. 'Should have been here minutes ago,' thought Rick. 'Useless fuckers. Have they missed us? Jesus Christ – there's no way I'm gonna see anything before one of those containers fucking well kills me. But if they don't drop real close, we'll never find them . . . Jesus Christ.'

But then he suddenly heard the first whisperings of the big Air Force jet engines, high above. 'That's gotta be them,' he thought, his heartbeat rising. And then he saw it: a ghostly shape, almost directly above and very close, falling slightly to one side. It seemed to swing against the wind. Fast, now slow, silent and menacing, like a dreadful hooded vampire, swooping low out of the night.

Before the SEAL Leader could move more than three paces, it was down, landing with a heavy thud in the soft ground, not 10 yards from where they stood. The field shook, and the parachute billowed and rustled in the wind as Rick manhandled it under control. He called softly into the dark, 'Got one. Heads up for the other two.' To himself he muttered, 'Holy shit! How *about* that?'

He heard Chief Cernic say softly, 'Here's one right now . . . *left . . . left* . . . right there.' And the second canister hit the field almost simultaneously, with the third following 5 seconds later, 20 yards farther to the south.

'That,' thought Lt. Commander Hunter, 'was the goddamnedest thing I ever saw.' Even more startling, he decided, than the day he and his team blew the engine of General Noriega's yacht 300 feet into the air by mistake.

Rick and Ray headed for the nearest canister. 'What d'you think, boss?' asked the lieutenant from Massachusetts. 'Do we open it and take a look, or do we just rush all three of them right back over to the woods?'

'The latter,' whispered Rick. 'Let's just get 'em the hell out of this exposed field. Fred, you take the parachutes – get over to the wood and look for a good spot to bury them with the canisters.

Leave another chemical marker at the edge of the wood. We'll start on the first load right away. What are the handles like?'

'Good. Well balanced right in the center,' said the Chief Petty Officer. 'Wide with padded leather grips. Big enough for a two-handed hold if necessary.' He grabbed one and lifted. 'Christ,' he said. 'These things are *really* heavy.'

Rick's soaking wet brow furrowed. And he prayed the guys back at Coronado had not misjudged it, prayed that he and Ray could lift the canisters. He slipped his big farmer's hand into the grip of the handle, and heaved. The canister came easily off the ground. 'Not too bad,' he said. 'We can get these over the field and into the trees, but it ain't gonna be easy, the grass is so damned slippery.'

'Okay, sir,' said the Chief. 'I got the first 'chute free. You're off.'

'Beautiful,' thought Ray. 'You've made it possible for me to get a hernia . . . I'll probably have died from exposure and pain before we get to the next one.'

The Chief confirmed quietly that he now had all three canisters and the chemical marker at the wall set up on the GPS. 'No one's gonna get lost unless the GPS dies on us. If you two get out of contact, make two short owl-hoots. But stay dead on one-three-zero, that'll take you to the marker on the wall, and on to the wood, where there's another. If there's real trouble, that's three owl-hoots, and we all head for the wall, no matter what.

'By the time I pick our burying spot and get back to the marker light, you two should be there with the first canister. Don't crash into the goddamned wall like I did.'

'Okay, Chief. Okay, Ray, take the left side for your right arm. We'll swap sides at 100 paces.'

The two SEALs lifted the 250-lb canister. Ray's heart skipped a beat at the weight of it. He thought of the trek across the sopping wet, slippery grass, in the now-driving rain, and the bravado drained from him. Rainwater streamed down his face, and he closed his eyes, and he said very privately to himself, as he had always done at such times, 'This is going to be hard. Pace yourself, Ray, old buddy. And please, please God don't let me fail.' It was the same prayer which had sustained him through the terrible ordeal of 'Hell Week.'

'It worked then,' he thought. 'It'd better work now.' And he began to move forward, trying to find a rhythm, trying to settle into a regular stride, trying to forget the ever-present truth, that this huge weight was so much easier for the massively strong Rick Hunter than it would ever be for him.

The first 20 strides were not that bad, but the rain was sheeting down, and the wind was rising. Despite the strenuous task, both men were shivering uncontrollably as they fought their way through the pitch-black darkness, sliding on the muddy patches, struggling for a foothold. Rick was trying to keep one eye on the dim glow of the compass, trying to hold the flickering arrow on one-three-zero. He was also trying to adjust their direction, pulling the canister around, when he went down for the first time, thumping forward onto his knees.

The force of the huge, unbalanced weight jolted Ray Schaeffer forward, and he pitched heavily into the field, breaking his fall with his right fist at the last second. They had gone but 40 strides, and Rick climbed to his feet and made two owl-calls into the night. They both heard the Chief answer, 'What's up?'

'Bring the clothes bag, will you? I'll talk you in. Ray, we gotta stop assing around here like a coupla second-class mud-wrestlers . . . gotta get our stuff off before it gets torn and filthy. That means trousers, shirts, sweaters and parkas. We can get back in the ship looking a bit wet, but if we stay dressed we're gonna look like a coupla walking shitheaps on the upper deck and we can't risk it. We'll finish this just in shorts and sneakers.'

'You mean I'm about to contract pneumonia as well as a hernia,' said Ray. 'Sweet.' But he climbed back to his feet and took off all of the garments which covered his upper body and stuffed them into Fred's plastic black garbage bag. And then he grasped the handle on the canister once more, and he and Rick Hunter set off again in driving rain, clad only in their shorts and sneakers. Course one-three-zero. The temperature had dropped to 37 degrees Fahrenheit. In the rain and wind, it was closer to freezing. Neither SEAL mentioned the cold. They just kept going forward, toward the three-foot-high wall.

After 60 more paces they changed sides. Ray was sweating and shivering at the same time. The cold water streamed down his body, and his left arm was throbbing. He turned to try and grab the handle with two hands, but as he twisted he fell forward into the mud. The canister came down heavily on the back of his thigh, shoving his knee into a sharp flint.

He heard Rick Hunter mutter, 'Jesus,' and felt the great weight move off his leg as the Lieutenant Commander, with an outrageous display of strength, pulled the heavy metal cylinder off him.

'You okay, Ray?'

'Yup. Fine. Just lemme get a grip.'

He struggled to his feet, feeling the warm blood streaming down his leg and the rain trying to wash it away. He hoped the cut was not deep, but there was no time to find out. He grabbed the handle again with his left hand and walked forward once more, counting the strides as he went. He knew the wall must be close, and he hauled at the canister with every ounce of his strength, trying to reach forward, to ignore the pain in his arm, to dig deep within himself, as he had done so often before when the chips were down. He did not dare to question whether he could repeat this two more times. He *had* to repeat it. Softly, in the blinding rain, he whispered, 'Please, please don't let me stop.'

'Here's the wall, Ray.' The words were whipped away by the wind. And then Rick Hunter said, 'Okay, let's rest for one minute, then we'll get this baby on top of the stones, and drag it down the other side.' Chief Cernic materialized out of the darkness, and announced he was heading back into the middle of the field to where the other two canisters rested in the mud.

Sixty seconds later, Ray Schaeffer dragged himself over the wall, and he and the big SEAL Leader maneuvered themselves into position. Then they carried the canister forward again, into the trees, where they lowered it to the ground, right by the green chemical marker the Chief had left.

The walk back, almost naked, in truly shocking weather – near-freezing rain and a 20-knot southwest wind straight off the Baltic – was not much short of paradise. Relieved of their terrible burden, the two superfit SEALs marched along boldly, smacking their feet into the mud. After 300 paces they called out Fred's name. And, surprisingly closely, just out on the right, they heard the Chief snap, 'Right here.'

Rick Hunter was concerned at the distance of separation, and he decided they should carry the last two canisters in 50 paces at a time, going back for the third one each time. 'That way we get a rest between the drives, and it keeps Fred up close in case we need help.'

It was a psychological masterstroke. Ray Schaeffer felt he could handle 50 paces if he could just get a rest in between, and, with renewed vigor, he picked up the new handle, this time with his right hand, and once more walked forward into the dark. He counted off the first 25 paces before the pain began to set in, right across his forearm. Even Rick Hunter was feeling the strain. And the ground seemed to grow more waterlogged by the minute. First Ray went down, then Rick, then Ray twice more. Rick's knee was cut almost as badly as Ray's.

But the SEALs' code was never broken. Neither one of them uttered one word of complaint. When they fell, they got up again. When the pain was too great they ignored it and walked forward. When Ray felt he could go no farther, he spoke his little prayer, and he drove on, assuming that he would either make it, or die out here in this horrific Russian farmland.

It took one more hour. And it was a truly terrible hour. No ordinary man could have withstood it. The two SEALs, covered in mud, the sheeting rain streaming down their faces, were almost at the end of their tether. Shivering violently, sweat pouring down their chests, exhausted from their titanic efforts carrying a third of a ton by hand across a saturated field, their muscles aching, neither man had much more left.

But they had once again reached the wall, and now Chief Cernic was stripped for action down to his shorts and sneakers, trembling in the freezing rain, helping to manhandle the two final canisters over the wall. The three of them half dragged, half lifted them over to the trees, where Lt. Ray Schaeffer collapsed on the soaking dead leaves of the woodland.

'Get him up, sir,' snapped the veteran Chief. 'Get him up, sir . . . he'll stiffen up in two minutes. Get the jackets out and get him upright.'

They pulled the shattered SEAL to his feet, and Rick Hunter wrapped one coat around Ray's shoulders. The Chief came up with a small flask of brandy, and tipped it between Lt. Schaeffer's lips. The reviving liquid, burning its way through the youngest SEAL's throat, worked its magic. Ray came around, shook his head, and said, 'Christ, guys, I'm really sorry. I'm okay. Just lemme sit here for a minute . . .'

'Keep moving, sir, straight away,' said Fred Cernic, who knew imminent hypothermia when he saw it. 'And keep talking. Don't even think of stopping – keep moving.'

He moved to the first canister and opened it. Bullseye. The first things he felt, right on top, were two shovels and a flashlight. He grabbed them out and shut the metal door, handed one to Rick and said, 'Pick a spot and let's start digging . . . what do you say, Ray?'

'That's it, Chief, I'll help in a minute. Just gimme a minute.'

Fred and Rick walked deeper into the wood, using the flashlight sparingly, looking for a spot in the undergrowth. The Chief picked it out, under a loose straggling bush. 'Let's pull that out and bury them underneath, then stick the bush back in.'

'Good call, Fred. Let's go.'

They pushed through the branches, ignoring the scratches, and slammed their shovels into the area around the root, loosening the earth. Then they grabbed the main piece of the stem and heaved, and the entire bush came out in one rush. They did not stop to discuss the matter. They just started to dig three trenches, each one six feet long, four feet wide and three deep, about the size of a well proportioned grave.

Fred Cernic was tough. He was from New Jersey and he knew how to dig. But he had never seen anyone dig quite like the country boy from Kentucky who worked beside him. Rick Hunter got into a rhythm, cleaving the shovel into the ground, and lifting out a mound of wet earth at every stroke. Fred reckoned he could pull out 10 such shovels without a break. Rick Hunter could do 30.

The first 'grave' took them 40 minutes of sustained shoveling. But the second one took an hour. The rain, if anything, grew worse. It was 0330. And there was still another hole to dig. Fred Cernic was spent, Ray Schaeffer was half dead, but Rick Hunter worked on. Cut and scratched by the foliage, all of them bloodied and shivering, covered in mud, their hands too slippery to hold the shovels efficiently, they really had only one man still pulling the wagon. And Rick dug on, uncomplaining, understanding that when a highly trained SEAL can offer no more, there is simply no more to offer.

He crashed the shovel into the ground, hauling out the earth, trying to find a rhythm, his breath now coming in short angry bursts, his ribcage heaving, the pain in his massive arms excruciating from the lactic acid buildup in his muscles. He was operating on the edge of blackout now, and he knew it. Rick Hunter tried talking to himself, snapping out the word 'NOW!' every time his shovel hit the ground.

He worked like this for three minutes before he became conscious of another shovel slamming into the earth alongside his, and through the sharp light of the Chief's lowered flashlight he could see the pale face of Ray Schaeffer, still fighting, still trying to help. This was a man back on his feet and still punching after being knocked down three times in three rounds, as Ray had once been as an amateur boxer.

But this was more dangerous. Covered from head to foot in mud and blood, flecks of white spittle coming from his mouth, his lips drawn back from his teeth with effort, Ray Schaeffer was alone now with his God, still praying softly that he would not let the SEALs down. They rammed their shovels into the ground alternately, each of them drawing strength from the presence of the other.

And they kept going like this, shoveling steadily, tackling the pain-barrier, for five more minutes, before Ray Schaeffer collapsed again. Right at the bottom of the hole, face down in the rainwater which had gathered there, five inches deep. Chief Cernic came out of the dark like a panther, and dragged Ray's head clear. Ray Hunter dropped his shovel and helped to carry the young lieutenant out.

They propped him against a tree while the Chief got ahold of the jackets and wrapped all three of them around the unconscious SEAL. This was beyond brandy. Ray needed a doctor, or a hospital, and there wasn't one. However, his breathing was steady, and Fred Cernic left him covered, and picked up the second shovel.

It took 20 more minutes to complete the 'graves' and they rolled the canisters into position carefully, before tipping them into the holes with their long doors uppermost. While Lt. Commander Hunter fell back exhausted onto his back, battered but conscious, the Chief checked the contents of the air-dropped cargo, rescued three towels, locked the doors, and began the much easier task of covering the canisters with the loose soil.

The trouble was the holes required only about one third of the available earth, and as the Chief began to tackle the last one there was one hell of a pile of soil still left. When he was almost through he dropped one shovel into the last 'grave' and then covered it. Then he and Rick took turns making the mound of spare earth smooth above the precious buried stockpile of SEAL demolition kit. Afterwards they brought in piles of dead leaves to make it look like a natural mound. Then, finally, they dragged the big bush back into place and replanted it to disguise the disturbed area. It was almost 0500 when they laid the last shovel into the loose earth, deep under the bush, and camouflaged it with soil and leaves. Rick checked the burial position with the GPS. And still the rain dripped steadily down through the trees.

'Okay, Chief, let's go,' said the Team Leader. 'You pack up the clothes and towels into the garbage bags, and we'll head back to the road as fast as we can.' At which point, he walked back to Ray, zipped up his jacket, and with another monstrous display of strength, lifted him up and over his shoulders, walking forward: course one-four-zero.

They made the return journey faster than they expected, mostly because Ray suddenly, and in a sense miraculously, regained consciousness and insisted on walking unaided. It was 0534 when they reached the dirt road. They could see the lights of the *Mikhail Lermontov* almost half a mile away, and they stood in the rain for 10 minutes, trying to wash and wipe off the mud and blood. The new towels felt like heaven as they worked beneath an ancient pine tree, getting dry. Then they put on their shirts and sweaters, which had never been wet, then their trousers, and dry socks and street shoes, then their parkas and hats. The wet towels and three pairs of mud-caked sneakers they put in a garbage bag with a couple of small rocks, tied it and heaved it into six feet of water about eight feet out into the lake. Rick recorded their GPS position, the landmark for their next visit.

At 0615, looking more or less normal, they strolled back up the gangway into the darkened ship. There was a seaman on duty but he was asleep in a deck-chair, and the three SEALs walked silently past, and on up to their cabins, unseen by their fellow passengers.

There was an envelope pinned to Lt. Commander Hunter's cabin door, number 289, with the name 'Ricky' on it. 'Guess who, lover boy?' grinned Fred Cernic.

Rick was too tired to respond, too tired even to speak. He grabbed the envelope, opened the door and almost fell on top of his bed. The other two walked on to cabins 290 and 291, and as they got there, Lt. Schaeffer turned to Fred and said: 'I'm sorry. I'm really sorry.'

Chief Petty Officer Cernic turned to face the junior officer, and said, in a barely audible whisper, 'You didn't let anyone down, sir. I've known men get decorated for a lot less.'

CHAPTER EIGHT

FRED CERNIC WAS essentially locked in his cabin. He had not
been allowed out all morning, and a steward had delivered his
lunch of potato soup, rare sirloin steak, beetroot, cheese, black
bread, and a pot of coffee. He ate alone, unlike the other two
SEALs, who were busily concocting a succession of truly majestic
lies with which to regale Jane Westenholz and her daughter.

'. . . And then we met these two Russian farmers just along the
road there . . . and they invited us into their house for a glass of
home-made vodka . . . Of course, before we knew it, Fred had got
ahold of a second bottle and drunk it . . . Started falling about all
over the place . . . In the end we had to lock him up in a barn
until he passed out, then Ray and I managed to manhandle him
back here in the small hours . . . The two Russian farmers were
pretty damned good about it.'

'Oh, how perfectly awful,' said Jane. 'And he seems like such a
nice man.'

'Jane, I'm telling you, you wouldn't recognize him when he gets
into the booze. Part of the reason we brought him up here for this
little trip was to get him away from the bars at home . . . never
thought he'd manage to find a bottle of home-made vodka right
out in the middle of nowhere.'

'Where is he now? Are you sure he's okay?'

'Yeah. He's just sleeping it off. Didn't want any lunch. I guess
he'll be fine by the end of the day . . . but it might be better if we
had dinner separately tonight. I just don't want him near wine or
anything.'

'Oh, yes. I understand, Ricky. And of course I won't mention
anything if we meet later . . . but I'm glad you told me about it.
Did you, by the way, get my note?'

'Sure did, ma'am. And I appreciate what you wrote about me.

Maybe we could get together for a drink later tonight, after we get Fred back to bed.'

Jane Westenholz smiled and touched the big SEAL Commander on the back of his hand. 'Then,' she said, 'you can tell me what you do with your life back home in the States. I think you've always been a teeny bit secretive about it.'

'It's pretty damned dreary, Jane,' said the Lieutenant Commander. 'But I'll be real happy to give you the highlights.'

He smiled his big farmboy smile, and he and Ray Schaeffer made their way out of the ship's dining room. The *Mikhail Lermontov* ran on south down the middle of Lake Onega, making an easy 25 knots through flat water, bound for St Petersburg, where she would dock at the Naberuzhennoe tomorrow afternoon.

Rick Hunter made his way up to the ship's office and asked if there were facilities for a cable to be sent by phone to the USA. 'Just to let the folks know we're okay.' He grinned at the dark-haired girl operator, who handed him a writing pad made up of cable forms. He filled in the name Sally Harrison, and wrote down the phone number with its 301 area code. And then he wrote carefully, 'Lovely time. Freddie fine. Rick.'

He handed the girl an American $5 bill, and asked her to send it as soon as possible.

Two hours later, at 0600 Eastern Daylight Time, 6,000 miles away in Maryland, Lt. John Harrison answered the ex-directory telephone line in Admiral Morris's office, and wrote down the message from Cable and Wireless. He had no clues whatsoever as to what any of it meant, but he was instructed to call Admiral Morgan direct, immediately, should he receive a cable signed from 'Rick.'

He picked up the other line direct to the Admiral, who was already in his office, waiting. 'Short cable from Rick, sir,' he reported.

'Beautiful,' said the Admiral, putting back the phone in a some-what preoccupied manner. Then he stood up and punched the air with delight. 'Those guys!' he exclaimed. 'They just delivered the bacon . . . I'll show those Russian pricks precisely who they can and cannot fuck with.'

Back in Russia, the tour ship steamed on, leaving the lake shortly after lunch and cutting her speed as she entered the waters of the Svir' River, which joins the vast lakes of Onega and Ladoga. The

193

Lermontov spent most of the afternoon and evening making the 100-mile journey along the winding and sometimes shallow waterway.

Rick Hunter avoided the attentions of Mrs Westenholz on the pretext of looking after Fred, who was not permitted to leave his cabin. The following morning he was still confined to his quarters as the ship ran across the wide southern waters of Lake Ladoga for almost 100 miles. They left the lake in the most southwesterly corner, when the *Lermontov* turned into the Neva River for the final 30-mile stretch up to the port of St Petersburg.

Lt. Commander Hunter and his men said 'Goodbye,' to Jane and her daughter and mentioned they would probably see them on the dock when they disembarked. But the driver of the unmarked car which picked them up was very efficient, and had the three SEALs on board and heading for the airport as soon as they disembarked.

They were on a Finnair flight inside an hour, and touched down before dark, 180 miles later, in Helsinki. Jane Westenholz would never know who any of them were.

Watched by the distant eye of America's KH-111 satellite, the two *Tolkach* barges moved majestically and slowly on north up the Volga. Captain Igor Volkov, the master of the articulated double barge, led the way through the channel. His 24-year-old son, Ivan, was at the wheel on the for'ard rudder, 900 feet in front of him – the equivalent of three football grids.

On the evening of April 25 they had arrived at the cement town of Volsk, its pincushion of slim factory chimneys belching yellowish smoke and dust across the sky. The chronic pollution, which could be seen in the orange street lights, was even visible on the photographs which Admiral Morris studied in faraway Maryland.

The articulated *Tolkach* and its 600-foot-long consort took up over 500 yards of the Volga as they moved in stately procession through the heavily industrialized reaches of the river heading toward the imperial university town of Kazan.

On April 27, in occasional thin rain, they had rolled past Syrzan, a town of old rusty chimneys and sprawling brick factories which looked like a throwback to the Industrial Revolution. The pictures were poor in definition through the moisture, but the eye of KH-111 was just good enough. 'They're gonna make Nizhny by May 6th for sure,' George Morris told Arnold Morgan.

Four days later, on May 1, at the approximate time the SEALs had been fighting their way through the rainswept woods beside Lake Onega, the giant barges had reached Ulyanovsk, the birthplace of Vladimir Ilyich Lenin. It was night as they hove into sight, and Captain Volkov could see the red-neon nameplate stark above the new river station. They were not stopping, and he gave a short blast on the ship's horn as he passed. Everyone around the docks knew Igor Volkov, and as a consequence everyone thought he had blown the great booming horn on the *Tolkach* just for them. Little scatterings of people stood and gazed out across the sandy shallows into the great black flow of the central stream of the river, where the barges left hardly a ripple as they passed.

Right now they were 100 miles short of Kazan, and these miles would be traversed in wide waterways – up to 18 miles across – as the Volga turns almost into an inland sea. At the town of Atabaevo the barges made a ninety-degree left turn for the port of Kazan, which they reached in the small hours of May 3. Then, beyond there, they swung hard left once more, along the now-narrowing river, and began their nonstop run of 250 miles to Nizhny Novgorod.

The US satellites tallied their progress most days. And late at night George Morris and Arnold Morgan would sit in Fort Meade to examine the photographs of the three Kilo-Class submarines in Red Sormovo, and the progress of the *Tolkach* barges. There was still some scaffold left on Kilo Three, but the two American admirals assessed the first two must be almost complete.

All the way along to Nizhny the Volga is flanked by green rolling hills and woods, with intermittent villages set in the folds, bright in the morning light, and almost invisible in the misty rain which sweeps through here every few days in spring. The eastern shore is much flatter than the hilly Asian bank, but the two diverse green plateaus along the shallow, slow-flowing stream of the Volga offer a feast of glorious rural landscape. The presence of the giant transporters, with their military overtones, was as hideously intrusive as a guest appearance by Rambo in *Swan Lake*.

But Captain Volkov did his job. In the small hours of May 7 they steered around the Strelka, and moored alongside the loading quay at the junction of the Volga and the Oka rivers at Nizhny Novgorod. Both barges made a huge 360-degree turn in the mile-wide waterway and came up in the shadows of a forest of dock cranes, behind which stood the great cathedral of Alexander Nevsky. With the dock on their starboard side, and the waters of the Oka to port, the barges now faced northeast. At this stage they were less than 400 yards from the three Kilos.

At Fort Meade, Admirals Morris and Morgan peered at the satellite pictures.

'How long, George? How long before they leave?'

'Well, if we assume they will all go together, the most significant factor is that the third Kilo still has some scaffold. I'm not sure how long it takes to load and secure something that big onto a barge but it's gotta be a day for each one, and they're not yet down at the loading dock. Right now I'd say the earliest those transporters could start moving would be 10 days from now – say May 17th. But if you want my best guess I'd still say first week in June.'

'Any idea how they load 'em?'

'They move the hulls around on the land the same way we move our big boats, on a multi-wheel trolley system, running on rails over some very hard standing. We use hydraulic lifts to put the hulls into the water, rather than onto floating barges. I've never seen anyone do that, but I guess it's possible. We might even learn something if we get a photo at exactly the right moment.

'We've seen them put submarines onto those ocean-going freighters they sometimes use . . . that's when they flood the ships down into the water and float the submarines onto the decks, same system as a floating dock. These barges look a bit different, but they must do it the same way. I don't see any other possibility.

'The Kilos will have to be lowered into the water, and then floated over the barges. Then the barges will pump out and lift the submarines clear of the water. I'd say the whole process is going to take a couple of days.'

Arnold Morgan thought quietly to himself.

'Right. Then we got five days' running time at 5 knots to make the journey up to the middle of Lake Onega . . . the very earliest I'm going to see them in the right area is going to be May 22nd.'

He calculated in his mind that would require a five-day tour boat with the scheduled Green Stop at the north of the lake at about 1900 to 2100 on that same night – a tour boat which had left St Petersburg three mornings previously on May 19, and which would meet the submarines on the waters of Onega in the afternoon of May 22.

'Just gotta make sure we have the right room space on one of those ships every day from May 19th,' he mused to himself. 'Once we get that in place, the only thing we need to do is to get the travel agent to change the names on the day we send the team in.'

And so the CIA took over the 'nuts and bolts' part of the operation, organizing different travel agents to book two suites on the top deck, plus one extra cabin, for one ship every day between May 19 and June 10 – every working day that is, not Sundays when the dockyards were closed.

The entire plan was carried out from Langley, and the space was all booked in the United States through the offices of the Odessa–American Line. As long as the Kilos stayed in Red Sormovo, a succession of young American executives would be enjoying nice, relaxed, paid-for vacations up the Russian canals and lakes.

By May 31, a total of almost 50 staff members from various consulates, embassies and corporations had made the journey up towards the gateway to the Belomorski Canal. And more were scheduled. Except that on June 1 everything changed, fast. The first Kilo was photographed by KH-111 moving down to the loading dock on rails. Twenty-four hours later a new picture showed it actually on board the lead *Tolkach*. There was suddenly no scaffold whatsoever on the third Kilo.

'Christ,' said George Morris. 'They're on their way. Looks to me like June 3rd or 4th departure.'

Arnold Morgan alerted Admiral Bergstrom in Coronado who confirmed the SEALs were ready to go at a moment's notice. The NSA just needed to let him know the day they were to leave St Petersburg, and on what ship they had reservations. Meanwhile Admiral Bergstrom would immediately move his SEALs back across the Atlantic and into a hotel in the busy Russian seaport.

Lt. Commander Rick Hunter's team, ensconced in the Hotel Pulkovskaya out near the St Petersburg Airport, was very different now. Lt. Ray Schaeffer was with him, but Chief Petty Officer Fred Cernic had remained behind in California. Two other SEALs, one a 30-year-old petty officer, Harry Starck, the other a much younger noncommissioned seaman, Jason Murray, were already in place. The CIA officer, Angela Rivera, a slim olive-skinned veteran in her mid-30s, had arrived on May 29, bringing with her a large bag of theatrical make-up kit and a box full of wigs which she had apparently never seen before.

One of them, a bushy dark-gray mop of hair, had practically engulfed her small head when she had tried it on. Her verdict had reduced Ray Schaeffer to rubble . . . 'Jesus,' said Angela. 'I feel like I'm looking out of a yak's asshole.'

The *Tolkach* barges were not ready by the afternoon of June 4, but they were, all three of them, loaded. And at first light on the morning of June 5 four tugs dragged the transporters and their $900 million cargo off the Red Sormovo moorings. The massive engines of Captain Volkov's mighty warrior of the inland waterway churned up a seething maelstrom in the middle of the Volga junction as it slowly pushed its way forward, followed by the 600-footer, 50 yards astern.

On board was the usual complement of Russian military personnel: three armed guards working shifts on each of the three barge sections, one of them on duty at all times. The Lieutenant in charge stayed with Captain Volkov. When they reached the White Sea, the Kilos would probably proceed on their own diesels, on the surface, round to Pol'yarni for trials and work-up. Then, eventually, they would set off down the Atlantic on their journey to China, escorted all the way – probably by four heavily gunned Russian antisubmarine frigates carrying guided missiles, torpedoes, antisubmarine mortars with a 20,000-foot range, plus racks of depth charges.

America's KH-111 satellite photographed the barges and the Kilos as they set off from Nizhny. And George Morris had the pictures in his hand within two hours, at 2346, in Fort Meade. Admiral Morgan called Coronado, and Admiral Bergstrom himself hit the start button for *Operation Northern Wedding* at 2122 Pacific time. The SEALs would depart St Petersburg on the Russian tour ship *Yuri Andropov* at 0800 on the morning of June 7.

That meant a further two-day wait for Rick Hunter's team, and while they settled down once more to the mind-numbing boredom of life in a commercial hotel in Russia, the *Tolkach* barges cleared the partly elegant thirteenth-century city of Nizhny, with its population of one and a quarter million, and its belief that it stands as Russia's third capital.

Captain Volkov settled into a speed of 5 knots and led the way slowly upriver, past the dark-green forests which stretch all along the right bank, forming the heart of the central Volga timber-growing industry. The sight of the three jet-black submarines being ferried along the river brought local people out by the dozen to see them go by, right along the lonely, wide, north-flowing stretch up to Yurevets, where the Volga turns left, and immediately begins to narrow.

This is one of the finest reaches of the river, passing first through the picturesque little nineteenth-century artists' colony near Plyos, where white houses built like Swiss chalets cluster along the river-bank. Then comes the neoclassical white town of Kostroma, a place of literature, silver filigree, and art, where Czar Nicholas II unsuccessfully pleaded to be exiled, and where Tolstoy was a frequent visitor.

But the submarines ran on, nonstop, past the city of Jaroslav, with its ghastly tire-making chemical factory, placed with typical Russian flair so close to the old-world, bourgeois charm of the town itself.

At 2200 on the night of June 7 they swept past the 100-foot-high statue of a female warrior which guards the entrance to the waters of the Rybinsk Reservoir. They were more or less halfway between Nizhny and the center of Lake Onega now, a distance of 500 miles; and Captain Volkov pressed on into the night, speaking on the telephone occasionally to his son, up in the bow wheelhouse, 300 yards for'ard. The Russian Navy guards remained stolidly on duty, walking back and forth in the night with Slavic doggedness.

That day, June 7, had been one of consolidation in the 9,500-ton tour ship *Yuri Andropov*, named in honor of the one-time head of the KGB who presided, briefly, over the Soviet Empire in the early 1980s after the death of Leonid Brezhnev.

The ship was packed and the suites on the uppermost deck, number four, were greatly sought after. They were newly designed and built, each one comprising two bedrooms with en-suite bathrooms, and a small salon between them. They were much superior to the 10 old single-bedroom suites which they had replaced, and much more expensive.

Four Americans occupied the first two. In number 400 was 76-year-old Boris Andrews, and his one-year-younger brother-in-law Sten Nichols, both from Bloomington in the southern suburbs of Minneapolis. In 401 resided Andre Maklov, a 78-year-old diabetic from White Bear Lake, St Paul. His 'room-mate' was the bearded Tomas Rabovitz, a somewhat youthful 74-year-old from Coon Rapids, north of Minneapolis.

All four of the men knew each other, and they had saved money for many months to make the trip, each of them being able to trace distant ancestors from the European north of Russia. They were all in reasonable health except for Mr Andrews, who would soon require a hip replacement, and walked now only with the aid of a cane, and needed to take constant painkillers to deaden the endless hurt at the top of his right leg.

They had banded together and paid for a nurse to accompany them back to the land of their forefathers. She was accommodated separately down on deck two. Her duties were to attend them throughout the trip, and to ensure none of them were left alone for too long. Her name was Edith Dubranin. She was 52, and also had some Russian ancestry, although she had never before traveled beyond the Midwestern states of the USA. Edith was a stern, no-nonsense kind of a lady who had spent much of her career as a staff nurse in a Chicago hospital. She was five feet in height, with fair skin and obviously dyed blonde hair. In her new job as nurse-companion she wore a gray skirt with a white jacket, and favored formality.

She addressed her four charges as Mr Andrews, Mr Nichols, Mr Maklov and Mr Rabovitz. She would attend to their laundry, arrange for their various medications to be taken on time, and accompany them to the dining room, where she would eat with them and deal personally with the waitresses. The table was for five only.

On the first morning they had walked slowly around the ship for some exercise after breakfast, watching the banks of the wide Neva River slip by during the first 38 miles up to Lake Ladoga. Mr Andrews, a big, stooping man made smaller by the pain in his hip, said very little, except to Mr Nichols. But Edith Dubranin seemed to strike up rather serious conversations with Mr Rabovitz. Mr Maklov, who also walked very slowly, seemed quickly exhausted by two strolls around the upper deck.

The nurse thus arranged for a steward to ensure there were always five deck-chairs immediately outside the two suites, in the small private area reserved for the passengers who had paid the most.

Late in the afternoon the little party of elderly Midwesterners made their first contact with the outside world when the senior officer on the ship, Colonel Borsov, called to pay his respects, in impeccable English, to his most valued passengers. Like all such men on these tour boats, he would have been obviously ex-military, even without the formality of the rank by which he announced himself.

Old Mr Andrews, somewhat surprisingly, took the lead in the conversation, made the introductions, and explained to the ship's commissar, in an infirm voice, how much they were enjoying seeing the lake. He also mentioned what a fine feeling it was to be right back here in Russia, four generations after his folks had left for the USA, back in the nineteenth century. Colonel Borsov asked where the family was from originally, and smiled when he was told, 'Right up there in Archangel, on the White Sea.'

'Then we are from opposite ends of Russia,' he replied. 'My family is from the Ukraine . . . like Leonid Brezhnev.'

'Well, you are a very nice, polite man,' chimed in Mr Maklov, brushing his white mustache upwards with the back of his right index finger. 'And I think you should run for President as well.'

This brought a smile to the face of the Colonel, who replied, 'Not of Russia, nor of the Ukraine, Mr Maklov. But perhaps one day of this shipping line.'

'Good luck to yer, Colonel,' said Mr Andrews. 'A bit of ambition never hurt no one.'

'That's right,' added old Mr Maklov. 'When you're young, that's the name of the game. And if I hadn't shown some of it when I started out in insurance, I wouldn't be where I am today.'

'And the *Yuri Andropov* would be the poorer for it,' said the Colonel, gallantly. 'By the way, have you been to see the little museum which we have dedicated to Mr Andropov, down on deck two? . . . No? . . . Well, you should. I know you will find it interesting. He came from central Russia, along the Volga, you know? He was a great man, a lover of American jazz, who died too young.' He did not mention that Mr Andropov was also a Communist ideological hard-liner, who had been a ruthless head of the KGB. Neither would the museum.

'Well, we'll certainly make a point of doing that before dinner,' said Mr Andrews, 'and we appreciate you visiting with us.'

When the Colonel left, Miss Dubranin walked a little way with him, and thanked him for making it such an enjoyable afternoon.

'They will be so proud that you came to talk to them, Colonel. They are such lovely old gentlemen – it's a real pity that walking is so difficult for Mr Andrews and Mr Maklov. But they are both very uncomplaining.'

'I was glad to come up and see them, Miss Dubranin. What line of business were they in back in the USA?'

'Well, Mr Andrews had a warehouse business distributing spare parts for automobiles. Mr Maklov was an insurance agent. I think Mr Nichols at one point worked for Mr Andrews, and Mr Rabovitz was some kind of a retail buyer for a clothing store in Minneapolis, Minnesota.'

'Men from the heart of the Western capitalist system, eh?' said Colonel Borsov.

'I suspect you are all getting used to it,' replied the nurse.

'No doubt,' said the Colonel. 'No doubt. But I must continue with my calls, and I hope we may speak again before too long.'

Miss Dubranin watched him descend to the lower deck, and she walked thoughtfully back and sat down once more. 'Very nice,' she said, carefully.

A little later, on their way to the second shift in the horseshoe-shaped dining room, they walked slowly past the museum, and looked at the pictures of the late General Secretary of the Communist Party: pictures of him in his birthplace, Rybinsk; pictures of him in the Kremlin; pictures of him in naval uniform, taking the salute at the Naval Academy in Rybinsk. Yuri Andropov, who died in 1984 before the full horror of the Soviet Union's collapsed economy became known. Andropov, one of the very last of the Communist Old Guard, a blinkered man, who thought until the day he died that another idealist from the Volga, Vladimir Ilyich Lenin, might yet be proved right.

'What a total asshole,' murmured Andre Maklov.

And with that the four old gentlemen and their nurse made their prolonged way to dinner, Mr Andrews' limp becoming noticeably worse. Two of their fellow passengers, both elderly ladies, smiled sympathetically as they passed. It was the natural telepathy of the elderly, a smile of shared anguish at the passing of middle age and the onset of twilight.

That evening they stood out on the deck with many other passengers and watched the distant shores of Lake Ladoga, as they wended their way up to the north end to see the islands. By 10 p.m.

the ship had not quite reached its turning point and would now cut its speed almost to zero during the night.

Tomorrow they would sail close to the islands before turning south once more, with a slow 90-mile run down to the estuary of the Svir' River. A further 100 miles up the river, at no more than 8 knots, would bring them to the port of Voznesene in the southwest corner of Lake Onega. They were scheduled to arrive there in the small hours of June 9, and anchor for the night in the sheltered southern waters of the lake.

They would spend that day running north again up to the island of Kizhi to see the spectacular wooden churches, and then steam down to an anchorage among the islands which dominate the central part of the lake north of Petrozavodsk. On the morning of June 10 they would set off for the Green Stop at the northwest corner of Onega.

And during this time the four gentlemen from Minnesota quietly made themselves known to a variety of passengers. They never shared their table at any meal, but they would sit up in the little bar at the stern of the ship, sipping coffee and the occasional glass of Armenian brandy, talking only rarely to fellow travelers, but listening appreciatively to the Russian songs which invariably broke out when sufficient vodka had been consumed. They befriended the young blond-haired steward, Pieter, who served during the afternoon and early evening. He really liked talking to old Mr Andrews about the second-hand American car he one day hoped to buy, though Mr Andrews never seemed to say much himself.

In the mornings, Nurse Dubranin always awakened her men at six-thirty and attended to their laundry, and organized clean clothes. The fact that she was into the two suites before six-forty-five, and none of them emerged for breakfast until eight, might have given rise to upper-deck chatter had they all been a bit younger.

However, June 10 was an early morning. All five of the party from the Midwest were out on deck as they cleared their anchorage off Kurgenicy, and set off at a low speed for the main north–south channel which lay to the northeast. The Captain spent much of the day cruising along the lovely western shoreline, and a guide, broadcasting on the ship's radio, pointed out what local history there had been in the past 500 years around these lost and remote farmlands.

In the late morning, the *Yuri Andropov* began to speed up, running straight now for the Green Stop which she would make by six-thirty in the evening. It was just 12.52 on Boris Andrews' watch when they spotted Captain Volkov's convoy, about a mile up ahead, driving slowly along the deep central channel. Traffic on the route had been unusually light during the last few days, but there were still five large freighters trying to get past the *Tolkach* barges.

The *Andropov*, being of shallower draft, was not forced to wait in line with the freighters, and overhauled the barges effortlessly. In company with every other passenger, Nurse Dubranin and her four employers were out on deck to see the truly astonishing sight of three Kilo-Class Russian submarines being carried across the lake and up to the White Sea on the biggest transporters anyone had ever seen.

The ship's broadcast network pointed out that this was not an unusual sight. It was the regular summer route of new Russian Navy ships which had been built, or undergone a refit, in the famous Red Sormovo yards at Nizhny Novgorod on the Volga River. And that the Soviet Navy had been using these 'secret' inland waterways for more than half a century to move warships around. Not of course, in the winter, said the female guide on the network, because all of these northern waters are frozen solid from October to April.

She added that it was a testimony to the immense foresight of the Communist leaders who had constructed these 'matchless' throughways, which joined rivers, lakes and oceans together, through the canals. She also mentioned that the Russian water transport system, engineered for major shipping, was unequaled anywhere in the Western World. She missed out the part about the thousands and thousands of deaths which had occurred among the enslaved labor force which had built the Berlomorski–Baltic Canal.

The *Andropov* slipped past, out to starboard of the Kilos, and both Mr Andrews and Mr Maklov noted the presence of three guards on the barges, all of whom waved cheerfully at the passengers while the captains sounded off the ships' horns in greeting. Mr Nichols and Mr Rabovitz looked almost speechless at the sheer size of the two two-and-a-half-thousand-ton submarines marooned high on the deck of the 900-foot *Tolkach*.

They spent the afternoon either out on the deck, or in the two suites. But at 6 p.m. they all went up to watch their final approach to the Green Stop, peering out at the sunlit shore on the port side as the Captain slid up to the jetty, reversed his engines and came to a halt in the shallows, the waving grasses of summer brushing the side of the ship.

Boris Andrews was unable to avoid a chuckle lighting up his lined face when Mr Maklov muttered, 'Holy shit!' followed by the immortal words of Mr Yogi Berra: 'It's *déjà vu* all over again.'

Nurse Dubranin walked back to the stern and stared back down the lake, marveling at its translucent light, a light which would scarcely fade throughout the long night ahead, a light which all summer long creates the White Nights up here in the northerly reaches of Russia.

Never had she seen such bright water. A group of seagulls swimming on the surface were lit by a light so pure, at an angle so oblique that the water had turned, literally, into a mirror, the reflections as sharp and focused as the birds themselves.

She saw the submarines were left far behind, and she watched the lines being secured before walking back to rejoin her gentlemen, just as the big gangway was lowered out of the hull, across the grass and reeds to form an easy bridge to the dirt road beyond.

They could all see passengers already walking out to investigate the territory, upon which awaited a small army of traders, with trestle tables set up selling local wares: filigree silver, carvings (especially carvings), jewelry of all types, antiques, little paintings of the area, pots of jam. Right here was capitalism taking firm roots.

Fifty yards to the left along the road was a small farmhouse which had been converted into a café-bar, with a white-and-yellow awning outside, and chairs set up in the shadow of a large willow tree. The hand-painted lettering on the sign said: 'WELCOME INN.' And on the timbered counter there were three brass samovars containing tea, plus two large coffee pots, and various bottles of brandy and liqueurs.

Farther along the road there were at least six buildings under construction, presumably shops, as the folks who lived on the lake anticipated perhaps a half-dozen ships per day arriving up here in summer, all full of foreigners eager to spend money on Russian souvenirs.

The ship's broadcast system announced that in view of the lovely warm evening the crew would prepare a barbecue on the shore tonight and passengers were welcome either to treat it as a picnic or alternatively to take their freshly grilled food back to the ship. The waitresses would clear up, and there would be a small charge for those wishing to sit at tables and chairs set up by local people in the field adjoining the Welcome Inn. One of the first rules of capitalism had plainly been learned – you always make more money when you cooperate with your rivals.

Nurse Dubranin quickly paid $10 for a $5 table on the edge of the field, and placed a reserved sign on it with her name at the top. At seven-thirty, as her gentlemen prepared to leave the ship, they all took one final walk on deck, very slowly along the starboard side. They walked even more slowly than usual, because, less than one mile off their beam, slightly for'ard, were the two giant *Tolkach* barges, anchored now with their cargo of submarines, lit by the still-bright western sunlight, their hulls stark against the distant horizon: K-6, K-7, and K-8.

Boris Andrews nodded slowly. And then they walked away without a word, eager now to get into some grilled steak and baked potato with butter and sour cream. After that they would most assuredly eat Russian cheese and black bread, with hot coffee. For their night would be long.

By 10 p.m. dinner was over, but the sky was still light, and out above the western flatlands the fireball of the sun could still be seen above the endless horizon, casting a pinkish light on the long waters of the lake. The winds were from the southwest, warm and light, and whatever else the night may have been, it was not dark. Sitting here, sipping coffee, awaiting the midnight shadows, the little group from the Midwest watched the diligent efforts of the Russian crew to make money.

Stewards, bearing little envelopes, mingled with the passengers requesting tips for the less public members of staff – the cooks, the galley staff and the maids. They were not greedy, the tips were not expected to be high, just a little something, just a dollar or so from the wealthy folk from the West for the underprivileged Russian workers. The envelopes would be collected on the way back. By ten-thirty Boris had five of them in his pocket.

Fifteen minutes later, with 50 or more passengers still sitting in the warm field sipping brandy at their tables, Nurse Dubranin rather ostentatiously stood up and announced she was taking her men for a short evening walk along the dirt road and back. Then, she added, addressing the people at the next table, an edge of asperity creeping into her voice, 'I will insist they go to bed . . . they have all drunk quite sufficient of that brandy, or whatever it is.'

There were two or three cries of 'C'mon, Edith, let the guys have a few laughs . . . they're on vacation, right?' But the nurse from Chicago was having none of it. She bossily told them to follow her out of the drinking area, and to breathe deeply, especially Mr Nichols, who occasionally suffered from asthma.

And they set off along the road, going slowly north, advancing only at the speed of Boris Andrews, who could be seen limping painfully at the rear of the group. 'Poor old guy,' said a Texan at the next table. 'She shoulda left him alone. He was having a good time.'

It took them more than 10 minutes to walk 600 yards, while still in sight of the other passengers. The final 200 yards, along the shallow left-hand curve in the dirt road, were completed more quickly. It was still light – not bright, but light. You could see the silhouettes of the *Tolkach* barges way out on the water.

Andre Maklov led the way, and he walked carefully along the left-hand side of the road, staring at the trees. He stopped suddenly before the trunk of a big pine. Then he said softly, 'Look carefully left, then right, guys . . .' And all five of them took a hard all-around view. Not a sound disturbed the night, not a soul moved anywhere within their vision.

'Okay,' said Boris Andrews very quietly, staring at a small square instrument he had taped inside his guide-book. 'This is it. Let's go, guys.'

He bounded across the grass verge and slid through the under-growth into the wood, followed by his four companions, Nurse Dubranin hurrying along last, trying to rip 'this fucking wig off my head.' They moved with swift, sure steps, guided by their Leader, who now had his GPS in his hand, leading them to the waypoint he'd entered several weeks previously.

It was darker in here than it was on the road, because of the dense foliage above them. But in the gloom of these critical minutes, Messrs Andrews, Nichols, Maklov and Rabovitz were ceasing to exist. And the four US Navy SEALS, looking ridiculous now in their disguises and their old men's polyester summer clothes, moved swiftly forward, easing branches and bushes aside. As they ran, they cleared a path for their late nurse Edith Dubranin, who was running fast, with the light, trained skill of the CIA field officer Angela Rivera.

They reached the rising ground just below the big straggly bush they sought; the light appeared brighter in front of them now, as the mile-deep wood prepared to give way to open farmland. They arrived silently, tearing off their disguises with relief, and placing them in a neat pile.

Ray Schaeffer was under the bush like a groundhog, scrabbling for the shovel, which he found in 20 seconds flat. He and Rick Hunter grabbed the bush and heaved it out. The Lieutenant Commander ordered young Jason, the late Mr Rabovitz, to stand guard. 'Patrol around us. If you see *anyone*, warn us with two owl-hoots, and hide. Let him come on in if he must, then take him out with this combat knife, instantly. Right now we have a zero margin for error.'

Rick Hunter handed over the knife, then he ordered the late asthmatic Sten Nichols, now referred to as Harry, to 'Start digging right there – not deep, the canister doors are right on top, no more than a coupla feet below the surface.'

It took less than five minutes to uncover and open the door. Lt. Commander Hunter took charge of the unloading of the first canister, while Petty Officer Harry Starck started digging for canister number two. Inside, Rick found, carefully packed in sealed plastic bags, four sets of wet-suits, each one containing a numbered pair of flippers – the white-painted number each SEAL had been awarded on the day he passed his BUD/S course, the number which would follow him throughout his career in the élite Navy corps.

Angela took over here, arranging the packs in a line, and then placing on top of each one a SEAL's Draeger Mk V, the underwater breathing apparatus which leaves behind neither bubbles nor noise to betray the presence of the combat swimmers to an alert sentry. The cylinder holds 13 cubic feet of oxygen at 2,000 lb PSI (per square inch). A trained SEAL, breathing steadily, has four hours of air in his Draeger, but stress and adrenalin can empty the oxygen supply in half that time. The equipment weighs a hefty 35 lb on dry land, but is virtually weightless underwater.

Already packed, in with the wet-suits, was each SEAL's modern, commercial scuba-diving mask, which fit perfectly, but are apt to be manufactured in fluorescent greens, oranges and reds to attract attention. Each SEAL had, naturally, taped or black-painted his personal mask, and each one had been carefully checked and wrapped by the instructors back at Coronado.

Beneath the underwater equipment, Rick Hunter found four SEALs attack boards, the small, two-handed platforms which contain a compass, depth gauge and watch, right in front of the swimmer's eyes as he kicks forward. It keeps him straight, keeps him on time, helps him check his likely oxygen consumption, and keeps him cool and steady with all the information he needs effortlessly to hand. SEALs usually share one board between two, but Rick Hunter thought they should have one each for this mission, since they would be subsurface all the way there and back, and would have to separate under the barges.

At the bottom of canister one were two light machine-guns, Russian-designed RPDs, with six ammunition clips for each. Rick grunted as he dug for the door of canister two, 'The guns are for Ray and me. There's gonna be pistols for all five of us.'

The second door came open, and inside there were two old canvas bags containing obvious street clothes for the SEALs, jeans, shirts and sport jackets, socks and Topsiders. Beneath them were four packages of Semtex explosive, in this canister 160 lb of the stuff, grouped into sets of eight charges, each one weighing 5 lb, with a separate timing device, and a separate magnetic clamp for each charge.

Ray had the third canister open by now, and he pulled out more explosive and more timers, plus five Sig Sauer 9 mm pistols with ammunition clips. There were also five sheathed Kaybar combat knives. There were the standard medical and survival supplies, plus the groundsheets and ponchos they might need if they had to take to the hills, and 'walk out.' On the floor of the canister there were a flashlight and powerful binoculars. Plus ten chocolate bars, and five large bottles of fizzy water. Plus another hunk of Semtex fixed to a wooden board designed as a booby trap, with a battery detonator.

They unloaded their old men's clothes now, and dumped them into the underground canisters. They pulled on their wet-suits, and prepared to walk to the lake. They would carry the flippers and Draegers by hand, with the two rifles, pistols, knives and explosives strapped and clipped on their cross belts, the way they had been trained. It took no more than five minutes for each of the four men to become underwater battle-ready.

Angela cleared up as they went, organizing what was now their home base. The plan had been reviewed time and time again. They were to make their way back here afterwards and get rid of as much stuff as they could, before heading off across the fields to the main road which ran north—south, one further mile to the west.

Angela was left behind to clear up. She wore a loaded pistol at her side, with a Kaybar handily strapped to her belt close to her right hand. It was agreed that she would make her way to the shore of the lake in one hour, and wait on the edge of the wood in case there should be an observant passer-by. She knew if someone came along at the wrong time, as the SEALs returned, she would have no option but to kill instantly. Angela had no difficulty with that.

They shook hands silently, and the SEALs set off in the twilight of the wood, arriving at the outer edge of the trees, gazing out from the undergrowth to the *still* light waters of the lake. It was 0145 exactly.

The SEALs stood quietly, ensuring the coast was clear, then they slipped across the dirt road, and, crouching low, made their way into the long grass which grew in the shallow water. They stayed low, listening for any unusual sound, above the sigh of the summer wind in the reeds, or the whine of a mosquito.

But there was something else. Something which sounded like a ship's engine. They peered out through the bulrushes, looking along to the *Andropov*, moored with lights blazing a half-mile to the south. The sound was nearer now, a steady buzzing from the other direction. It was bad news, and it was arriving at the worst possible time. Jason, unaware, was trying to return Rick Hunter's sheathed hunting knife, and he tossed it forward to the SEAL Leader. But he tossed it too far, and to his horror it missed Rick's outstretched hand, hitting the water with a significant splash, 10 feet beyond the edge of the bulrushes where Rick stood.

'Fucking *hell*!' snapped Schaeffer. 'That's an outboard motor – about 50 yards away. One of the ship's little inflatables . . . I guess the one Pieter said he takes passengers out on for a dollar a ride. *Fuck*. He's coming this way . . . *and there's some bastard with him. Rick* . . . he must have seen the knife splash – they can't miss us. They'll probably start fishing right here.'

Lt. Commander Hunter snapped immediately, 'Get your stuff off. Stand up and greet them, keep only your knife handy. Get rid of everything else. Jason, get over and help him. Ray, call them over in Russian. Smile and wave.'

The SEAL Leader, keeping on his own heavyweight equipment, moved forward into deeper water, sliding under the surface. The noise of the outboard was louder now, and Rick in the shallows could see that Ray was standing, bareheaded, just in his wet suit, shoulders out of the water.

'Hi there, Pieter,' he called, in the elderly voice of Andre Maklov. 'There's good fish in here. Come and see. Help me catch him. We grill for breakfast on the barbecue back there.'

Rick heard the young Russian answer quizzically, in the hesitant words of a man who recognized someone, but on the other hand had not seen the person before. 'Who's that? Mr Maklov? Okay? Where's Mr Andrews?'

The boat drew nearer, slowing right down as it came up alongside Lt. Schaeffer. The SEAL now recognized Pieter's companion as Torbin, the head waiter from the ship, and he greeted them both warmly, ignoring the fact that he was no longer made up to look 78 years old. Rick heard the *Andropov* steward speak again: 'Do I know you . . . ?'

Then Rick came to the surface. His feet found the bottom and he shoved the rubberized hull upwards with all of his strength. Pieter, standing, overbalanced and pitched forward, not quite out of the boat.

But Ray Schaeffer grabbed the Russian's blond hair and heaved him into the water, plunging his long Kaybar combat knife straight between the fifth and sixth ribs, cutting clean through Pieter's pounding heart.

His friend, still hanging from the rear seat, was about to cry out when Harry Starck vaulted off the bottom and into the boat. His right hand found the Russian's wind pipe, crushing it from behind, and simultaneously slamming his Kaybar right through the head waiter's back, stopping his heart as abruptly as Schaeffer had stopped Pieter's. With the boat now upside down, the engine, starved of air, also died.

'You drag the boat, Ray, I'll bring the bodies,' said Lt. Commander Hunter, displaying every one of the instant, under-pressure, do-it-*now* qualities which made him one of the best SEAL Leaders in Coronado. 'Get 'em inshore, dump 'em in the water, face down. Get the engine off, deflate the boat over on top of 'em and weight it down with the outboard. Could be weeks before anyone finds anything, in six feet of water in the middle of these fucking weeds.'

The exercise took six minutes. And the two SEALs headed back to where Harry and Jason waited. Right here, for the umpteenth time, Rick went over the plan. He glanced at his watch which now said 0210. 'We'll delay for a couple more minutes while your adrenalin dies down,' he said. 'Otherwise we might run out of air. Meanwhile, you all know what to do: take a bearing on the middle barge and head straight for it; deploy underwater one man for each vessel; attach the eight charges at 50-foot intervals down the starboard side of the front two, starting 50 feet from the bow. That's Harry and Jason. Ray, you know you're taking the rear barge – the separate one – and placing your charges on the port side, same distance apart, starting 100 feet from the bow. Timers arrived set and synchronized for 24 hours, from the time of the first charge, right?'

'Right, sir.'

'Jason, remember now: measure your distance. Each kick takes you 10 feet, that's five between charges. Breathe slowly and carefully. Look for the bilge keel and get them clamped up behind it. I'm not sure of the depth or the clarity of the water, but stay deep anyway. We're looking at 40 minutes to get out there, 40 minutes under the barges and 40 minutes back. Anyone not here in two hours and 15 minutes, I'll assume you're dead, and I'll come out to replace you myself.'

Each of the SEALs nodded curtly. Ray announced he felt no adrenalin running right now, and that he was ready to go. Lt. Commander Hunter nodded. Then he said softly, 'That's it, guys. Go do it.'

The time was 0220 when Lt. Ray Schaeffer and his men slipped silently under the water, each of them kicking forward with their attack boards held at arms' length in front of them, the compass bearing set on zero-four-four, one tick light of due northeast. Rick had calculated the barges were around three-quarters of a mile off-shore, which at 4,500 feet meant the SEALs must kick 450 times to get there, a little more than 11 kicks a minute. Their rhythm would be steady: KICK . . . one . . . two . . . three . . . four. KICK . . . one . . . two . . . three . . . four . . . Kick and glide, kick and glide, all the way to Admiral Zhang's submarines.

The SEALs would not come to the surface. The first they would know of their proximity to the Kilos would be from the darkness in the water. The key was to stay accurately on bearing. And they swam together silently, three jet-black figures running deep, 12 feet below the surface, so as to leave no ripples.

Rick Hunter, the strongest swimmer of them all, waited behind, sitting in the shallows watching the barges through the binoculars. If one of the SEALs was still missing at 0435, he would immediately swim out there himself, fully equipped with charges, and check out the barge which had been worked on by the missing man.

He would, if necessary, attach his own charges to the bottom, and then search for his missing colleague.

If that was unsuccessful, he would return to shore alone, swimming as fast as he could go. Meanwhile, he sat in the shallows, watching for any discernible movement on the *Tolkach* barges, and as the minutes ticked away, he saw none.

Ray Schaeffer kept kicking. After 20 minutes he had counted to 240 — ahead of schedule — and on either side of him he could see his two colleagues, both moving sweetly through the water like the SEALs they were. The compass bearing remained resolutely on zero-four-four, and they were more than halfway. At the 30-minute mark, he had counted 340 exactly. They were slowing down a tad, but still just in front of schedule. The final 10 minutes would be the worst part. The trick was not to press, not to force anything, otherwise it would kill the oxygen supply.

Deliberately Ray slowed just a little. There was a pain now in his upper thighs, right in the place where it always hurt on a long swim. But he could fight through that. The lactic acid was bad, but not that bad. Not as bad as it had been the night they had carried the canisters. One hundred and ten kicks more, that was all he needed. No sweat. He could make that on willpower alone.

But they all received an unexpected bonus right here. Lt. Rick Hunter had slightly overestimated three-quarters of a mile, and after only 36 minutes' swimming they were all suddenly overwhelmed by the darkness just above them, as they entered the waters beneath the gigantic *Tolkach* convoy which carried the three brand-new submarines ordered by the Navy of China.

Ray stuck out his right arm as agreed. They would swim down the hull until they reached either the giant iron link on the articulated double barge in front, or, alternatively, the clear water between the two separate vessels. Either way they would then know where they were, which, right now, they did not.

As it happened they were bang on the middle barge. And when

they reached the open water at its stern, it was obvious that Ray alone would proceed through the empty water and make for the 600-footer in the rear. Jason and the Petty Officer would head back along the starboard side of the middle barge, and part company at the coupling joint. Jason would then count his five kicks back, and go deep in search of the bilge keel. Harry would go farther for'ard and attend to the lead barge. They would not see each other again until they reached the shore, returning on bearing two-two-four.

Ray Schaeffer was first into position. He kicked 10 times down the port side of the rear *Tolkach*, right next to the straight-sided hull. Then he went deeper, sliding his hand down the great ship's plates until he came to a thick iron ridge, protruding obliquely outwards about six feet at a 45-degree angle from the perpendicular. This was the bilge keel, a kind of giant stabilizer. Ray knew he had to get up under it, on the inside, closer to the central keel, in order to clamp on his explosives.

He pushed out to the end of the ridge, and found to his horror he was standing. There were only three feet of water below the keel, and he thanked God there was no falling tide up here at the northern end of Lake Onega. He dived down, head first, kicking to get right under the barge. Then he stood again on the sandy floor of the lake, running his hands across the inside of the bilge keel, working his way up to the point where it joined the hull right above his head. It felt awfully rough, like the underside of a rock, full of barnacles and weed. That was not, he knew, good news. Worse yet, he was now working in the pitch dark.

He took out the first 5-lb pack of explosive, and screwed in the magnetic clamp, tight. Then he fixed the timer, with its small glowing face showing a 24-hour setting. He placed it against the hull, but as he suspected, it would not stick. So he held it in his left hand and drew his Kaybar for the second time that night. Ray scraped a small spot clean on the hull of the *Tolkach*. And this time he felt the powerful magnet pull, and then lightly thud home, hard on the bottom of the ship.

He elected now to stay on the inside of the bilge keel, and he swam on for five kicks in the pitch dark, proceeding down the port side of the hull to his next stop. There he repeated the process, and, checking the time, saw that it was taking him six minutes to make each connection. And he had six more to go. However, he was more or less safe down here, and his bigger worry was young Jason, and he wondered how the kid was getting along, as he adjusted each timer to run for 360 seconds less than the previous one.

Lt. Schaeffer wrapped up his project at 0340 precisely. It had taken exactly 48 minutes. And now he swung out from under the bilge keel into the light. He unclipped his attack board, grabbed it with both hands and kicked straight along bearing two-two-four. Breathing slowly. Wondering where the others were.

All the way back, he kicked, counted to four, and kicked again. During the final 15 minutes he was murderously tired, and his upper legs throbbed. But he kept going, kicking and counting, fighting the pain barrier, repeating his little prayer. No one, he thought, could have done this faster.

Which was why he was truly amazed when he finally surfaced, and saw Rick Hunter still sitting in the bulrushes which grew in the shallows, chatting with Jason and Harry.

'Where the hell have you been?' asked the SEAL Leader. 'I was just beginning to wonder if you might be dead.'

'Well, I'm not,' snapped Ray, unnecessarily. 'It was just the bottom of that rear barge. It was so dirty, nothing would stick. I had to clean every spot free of fucking barnacles before the clamp would go on.'

'Oh, right,' said Harry. 'Ours was completely clean, probably been in refit. I was whipping those babies on there in three minutes. So was Jason. We both adjusted the timers for 180 seconds. By a fluke we finished at the same time. Came back together.'

'Short straw again,' said Ray. 'I probably ruined my knife scraping the bottom . . . just hope I'm not asked to assassinate anyone else tonight.'

'No – I hope not anyway,' said Rick. 'But right now it's going to start getting lighter by the minute and we have to get back across the road and into the woods. Angela, by the way, has gone, as planned . . . we'll catch her later.'

The SEALs came out of the water, crouched and observed the empty road. Then they bolted across, free now of their 40-lb weights of explosive, and, clinging onto their attack boards and flippers, jogged on through the woods to the spot where the canisters were buried. Angela had left just one uncovered, with their new street clothes, chocolate and water right on top.

They stripped off their wet-suits and Draegers, and placed them with the two machine-guns, ammunition clips and attack boards inside the canister. Then they dressed in socks, shoes, jeans, shirts and jackets. They each ate some chocolate, drank some water, and piled everything else inside the last canister, ensuring they would leave unencumbered.

Then Rick Hunter set the incendiary booby traps and placed them inside, against the door handles before carefully closing each door. If anyone, in the next 50 or so years, ever found the canisters and tried the doors, they would blow to smithereens with everything inside. Right now, Ray Schaeffer shoved the old bush back into the loose earth, and took the last shovel and covered the disturbed area with soil and dead leaves. He and Rick twisted and turned the bush back into place, and the four of them left, carrying the last shovel, but armed only with their Kaybars and pistols.

They did not head back to the dirt road but went farther west, walking softly along the edge of the wood in the early morning light. They found the highway after one mile and hid on the steep bank which led up to it from the forest. They could see, a couple of hundred yards to the right, an old Russian peasant woman wearing a shawl, sitting on the roadside awaiting a lift, and they too waited.

At 0655 a deceptively old Volkswagen bus pulled up, collected her, and then drove on to a spot right above their hiding place. Angela's face peered out from under the shawl, through the passenger-seat window. 'Okay, guys,' she said, 'let's get the hell out of here.'

The SEALs came up off the bank like bullets, and hurled themselves, and their surviving shovel, into the vehicle. Angela Rivera spoke freely. 'This is young Vladimir,' she said, nodding at the driver. 'He's a colleague of mine, works for us in Moscow. All our clothes, papers and passports are here, and this thing will take us straight down to the M18, then south all the way to St Petersburg. For the record, in case we're stopped, we all work for a citrus-growing outfit in Florida. You all know the cover, go through it all in your minds.

'Vlad's taking us straight to St Petersburg Airport, then we're going by private corporate jet to London. Everything's fixed – the Russians never bother with commercial executives on private planes these days. Specially Americans.'

'Beautiful,' said Lt. Commander Hunter.

'By the way, did you fix the Kilos?'

'Sure did,' said Ray Schaeffer.

CHAPTER NINE

CAPTAIN VOLKOV MOVED the Kilos off, traveling northeast across Lake Onega, at 8.30 a.m. on June 11. The journey to the White Sea for such cargo moving along at only 5 knots was one of approximately 24 hours' duration, and the eight-thirty departure would see them comfortably into the canal by ten-thirty, and then at Belomorsk for refueling just as the port came to life the following morning.

The big *Tolkach* barges always pulled out at this time after their overnight stop, and there were no surprises in Fort Meade shortly after 2 a.m. when the satellite photographs showed them doing exactly that.

Admiral Morgan was pleased. No communication had been received from the SEALs by midnight, and there had been no uproar from the Kremlin, which meant everything had gone according to plan. Arnold Morgan was even courteous to Charlie as they made their way back to Washington from Fort Meade in the small hours. Indeed, a thin smile played around the edges of his mouth as he contemplated the mayhem due to erupt in both Moscow and Beijing around seven o'clock (EDT) this evening.

'You're driving beautifully, Charlie,' he observed. Which almost caused his nerve-racked chauffeur to run straight up the back of a Greyhound bus.

It was 1300 local time when Lt. Commander Hunter and his team, having changed clothes during the journey, arrived at St Petersburg Airport. They all disembarked from the van, leaving Vladimir to get rid of the clothes, combat knives and pistols, which he would do at the US Consulate on Petra-Lavrova Street.

By 1500 the SEALs were on board the American Learjet, ready to take off for London. Five hours later they would be traveling business-class on the American Airlines 747 making its daily flight to New York. Rick calculated they ought to be somewhere over the coast of Maine when the barges blew up in the narrow northern reaches of the Belomorski Canal.

Pieter, the steward, and Torbin, the head waiter, were not due to report for duty on board the *Yuri Andropov* until lunchtime. When they failed to show up, the matter was reported to the Captain, and to Colonel Borsov. The senior officers ordered a thorough search of the ship, which took almost two hours, and at 1400 the executive decided the two men were undoubtedly missing.

The ship was heading south down Lake Onega now, and it was a difficult decision to make, whether just to inform the nearest police, or to return to the Green Stop. It was hard to imagine that anything had befallen the men up in that lonely rural area. But the search had revealed one of the ship's rubber inflatables from the upper deck was also missing – and several people knew it was the very one Pieter had been using to take passengers late-night sightseeing.

Colonel Borsov decided something was afoot. And he ordered the *Andropov* to come about, and head right back to the Green Stop, where all members of the crew would be expected to assist in the search for their lost colleagues.

The four old gentlemen from Minnesota, and their nurse, Edith Dubranin, were also missed at lunchtime. Their table was empty, they had not been in for breakfast, and no one had seen them. Colonel Borsov himself noticed they were not at lunch, and ordered a steward to go to the upper deck and check the two suites.

The steward used his master key and found the rooms intact, with a few possessions scattered around, but no sign of the old gentlemen. Colonel Borsov suddenly understood that the *Andropov* had somehow left seven people up at the Green Stop, which was precisely when he ordered the ship to come about.

All day long, Captain Volkov pushed north at his normal slow speed. There would be no more stops before the White Sea, and he always found the 120-mile journey endless and laborious. He had done it many times before, in various ships, but the submarines meant he could hardly see anything in front of him. The Captain's forward view was completely blocked by the great bulk of the Kilos. And he just had to sit and keep the engines steady, driving forward and relying on his son to steer from the wheelhouse on the bow of the lead barge. But young Ivan was good at that.

By sundown, or what passes for a sundown in the season of the White Nights, he was well on his way, running up through the long wide lakes towards the town of Segeza. They reached this area around midnight, and then turned into the narrow inland canal which begins south of Nadvojcy. It was a four-hour run on this very slow stretch up to the next lake, and the master of the *Tolkach* was glad both he and Ivan had slept for most of the evening, while the first mate and the navigator had taken over the helms.

At 2.58 a.m. on June 12, lit up by the bright glow in the northern sky, the Kilos were just four and a half miles south of the lake, and six miles south of the town of Kockoma. The water was flat, there was no breeze, and little traffic, when Captain Volkov sensed a long and distant rumble beneath the keel. He had heard such a noise before, and he knew what had happened. 'FUCK,' he shouted. 'WE'RE AGROUND . . .'

Reaching for his phone he yelled for Ivan, uncertain whether there had been a steering failure. And now he heard a truly sensational thundering sound, again, he thought, right beneath the keel. 'CHRIST! WE'VE HIT SOMETHING . . . JESUS . . . IVAN! WHERE THE HELL ARE YOU?'

But there was no reply, and Captain Volkov put his engines to stop as he left the bridge and rushed down the companionway, running along the deck beneath the port side of the Kilo. When he reached the bow, where the two *Tolkach* barges were joined, he could not believe what he was seeing. The lead barge was listing to starboard before his eyes, the deck now at a lunatic angle.

He could see the guard hanging on to one of the great wooden blocks which held the submarine in place. Suddenly there was another sound of thunder from under the keel, and the front barge twisted yet further to starboard. As it did so, two and a half thousand tons of Kilo-Class submarine swayed, and then toppled sideways, smashing into the barge's deck edge, before hitting the water with a gigantic splash, and disappearing beneath the surface.

But it vanished for only a split second. Then it surged upwards again with terrifying force, like a giant broaching whale, before settling on the soft bottom of the canal, with the lead barge capsized on top of it. Deep beneath the surface the waters of the canal rushed inboard through the huge split the submarine's hull had sustained on impact with the deck-edge.

But Captain Volkov had more immediate worries. The lead *Tolkach* had now broached and the clockwise pressure on the coupling which attached his own rear barge was immense. They were swinging right across the canal, and he could feel she was twisting to starboard anyway, and now he felt her lurch right, just as the force on the coupling became too great. The entire barge rolled right over in agonizing slow motion, which sent the Captain hurtling to his death, right across the deck and into the tortured, fractured coupling area under the bow. And, more spectacularly, sending the second Kilo hurtling off the deck, right onto the eastern wall of the canal.

The Kilo hit the bank with crushing force, smashing the concrete, smashing herself, and rolling back into the side of the barge, then down into the water with an impact almost equal to that of the first one. Split wide open below the sail, she lay half submerged with water gushing in, pinned to the bottom by the great *Tolkach* which had carried her halfway across Russia. Ivan Volkov had somehow survived and fought his way to the left-hand shore, not knowing yet that his father had died.

He clambered out just in time to hear the muffled underwater roar of Lt. Ray Schaeffer's slightly later Semtex charges blast eight gaping holes along the underside hull of the rear *Tolkach*. He heard the dull thunder, as his father had done four minutes earlier, and then he stood and stared as the 600-foot following barge began to list, and then to lurch dramatically, as the water rushed in below. She seemed to rise, and then groan her way onto her port side, just as John Bergstrom had planned.

From Ivan's perspective, she seemed to roll right with terrible slowness, and he watched in further horror as the rear Kilo wobbled, then crashed majestically sideways, plunging down from her keel blocks 20 feet above the water. If you could imagine one of the double towers of the Brooklyn Bridge toppling into the East River, you'd be on the right wavelength. The Kilo hit the surface of the Belomorski Canal with breathtaking reverberation. The rear barge had slewed towards the west, and this submarine, too, obliterated the canal bank before rebounding back into the water with a gaping hole behind her tower, and a giant split all the way aft, through which water was gushing, short-circuiting and wrecking the battery, flooding the diesels, ruining the computerized firing systems and all of the electronics, wiping out the sonar, the radar, the operations center, and flooding every compartment.

No crane could lift even one of the Kilos out of these waters. The fact was, in under six minutes, the explosives set by Admiral Bergstrom's SEALs had written off three Kilo-Class submarines worth $900 million, sunk three of the biggest barges in Russia, and completely blocked the Belomorski Canal for months, or even a year. Or at least until the Russians could begin to bring in frogmen and lifting 'camels,' and start raising the hulls off the bottom.

Ivan Volkov was the only survivor. And he stood on the chilly, battered banks of the canal, shivering with cold and shock, miles from anywhere, as the waters settled slowly and quietly over the wreckage. To the northeast he could see the sun, glowing pink at 3 a.m. on the distant horizon. But there was no movement any-where, and he knew instinctively that no human being could have survived such a crash; at least not on the side over which the barges had toppled.

He knew now why he had survived. As his *Tolkach* had listed to starboard, he had sensed the danger, and dived straight over the bow of the lead barge, from the area directly in front of his wheelhouse. He had plunged into the dark water, out to the left, swimming away from the hull, kicking off his boots as he did so. At the moment she capsized, he was 40 yards clear . . . and safe.

In all of Russia's northern territories, Ivan was the only man who knew it could *not* have been an accident. Because he had heard the thunder beneath the surface, not only on the articulated double barge which he was himself steering, but also from the quite separate rear barge. Young Volkov alone *knew* something diabolical was afoot. Someone had blown up the convoy. Of that he was quite certain.

Since he had no recollection of passing any sign of life in the previous few miles before the barges overturned, he decided to walk north, taking off his soaking wet shirt and jacket, and deeply regretting losing his boots. Sometimes he walked, sometimes he ran, trying to keep his circulation going until he reached a waterside village. But it was a long way.

Meanwhile, moving slowing north up the canal, some 22 miles south of the disaster, was the 1,700-ton river cargo ship *Baltika*, laden to her gunwales with timber from the central Volga, and bound for the northern shipyards. It took her more than four hours to reach the site of the catastrophe, and it was shortly after 7.30 a.m. when the first mate spotted the completely unexpected wreckage in the water nearly a mile up ahead. He called for the Captain to return to the bridge: 'Look out, sir . . . What the hell's that, in the water right on our bow?'

'Where?' asked the Captain peering north at the jutting hull of the rear *Tolkach*. 'JESUS! . . . FULL ASTERN!'

The freighter was slow to stop when she was unladen, even at only 7 knots. But right now, weighed down by hundreds of tons of timber, she was almost impossible to bring to a halt in the short remaining distance. Her ancient engines slowed, then stopped, then restarted in reverse, seeming to take forever. The ship shuddered from end to end as her screw fought to destroy her momentum, dragging down her speed as she slid inexorably towards the half-exposed propeller of the rear *Tolkach*. But it was not quite enough, and she still bumped hard, saved hardly at all by the heavy tractor half-tires Captain Perov had fixed on his bow to avoid damage in the often-crowded Russian trading ports.

The engine pulled her off, and there was no real harm done, but the sight before the eyes of the Captain and his small crew was nothing short of overwhelming. There was wreckage all over the surface of the water. There was another colossal barge overturned on its side in front of the one they had just hit. Up ahead there was yet another, jutting out of the water. On the left near side of the canal was the unmistakable shape of a *submarine*, its stern visible, slammed against the obliterated bank of the canal.

To the right, Captain Perov could see a second submarine, sideways on across the waterway, sunk, but with her stern, after-planes, rudders, and screw out of the water, resting against the eastern bank, which looked as if it had been blasted by a mine. On the same side, but farther forward, there was yet a third hull, rigid and still, the way a racing yacht looks when hard aground. He did not know that this was another submarine, hard aground on its own sail, which was dug into the bottom of the canal. And its hull was split. And it was full of water. And the lead *Tolkach* was remorselessly pinning it, upside down. If Captain Perov had not known better he would have assumed himself in a war zone.

Of life, there was no sign. And for a river cargo captain there was but one salient point: the Belomorski Canal was completely blocked. Both ways. And it was liable to stay that way for some time. Captain Perov picked up the radio handset and told the river police. It was 0736 on the morning of June 12.

By 0900, news of the devastation on the canal had reached the Kremlin. And in the office of the Chief of the Main Navy Staff there was an atmosphere of scarcely controlled fury. Its thunderstruck occupant, Vitaly Rankov, the massive ex-Soviet international oarsman, was a full Admiral now, and he wielded enormous power as the third most important man in the entire Russian Navy. As Chief of the Main Staff, he batted right behind the C-in-C, who also held the position of Deputy Minister of Defense; and the Deputy C-in-C of the Navy.

Each of the two men above Admiral Rankov was involved politically in the machinations of the various ex-Soviet fleets in the Baltic, the Black Sea, the Pacific and the North. But in the day-to-day running of the 270,000-strong Russian Navy, Admiral Rankov was the name most people feared above all others. Straight-forward situations, where major decisions needed to be made, ended up on his desk very quickly indeed. Situations where any threat to national security was suspected arrived for his attention instantly. And now the ex-naval intelligence chief sat staring at the brief report in front of him: the wrecked *Tolkach* barges, the ruined Kilo submarines, the blocked canal.

There were a thousand questions to be asked, and most of them, he had no doubt, would never be satisfactorily answered. But there was one question he could answer immediately, though he might have trouble proving it.

Who was responsible for this outrage?

Answer: Admiral Arnold Morgan, National Security Advisor to the President of the United States of America. Somehow, that is. In some totally devious way, which might never be proved.

How do you know that, Vitaly? 'BECAUSE I KNOW THAT BASTARD,' thundered the Admiral to the vast and empty room. 'He virtually threatened our ambassador in Washington . . . *That fucking maniac has destroyed a total of five Kilo-Class submarines, two in the North Atlantic, and now three in the canal.'*

It took him a full 10 minutes to regain his cool, pacing from one end of his great vaulted office to the other, the steel tips on the heels of his polished shoes clicking on the marble floor as he walked. He tried to gather his thoughts into some kind of coherent order. Politically he had no idea what would be decided, and plainly it would be absurd to alarm the populace with some wild accusation involving the USA. At least it would without a great deal of hard evidence.

No, that was all out of the question. The entire matter must be treated as an accident, and maybe it would not be necessary to make anything public, except for news of a cataclysmic crash in the canal. There were after all very few casualties, and the entire incident happened in an extremely remote area. It was just the sheer brass balls of that lunatic in the White House – that was the infuriating part.

Worse yet, in the mind of Admiral Rankov, was the possibility that Arnold Morgan was going to believe he had gotten away with the entire escapade. And when his personal white fury had subsided, he picked up the telephone and told the Kremlin operator to get through to the White House switchboard, and somehow patch him through to Admiral Morgan on a matter of extreme urgency.

'You do realize it is 0100 in the morning in Washington, sir,' said the operator politely.

'I do,' replied Admiral Rankov, forcing a smile at the prospect of awakening Admiral Morgan, as the American security chief had done so often to him.

It took only three minutes, because the White House board was able to put the call straight through to Fort Meade, where the Admiral was still chatting to George Morris.

'Vitaly! My old buddy, how the hell are you?'

'Good morning, Arnold. Should I apologize for the lateness of the hour?'

'Hell, no. I've always told you. If you want me, call me, never mind the time. That's the way I operate.'

'Yes. I have noticed that a few times in the past,' replied the Russian coldly.

'Now, old pal, what can I do for you?'

'Arnold, we were transporting three Kilo-Class submarines up the Belomorski Canal this morning when the three barges carrying them suddenly overturned. The resulting wreckage was just about total. More than a billion dollars' worth of damage, and the canal closed for probably six months.'

'No kidding? Hey, that's awful.'

'Arnold, I wondered whether you might not know something about it. Since you made it so clear to Nikolai Ryabinin that you did not wish our export order to China to proceed.'

'You mean these three Kilos were on their way to China?'

'Exactly that.'

'Well, I can't say I personally have any knowledge about them . . . I mean, I haven't really left my desk much today. But let me get this clear . . . you think someone tipped over your barges and smashed up the submarines, bang in the middle of Russia, right under the eyes of your security network. Who's your first suspect – King Kong?'

'Arnold, we are old friends. And you sometimes make me laugh. But not today. I am just mentioning that the United States has the *motive* to want such an "accident" to take place. And I am also going to warn you, formally, on behalf of the Russian Navy, that I will not rest until I get to the bottom of this. And if I discover the hand of America behind it, I will personally ensure that the entire world views you as a bunch of selfish, lawless, vicious bastards, and we will take a resolution to the United Nations insisting that you be required to make full and total compensation to us for loss of lives and all repairs, and that you publicly apologize for bringing this world to the brink of war. I know you think we are some kind of a backward, Third World country compared to the mighty USA. But we are not powerless, remember that.'

'Now come on, Vitaly. We don't think that. We certainly do not regard you as backward, or Third World, or powerless. We're not your enemy. We didn't want the Kilos delivered, that's true. But we would *never* do something like you describe. Anyway, how could we? How could any outsider pull off an operation like that? You think someone blew 'em up?'

'No, Arnold. Not *someone*. I think you blew them up.'

'No. No. No. I would regard that as an unacceptable act between friendly nations. I might consider it . . . but I'd never carry it out.'

'Arnold, I just had to hear your formal denial.'

'Well, you got that, old pal. If I were you, I'd take a careful look at some of your other enemies. How 'bout those Chechen characters? They're still pretty fed up with you guys. And I'll tell you, it would be a whole hell of a lot easier for them than us to knock a few holes in a big barge. Sounds to me like a classic inside job.'

'Thank you, Arnold. I appreciate your concern. But don't take me for a fool.'

'Would I do that, Vitaly? We're friends, and anything I can do to help, lemme know. By the way, you got any kinda security forces in that canal? I mean, what type of guards and surveillance do you have up there?'

'Well, very little really. We've never had a serious enemy *inside* Russia.'

'Jesus, Vitaly. You gotta shape up. I'm telling you, this world's a dangerous place. Stuff happens all the time. My advice is to beef up security when you're moving expensive export submarines around.'

Admiral Rankov could, quite cheerfully, have strangled Arnold Morgan with his own huge, bare hands. But instead he just said, 'Thank you, Arnold, for your time. And, of course, you will understand my position when I tell you that I do not believe in your innocence.'

'I understand your position, of course. You must believe what you must believe. But I am genuinely sorry, and I would like you to try to count me out . . . please.'

'You're a terrible bastard, Arnold Morgan,' muttered the Russian, shaking his great leonine head as he replaced the telephone.

It was a call he knew he had to make. And the result was as he had known it would be. Morgan, deadpanning his way through the conversation, denying all knowledge, shocked that the USA should even be under suspicion.

And now it was time for Admiral Rankov to initiate a major investigation as to what, precisely, had happened up there in the Belomorski Canal. Right now his facts were sketchy. He had spoken to the Chief of the river police, who confirmed that the lead barge had tipped over first, followed by its adjoining articulated 'pusher' which housed the Captain and crew. The third barge had tipped the opposite way, moments later. The police Chief did not know whether the rear barge was in any way attached, but he thought not.

'Losing one,' murmured Admiral Rankov, 'might be just an accident. Losing two barges coupled together could be blind carelessness. Losing three, the last of them unconnected, must be, plainly, sabotage. Terrorism.'

And now he stood again, and paced the length of his office. Could it be the Chechens? Possibly, though there must be so many better ideas for them. Aside from the money, the real losers were China, not Russia.

'For sheer motive, I need look no further than the USA. Though I must admit I find that incredible. How could they have the nerve? How could they operate inside Russia, deep in the heartland, a long way from the ocean? How did they get here? How did they get explosive in? How did they get away? Where are the culprits now? Are they still here? Might they do something else?'

Admiral Rankov shuddered. The facts all seemed suddenly disconnected. And the clues were sparse. There was only one real thought in his mind. Morgan.

He decided to initiate his investigation before reporting the matter to the Deputy Commander-in-Chief of the Navy. And he called his staff lieutenant commanders, Levitsky and Kazakov, to begin making his lists. He told them to sit down with notebooks while he paced and dictated. Then they could go off and prepare a comprehensible report.

The situation around the disaster area was well in hand. The river police had cordoned it off for a radius of five miles. There were road blocks set up every two miles, and all vehicles, regardless of nationality, were being stopped and searched. Extra police were being drafted in from all the local areas. Navy frogmen were on their way down by helicopter from Severodvinsk. A naval commander was already on his way south down the canal with a full staff from the Northern Fleet, traveling in a small fleet support ship specially equipped for salvage operations.

A command operations center would be set up on board while a Navy investigation of the actual wreckage took place. Admiral Rankov ordered a list to be delivered of every passenger, and every crew member, on every tour ship and every freighter which had, in the past three days, stopped anywhere on Lake Onega. He also ordered an immediate survey of all missing persons in the area for the past 12 months. This he insisted would include a survey of every town and village, every tour ship, every local freighter and every military vessel which had been anywhere near those upper reaches of the Belomorski Canal. If anyone had gone missing, under any circumstances whatsoever, he, Admiral Rankov, wanted to know precisely who that person was.

He also wanted records pulled up of every foreigner who had entered Russia in the previous three months, and he wanted those records compared to every departure record. 'I want to know who's still here, where they are and what the fuck they're doing. All of them. Also make sure they check out departure records in reverse. If anyone's gone who apparently did not enter officially, I want that person traced, and I don't care where he lives.'

One of his lieutenant commanders ventured unwisely that such an operation was going to use up about a thousand people. The Admiral replied that he did not give 'one solitary shit if it took up 10,000 people.' He was going to find out, and *prove*, who had killed his Kilos. 'As if I don't already know,' he growled under his breath.

Back in Washington, fighting down an overwhelming desire to feel gratified at the obvious plight of the Russian Admiral, Arnold Morgan steadied his grim pleasure. And he told himself, 'This is an interesting contest. John Bergstrom and I have tried to cover all the angles. But there will be a lot of rabbit holes down which I expect Vitaly Rankov to run. I just hope they all come to a dead end.'

Right now, Admiral Rankov was digging out rabbit holes all over the place. His heels clicked on the marble as he paced back and forth, his face clouded, his tones urgent. 'Make sure we get lists of all ships which came through the northern waterways that *could* have been carrying explosive; check all radar surveillance for any unknown aircraft which came by. Get me lists of every single aircraft that came through Russian airspace in the vicinity of Lake Onega for the past two months.'

'Including passenger planes?' asked Lt. Commander Levitsky.

'Including every fucking thing that flies,' snapped Rankov. 'If a foreign power did this, I think we're going to find a few holes blown in the underside of the *Tolkach* barges. And I must ask how the hell that much explosive got into this country. No one in their right mind would have risked a train or a truck, or even a boat. The consequences of discovery would simply have been too serious. My instinct tells me that somehow, somewhere, the kit that was used by the saboteurs was air-dropped, but don't ask me how.'

'How much explosive, sir? How much d'you think it might have taken?'

'I'm not sure. But those barges are huge, they formed a 1,500-foot-long convoy. I suppose you'd want a charge every 50 feet to be absolutely sure they capsized immediately. That's a big consignment of explosive. It must have been air-dropped. There's really no other way, unless they planned it for months and months, and smuggled it in little by little, storing it somewhere up the canal. But I really doubt that. Too messy, too risky and too difficult to hold under tight control.'

'Sir, are you suggesting someone dropped 150 lb of high explosive out of a plane, and that a group of foreign frogmen found it, shared it out, and then got under the barges and blew 20 or 30 holes in them?'

'Well, I thought I was, but when you put it like that it sounds not so likely.'

'Sir, I was just thinking about the accuracy factor. Things that get thrown out of planes can go anywhere in a four-mile radius. You could have 15 or 20 men running round in circles for days trying to find stuff. Someone must have seen them.'

'Yes, I know,' replied Rankov. 'But we have no idea where the stuff might have been dropped. We don't even know *where* they attached the explosives to the barges. Remember, you can detonate a small sticky bomb anytime within one minute and 24 hours. They could have done it anywhere.'

'Not while the barges were moving,' said Lt. Commander Kazakov.

'No, not while they were moving,' said the Admiral, stopping dead in his tracks. 'The report says the Captain's son, Ivan Volkov, was the for'ard helmsman, and he's still alive, helping the river police up in Kockoma. Get him on the line, will you? Find out where they stopped. And anything else he has to say. We might just have to bring him down here to Moscow.'

'Of course, sir,' added Lt. Commander Kazakov, 'they might have fixed the explosive right back in Nizhny where the barges were stationary for several days . . . maybe using some kind of a special seven-day detonator.'

'They may have, Andrei,' replied the Admiral. 'But I think not.

That's too loose. Too much out of their control. Not knowing where the charges would blow . . . whoever did this was under tight control, and an accurate, long-delay, position-specific, underwater detonator, if such a thing exists, does not really fit the pattern, do you think?'

'No, sir. Not really. And anyway it brings us right back to the original problem . . . if this was done by a hostile foreign power, how did they get the explosive into Russia without anyone knowing?'

'Well, I heard the Americans may have one little invention that *no one* else has. I think it's made in California and it operates on a similar principle to those laser-guided bombs of theirs. I've only read about it in a Western defense magazine, so I've no idea if it's properly operational. But I think it's called HALO – High Altitude, Low Opening. It's a parachute system which allows a man to dive out of an aircraft at 35,000 feet and free-fall, homing in on a ground beam. At 1,000 feet his 'chute opens, and he lands exactly where they had planned. Takes a lot of training . . . I don't expect it would be so difficult to drop military materiel in canisters in the same way – homing in on a beam, rather than on a pre-set building or ship, like a bomb or a missile. I'm talking about dropping the canister, literally, from nearly five miles up, onto a target 30 feet wide.'

'Christ!' said Lt. Commander Levitsky. 'I didn't see that article, sir.'

'Well, I don't even know if the system is up and working yet, but it's a thought, eh?'

'Yessir. I'll get onto it, see if I can find more about it.'

By lunchtime on June 12, the *Yuri Andropov* was still anchored at the Green Stop mooring and the passengers were growing restless. Many of them had walked through the area with the crew in search of Pieter, the steward, Torbin, the headwaiter, and the five missing Americans. But there was no sign of any of them, despite several search parties walking within 30 feet of the two Russian corpses hidden in the shallows among the high reeds, under the flattened rubber hull of the lost inflatable outboard. The elderly Americans, too, had simply vanished.

Colonel Borsov assumed command of the search but realized he had a duty to his other passengers, and announced they would leave at 2 p.m. He called the river police and reported his seven missing persons. He was ordered to report in again when the *Andropov* arrived in St Petersburg, 36 hours from now.

By 1600 Admiral Rankov had a considerably expanded dossier on the disaster on the Belomorski Canal. The survivor, Ivan Volkov, had confirmed the precise location of the convoy's overnight stop across the lake from the entrance to the northern section of the canal. He also confirmed that the rear barge was definitely not connected to the articulated leading *Tolkach*. And he offered a first-hand account of the deep rumbling sound he heard beneath the barges, and then the more obvious sound of explosions beneath the waterline of the rear barge.

He had, he said, seen that final barge go over, hurling the submarine first into the bank, and then into the water. He added there was no doubt in his mind that the bottoms of the barges had been blown out, two on the starboard side, one on the port side. This had caused them to capsize, with swift and deadly effect.

By 1800 Admiral Rankov was back in his office after a meeting with the Commander-in-Chief and his political masters. To a man they were incredulous that the United States might have pulled off something of this magnitude, right in the middle of Russia. For the first 30 minutes they were inclined to believe it was simply impossible. But Admiral Rankov was insistent that, despite his denials, the US President's National Security Advisor was well capable of such an outrage, and was almost certainly behind the destruction of the Kilos.

In the end it was agreed that Admiral Rankov should pursue his inquiries vigorously, with the single objective of finding proof against the United States, and then hanging the USA out to dry, as lawless gangsters, in front of the entire world.

Admiral Zhang Yushu, Commander-in-Chief of the Peoples' Liberation Army–Navy, could not quite believe what he was hearing. But the naval attaché in the Russian Embassy in Beijing was in no doubt: the three Kilos which had left Nizhny Novgorod on the first stage of the journey to China had been destroyed in some kind of an accident in the Belomorski Canal. It was not an alarming situation. They had not been fired upon nor hit with a missile, nor even a bomb. They had simply rolled off the decks of the

Russian barges, and were, right now, resting on the bottom of the canal itself. The Chinese order, for those three submarines, at least, could never be fulfilled. Essentially, they were write-offs.

Admiral Zhang listened to the careful, emotionless words of the interpreter. There was no doubt whatsoever what had happened. The three Kilos, on their way up to Severodvinsk to meet Chinese crew and engineers, were never going to get there. He replaced the telephone and cursed silently to himself. The Kilos had, he knew, become virtually his own private domain since the loss of the last two. For there were many service chiefs and politicians in China who instinctively hated association with projects which might be going wrong, as this one most certainly was.

Zhang, however, was made of steelier stuff. The only thought he had was that the Americans had wiped out three more, as they had wiped out the last two. They had practically promised as much to the Russian ambassador in Washington. He knew that, because Admiral Rankov had told him so, months ago. There could surely be no doubt now. Washington, it seemed, was prepared to go to any lengths to prevent the delivery of the Kilos. Which put the Commander-in-Chief of the People's Army–Navy in very moderate shape politically.

The Paramount Ruler had made it quite clear that he was not interested in a fight of any description with the United States. He saw no reason to become involved in anything which would damage trade between the two countries; trade which was making everyone richer than ever before on the Chinese mainland.

Zhang knew he would get scant support from any of the military or naval leaders if he again suggested a strike of some description against the United States in justifiable retaliation. In fact the most he could hope for would be a green light to proceed with the delivery of the final two submarines, which he, personally, wanted. Desperately.

But first he needed to sort out the problem of the money. His government had paid a US$300 million down-payment on the three Kilos, with a further $300 million due on completion of sea-trials in the Barents Sea this summer, and the final $300 million upon their arrival in Chinese waters. The Russians were not going to be overjoyed at paying that first $300 million back. But those were the terms the Chinese Navy must demand. Only when that hurdle had been safely negotiated would Admiral Zhang feel he was safe in making further demands for heavy Russian warship escorts for the final two Kilos, all the way back to Shanghai.

Meanwhile there were, he knew, many of his peers who thought the Russian diesel-electrics were much more trouble than they could possibly be worth. In Beijing, the project would now hang in the balance.

And if the cautious elder statesmen prevailed, Arnold Morgan would, in Washington, be proved right. 'If you slam 'em hard enough, and seriously enough, they'll probably back right down, and just accept we're not going to let 'em have those submarines.'

Admiral Zhang knew, perhaps above all other men, precisely how hard they had in fact been slammed. And, like Admiral Rankov, he knew, beyond personal doubt, which nation had done the slamming.

In the days that followed, Admiral Rankov worked tirelessly in pursuit of an American mistake. He thought he was onto something when his sleuths discovered five executives of a big Florida citrus fruit company had entered Russia on a commercial jet through St Petersburg, but had apparently not left on the date specified on their entry visas.

He was not of course to know that the five Americans had left on a mysterious fishing boat on the very night of their entry, in the small hours, out of the little port of Kurgolovo, on a remote headland 80 miles east of the city. In time their passports and visas were to be utilized by five other Americans, who, between them, knew zero about growing fruit.

Then it came to light that the five Americans had indeed formally left Russia, only 24 hours late, on a private corporate jet from St Petersburg to London. There were, literally, no other US citizens in the last couple of months who had overstayed their welcome, nor indeed gone missing.

It was not until June 19 that something did come to light involving missing Americans. Apparently four men from the Minneapolis area, and a woman from Chicago, had disappeared from a tour ship, the *Yuri Andropov*, up in the northern reaches of Lake Onega. Furthermore they had done so two evenings before the barges had been blitzed in the canal.

Rankov discovered this via the US Embassy in Moscow, as a result of a formal complaint from the State Department in Washington, that five of their citizens had gone missing on some godforsaken Russian lake, and what the hell were the Russian authorities doing about it?

It was a classic Arnold Morgan preemptive strike, making the Russians nervous over something that was ostensibly their fault. The irritated tone of the State Department made everyone exceedingly jumpy at Moscow's Ministry of Tourism, and caused huge consternation among the shipping tour operators who wanted such incidents played down, to prevent the knock-on effect of notoriously edgy US vacationers canceling en masse.

None of this fooled Vitaly Rankov, who again sensed the hand of Admiral Morgan behind the fuss, and he immediately summoned the ex-KGB man, Colonel Borsov, to his cavernous office in the Kremlin.

The senior executive from the *Andropov* was more than helpful. He had met and spoken to the Americans, indeed it was he who had discovered them missing and ordered their suites to be searched.

'What kind of men were they?' asked the professional head of the Russian Navy.

'Old.'

'Old? How old?'

'Very old.'

'Like what? Sixty? Ninety?'

'Well, sir, I'd say one of them, Mr Andrews, was close to 80. He walked with a cane, very slowly. Mr Maklov was older, must have been 80, did not walk well at all, but he was a nice man. The other two were a little younger, but not much, both in their mid-70s. It's a complete mystery to me what happened to them.'

'How close did you get to them?'

'As close as I am to you, sir.'

'No doubt in your mind they were that old?'

'Absolutely none, sir. They were that old. I saw them often, twice a day at meals, once up in their sitting area, a few times in the bar.'

'Did they look like they might be good swimmers?' Rankov smiled.

'*Swimmers?* No, sir. They were old men, perhaps having the final vacation of their lives. They all had ancestors from Russia.'

'How about the fifth person in the party?'

'Oh, she was their nurse. Edith Dubranin. A woman of over 50, certainly. Looked after them all, told me she was from Chicago, worked in a big hospital there for many years.'

'Do you think there was a possibility they might have been terrorists?'

'*Terrorists?* I wouldn't think so. Two of them could scarcely walk across the deck.'

'Any theories about what might have happened to them?'

'No. None, sir. And we had a further mystery . . . two of our staff went missing on that voyage, up in the same place, our Green Stop on Lake Onega. These were young men, Pieter, the steward in the very busy stern coffee bar, and Torbin, the head waiter. They had gone out in a small boat, and have never been seen since.'

The crisp, factual replies of Colonel Borsov pleased Admiral Rankov. He had to accept the description of the Americans, and he willingly accepted the word of the *Andropov*'s senior executive that he would keep him posted the moment he heard anything about any of the missing seven.

He walked the Colonel out to the street, and on his way back along the stark, military corridors, he found himself piecing together the incontrovertible coincidences of the events on the *Andropov* on the night on June 10 and the events less than 135 miles away up the Belomorski Canal, 29 hours later. He had little choice but to accept the word of a former officer in the KGB: that the elderly Americans *could not* have committed such a crime.

As for the steward and the waiter, two men who had worked for the shipping line for over four years, both Russian citizens, well known to many people in the tour boat business . . . well, Vitaly Rankov did not suspect them of high treason against the State. But he would have them investigated, nonetheless.

Two days later, on June 22, another steward, from another tour ship parked up at the Green Stop, found the upturned inflatable outboard from the *Andropov*. He was driving an identical boat, carrying six American ladies, at $1 a head, on a short tour along the lake, when in the bright sunlight he saw the white engine about five feet below the surface, visible from the water but not from the land. He swerved in close, and dimly saw a name on the crushed rubber hull, too deep to read, but possible to grab with a boathook.

The steward sat in the boat, rising and falling from his own wake. He decided to drop off his paying passengers, and bring a couple of crew members out to conduct a salvage operation, and rescue what looked like an expensive outboard and inflatable hull.

They set off after 11 p.m., but up here in late June, the sun would scarcely set. Instead it would slip only inches below the northern horizon, and it would light up the sky in a bright rose-colored glow throughout the night. On European Russia's vast northern lake, the horizons are wide, and the skies spectacular. It is impossible to remain unmoved by what the locals call the White Nights.

The sharp-eyed wine steward, Alek, assisted by the main dining-room waiter Nikolai and the engineer Anton, made their way quietly through the shallows near the shore in one of the ship's grey Zodiac inflatables, with its 150 h.p. outboard ticking slowly over in low gear.

They were searching for the submerged shape of a similar engine to their own, still bright, white-painted, resting on the bottom, five feet below the surface.

The young Russians were armed with three sacks, and a couple of large boathooks. They planned to raise the engine, hide it in the hold of their tour ship, the *Aleksander Pushkin*, and then get it home to St Petersburg. They could dry it out, Anton could recondition it, and then they could sell it for possibly $4,000 – a sizable sum of money in Russia for young men earning less than $60 a week.

The trouble was Alek had not marked the spot with a landmark on the shore and it was taking a long time. But at least it was light. And at 15 minutes before midnight, Nikolai spotted it, bright beneath the clear water right in the shadow of the reeds.

Alek maneuvered them in close, and the other two locked the boathooks onto the engine, and heaved. It started to move, but not enough. It kept weighting itself back down to the bottom. 'The damn thing's attached to a boat,' said Anton. 'One of us may have to go over the side and free it up – we'll never pull the whole lot off the bottom.'

'Get going, then,' said Alek. 'I'm in charge of the boat, and Nikolai's the biggest and strongest of us . . . he's got to pull the engine in. I bet it weighs a ton.'

The 6 ft 3 in Anton, suspecting he had been awarded the rougher end of the stick, shrugged, grumbled a bit, kicked off his boots, removed his shirt, socks and trousers, and eased himself over the side into the cold water. He took a deep breath and somersaulted down to the white engine, spotting the problem instantly. The metal point of the casing below the propeller had gone through the wooden floor of the Zodiac, tipped over and jammed as it fell.

Anton went to the surface and told Nikolai to pull the engine into an upright position so he could free it. Then he went back under and pushed the engine clear of the thin wooden decking. By the time he surfaced, Alek and Nikolai were manhandling it inboard.

With the weight of the engine now removed, the deck and the rubberized hull began to float slowly upwards. Anton, hanging onto their own boat, kicked it away and slammed his foot down to keep his balance. As he did so he let out a yell of revulsion. 'SHIT! I'm treading on a dead dog or something . . . pull me out!'

Alek laughed, and said, 'It's just weeds. Lake water is full of plants and stuff.'

'Forget weeds,' replied Anton. 'I was treading on something furry and dead. Horrible.'

'Well, I'll show you what you were treading on,' said Nikolai, plunging his eight-foot extended boathook into the water and casting around for a 'catch.' 'Here, help me pull this up.'

Both men heaved again, and they felt whatever it was squelch free of the holding bottom silt. It was big, bigger than a dog, and it turned turtle as it rose, like a long muddy log. Except this log had eyes, white staring eyes, peering flatly out of the thick mud which covered the face and hair.

It was a slimy, oozing carcass from hell, its black-and-red sludged length decorated by a small gaping red scar, about two inches long, set like a thin hideous line of combat medals to the left of the central area of the chest.

Anton thought he might throw up; he let go of the boathook and turned away. But Nikolai was made of sterner stuff and he peered down into the water, making out the shape of another 'log' on the bottom, this one with a distinctive blue cast.

He seized the other boathook and grappled it around below the surface until it grabbed. Then he heaved a second body out of the mud, but this one did not turn turtle. It came up cleaner, with the muddy side downwards, and the discolored back of the denim jacket clinging tight to the corpse.

The peculiar aspect was that it was decorated with an identical stark, thin, red slit, but in reverse, about halfway down the back, on the left-hand side of the body.

It was as if, in life, the cadavers had fought some kind of a monstrous duel with long hunting knives. Or, alternatively, run into a skilled killer, who could extinguish life with the precision and correctness of an open-heart surgeon.

Alek and his friends had salvaged the dead Pieter and Torbin, and the river police were there inside 45 minutes. And the plot seemed only to become more obscure.

Colonel Borsov heard the news on his ship's telephone, and he called Admiral Rankov immediately to inform him that he now had only five people missing, rather than seven. The two crew members were accounted for.

Rankov was now truly mystified. In the back of his mind, he had considered the possibility that the two Russians might have murdered the old American men for their money and then taken off. He realized it was a somewhat outlandish thought, but it happened to be the only one he had at present.

Now he lacked even that unpromising lead. And there were yet more questions. Who had killed the crew members? And could the aged Americans have had anything to do with the wrecked Kilos? Admiral Rankov was beginning to think not. How could they? The submarine convoy had been parked three-quarters of a mile offshore, and the party from the Midwest was comprised of elderly tourists, not trained frogmen.

The Admiral decided this was a blind alley, but he wondered whether the gallant Colonel Borsov might just have been guarding his back when he was being so completely certain about the ages and infirmities of the four American men and their nurse. And he made a note to check out the backgrounds of all five missing Midwesterners. The Americans might conceivably have blundered in their cover story. But he *knew*, in his soul, that Arnold Morgan would have spun his tangled web too skillfully for that, and a dull feeling of despair settled in the pit of his stomach.

Nonetheless he elected to turn his mind to possibly more fertile areas. Like aircraft.

Before him was a list, a somewhat short list, of aircraft which had come out of the Arctic and journeyed south, high above the Russian mainland, down towards Turkey and the Arabian Sea, and indeed the Persian Gulf. Generally, these were aircraft from the west coast of the USA and Canada, taking the short cut across the North Pole to the Middle East. Rankov's men had turned up only eight of them in the past two months. All of them checked out, and all of them had arrived at their destination as recorded on their flight plan. Except for one.

The list in front of the Russian Admiral showed an American Airlines flight, AA294 out of Los Angeles on May 1 (Russian time), a Boeing 747, according to its flight plan bound for Bahrain international airport, right on the Gulf. 'Well,' mused the Admiral, 'Everything went according to plan as far as Russia . . . they arrived in our airspace on schedule over Murmansk at about 2230 – just a few minutes late – and then flew more or less straight down longitude 34 degrees. According to this they were at about 35,000 feet, making 440 knots, and never slowed down.

'However, according to our men on the ground in the Emirates, that aircraft was never recorded at Bahrain. And was never scheduled to do so. They did not have a Boeing 747 in there any time that morning. Not according to the records.'

The Admiral ran his finger further down the report. 'Here we are . . . American Airlines say they landed in Bahrain on time . . . the commercial flight was a charter for Arab businessmen . . . and they can't understand why the Arabs have no record of it.'

Surprisingly, the Russian agent had also provided a verbatim report of his phone conversation, in which the American official mentioned they couldn't 'give a shit one way or another, since the aircraft is safely back in LA . . . and why anyone should want to fuck around checking the unbelievably unreliable Middle East airport data beats the hell out of me. Sorry I can't help more. G'bye.'

'That,' said Admiral Rankov, 'is the end of that. The aircraft didn't even come to Russia. Just flew straight over. We don't have any rights here. And anyway we've no reason to think that Flight AA294 was doing anything more than transporting Arab businessmen, certainly not dropping explosives on to the shores of Lake Onega. That's a real dead end . . . I suppose it could have been a US aircraft heading for their Air Force base at Dahran, but there's no chance of getting anything out of them . . . Still, I'd never be surprised if that bastard Morgan . . .'

Every time the giant ex-naval intelligence officer came up with a possible lead, any lead, he seemed forced to discard it as either too unlikely, or just plain impossible. And yet he still sensed the hand of Arnold Morgan behind all of this. He was not done trying yet. But he was developing an uneasy feeling that he was never going to prove anything; that the birds he sought had already flown the coop. Leaving not a feather behind.

On June 24 an initial report came in to his office from the naval lieutenant commander in charge of the diving operation up in the canal. Work was slow, because barge hulls one and three were deeply embedded in the silted bottom of the waterway. It was hull two, the back end of the articulated *Tolkach*, the one which had flipped right over, which gave the evidence. The divers had found a succession of eight gaping holes, between four and five feet long, on the starboard side, right where the bilge keel joins the underside of the ship. They had been placed evenly, 50 feet apart.

'Neat,' grunted Admiral Rankov, scanning the rest of the report for information which he knew before he read it. 'Burn marks plainly showing . . . hull metal taken out with oxyacetylene under-water cutters and forwarded to the old KGB forensic laboratories in Moscow . . . results not in.

'And when they do arrive,' murmured the Chief of Russia's Naval Staff, 'they're going to say, "Semtex," and then, "Made in Czech Republic" . . . Neat, neater, neatest. Fuck it.'

It was now his duty to inform his superior, the C-in-C and Deputy Defense Minister, Admiral Karl Rostov, in strictest confidence, that the Navy *knew* the barges had been professionally blown up and sunk by persons unknown. The question would be, how to present this unpalatable truth to the people? If at all.

Vitaly Rankov understood it would, in the end, be announced as an accident, which would he knew be picked up by the international media, not as particularly major news, but nonetheless as news. He could deal with that. What he could not deal with was his vision of the gloating, complacent face of Admiral Arnold Morgan . . . *Now then, old pal, you gotta start thinking about beefing up your security. Stuff happens . . .*

'Jesus Christ,' said Admiral Rankov. It was the first time he had ever accepted the distinct possibility that the United States might actually get away with this. Just as they had got away with the destruction of the two previous Kilos.

Meanwhile he picked up the telephone and instructed Lt. Commander Kazakov to find out where the pathologist's report was, the one dealing with the death of the two members of the crew of the *Andropov*. Their bodies had been flown down to St Petersburg by the Navy, and there ought to be at least a preliminary view of the precise cause of death.

Lt. Commander Kazakov was back in 35 minutes with the faxed notes of the examining pathologist. The cause of death was identical for both men, heart failure caused by one single, dead straight incision between the ribs by a large knife-blade which almost cleaved both hearts in two. One entry was from the front, one from the back. The body which contained the frontal injury, that of the steward Pieter, contained more water in the lungs than the other victim. However, neither man drowned. They were both knifed to death.

'Classic special forces,' muttered Admiral Rankov. 'Just one wound. No mistakes. Professionals. Professional frogmen I'd guess. These two comedians from the *Andropov* spotted them, and were summarily taken out before the killers swam on out to the barges and placed their charges on the hulls.'

'Strange how I know so well what must have happened. Even stranger, that I don't have one shred of evidence for either crime. Just four geriatric Americans, two of whom can barely walk, and all of whom are even beyond the suspicion of a seasoned KGB officer like Colonel Borsov. And they're missing.'

The Admiral stood up and pushed his thick, wavy, dark hair back in a gesture of exasperation. He walked across the long room slowly, his heels metallic on the marble, like the ticking of a great unseen clock. 'I know,' he told his deserted office, *'everything . . .* and yet, I know *nothing.'*

However, Rankov was nothing if not a complete professional himself. He called in his two lieutenant commanders and ordered them to organize an immediate search of the lakeshore, fields and woodlands around the area of the Green Stop of the *Andropov*.

'Might we know what we're looking for, sir?' asked Kazakov.

'You may. I think we might be looking for five more bodies.'

'The Americans?'

'Uh-huh. I have a feeling this hit-squad which blew the barges

241

was seen by the two crew members, and possibly by the Americans. It is my opinion that the terrorists may well have taken out all seven people. Authorize search parties to go through the woods immediately adjacent to the lake, and to comb the shore, above and below the surface. Get Navy frogmen in there. If you had just killed four old men and their nurse in the middle of the night, in the middle of nowhere, and you were right next to a large lake, my guess is you'd dump the bodies in the water, weighted down somehow. But tell them to check the woods anyhow.'

Within three hours, a wide search was under way along the area of the Green Stop. Tour ships were moved on, the area was cordoned off, all along the shoreline, all along the dirt road and back into the woods. The river police Commandant, working in conjunction with two commanders from the Northern Fleet, who had arrived by helicopter, decreed that a line should be marked off, parallel to the dirt road, deep in the woods, more than a quarter of a mile from the shore.

At this the local police Chief objected, since the woodlands were 12 miles long and they were looking at a two-mile stretch. 'With five bodies to drag into the undergrowth, they're not going in there more than 100 yards at most,' he said. 'You draw that line a quarter of a mile in, we're looking at a search area of one and a half million square yards. With 100 men, that's 15,000 square yards each. But we only have 100 in total, and 50 of our men are working along the water. Therefore we have each of our land-searchers taking care of 30,000 square yards, all of it covered in bracken, dead leaves, trees and bushes. We'll be here till Christmas.'

'If we don't crack this, we might end up somewhere for a lot longer,' replied one of the commanders. 'Let's just keep going until someone tells us to stop . . . the classic old Communist way.'

The police Chief laughed. 'You're in charge,' he said. 'A quarter of a mile it is. Let's get in the woods. You want metal detectors used?'

'Not searching for bodies. Just rakes, forks and sharp sticks. I think in pairs is most efficient.'

'Yessir. That's our usual method.'

Nine days later they had found precisely nothing.

Which was scarcely surprising, since the searchers were, even at their nearest point, more than 7,000 miles from the still-breathing bodies of the missing Americans. Not to mention still three-quarters of a mile from the deeply buried, booby-trapped SEALs canisters, each one of which had, anyway, been thoughtfully metal-stamped by Admirals Morgan and Bergstrom, '*Made in Ukraine.*'

Admiral Rankov himself was almost disappointed. He had talked himself, for the moment, into believing they might actually find the Americans dead. But every instinct he possessed now told him the missing Americans were the hit-squad which blew out the Kilos. And those same instincts were telling him he was never going to find one shred of positive proof to shed a single ray of light on the catastrophe.

The next question was, should he hand this entire investigation over to the Military Agency in Moscow which specializes in terrorism? He would have done so without hesitation had he considered any nation had a motive. But there was only one nation which fit into that category. And the special forces which operate in deadly secret behind the Stars & Stripes did not count as terrorists. These were the US Army Rangers, or US Navy SEALs, and either one of them was way beyond the reach of any Russian reprisal, short of a shooting war.

Admiral Vitaly Rankov had never felt more utterly powerless. There could be no admission from the Kremlin of what he knew had happened. No possible confession from his already beleaguered government that special forces from the USA had attacked his country, way inside the borders. No disclosure that the old Iron Curtain was now made, essentially, of gossamer.

And he cursed the ground upon which Arnold Morgan walked.

It had been a black operation. And Admiral Rankov knew that black operations were specifically designed to leave no footprints, to ensure there was no evidence. That had been the case when the two Kilos vanished in the North Atlantic. And it was most certainly the case now. The Chinese had not as yet caused a huge fuss, but they wanted their $300 million back.

The Russian Admiral was a loyal member of the high command of the Navy, and he cared deeply about the service in which he had worked for all of his life. If the Chinese pulled out now, he knew it would cause shocking hardship in every corner of the Russian shipbuilding industry, and indeed among the Navy personnel.

The priority, he believed, must be to save the order from Beijing for the unfinished aircraft carrier in the Ukraine, and to come up with a foolproof scheme to deliver the final two Kilos to China. 'With some luck,' he thought, 'we might even get them to hold over the $300 million, maybe even roll over the order for more Kilos. Just as long as I can come up with a method of delivering them, without that fucker Morgan and his bandits sinking them first.'

He sat alone in his office, gazing at a large map of the Northern Oceans, those to the south of the floating Arctic wasteland which surrounds the North Pole. He looked again at the unfathomable areas where the surface waves rolled over a 12,000-foot depth. And he checked his calendar for the weeks when the ice would be at its northern summer limits.

And then he looked at the availability of the largest nuclear submarines this world has ever seen – the Typhoon-Class – built, he thought proudly, in the old Soviet Union, their own massive platform for sea-launched intercontinental ballistic missiles. No one, not even the USA, would monkey around with a Typhoon. It can operate under the ice if necessary, 1000 feet below the surface, and can smash its way upwards through ice 10 feet thick.

Admiral Rankov gazed with some satisfaction at the statistic he knew so well: this colossus of the underwater world packs the punch of nearly 40 torpedoes and antisubmarine missiles. Also it can run swiftly beneath the waves at almost 30 knots, powered by two massive nuclear reactors.

'Just let him try,' growled Admiral Rankov. 'Make my day. Just let him fucking well try.'

CHAPTER TEN

More than 300 relatives and friends attended a memorial service for Dr Kate Goodwin at St Francis Church, Brewster, yesterday. Dr Goodwin was one of 29 Americans presumed dead after the Woods Hole research ship, *Cuttyhunk*, vanished in the Southern Ocean off the island of Kerguelen 18 months ago. The principal reading was delivered by Mr Frederick J. Goodwin, the senior feature writer on this newspaper, and a first cousin of the deceased.

– Cape Cod Times, June 28.

THE SHARPLY WORDED MESSAGE summoning Admiral Zhang Yushu back to Beijing had a rare urgency about it. The regular helicopter flight from the Navy's Southern Fleet Headquarters at Zhanjiang, up to Canton, and then a commercial flight north, would not be fast enough.

Which was why the Commander-in-Chief of the People's Liberation Army–Navy, in company with his Southern Fleet Commander, Vice-Admiral Zu Jicai, were right now ensconced in a Tu-16 Badger marine reconnaissance aircraft making 500 knots, 40,000 feet above the Changjiang Lowlands.

Admiral Zhang had been obliged to commandeer one of his Navy's 700 aircraft and use it as a taxi, such was the tone of the words contained in the Politburo's message. Neither one of the two senior officers had any idea what was in store, but the meeting they must attend was scheduled to start at noon, and right now it was 0700. They were 800 miles due south of the Chinese capital, and the big converted bomber was flying directly above the central reaches of the Yangtse, where the great river threads its way through a sprawling network of inland lakes, dams, gorges and canals. Occasionally, from this height, the view of the waterways east of Sichuan is quite spectacular, but not today. Down below in the agricultural and industrial heartland of China there was torrential warm rain, and the Yangtse flowed muddily eastward, beneath lowering, gray clouds, its waters slashed by the downpour.

'What d'you think, sir? The submarines?' asked Admiral Zu.

The C-in-C was thoughtful. 'No, Jicai. I don't really. When all of this started we had seven Kilos trying to make it to China. Five of them have been destroyed, and the other two are not yet ready to leave Russia. I can't think of any possible development as urgent as this obviously is.'

'Well, if that's the case, it must be something to do with Taiwan. It seems to me, it's always Taiwan when the politicians get anxious.'

'That is undeniably true. But I'm not at all sure what this is about . . . Still, we'll know soon enough.'

'What happened about the submarine money?' asked Admiral Zu. 'Are the Russians cooperating?'

'Not much choice for them,' said Admiral Zhang. 'They could hardly expect us to forfeit our $300 million deposit on three Kilos which somehow fell off their own barges right in the middle of Russia.'

'Did we ask for cash back?'

'No, we just agreed to roll the money over for the final two, meaning we pay $300 million more when they arrive safely in Chinese waters, which completes the deal. Admiral Rankov is working on an escort program which he swears will be unbreakable, even by the American bandits.'

'Expensive for his government if they fail again, eh?'

'Very. They have agreed to repay the $300 million in full, if those submarines, for whatever reason, fail to arrive in a Chinese port.'

'Were they as reasonable over the loss of the first two in the North Atlantic?'

'Not quite. They held us to the letter of the contract. We'd paid $200 million down, with $200 million more due at the completion of sea-trials, which was deemed to be when the Kilos dived and left Russian waters. The last payment was due, naturally, when they arrived in Xiamen. Unhappily we had the second payment on an automatic transfer through the Hong Kong–Shanghai Bank, direct to Moscow on a specified date. We paid it, and three or four days later the Kilos were lost.'

'An ill wind,' said Admiral Zu.

'Yes. And the Russians were within their rights. They just said it was unfortunate, but they were not asking for any favors. The contract was quite specific. The sea-trials *were* completed successfully, and the money was theirs. They had, after all, built the submarines, and the "accident" was not their fault.'

'So we're out $700 million on the deal so far?'

'Correct. And if they do deliver the last two safely, we will have paid $1 billion for two submarines. Very expensive, hah?'

'Yes. But will we receive compensation, if the Russians can successfully prove to the United Nations that America was responsible?'

'Yes, we will. I personally wrote that clause into the new agreement. Russia will demand repayment in full – $1.5 billion for five submarines. We'll get our $400 million back. The Americans will also have a huge bill for reparations to the Belomorski Canal, and I imagine the Russian Government will demand colossal compensations for the loss of life – caused by deliberate acts of US piracy.'

'Will we claim damages for the 100 or so men we lost in the first two Kilos?'

'Oh, undoubtedly . . . If the Russians manage to prove anything, the Americans will be in serious trouble.'

'Any chance, sir? Does their investigation go well?'

'They say it's so far very successful. But those villains in the Pentagon are quite remarkably clever. My personal view is that nothing will ever be proved . . . I just hope that Admiral Rankov is able to get the final two Kilos here without further trouble. Then we will have five of them – almost sufficient for us to be very dangerous to any cruising American aircraft carrier. That's what I want – that's my ambition. The three Kilos we have are simply not enough. Two of them are in dock for repairs after a collision. The third is awaiting overhaul. We already have to depend on the Song-Class, which are unreliable at best.'

The big Navy aircraft, with its two solitary passengers, came lumbering into Beijing Airport shortly before 0900. A Navy staff car was out on the edge of the runway when it came to a halt. The admirals were on the road to the city within six minutes of touch-down. The aircraft refueled and left immediately for Canton.

Admiral Zhang told the driver to go straight to his official residence, where he and Admiral Zu would shower, change uniform and have some breakfast. He would like the car to wait and drive them to the Great Hall of the People at 1130. The Paramount Ruler disliked lateness, and he would make no exception even for two very senior military figures, who had raced 1,300 air miles from the southern borders of China that same morning.

They actually pulled up in Tiananmen Square at 1150, and were greeted by a personal Navy escort of four guards, who marched protectively, two in front and two to the rear, down the long corridors to the committee room in which the meeting would take place.

Inside the room, already seated, was the General Secretary of the Communist Party. He was next to the Chief of the General Staff and the two men were speaking to the rarely seen head of the central Chinese Intelligence Agency. The new Political Commissar of the Chinese Navy, Vice-Admiral Lee Yung, was also in attendance, in deep conversation with the East Sea Fleet Commander, Vice-Admiral Yibo Yunsheng.

Zhang and Zu arrived two minutes before the Paramount Ruler himself, and everyone stood as the great man walked in, accompanied by two senior assistants. He smiled and nodded his greetings to his most trusted colleagues. The eight armed personal guards who attended him at all times were already positioned in the corridor.

The Ruler wished everyone 'Good morning,' and said that he would like General Fang Wei, the intelligence chief, to address the meeting and to bring them up to date with a developing situation in Taiwan. Admiral Zu turned to his C-in-C and nodded discreetly as the General stood up and began to recount to the meeting the results of a report he had just received from one of his field officers operating under deep cover on the island of Taiwan.

It concerned the continuing disappearance of some of the most eminent nuclear physicists in the country, many of them attached to the permanent faculty of the most distinguished universities in Taiwan. Professors had suddenly vanished from such academic strongholds as the National Central University in Chungli; the National Chengchih University in Taipei; the National Tsing Hua University in Hsinchu; the National Chunghsing University in Taichung; even from the National Taiwain University in Taipei; and from Tamkang University in Tanshui.

'At first,' said General Fang, 'we noticed nothing. There was no information. No one knew anything. Not friends, colleagues, nor even relatives. But then we noticed that after two or three years, the professors were suddenly, quite inexplicably, back in their university posts, as if nothing had happened. And still no one could find out what was going on.

'Then,' he continued, 'about a year ago, I tried to tighten our grasp on the senior nuclear scientists and engineers, checking about 25 of the top men every 24 hours. And, sure enough, three months ago, two of them suddenly disappeared on the same day. They have, of course, never been seen since. And no one knows where they are. At least, no one is telling us.

'We did of course run all the routine checks — airports and seaports — and there is categorically no record of any of them leaving the country. But Taiwan is a small and surprisingly talkative place. It is not possible that these men remained on the island without *someone* knowing something. Nor is it possible for such people to disappear without relatives or friends bringing it to public notice . . . unless they've been told not to.

'And in this case, we had, at one time, a total of 11 truly distinguished Taiwanese scientists, all nuclear physicists, all missing.

'Now, as you all know, we have been aware of this situation, in various degrees, for several years — since we are always concerned that our irritating neighbor may take it upon itself to develop its own nuclear capability. But we have never had any evidence. And it's been very hard for us to pinpoint dates of departures and arrivals back. I should mention that the illustrious Professor Liao of the Taiwan National University has vanished twice, for about 18 months each time.

'Now, to bring you to my point: One week ago we were secretly informed that two of the disappeared professors, Liao himself and Nhung of Tamkang, would be returning to work two days hence. And we watched every incoming flight, every arriving ship. We checked every passenger list. And there was nothing. Then — by some miracle — the two professors arrived back at their universities exactly when our contact said they would.

'Needless to say, we were absolutely mystified. Where had they been? We decided, therefore, that their mode of transport must have been military, but there were no military aircraft or ships arriving from abroad at the appropriate time, barring only their submarines. And, sure enough, we were informed that a *Hai Lung* submarine had just docked at the Taiwanese base in Suao, three days previously, after an 11-week absence.

'That fitted our inquiry. It was the *only* ocean-going vessel which could possibly have brought the professors back at the right time. We then checked out its departure date, which was April 5th. And then we discovered a real coincidence. Remember the two professors I mentioned previously? The ones we had under surveillance, who disappeared on the same day . . . they vanished on April 4th.'

The General paused and gazed at his audience, before adding slowly, 'It is therefore my conclusion that the scientists are leaving Taiwan, and returning, by submarine. If we knew where the *Hai Lung*s were going, we would know where the nuclear scientists were.'

The Paramount Ruler nodded his head gravely. And when he spoke, he addressed Admiral Zhang. 'We do know something of the activities of the *Hai Lung*s, I believe?'

'We do, sir. But, I am afraid, not enough. We have established their sailing pattern – the 11-week tour of duty mentioned by the General is accurate. The *Hai Lung*s dive very quickly once out of the harbor at Suao and we have never seen them again until their return 11 weeks later. We have concluded their probable speed is 8 or 9 knots dived, and that they are covering about 200 miles a day. That would mean 1,000 miles every five days.

'However the real clue lies in the 11-week absence, which is far longer than any submarine would normally remain on patrol, *if it was local*. The sheer length of time rules out the possibility that the *Hai Lung*s are merely lapping Taiwan, or patrolling the Strait, or watching Korea. Otherwise they'd be back within about 60 days. The 11-week time span is what matters, because it means they are going far away, and they are getting refueled.

'In five weeks they can make 7,000 miles, possibly a little farther. We calculated one week on station and five weeks back. It appears to be a kind of shuttle service. The trouble is, when you are just a few miles out of Suao harbor, to the southeast, the Pacific shelves off very steeply to about 10,000 feet, and we have never been able to see which direction they are headed, because they run deep and silent.

'However, this new information about the scientists provides a support for the existence of a possible specific project, being conducted, most likely, 7,000 miles distant.'

'Well, perhaps you may think it is time we learned a little more,' replied the Paramount Ruler. 'Because I think it is becoming obvious that Taiwan is taking more than a passing interest in the development of a nuclear capability. The question has become quite sharply defined. How? And where? Where are they doing it?'

At this point General Fang requested permission to speak, and revealed yet another observation made by one of his field officers. 'As long ago as three years, we received a report that a local furrier in Taipei had received an order from the Taiwan Navy for a large number of garments, jackets, hats, trousers, and boot linings. All in fur. We checked that out again two months ago, and found that the order had been constantly renewed. One of our officers did track the crate from the furrier right to the submarine loading bay.'

'Which proves beyond doubt,' smiled the Paramount Ruler, 'that the submarines are either going to the cold north or the cold south, but probably not east or west.' Everyone else smiled also at the gentle wit of China's venerable leader.

'Sir,' said Admiral Zhang, 'I do agree we must find out what the Taiwanese are doing. And I am honored that you invited me here today because I think I may be able to assist with a plan. At least a preliminary one. I have considered the route of these two submarines on several occasions and I have always found the northern option the less likely of the two.

'I suppose they could be going up to the Aleutian Islands, which are very spread out and have some very lonely areas. But beyond there is the heavily patrolled Bering Sea leading up to the Bering Strait. Russians to the left, Americans to the right, and both of them in the middle. If I were seeking a clandestine place to put in place an undercover operation, it would most certainly not be up there, and it would not take me 11 weeks.

'Also there is no reasonable choke point on the north route where we could keep watch for the *Hai Lung*s . . . I am therefore drawn to the conclusion that we should bear the Aleutians in mind, but concentrate on the more likely prospect that the Taiwanese submarines are going south.'

'And what about choke points?' asked the Navy's new Political

Commissar, Admiral Lee Yung. 'Are there any which we can utilize?'

'There are several,' replied Admiral Zhang. 'The most usual place to keep watch would be the Malacca Strait, but in this case I'm inclined to think not . . . the Taiwanese submarines will almost certainly make their journey dived all the way and the waters through the Malacca Strait have a few tricky shallow areas. My personal view is that the submarines will run straight through the middle of the South China Sea heading directly south-southwest for 2,000 miles. Then, once they arrive in the Indonesian Islands, they will head almost due south between Sumatra and Borneo, arriving at the Sunda Strait – the water which divides Sumatra and Java – three days later. They can then run through there submerged, and make straight for the open ocean.'

He paused for a moment, allowing his naval officer's assessment to be absorbed by those less familiar with such journeys. Then he added, 'The only alternative I can see is a route past the island of Bali. There is a seaway, rather narrow, between that island and Java, but to be quite honest, I am not sure whether a submarine can make the voyage dived. I have not heard of anyone doing it.'

'Admiral Zhang, sir,' said the Political Commissar, 'you are surely not suggesting we wait down there and attack the Taiwanese submarine, are you?'

'Absolutely not,' replied the C-in-C. 'I am suggesting we might consider waiting down there, locating the first *Hai Lung* which comes by, assessing its course and speed of advance since it sailed. That would set us on an initial path to its ultimate destination . . . where we might find a lot of nuclear physicists involved in nefarious activities.'

'Would it be difficult to track it?'

'Impossible, without alerting them. But we could get a fix as they pass the choke point, with a new device we have been perfecting for several months.

'It's a little complicated but let me explain . . . We are all familiar with the Russian and American ELINT trawlers, which have fishing-boat hulls, equipped with very sensitive electronic interception gear – radar and radio. Anyone can spot them really. Well, we have been working on an ACINT system, which means acoustic interception, a highly sensitive listening device with passive sonar, brand-new, undetectable, carried below the waterline by naval trawlers. They are covert, and hard to identify as anything other than commercial fishermen.

'If one of those *Hai Lung*s passes anywhere near, we'll pick him up . . . and I'm going to suggest we move one down to Indonesia very soon and station it at the southern end of the Sunda Strait where we'll be patrolling, and ready.

'We'll know when it's due, because we'll let the trawler know the moment the outward-bound *Hai Lung* clears Suao. Since the distance is about 2,200 miles they ought to arrive 11 days later. We will of course be there very early . . .'

'What if he doesn't show up?'

'Then we check the Malacca Strait, then the Bali Strait, and if he doesn't show up there either, well, he's not coming . . . and then we have to turn our attentions to the much more difficult northern problem. But I don't think that's going to happen.'

'Tell me, Zhang,' interrupted the Paramount Ruler, 'where could they be going?'

'Sir, I am as ever honored that you should value my judgment, but in this case I am afraid I may be wasting everyone's time by speculating. I do have my chart book here, and I have marked out possibilities . . . I am more than happy to give everyone the benefit of my studies, but I have of course nothing certain.'

'I would like to hear of these places, Zhang,' said the Ruler.

'Well, the Taiwanese could be going to the islands of Amsterdam, or St Paul, which are 4,000 miles southwest of the Sunda Strait. And I suppose they might just make the Îles Crozet which are 1,800 miles farther. However, there are three places which fit rather better into our estimated five-week time frame: Heard Island, and, 230 miles to the northwest, Kerguelen, which is really a large archipelago of both large and small islands. The three desolate McDonald Islands lie 23 miles west-southwest of Heard. So far as I know, all of them are completely inhospitable, and without power of any kind, except for the French weather station on Kerguelen. The weather on each of them is shocking, and they are all ice- and snowbound for most, if not all of the year.

'If the Taiwanese are in the south, working on some nuclear program, they must be in one of those places. I must say, sir, I am nearly at a loss to suggest a way in which we might find them. They are without doubt the most remote places on the earth. Very nearly inaccessible; no airstrips. And really bad weather and sea conditions. You would need a nuclear-powered warship with a helicopter, and that would be noticed within a week of arrival.'

'Or perhaps a submarine,' said the Ruler.

'Yessir. A submarine would be helpful,' replied Admiral Zhang. But he did not look too convinced.

'I am somewhat at a loss,' said Admiral Lee Yung. 'How could the Taiwanese possibly have set up some kind of a laboratory in a place such as those you have mentioned, where there is no power and no buildings?'

Admiral Zhang answered, 'The power is not a huge problem, sir. You could use a nuclear submarine – its reactor would power a small town. No problem with a couple of very large generators.'

'But the Taiwanese do not have a nuclear submarine,' interjected the Ruler.

'No, sir, they do not. At least not one that we know about, or one which has ever been to Taiwan. However, there was much speculation a few years ago that they had bought one from France somewhat inexpensively . . . it was an old 2,500-ton Rubis-Class nuclear boat. I believe it was in 1999. But the story became a mystery: it was never delivered, and there was much conjecture that it had been lost on the journey. We never even had confirmation that it had left the main French Atlantic base at Brest.'

'Perhaps it just went straight to Heard Island and began its work as a power station,' said the Paramount Ruler.

'Perhaps, indeed, sir,' replied Admiral Zhang. 'But if it were not to be detected eventually, it would have to remain underwater for long periods and, to provide power for any facility ashore, it would also have to be moored underwater. Who could ever see it then?'

'Are any of these places on the shipping routes?'

'No, sir. Certainly not Kerguelen, or Heard or the McDonalds. None of them are even on air routes. They are basically just slabs of granite jutting up from undersea ridges. It's hard for me to imagine anyone operating anything from there . . . In my view, the sooner we are able get a trawler into the Sunda Strait, the better it will be. Then we can acquire some facts.'

'I agree with you, Zhang. And unless anyone here has some serious objection to this course of action, I would like you and Admiral Zu to develop your plan, and bring it back for our approval as soon as possible.'

The General Secretary of the Communist Party, whose office

entitled him to chair the Military Affairs Commission, nodded his assent, and everyone else took their cue from this most powerful Paymaster to the Navy. There was no dissenting voice, and Admiral Zhang Yushu confirmed he would take charge of the mission forthwith.

'I would also like to say, sir, that this makes the delivery of the final two Kilos even more pressing.'

'I wondered if that might be the case,' said the Ruler, smiling again. 'Tell me why.'

'Because, sir, if we find what we think we may find, behind some remote rock in the Southern Ocean, I imagine we will consider the possibility of an attack . . . and I would prefer to do so with our very best submarine. A brand-new Kilo would be perfect.'

'If we find what we think we may,' said the Ruler, 'there is not the merest possibility of an attack. My orders will be absolute. I want any Taiwanese nuclear laboratory, or factory, or any such facility, destroyed. I hope I make myself clear . . . Now, perhaps we should have some tea.'

'Yessir,' said Admiral Zhang, standing formally to attention.

The pressure on the CIA from the office of the President's National Security Advisor had been intense for several days now. Scarcely an hour passed without some new instruction, demand, or memorandum landing on the desk of the profoundly harassed chief of the Far Eastern desk, Frank Reidel . . . 'Admiral Morgan wants this . . . Admiral Morgan wants that . . . Admiral Morgan says, "Get in to the White House right now" . . . Admiral Morgan wants to know what the hell's going on . . . Admiral Morgan says if he is not told what those "fucking *Hai Lung*s" are up to within one day, heads are gonna roll.'

'Jesus Christ,' said Reidel.

In turn he had turned the heat up on all of his far-eastern field officers, especially those in Taiwan, who were permitted by the friendly government to operate almost at will, making their inquiries on behalf of the United States, freely, almost like journalists, which indeed a couple of them were.

There was, however, one place on the island of Taiwan where *no one* was permitted to operate, visit, or contact . . . and that was the Eastern Command submarine base out along the Sutung

Chung Road, which runs seawards out of Suao, a coastal town 33 miles southeast of Taipei, in Ilan County.

This road comes to a shuddering halt 300 yards from the post office. A big military-style gate, set into hundreds of yards of wire fencing, is manned 24 hours a day by armed police. No one is permitted past those gates without serious documents. Dock-workers who forget or mislay their pass are not admitted.

Frank Reidel's Taipei chief had two men in there, who under-took enormous risks for very little information. It was agreed that both of them would one day be 'lifted' back to the USA. Carl Chimei, the 44-year-old foreman on the submarine loading dock, was one of them. A deeply embittered man, he hated China and everything to do with it, including Taiwan. He had done so ever since his schoolteacher parents had both been murdered by Mao's Red Guards on the mainland 30 years previously. He himself had escaped the insurrection, and made it to Taiwan when he was just 18 years old.

He was probably the easiest recruit Reidel's men had ever met. He lived for the day when he would be flown to the USA. His wife and two children were leaving early next year, if not sooner.

But on this night, June 28, crouched in the shadow of the stacked crates on the jetty, Carl Chimei was in mortal danger. He had not returned home with his comrades, and his exit pass had not been stamped. Tomorrow, or even later tonight, he would attempt to talk himself out of that, or perhaps no one would notice. He had worked in the dockyard for 20 years.

But now he was petrified. Every 15 minutes, two armed Navy sentries walked within 10 feet of him, and 30 feet of the *Hai Lung*. If one of them saw him, he would be shot dead, no questions asked. Only the glorious thought of life in the USA, with a promised payment of $250,000 for risking his life on more than one occasion, kept him steady. In his hard right hand he carried a two-foot-long crowbar. But the crate he wanted to prize open was stacked 20 feet up, and he would have to work ferociously fast, with only the distant dock-lights to guide him.

He had the pattern of the sentries' patrol clear in his mind. They walked past the orderly pile of crates, and then hesitated at the light above the gangway to the *Hai Lung* which was moored alongside. Twice they had called out something to the guard on the casing of the submarine. They had then proceeded on down the jetty and it took precisely 15 minutes before they returned from the other direction. Carl had already decided to scale the crates while they checked the shore bridge to the *Hai Lung*.

And now he could hear the steady beat of their footsteps as he flattened himself behind the wall of crates. He closed his eyes, and willed his thumping heart to be silent, as the footsteps grew louder, and then began to recede.

Carl counted to 10, hooked the crowbar through his belt, and pulled himself up onto the rim of the first crate, three feet above the ground. They were unevenly stacked, so the climb would not be difficult for a hard-working man as fit as he was. But there were six more crates to scale and one mistake might prove fatal. He dug his fingers hard over the rim of the wood as he cleared the next two, and hung on nine feet above his starting point, his slim, soft work shoes jammed into the cracks between the cases. It took him three minutes to reach the top of the stack, and when he got there he could just see the red-painted letters he wanted: '*HAI LUNG* 793.' Expertly he jammed the crowbar between the lid and the wall of the crate, and heaved with short strokes to prevent the nails from squeaking as they came out. But the lid would not move.

Carl's fingers raced over the surface of the crate. And he cursed the two steel bands which bound it right around. He reached for his cutters, deep in his trouser pocket, adjusted them for size, and severed the two bands. He was appalled at the noise they made as they fell away . . . that twanging, sprung, metallic protest. He thought it would never die.

But now the six-foot lid of the case moved against the heave of the crowbar, and Carl wrenched it upwards and back, leaving it folded open. Seven minutes had passed, and he ripped at the waterproof wrapping inside the case. Then he tore through more plastic, before switching on his tiny pinpoint torch. The feel on his hands was soft, and furry. For a moment he thought he was touching a dead panda. But the light told him differently. He was looking at fur-lined clothes, and at the bottom were boots and hats. Carl knew what he had come for – and he knew that wherever those submarines were going was very cold indeed.

And now he heaved the top of the crate back into position, and loosely pushed the nails back in with the flat end of his crowbar. The trouble was, once more, the steel bands. He could cut them and get rid of them, but if he left them dangling, and ran for it, the break into the crate would be obvious in the morning.

He had only three minutes left before the sentries were due back again, and he decided to stay and clear up the steel bands, and hope that neither of the guards would look aloft as they passed.

Carl's luck held. The sentries came and went, and by raising the crate with his crowbar, first at one end and then the other, he was able to pull out the bands underneath, one by one, and then fold and carry them to the ground, like fully extended steel measuring tapes.

He cut them into smaller pieces and then dumped the jangling pieces into a bin. Tomorrow, with any luck, he would himself supervise the loading of the *Hai Lung*. For now, he just had to get away, and at 11 p.m. that was not going to be easy. Carl, however, was a senior worker, who had lived right in the town of Suao for many years. If he had even a halfway decent reason for being on duty so late, he would almost certainly get away with it.

And so he pulled on his jacket, picked up a clipboard full of notes and crate numbers, and marched straight down the jetty towards the road that would take him up to the Sutung Chung Gate, 800 yards distant. As he approached the guardhouse, the duty officer stepped out to meet him. 'Hey, Carl, what are you doing here at this time of night?'

'Ah, someone had misplaced one of those crates – we're loading tomorrow. At least the documents said it was misplaced. Took me five and a half hours to find it . . . in the wrong damned pile. I was so angry I've walked up here with all the stuff . . .' He handed it to the guard and said, 'Stick this in your office for me, will you? I'll collect it in the morning – if my wife hasn't killed me. We were going out to dinner.'

The guard laughed. 'Okay, Carl. I'll be gone by the time you get back. Tell the duty officer your worksheets are in my desk drawer. Here, let me stamp you out.'

The two men chatted for a few minutes more, and then the foreman walked off down the dark Sutung Chung Road towards the town, humming quietly to himself the National Anthem of the United States of America.

Frank Reidel had no real idea what the fuss was about. But Admiral Morgan had been specific. 'If you get any word whatsoever from Suao, let me know, right away.' It had taken Carl Chimei and his

CIA contact almost a day to get his message out, but they did so, from a safe house in Taipei, via Pearl Harbor, and then satellite to Langley. It read simply, 'Opened the box. Fur coats, hats and boots. Cold vacation for the Dutchman.'

It arrived at 1800 on June 29. Reidel opened up the secure line to the White House, and dictated to Admiral Morgan the 13 words which had come out of Taiwan. 'Beautiful, Frank,' said the NSA. 'I'm grateful.' Without even considering the possibility of saying 'Goodbye,' the Admiral slammed down the phone and punched the air triumphantly.

'That does it for me,' he said to himself. 'The Taiwanese are fucking around in Kerguelen. The distance is right. The time is right. The message from *Cuttyhunk* was right, except that the Japanese were Taiwanese. And my boys saw the periscope of a Dutch-built *Hai Lung* submarine, right there in Choiseul Bay. There are two questions: What the hell are they doing down there? And, do I give a rat's ass? The answer to the first is, I don't know what they are doing. To the second, I answer, Yes, I think I give very much of a rat's ass.'

He stood up and roared the word 'COFFEEEEEE!' to anyone who might be listening beyond the closed oak doors to his office. Then he glanced at his watch and placed a large cigar between his teeth. He lit it up luxuriously, using a gold lighter given him one far-lost Christmas by his long-departed second wife. He always thought of her when he lit his early evening cigar, and sometimes he wished things could have been different. But that would never be, since the former Mary-Ann Morgan was now happily married to a Philadelphia lawyer, whom the Admiral considered to be one of the dreariest men he had ever met. The fact that the sonofabitch had been his wife's lawyer in the divorce irked him still.

But he put the lighter away, and turned his thoughts to the frozen island at the other end of the earth, where Boomer Dunning and Bill Baldridge had seen what was obviously the Taiwanese submarine.

'Whatever they are doing is clandestine,' he declared firmly, as Kathy O'Brien, his secretary, brought him in a mug of coffee.

'Clandestine?' she said.

'Clandestine, woman, *clandestine*. Secret. Covert. Furtive. Surreptitious. Right?'

'Right,' said Kathy, a striking 34-year-old divorced redhead from

Chevy Chase, who unconditionally adored her boss. Not in any romantic sense, but just because she had never met anyone like him: so rude, so clever, so tough, so utterly respected by everyone. And yet he was so patient when he was explaining things. Even when he called her, in occasional fury, 'the stupidest broad on the entire east coast, including all of my wives,' it was somehow hysterical to them both. Admiral Morgan's method of delivering the most withering insult, with just a touch of real humor, was not much short of an art form. He was abrupt, tactless and discourteous to just about everyone. He had always been so, but only the over-sensitive, and the genuinely incompetent, had ever taken serious offence.

'Who's clandestine?' asked Kathy.

'The goddamned Taiwanese.'

'Why? What have they done?'

'Nothing yet. But I don't like 'em creeping around in a god-damned submarine when I don't know what they're at.'

'Well, why should you? America doesn't own them . . . do we?'

The Admiral smiled what he would call on other lips a shit-eating grin, and drew boldly on his cigar. 'Kathy, they are sneaky little sonsabitches.'

'Yessir . . . but what . . . ?'

As she spoke two phones began ringing on her desk, and she walked quickly back through the open door. And then the President himself stopped by. 'Morning, Admiral,' he said. 'Unofficial visit. How's things east of the Himalayas?'

'Hello, sir. Not too bad, but I'm darned certain the Taiwanese are hiding something from us which might be quite significant. They seem to be running submarines back and forth from the Southern Ocean. And if they're hiding something from me, they must be doing something wrong.'

'Well, what do you think they're doing?'

'I don't know. But when you have a small offshore nation like Taiwan, which exports more stuff annually than the whole of the Chinese mainland, you gotta watch 'em, just because they're so rich and potentially menacing. The place is awash with cash, and those submarines of theirs are up to something . . . down south, in a frozen hell-hole called Kerguelen.'

'How do you know?'

'We had a couple of sightings right among the islands, sir. But Kerguelen is a place no one would be, not on a regular basis, unless they were up to something. You see, it's so lonely down there they could not be on a military patrol, so they must be either on a supply run, or on some kind of an exploration project. I ought to know, but I don't. Also it's just possible they may have attacked and sunk *Cuttyhunk*.'

'The Woods Hole research ship that vanished?'

'That's the one, sir.'

'Jesus. Have you asked them about it?'

'No point. If they did it, they'll deny it. If they didn't, they'll just think I'm nuts.'

'Did they do it?'

'I think so. But I'm much more concerned right now with what the hell's going on in Kerguelen.'

'What kind of thing could it be?' asked the President.

'Well, you have to try to get inside the Taiwanese mind. Here you have a hard-working people who lived for centuries with very little. Now, thanks to the protective arm of Uncle Sam, they are mopping up riches which would have been beyond their dreams 50 years ago. Suddenly they have a whole world of their own to conserve and protect. I mean money, industry, a growing infrastructure, a population which hardly knows what poverty is. They have their own banks, their own culture, their own universities. They are 94 percent literate. Out of a population of 21 million, they have 500,000 students, a third of them studying engineering. They have their own armed forces. An Army and a Navy and an Air Force. They have taken their place right up there with the big hitters of the modern world.'

'Yes,' said the Chief Executive slowly. 'When you think about it, they really are in good shape. So what are they doing creeping around in submarines?'

'Sir,' said the Admiral, gently. 'As we all know, they have, just beyond their backyard, a hundred miles away, one fire-eating dragon called China, which is massively jealous of their success, and would like to retake them militarily if possible, and make them once more a part of the mainland, under strict rule from Beijing.'

'Which they would hate.'

'Correct. So right there you get a people who, deep down, are desperate to protect themselves . . . and worried that America will not always look after them. In any rising nation like Taiwan, you eventually get a government which will try to work out ways to protect themselves and their wealth.'

'Like a very big bomb.'

'Yes. But less dramatically, in the event of a sudden, successful attack by China, probably by air and then by sea, they would want to evacuate their senior politicians and military leaders. Those submarines we're attempting to track could be surveying remote areas of the world, with a view to constructing safe, luxurious hiding places. Fixing up communication systems.

'On the other hand Taiwan may have discovered China is up to something somewhere down in the Southern Ocean, and the submarines are prowling around trying to get to the truth.

'Or I suppose it is possible that Taiwan is trying to develop its own nuclear deterrent, which would be impossible in their own island. Someone would find out in about three days. Maybe they're looking for a site to open up a nuclear weapons plant. But that would be a hell of a thing to do in a place like Kerguelen, which is without power of any kind, and completely desolate . . . I guess if I thought about it, I could come up with a lot of schemes Taiwan could be up to, but right now I'm not sure . . . However, I am going to make a note to send a warship down there for a proper look around, soon as possible. And I don't mean a frigate, I mean a nuclear submarine, which can operate indefinitely, and can probe those long, deep waterways . . . maybe find something real interesting.'

'Sounds reasonable to me,' said the President. 'As ever, my short visit was highly instructive. Catch you later, Arnie.'

The big man left, and then Kathy made a short comeback. 'You need anything else, sir? I was wondering if I could go home now.'

'Okay. I'll put that down to a total lack of interest,' growled the Admiral. 'See you in the morning, and don't be late. If you see Charlie tell him to mark time. I'll be another hour.'

'Yessir.'

Arnold Morgan paced the room for another 10 minutes, trying to decide if the Kerguelen situation was in any way urgent. On reflection he decided not. The worst-case scenario was that the Taiwanese were making 'a fucking hydrogen bomb' in deadly secret, in order to obliterate China. But he decided that was barely credible. Whatever they were doing was probably going to take years, so he would file a report away in his computer, and he would remember to get a nuclear boat down to the Southern Ocean at the first opportunity.

Meanwhile he'd better check with Morris if there was any activity whatsoever on the last two of China's seven Russian Kilos, up in Severodvinsk. Because when they moved, the solids were going to crash into the fan, from all directions, 'and Rankov is unlikely to be so goddamned dozy this time.'

The Presidential Office Building, which stands imposingly in Taipei's grassy civic district, east of the Tanshui River, had rarely been under such strict security. Army guards patrolled the main street entrance and the foyer of the building. There were Navy guards on every landing and in every corridor. A whole section of Chungching South Road was cordoned off by the police. Traffic in the area was chaotic.

Out-of-town Taiwanese might have been excused for mistaking the date for October 10, National Day, when this area is literally swamped with rallies and military parades. But this was most certainly *not* the Double Tenth. This was June 29, and the reason for the iron-clad security was to be found on the second floor, where 36 guards, on both sides of three converging corridors, protected one locked room, in which there were just 10 men.

It was a big, carpeted room, containing two giant portraits of the late father-and-son presidents, Chiang Kai-shek and Chiang Ching-kuo. Below their benevolent gazes sat the current President and his Prime Minister, Mr Chi-Chen Ku, Head of the Legislature. Surrounding them were the Head of the Ministry for Foreign Affairs, Mr Chien-Pei Liu; the newly appointed Minister for National Defense, General Jin-Chung Chou; and the Chief of the General Staff for the Republic of China Navy in Taiwan, Admiral Shi-Ta Yeh.

Essentially these were the men being so vigorously protected. But there were five others in attendance, who were also not without their enemies. There were two senior professors from the National Taiwan University, both nuclear scientists, George Longchen and Liao Lee. There was one of the biggest construction moguls in Taipei, Mr Chiang Yi, plus two military men: one the commander of the Amphibious Regiment attached to the Marine Corps' 66th Division; the other a submarine captain.

Both of them had flown up earlier that morning by helicopter from the great Taiwanese Navy Base of Tsoying, Headquarters Fleet Command, Headquarters Naval Aviation, Headquarters Marine Corps, home to the Taiwanese Naval Academy. This is a relatively small, shielded place, standing quietly in the suburban shadows of Taiwan's second city, Kaohsiung, the fourth largest container port in the world. But to military men, Tsoying stands defiantly, housing the offensive and defensive capability of its motherland, right on the Strait of Taiwan; right on the sloping southwest coastline of this stubborn island, which faces China head-on. It is a place so secret, so mysterious, it is not even mentioned in the national guidebooks.

The real reason for the security on this sweltering late June morning was not so much the eminence of the politicians and the senior commanders, nor even the vast knowledge of the other visitors. It was their combined knowledge, in a city crawling with Chinese spies, in which no restaurant, no barber's shop, no laundry, no taxi was free from suspicion.

And today was a particularly secretive day. These 10 men, bound together in the greatest national security program in the whole history of Taiwan, met rarely. Today was the day. The first time for two years. It would be referred to hereinafter as the June Conference. But only among themselves. No secretary, no assistant, military or otherwise, would be admitted to the privacy of the agenda. The President had chosen his team well. After five years of operations, not one word of their astounding activities had leaked out. At least, not in Taiwan it hadn't.

The meeting was one hour old, and the 46-year-old millionaire builder Chiang Yi was concluding his report about the safety and continued steadiness of the huge network of tunnels his men had dug into the base of the shoreline rock below the 3,000-foot Guynemer Peak, right at the sheltered western end of the eight-mile-long Baie du Repos, Kerguelen. The massive concrete columns, two feet in diameter, supporting RSJs, were holding up perfectly. They had all been made on site, from concrete mix transported south by submarine.

All through the year-long drilling operation, Chiang had stayed on station, supervising the removal and clearance of thousands of tons of granite rubble, the mechanical diggers dumping it straight over the side into 300 feet of water. All power requirements were met from the nuclear reactor on board the 2,600-ton Rubis-Class French submarine, *Émeraude*, which had made the journey from

Brest to Kerguelen without surfacing once. Today it was moored underwater, where it had been for five years, between two old, rusting gray buoys, spaced about 400 feet apart, 50 yards off the western lee shore. Only occasionally did the *Émeraude* ever come up for stores or ventilation.

Its reactor was still running sweetly, powering with ease the generators in the 180,000-square-yard factory/hotel: its lighting, its heat, its water convertors, its air intakes, and all the tunneling machinery. It also powered the electrical systems for the future Pressurized Water Reactor, which would ultimately replace the Rubis itself.

The aging Rubis was indeed the workhorse of the entire project. Because, above all, it powered the 50 big metallic 'spinners,' the gas centrifuge systems which would slowly, laboriously, breathtakingly expensively, over a period of years, separate Uranium-238 from Uranium-235, that most sinister element, with its highly unstable nucleus . . . the bedrock of a nuclear warhead.

Chiang had been priceless to the Taiwan Government. When the 'cavern' and tunnels were finally completed, and the electricity, air and water lines laid down, he returned to the Baie, and spent yet another six months personally supervising the building of the U-235 plant, and the preparation for the PWR itself, and the protection of the workforce from its lethal contents. He actually drove the big mobile concrete mixer himself during the construction of the long jetty. For this he designed a special slate-gray, automatic steel curtain which would cover the docking area when it was not in use. For all of this Chiang Yi would accept not one penny for the labor of either himself or his men – though he would forever have the pick of all government building contracts in Taiwan.

Chiang's report today pleased everyone in the locked room in Taipei. There were no stress fractures. All systems were perfect, and even the richly carpeted bedrooms for the professors were still in excellent condition. The two Dutch submarines, which brought in their supplies every three months, made living bearable if not luxurious. But the tours of duty were long, the work slow and difficult, with little time for recreation. No one looked forward to returning for a second 18-month spell. But each of the professors was paid a half-million-dollar bonus for their time. And no one had ever refused to work for the Taiwan nation, deep inside the deserted island at the end of the world.

In winter, conditions were, of course, appalling. It was light for only a short while every day, and the weather was so vicious, it was impossible to walk even for a short distance on the rare occasions anyone was allowed out. The so-called summer was slightly better, but it was dangerous to move far from the base, because the howling gales could bring raging 70 m.p.h. winds screaming up the fjord in moments, sometimes accompanied by sleet and even snow. The katabatics, the fluke circular winds which swing off the tops of the mountains and then 'suck under' like a wind-tunnel, from an unexpected direction, were able to frighten even experienced ocean navigators operating inshore.

The President of Taiwan, nominally the Commander-in-Chief of all the Republic of China's armed forces, now thanked Chiang Yi formally for his report, and spoke to the gathering carefully. He reported that twice in the previous 12 months, the Navy of China had brought warships very close to Taiwanese coastal waters, in a gesture which everyone had perceived to be threatening in the extreme. There had been two further outbreaks of live rocket tests, each one involving the firing of the lethal HQ-61M surface-to-air missile from a Jiangwei-Class frigate. All designed to intimidate. The Chinese, he said, had continually sent destroyers and frigates in close to the Spratly Islands – the 53 rocks, shoals and reefs in the South China Sea which Taiwan claims as its own, and indeed occupies with a military force on the largest of the islands.

'We do, of course, enjoy the theoretical support of the United States in these matters,' said the President. 'But in the past two years we have been singularly unsuccessful in our efforts to build up our own submarine capability. We have tried to order from the French, the Dutch, the Germans . . . every time we have an acceptance from the shipbuilders, the project is overruled by the respective government. They are, quite simply, afraid of damaging their own trade relations with mainland China, and will not supply us. Even the Americans will not sanction a submarine sale to us. Nor will they provide us with their Aegis missile system, even though they *know* we constantly face the known threat of a massed air attack from mainland China. We are within range of their fighter-bombers.

'Therefore, I conclude, we *must* make our own arrangements. These military exercises by China are nothing less than a threat to us, letting us know that if they so wished they could blockade the strait with a surface and submarine force. This threat, in my judgment, is ever present.

'Gentlemen, as I have said so many times before, we cannot count on the USA to help us. Things are changing. The USA may one day value China more than it values us. A new American President may feel his armed forces have no business whatsoever engaging in military adventures in the Far East. Who knows what they may conclude?

'During my time at Harvard, I learned much about American flexibility. It is a nation which will adjust its views as the tides of history ebb and flow. You will doubtless recall that in the late 1980s Saddam Hussein went from America's Great Stabilizing Hero of the Middle East to Public Enemy Number One in less than three years.

'Gentlemen, I have said it so many times. If we are to resist China's attempts to bring us back into their fold, which means we would be occupied by them, militarily, we must have the means to frighten them. And since the West will not sell effective military hardware to us, the only way we have to guarantee our survival *is to possess our own nuclear deterrent*. This is not a weapon of war. It is a weapon of peace. It will not be used, but it will always be in the back of the minds of the mainland's politicians, and indeed the Chinese military commanders, that if Taiwan was pushed against the wall hard enough, we have the ability to unleash a weapon of such terrifying power, it could obliterate a major mainland city in one strike.

'No one has ever used such a weapon, not since Hiroshima. And I doubt anyone ever will. And that is why even the most powerful military forces in the world have contented themselves during the last half-century with minor wars, skirmishes . . . nothing on the grand scale with hundreds of thousands dead. This is simply because no one dares. Gentlemen, I say to you again, there is nothing more important to this nation than our nuclear project in the southern Indian Ocean.

'I owe a personal debt of gratitude to all those of you who have contributed to this work, but my own debt is as nothing, compared to the debt the Taiwanese people have to you all. And now, as always, I am most anxious to hear of our progress, and perhaps Professor Liao, who we know has recently returned, would enlighten us . . .'

The nuclear scientist from the National University, a man in his late 50s, small in stature, and dressed in the tweed jacket, checkered shirt and club tie beloved of teaching intellects the world over, climbed to his feet and bowed to the President. His news was careful to the point of pedantry. He spoke of the extreme difficulties of making a fission bomb, and the endless time it takes to produce the elusive isotope of uranium, U-235, the isotope used in nuclear power stations, in which weapons-grade plutonium can most readily be made.

For the benefit of the two visiting military men and the politicians, he explained briefly the process of turning the heavy metal into a gas, and then trying to 'spin off' the weightier 90 percent in order to leave the invaluable U-235. 'To achieve this, the process has to be long, slow, painstaking and precise,' he said, 'but, at last, we are getting there. We have now achieved solid production . . . sufficient Uranium-235 for our first core for the PWR, which we should have in six months.

'This is not yet sufficient to build a nuclear warhead, and it is an incredibly long process. But we have the designs, and I estimate we will be transporting our first untried warhead back to Tsoying in three years. I doubt we'll ever be in a position to test them, but we are making steady progress. Professor Longchen, as you know, is returning to Kerguelen in November . . .'

The President smiled. But it was not a smile of triumph. It was a smile of relief, for here was a man who lived on the edge of his nerves every day, wondering what the military dragons on the other side of the strait were planning. He dreamed of the day when he could make it known that *any* nation threatening Taiwan would in future do so on equal terms, and that Taiwan was a match for any aggressor, even one like China, with its burgeoning Navy 285,000-strong, manning 140 major warships, and 450 fast-attack craft. The nuclear warhead, pondered the President, was the world's great equalizer.

And now he turned his attention to the question of security in the waters around Kerguelen, and he called upon the Marine Commander, who had spent four years in Kerguelen, both organizing the security system and setting up the military surveillance post, deep down the fjord at the head of Baie Blanche – eight miles north of the laboratory, high on Pointe Bras.

'It is a very lonely place down there, sir,' he said. 'Except for a rare deep-sea fishing vessel, none of which came anywhere close to us, we did not see one single vessel, except our own, in the six months from November to June. According to my records, the only boat *anyone* saw was there one morning last February . . . some Australian-registered yacht, probably sheltering from the weather in Choiseul Sound. We never saw it, but the *Hai Lung* did. Through the periscope. It was gone by the afternoon.'

The President nodded. 'No further incidents like that most unfortunate business with the American ship 18 months ago?'

'Nossir. Nothing like that. We simply have not seen a ship in the fjord . . . no ships whatsoever.'

'Commander, I believe you were personally involved in that incident?'

'Yessir, I was.'

'Unhappily, the Americans made a huge fuss about it. I expect you know?'

'Nossir, I did not.'

'Oh yes. The US State Department contacted several nations, including ourselves, Japan and South Korea, and even, I believe, mainland China. They were extremely anxious about the fate of their research ship and its crew. They actually sent a warship from the Seventh Fleet to Kerguelen.'

'Yessir. We saw that. It was there for several weeks, and once it did come right down Baie Blanche. But it turned away at the last minute. We were watching it from Pointe Bras.'

'I understand you did open fire on the American research ship. What would you have done if the warship had proceeded right down Repos and come to a halt outside the laboratory?'

'I am uncertain, sir. We have no contingency for such a circumstance. I don't think it ever occurred to anyone that any warships would ever visit us. We obviously could not have taken on a fully armed American naval frigate. That would have been suicide. I imagine we would have tried to reason with them about our intentions, and then attempted an evacuation, if we had a chance.'

'Yes. I suppose we have to accept that in those circumstances we would have to use diplomatic means . . . However, I have always been profoundly concerned that we did open fire on the crew of that research ship.'

'Sir, we boarded it, just when it came in sight of the two buoys which secure the nuclear submarine. I was in command, and my intention was to turn the ship away peacefully, on the pretext that we were conducting some secret experiments in the fjord, and that we had not informed the French Government. Therefore we would prefer not to be disturbed. I am sure you will understand we could not afford the Americans to come any closer . . . they would have seen the dock, which was uncovered at the time.

'However, my men were very agitated. And then one of the Americans came around the bulkhead with a machine-gun and opened fire on us. He shot and killed three of my men before we could move. I personally answered his fire . . . but not before he killed another of us. Then the situation deteriorated. We had to stop their radio operator, and with four men already dead . . . well, I am afraid my men killed the radio man, and the captain, and his number two and anyone else who looked like an enemy.

'By this time, several other members of the crew were also armed. It took us another hour to subdue the ship. We lost a total of six men, with two more slightly wounded.'

'How about the Americans?'

'There were no survivors from the crew, sir. And I am afraid we may have killed one or two passengers. Plainly we were not able to leave any of them alive to tell their story.'

'Quite. But I did understand there were some prisoners.'

'Yessir. We found a small group of scientists in a cabin below. They were unarmed and very frightened. I could not bring myself to have them shot in cold blood. I am a soldier, not a murderer.'

'You took them prisoner?'

'Yessir. We towed the ship into a small cove, slightly beyond the main entrance, and secured it under a curtain overhang. Then we collected every document, every scrap of paper from the ship, and burned everything.

'The generators and engines still worked and we just kept her running, the same as the nuclear submarine. We had plenty of fuel, and food. And it took just one guard to ensure they remained aboard. I thought the best thing would be to keep them incarcerated, until we eventually close down the facility and leave the island. So far as I know, none of them knew who we were, nor what we were engaged in. We did interrogate them, and none of them even knew *where* they were.'

'I see. Presumably they are still in the ship?'

'Yessir.'

'It will be difficult to release them.'

'Yessir. But you will recall, sir, that some of those Middle East terrorists incarcerated some quite eminent people for years on end, and were mostly not caught, because the hostages did not know where they were. I have been telling myself this is precisely our situation . . . I am, sir, most reluctant to have unarmed, non-military US citizens put to death for no reason.'

'No doubt. But if anyone ever found out, the consequences would be monumental. The United States Government would react violently to public opinion. It may be better to dispose of them.'

'Sir, I have spoken to my superiors about this matter. And I do not think any branch of the Taiwanese Armed Services would be anxious to carry out such executions.'

'Admiral Shi-Ta?'

'Nossir. That is not an order I would wish to issue. It would be different if the prisoners were in the military.'

'I too think the execution of American civilians is a very bad idea. And I accept the wisdom of my commanders. We must, however, think long and hard about the method of release, when the time comes. Although they do not know *who* we are, or *where* they are. Which is to our advantage.'

'Yessir.'

'Meanwhile, do we have any contingency plan, should a Chinese warship come visiting?'

'Nossir, we do not. Though in that case I believe we would *have* to sink it, instantly.'

'Yes, I'm inclined to agree with that. Which would mean we might need another submarine down there, which we do not have . . . Admiral, I think we should discuss that, with General Jin-Chung, at the conclusion of this conference.'

'Sir.'

And now the Captain of the *Hai Lung* was summoned to give his report, which was brief and efficient. There had been no problems with either submarine; they were running down to Kerguelen submerged, right on time, and had become experts at sliding into the fjord still underwater, and not coming to periscope depth until they were well down Repos.

The tactic of using the submarines as freighters was also working extremely well, particularly in the transportation of the unrefined Uranium-238, which was relatively easy to obtain, even while avoiding the international supervisory bodies. Packed in specially designed lead and polythene canisters, the radioactive uranium was thus transported in the safest possible environment – underwater, where it was undetectable from any form of surveillance, on or above the earth.

The meeting broke for lunch at one, and tea was brought in, served in the most beautifully painted china, which looked a lot like Royal Doulton, but was, unsurprisingly, made in Taiwan.

The President stood by the window with his Foreign Minister, Chien-Pei Liu, and the two men were thoughtful as they stared eastward beyond the spectacular gardens which surround the wondrous architecture of the Chiang Kai-shek Memorial.

There was so much to protect here in this scenic, mountainous island, where the glorious rivers flow with money, and the great oceans wash billions of American dollars into the economy each year. 'Here in Taiwan we are on the verge of creating the world's first genuine Shangri-la,' he said. 'We have opportunities which no nation has ever enjoyed, not in the entire history of this world . . . and only one nation stands in our way. I pray we will be in time to frighten them off for good.'

He was not, of course, to know that China was keenly aware of precisely what he was up to – although Beijing did not know where. Neither did he realize that America knew precisely *where* he was up to something, although they did not know *what*.

CHAPTER ELEVEN

A WARM, SUBTROPICAL RAIN swept across the narrow two-mile-long causeway which leads out to China's island seaport of Xiamen. Hunched against the stiff, offshore sou'wester, all alone, strode the unmistakable figure of Admiral Zhang Yushu. He was bareheaded, wearing dark blue foul-weather gear, and without his customary horn-rimmed spectacles. It was 0700, and the overcast sky and rain stretched all the way to the eastern seaward horizon, beyond which lay the rebel island of Taiwan.

Occasionally a passing worker on a bicycle would nod to him in greeting as he pedaled past. The Commander-in-Chief of the People's Liberation Army–Navy was a familiar sight around Xiamen, particularly in the summer months when he and his wife and family tried to live a normal life in their big villa on Gulangyu Island, which lies right at the front of the town, across the Lujiang Channel, the Isle of the Thundering Waves.

Out here, in this lush green suburb of the busy seaport, Admiral Zhang was in the land of his boyhood. Not the villa of his boyhood, for that was not much more than a dockside shack. But in the setting of his boyhood. Admiral Zhang had been born right here in these waters, on his father's elderly freighter. He was on deck before he was ever on land, but for as long as he could remember, right back to his schooldays, he had loved the long walk along this rocky causeway from the mainland, with the sea on either side, and the lazy, gaff-rigged junks in the distance, making their way ponderously across the mouth of the Nine Dragon River.

When his father had died and the still-valuable ship was sold, the young naval officer had invested the money in a broken-down property on the nicest side of Gulangyu overlooking the rugged coastline of the Strait, close to the southern beach. Over the years he had improved it, building a beautiful house with a curved red roof, set amid abundant trees and flowers. Now, should he ever

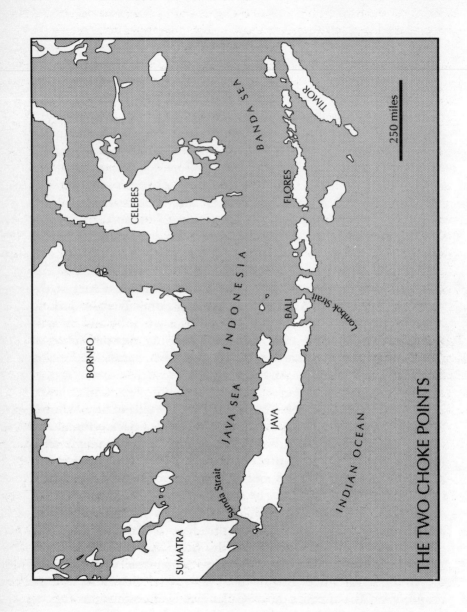

THE TWO CHOKE POINTS

BORNEO

CELEBES

SUMATRA

INDONESIA

JAVA SEA

JAVA

BALI

FLORES

TIMOR

BANDA SEA

INDIAN OCEAN

Sunda Strait

Lombok Strait

250 miles

274

sell, the proceeds would make him a relatively rich man. His wife, Lan, whom he had met at university, was also a native of Xiamen, and their dream was of retirement here, deep in South China's green and mountainous Fujian Province, home to both of their families for a thousand years.

Zhang had much for which to be grateful to the Navy – not least that they had thoughtfully maintained a major naval base right on the edge of Xiamen, a base which was equipped to deal, additionally, with submarines, and where he had established a summer office. Each morning a naval launch arrived at the Gulangyu dock, to ferry the C-in-C to his place of work in the Xiamen base. For the remainder of the year, he and the family lived in Beijing.

In the early hours of this morning, July 21, he had made the eight-mile journey down to the causeway by ferry and car, especially to walk its length and back. It was a place where he could think, where the fresh ocean breezes would clear his mind, where he would be undisturbed for one hour. The Admiral walked like a marching army, illusively fast.

His task today was of such a highly secretive nature that he had elected to spend two hours at his villa, from 0900, with the Southern Fleet Commander, Admiral Zu Jicai, to put in place a plan to nail down, once and for all, the precise destination of the vanishing Taiwanese *Hai Lung*s. It was obvious to him that the government across the strait was in the process of creating its own nuclear deterrent. The question he must answer, on behalf of his great mentor and supporter, the Paramount Ruler, was where? And to do that he must find a way to track Taiwan's two clandestine submarines.

And now he walked more determinedly than ever, ignoring the sheeting rain. He splashed along the road in his seaboots, with a face reflecting the thunder that rolled up the coast from the southwest. The key to the journey of the *Hai Lung*s rested, he was nearly certain, in the endless archipelago of islands that form Indonesia. The submarines plainly made their entire journey dived, and they must have found a way to travel out into the Indian Ocean, right past Malaya, Borneo, Sumatra, Java, Bali and the rest, without being driven to the surface by shallow waters.

He had already studied and written off the possibility of the Malacca Strait: too shallow in parts; too busy; and it would be too difficult to avoid detection, running through the myriad shoals and islands which straddle the waterway to the southeast of the great port of Singapore. Last night, when he had first arrived back from Beijing, he had spent an hour in his office trying to confirm the less obvious strategy of running down through the Sunda Strait, the 13-mile-wide channel which divides the northwestern headland of Java from the southeast coast of Sumatra.

It was just deep enough, 180 feet in the channel, but there were several shallow areas. It was also a busy ferry route, and the charts featured warnings of submarine exercises by the Indonesian Navy. 'If I were a Taiwanese submarine CO, on a secret mission, I would probably not go through there,' he had decided. 'I would find another gap.' But the Admiral had been too tired to proceed further, and he decided to go home and sleep, then walk the causeway, and then approach the problem anew in the morning, fresh of mind and spirit, with his friend Jicai. He had not counted on the driving rain, but he would not let that stop him.

And now he ploughed forward, on this muggy, rainswept early morning, head down, arms pumping, relishing the exercise, and plotting in his mind the possible destruction of some distant Taiwanese nuclear weapons factory, which was a mystery right now, but not for long. Not if he had his way.

He had almost reached the island end of the causeway, and as he walked he could see four men sitting in the lee of the side wall, beneath a large umbrella, playing cards, with a bottle of whiskey between them. 'Gambling,' he muttered disapprovingly. 'What a weak-minded pursuit, relying on chance. That's no way to run anything.' But at least tradition was on the side of the little scene by the wall. The Chinese did, after all, invent umbrellas, and playing cards, and whiskey. And they were not too bad at walls either.

Admiral Zhang himself was a traditionalist, one of those obdurate Chinese thinkers who believed implicitly that his country represented the very bedrock of civilization. It was the cradle of scholarship, and had been since the dawn of Chinese invention – from the world's first printed book, the *Diamond Sutra* in the ninth century, to the first printing press in the eleventh, the first seismograph, the first steel, the first suspension bridge, the first ship's rudder, and of course the first paper money. Admiral Zhang believed that China was already the great gateway to modern civilization when the English and other primitive Western tribes were still running around eating tree roots and pawing at their furry parts.

It pained him beyond words to see his nation still treated by the West as a Third World country, unable to be entrusted with its own military matters as and how it saw fit. 'But,' he thought, 'we will see about that, if we can just get our own Kilo submarine fleet into operational order, and then get Taiwan under control.'

Admiral Zhang, whose most prominent unit command had been as captain of a guided missile destroyer, reflected ruefully upon the fact that most of his time these days involved subsurface vessels. Indeed his two raging hot priorities these past weeks had involved *only* subsurface vessels: the disappearing *Hai Lung*s, with their potentially lethal nuclear cargo, and the equally disappearing Kilos, with their definitely lethal US enemy.

'Bastards,' said Admiral Zhang, under his breath, as he mentally dumped the military high commands of both Taiwan and Washington into the precise same garrison of deceit, villainy and dishonor.

He drove home across the little island and took the ferry on to Gulangyu. The rain had eased, and the sun was coming through, warming the lush, verdant grounds of the ocean-front properties. Jicai was already there by the time he arrived, having tea and pastries with Lan and the children. The Southern Commander apologized for being more than an hour early, but he had been dropped off by helicopter from the base at Canton.

The two admirals, both in white summer uniform, retired immediately to Zhang's private study on the western side of the house, where maps of the Indonesian islands were already laid out.

'What d'you think of the Sunda Strait?' asked the C-in-C.

'I don't think so. Not for an underwater passage,' replied Jicai. 'I don't much like the waterway. It's quite busy. But what I really do not like are the northern approaches. The entire place is covered with damned oil fields.' He pointed at the charted area 50 miles east of the coast of Sumatra. 'Look at this lot . . . you have the Cintra, Kitty, Nora and Rama fields; then, further north, the Yvonne, Farida, Zelda and Tita. The whole place is a mass of oil rigs, production platforms, tanker moorings, tanker storage areas, platforms on pipelines . . . it goes on for miles and it's shallow. No one would choose to make a submerged voyage anywhere near there. In my opinion the Sunda Strait is a non-starter.'

'How about the next one along . . . 650 miles east, the Narrows which separate Java and the island of Bali?' Zhang was happy to defer to the Southern Commander in all of these investigations since Admiral Zu was a submariner, and had served as the commanding officer of the 5,000-ton nuclear boat, *Han 405*, with its high-tech French intercept radar, and modern Russian homing torpedoes. Commander Zu Jicai had made quite a name for himself in the mid-'90s when he was caught and tracked by a US carrier battle group off the coast of North Korea.

Chinese naval propaganda made much of his skillful handling of the submarine, and of the fact that he lived to fight another day, after facing down the marauding American eagle. They made little of the fact that the Americans could, without question, have sunk Jicai at any time they wished, had they been so inclined.

Nonetheless, Admiral Zu Jicai had been one of the very best Chinese submariners – a status Arnold Morgan had uncharitably described as 'like the world's tallest midget.' But in an essentially nonmaritime nation, which China has been, at least militarily, for several hundred years, Zu Jicai knew more about submarines than almost anyone else.

'Don't really like the Bali Narrows, sir,' he said. 'Too shallow at their narrowest part, which is less than half a mile wide. And there's only 90 feet of depth coming out on the southern side. That's no real problem but the Narrows are too dangerous, too risky, especially with uranium on board. I'd never even consider it.'

'Are we reaching the point where we must declare the whole exercise impossible as a subsurface transit? Coming through the Indonesian islands?' Admiral Zhang looked puzzled.

'No, sir. They could get through the Lombok Strait dived . . . right here. Eighty miles east of the Narrows, this stretch of water. It's about 25 miles across between Eastern Bali and the island of Lombok. And the seaway splits into two good channels. It's deep, at least 600 feet all the way through, even in this shallow part. Just here at the southeastern exit point shows 400 feet on the chart.'

'It's a long way east, Jicai,' said Zhang, peering at the chart. 'They would have to take a different route from the short run down the South China Sea.'

'Yessir. They would. They'd have to head southeast as soon as they dived off Taiwan. Then they'd make a course east of the Philippines . . . through the Celebes Sea, right here. Then through the Makassar Strait, which is not only deep, it's 150 miles wide . . . See these depths, sir? Six thousand feet, shelving up to 2,000 feet. All the way down to the Lombok Strait it's never less than 1,500.

'Sir, I cannot be certain, of course. But if I was asked to transport a dangerous cargo from Taiwan, underwater, in a highly classified operation, that is the route I would take: east of the Philippines and through the Lombok.'

'How far would that be, Jicai?'

'About 1,000 miles from Taiwan to the southern point of the Philippines. Then a 1,200-mile run down to the Strait. Look here, sir, the water's 4,000 feet deep just north of the gap. There's no shoal water across the route, there's no need to surface, and there's shallow water for cover. It's exactly right for them.'

'Do we know when the next *Hai Lung* is due to clear Suao?'

'Yessir. Two days from now. July 23rd.'

'That means she could be at the Strait in two weeks?'

'Correct, sir.'

'What do you think, Jicai? Two ACINT trawlers right here at the entrance to the Strait? Would that pick them up? We'd know its direction and we'd be a lot wiser than we are now.'

'Two would do it. Three would be better. And then we would finally know if the *Hai Lung* was indeed three weeks away from its ultimate destination, sir, heading south.'

'Yes, Jicai. Yes we would. Perhaps three weeks away from some nuclear factory . . . which we *must find*.'

'The ACINTs are at 24 hours' notice for sea, sir. We have three of them based well south at Hainandao. We have good time to brief them before sailing, and we'll have them on station well ahead of the *Hai Lung*.'

'We'll do that right now, Jicai. We'll go together . . . . I'll get your signal orders out later.'

The last weekend in July was a Cape Cod masterpiece. The warm, damp sea mists, which had obscured the sun for so many days throughout the month, had drifted away at last to the north where they belonged, and the gleaming bright light of mid-summer lit up the waters of Nantucket Sound.

Not a cloud littered the pink evening sky as the sun went down behind the white steeple of the church in Cotuit – at least it did if you happened to be drifting home across the bay on the evening tide, as Commander Boomer Dunning and his two daughters were at this moment.

His wife, and their mother, Mrs Jo Dunning, had a different view from the foreshore of the big family house which faced southeast. She could see the surreal light of the setting sun along the sandy beach of Deadneck Island which made it look floodlit.

Whichever way you looked, Cotuit Bay was not too shabby a sight on this warm summer evening, and Jo Dunning, secure in her earthly paradise, waved at her crew as 13-year-old Kathy ran the family skiff, *Sneaker*, expertly in to the beach, centerboard up. Boomer jumped off the bow, and with his enormous strength, dragged the boat up the sand. Then they all pulled it a bit farther and Kathy and her younger sister took down the big gaff-rigged sail. Of course it would have been more orthodox to put the boat on a mooring, like most everyone else. But Boomer said he'd been running little sailboats up the beach all his life on calm summer evenings, and as the senior officer that was the way it was going to be.

For Jo, this Sunday evening, and the barbecue they were about to light, represented one of the rare bonuses she had received all summer. Boomer had arrived unexpectedly on Friday night and announced he was not due back in New London until the Monday morning. Her in-laws were away for three weeks in Maine, and the white clapboard house on the bay was theirs alone. Their real vacation here was not due to begin until August 5, when Boomer had a 10-day furlough, and right now Jo Dunning was at least as happy as she had ever remembered being.

On a long sunny Saturday, the previous day, she and Kathy had won the weekly Cotuit Skiffs race, while Boomer and Jane had walked up the road to watch the village baseball team, the fabled Cotuit Kettleers, wipe out the Hyannis Mets 9–0 at Lowell Park.

What Boomer did not know as he cheered his men on, was that one Mr Frederick J. Goodwin, the *Cape Cod Times* feature writer, was sitting in the visitors' area of the bleachers, glumly watching his team make four errors, and walk seven Kettleer batters. It was an unfortunate omission, because the US naval officer and the journalist would have had something in common, as certainly the only two men in the ballpark who had once journeyed to the island of Kerguelen. In fact they were probably the only two men in the ballpark who had ever heard of Kerguelen, never mind been there. Never mind each man's sense of a deep and personal involvement with that remote and terrible place.

The second omission in Boomer's life this weekend was more serious. He had not yet plucked up courage to tell Jo that their vacation together was off. When he left for the submarine base on Monday morning, it would be for several weeks. Maybe months. And the operation was black. Jo would never know where he was, or when he was coming home again. Boomer was not wildly looking forward to that particular conversation.

To prepare himself for the ordeal he busied himself with the barbecue, and while it reached its optimum heat to cook the big New York sirloins, he wandered inside to pour a couple of Navy-sized drinks for himself and Jo: two tall rum and cranberry juice cocktails, on the rocks, in frosted glasses. He shot a few squirts of bug-repellent on his deeply bronzed legs, arms and face, drying off his hands on his thick blond hair. 'Keep those little "no-see'um" bastards away while I'm busy,' he muttered.

Then he strolled outside and gave his beautiful wife a kiss and a drink and told her that no hour ever passed by, no matter where he was, or where he was headed, when he did not think of her, and all that she had always meant to him.

As statements go, that was not precisely vintage Boomer. And Jo Dunning's radar went up. 'Boomer,' she said, smiling, and looking at him as if he were a naughty schoolboy. 'You simply must have something you are waiting to tell me . . . something lousy, I'd guess.'

The commanding officer of *Columbia*, realizing a hand seriously overplayed, elected to seize the moment, rather than prolong the agony until after supper. 'Jo,' he said, slowly. 'I have to go away . . . for several weeks.'

She stared at him for a moment, a sudden sadness sweeping across her face. Whatever he said, it would make no difference. It was not his fault, she knew. She was a Navy wife. This was not unusual. But it happened so often.

'When?'

'I won't be back after tomorrow morning.'

'How long?'

'I can't tell you. A while.'

'Can I know where?'

'No.'

'Is it black?'

'Uh-huh.'

'Oh . . . oh my God. Not months?'

'Probably weeks.'

The endless nightmare of all commanding officers' wives stood before her. The weeks stretched out to infinity. There would be, she knew, no one to whom she could turn for information. His loneliness, out there in command of the great hunter-killer submarine, would, in the end, be hers. In the face of danger too great to contemplate, they would both be alone.

She willed herself not to cry, with yet another summer shot to pieces, another year really. And she turned away towards the grill, and just told him, defenselessly, 'I love you, Boomer.' And then she felt his great sailor's arms around her, and she fell apart without shame against his massive chest. In front of the glowing fire. In front of their daughters.

In the far distance, the almost-full moon began to rise coldly over the boatsheds by the Osterville town bridge. And very soon, on this clear night, there would also rise out over the Atlantic one of the brightest constellations in the heavens . . . that of Orion himself. The other hunter.

Commander Dunning arrived at the gates of the New London submarine base at 0845. It had taken him two hours down Interstate 195 from the Cape. And now he made swiftly for the jetty where *Columbia* awaited, her crew making final preparations for a long patrol.

There was a huge sense of purpose right now, as they loaded the hardware: torpedoes; missiles; major mechanical spare parts; welding kit; acetylene; computers; engineering extras such as seals, hydraulics, rubber and plastic pipes, valves; endless tubs of grease, paint and polish; carbon dioxide for the coke machine.

Supplies such as steaks, pork roasts, ham, bacon, eggs, potatoes, fruit, salad, vegetables, fish, coffee, tea and soda would be taken on board closer to the time of departure. The cooks baked their own bread during the voyage.

The nuclear reactor would go critical two days from now in readiness for her final sea-trials. The submarine's ETD was 1400 on August 7.

Boomer went below immediately, and found his executive

officer, Lt. Commander Mike Krause, who apologized for not meeting him at the gangway. Then the CO called a brief meeting of the senior executives, the XO, the combat systems officer, Lt. Commander Jerry Curran, the chief engineer, Lt. Commander Lee O'Brien, and the navigator, Lt. David Wingate. Boomer told them what he could, but explained he was leaving immediately by helicopter for SUBLANT in Norfolk, Virginia, and would be back in two days. Until then he would leave *Columbia* in their more-than-capable hands.

No one had time to watch the helicopter bearing their leader clatter off the pad and rocket away toward the hot south, to the Black Ops Cell where the keenest brains in the US Navy were planning the demise of the last two Chinese Kilos, K-9 and K-10.

Boomer Dunning was very within himself during the 390-mile flight through clear skies to Virginia. The Navy pilot crossed Montauk Point and then stayed out over the ocean, setting a course south-southwest which would take them well east of Long Island, New York, Philadelphia, the great estuary of the Delaware River and, ultimately, the long tidal waters of Chesapeake Bay.

Every mile they flew seemed to take him farther away from all that he loved. He tried not to think of Jo and the girls, and the tranquil waters of Cape Cod. Instead he tried to concentrate on the task which lay ahead of him; the deep dark waters, and the two Russian submarines. They would both be fully operational, armed with the latest weapons, of that he had no doubt. They would also be under heavy escort. He knew he would single-handedly be taking on a small Russian convoy, and that no ship in that convoy would hesitate to sink *Columbia* and all who sailed in her.

He and his team were, he knew, faster, cleverer and inestimably more lethal. Everyone knew that. No destroyer, or frigate, or even battle-cruiser was anything like a match for a well handled American SSN. Well, he supposed, now was the time to prove that. But his thoughts nonetheless returned stubbornly to the big white house on Cotuit Bay. And he wrestled with the unspoken anguish of all submariners: What if I don't return? What will happen to Jo without me? And then, inevitably, not, 'Have I loved her enough?' But, 'Have I told her often enough?' He closed his eyes and pic-tured again the long-legged redhead from New Hampshire who did, he knew, adore him. But her loneliness made him too sad, and he wished he could sing to her their favorite Willie Nelson track, the wistful, regretful, 'You Were Always On My Mind.'

Boomer understood he must shake himself out of this melancholy, and prepare to face the heavies in SUBLANT, Admirals Morgan, Dixon and probably Mulligan, the CNO himself. And after them the North Atlantic, and then God knows what else. Not for the first time he was assailed by doubts as to his own fitness for the duty which lay before him.

Down below he could see the south-facing headland of Cape Charles, and they were already dropping down to 1,000 feet. The sprawling Norfolk dockyards lay dead ahead. Boomer watched the pilot slide the helicopter into the wind, hover 20 feet above the pad, and then touch down lightly. He unclipped, patted the driver on the back, and climbed through the door now opened for him. The rotor was still beating as he stepped into the waiting staff car, which would drive him round to SUBLANT HQ.

Inside the Black Ops Cell, Admiral Dixon and Arnold Morgan were waiting. They both rose and greeted him warmly. The President's National Security Advisor poured coffee for them all, black and strong. He then fired 'buckshot' into all three china cups without asking and handed them around . . . Then, as if remembering his manners, or lack thereof, he chuckled, 'Black op, black coffee . . . right?' He never gave a thought to the plateful of cookies parked by the coffee pot, presumably with the CNO in mind. Arnold Morgan considered that real men didn't eat cookies.

But there was something so positive about this despot of naval intelligence it was impossible to feel irked by him, even if you would have preferred a half-gallon of cream in your cup, and six cookies, as indeed Boomer did.

'CNO's arriving soon,' said Admiral Dixon, 'and I thought we'd give you a thorough briefing before he arrives, bring you right up to date on K-9 and K-10.'

'Yessir. I'd appreciate that.'

'Well, as you know, the Russians got 'em in the water in April. Took 'em a while – guess they had some trouble with those hydraulic lifts they use up in Severodvinsk. Big Bird kept circling, sending us a picture a day, and nothing moved for nearly a week. Looked like the whole process was jammed up. But they got 'em freed up and floating, and from then on we just saw quite a large workforce on those Kilos, moored alongside. Another source informed us there were a lot of Chinese too.

'Early in May they moved . . . That was when we had a mild panic because it looked like they might be going straight home to Shanghai. But they were just leaving the White Sea and heading around to Pol'yarni, just like K-4 and K-5 – your two old friends, right?'

'Enemies, sir,' said Boomer.

'Precisely so,' confirmed Admiral Dixon. 'Anyway, since then we've been watching them carefully. Our best estimate always said they'd need three weeks in Pol'yarni for their safety trials, and then at least another three months' operational work-up in the Barents Sea to bring them right up to scratch as front-line operational fleet units.

'I am sure it has not escaped you, Commander, we did not face that problem with K-4 and K-5, which were . . . shall we say . . . unsuspecting. The game, from the Chinese and the Russian point of view, has since changed. Drastically.'

'Yessir.'

'Now, as far as we are concerned, the clock started on the day they began trials off Murmansk, first week in May. We've watched them ever since, going out every Monday morning, and returning every Friday night. So far as we can tell, their safety trials went without a major hitch, which means they ain't going to sink without us.

'We watched them complete their torpedo trials. They fired quite enough to make sure their guys knew their stuff, much as we expected. They were very thorough.'

Admiral Dixon's voice softened, and he said, quietly, 'Boomer, they must know we're coming for them. There is no way Admiral Rankov has not blown a very loud whistle. The whole Russian Navy has got to be on full alert . . . there are more guards around those two Kilos than we've ever seen before.'

Arnold Morgan, who had been sitting thoughtfully, suddenly added, 'The loss of K-9 and K-10 would represent a financial catastrophe for Moscow. Never forget that. The Chinese would, with some justification, demand *all* of their money back, every nickel they have paid out. And if they didn't get it, they'd bag the order for the aircraft carrier. That's a five billion dollar problem for the Kremlin. I am only mentioning this to highlight the level of sensitivity this entire operation will engender.'

'Thank you, sir,' said Boomer, ruefully.

'You're most welcome, Commander,' added the NSA, grinning. 'You want me to come with you – make sure it gets done right?'

Boomer shuddered at the thought, but sensibly kept quiet, and all three men laughed. It was Admiral Dixon who spoke next. 'Boomer, I'd like to send another boat with you, but all of my instincts are saying no, except as a backup perhaps. You get two of your own in the same patch, where the quickest on the draw wins, you're liable to end up killing your friends.'

And a sudden silence enveloped the room, as each of these vastly experienced US Navy commanders contemplated the truth that Boomer Dunning must, on this occasion, carry his huge burden all alone. Except that, in a sense, Admiral Dixon and Admiral Morgan, linked by the miracle of the satellites, would go with him.

'When do you estimate they will leave Pol'yarni?' asked Boomer.

'We've got it as the third week in August.'

'So my August 7 departure stands?'

'Correct. You'll head straight up to the Faeroes, as before, and wait on station there until we see the Kilos move.'

'What if they don't?'

'You'll hang around for six weeks and then we'll send another submarine up to relieve you in early October. But I won't start briefing another boat until the last possible time, because we want this kept as tight as possible. For obvious reasons. Right now you can count the people who know about it on the fingers of two hands, which is one too many, right?'

'Right,' said Boomer. 'Presumably the procedures up in the GIUK Gap will be as before?'

'Absolutely. If there's no escort. You'll be briefed every step of the way, and I expect you to pick the two submarines up when they snorkel, as before, *if* they're alone.'

'What happens if there is an escort?'

'We'll have to leave that largely to you,' said Admiral Morgan. 'But don't, for Christ's sake, risk hitting a surface ship . . . not even in self-defense. And if you can't get in close, just keep tracking them until the escort starts to peel off or something. There should be an opportunity, sometime, somewhere . . . maybe far down the Atlantic, maybe even in the southern Indian Ocean . . . but that's when you'll strike, in deep water. Remember the rules of this ballgame: hit 'em low, and hit 'em hard. No mistakes. Like always. You have our complete confidence. We're gonna have to leave it up to you as to where, when and how.'

'Thank you, sir. I appreciate that.'

Just then the door opened and the rangy figure of Admiral Joe Mulligan was escorted into the room by two Navy guards. The CNO reached for the cookies before he sat down, and Boomer, as very much the junior officer, stood to pour him some coffee.

'No, no, Boomer. I'll get it . . . you're our guest of honor today.' He smiled. Which was precisely the moment when the submarine commander from Cape Cod knew exactly how thunderously dangerous this next mission was going to be.

The Admiral sat down with the cookies placed strategically to his right, and he looked very preoccupied as he munched. 'I expect you have been pretty well briefed already,' he told Boomer. 'Same basic program as before. We'll track 'em up around the GIUK. And you'll get rid of them at the earliest opportunity.'

But he paused, and then said, 'Gentlemen, this operation, as you are each aware, could scarcely be more unlike K-4 and K-5. Because right here we have one major difference. The Kilos will not only be on their guard, they will be looking for you, as you will be looking for them. And if they find you first – one heavily armed US nuclear boat too close for comfort – they will not hesitate to open fire on you, on the basis that they're already 5–0 down in this particular contest.'

All four of the men were silent for a few moments. Then Admiral Mulligan added, 'It's quite a long time since any American CNO sent any warship into quite such clear and obvious danger . . . and I do so with great reluctance. But for the enormous importance of this project to this nation, and indeed to the world's freedom of sea trade, I would not . . . could not be persuaded to ask any single commander to take on such an onerous task.

'Boomer, I know what the United States Navy means to you, and I believe that if you felt this could not be done, you would tell us so, and we would certainly be obliged to return to the drawing board. But you have never said anything to that effect, so I presume I am correct in assuming you believe the mission is possible.'

'Yessir. I do believe that. I would also like to say that since I was about 10 years old, my main ambition in this life was to become a

United States Navy captain. It's an ambition I still have, and hope one day to attain. Getting killed at the hands of some half-assed Chinaman does not figure in my immediate itinerary.'

All three admirals laughed. But it was Joe Mulligan, the former Trident captain, who stood up and walked over to the commanding officer of USS *Columbia*, and, without a word, shook him by the hand.

'It's a pain in the ass,' said Arnold Morgan, 'but you can't let those sneaky pricks get the first shot in. Because then we'll be in the same spot they've already been in. Loss of a serious warship, her crew and commanding officer . . . and unable to admit anything to anyone.'

'I understand that fully, sir,' replied Boomer. 'But they're not gonna get the first shot in. We are, for one simple reason: we'll know where they are, and where they're going. And we'll be lying in wait. They may think we're out there somewhere, but they won't know where. And as long as I'm in command, that's something they'll never know . . . not till it's too late.'

'That's the precise way to look at it, Boomer,' said Admiral Mulligan. 'You have a superior ship, a superior crew, superior weapons, superior reconnaissance, and superior speed. You also have our complete confidence. Anything you need, just shout.'

'Yessir.'

'But for Christ's sake don't hit a Russian warship, especially if it's on the surface. Because that *could* start World War III. And we may not do that. We just have to take out the two Kilos in deadly secret. Is that too much to ask?' He smiled.

'I very much hope not, sir,' said Boomer, who was beginning to appreciate how difficult his task would be, under such stringent injunctions from these highly placed people.

At this point the CNO and Admiral Morgan took their leave, and headed out to the helicopters which would return them to Washington. Boomer and Admiral Dixon remained in conference for the rest of the afternoon, poring over the details of the plan which would rid the USA of the menace of the Russian Kilos. They dined together that evening, and the following morning Boomer and the entire black ops team went over the communications system one more time. Right after lunch, he took off once more for New London.

Boomer came in to land in the late afternoon, went to his office and called Jo at the Cape. He told her that everything was fine, his mission was very routine, and that she should not worry. He expected to be back in four or five weeks and that he was taking leave right through December, which would give them the best Christmas together they had ever had, up at the Cotuit house.

Before the call was over, Jo sensed the tension in his voice and impulsively blurted out, 'Boomer, you have to tell me, is this dangerous, what you're doing?'

'Hell no,' he replied. 'We're giving the ship a little sea-trial tomorrow, and after then it's dead simple. Just something we have to keep quiet about, that's all.'

'Please promise me you'll be careful,' she pleaded before he rang off.

'That's the one thing you really don't have to worry about,' he said. 'I'm gonna be damned careful, and make sure I get back on time.'

He told her he loved her, as he always did. But he didn't fool Jo. She might not have been that good at it herself, but she knew an actor when she heard one. Especially a bad one. And she had never heard her husband quite so uptight. When she put down the telephone, her hand was shaking; as she walked back to the big waterfront kitchen, she found herself saying, over and over, 'Oh my God . . . oh my God . . . please let him come home.'

One hundred and twenty miles to the southwest, Lt. Com-mander Mike Krause was making every possible effort to ensure her prayers were not in vain. *Columbia* was ready. Her electronic combat systems had been checked and re-checked. On board she would carry her full complement of 14 Gould Mk 48 wire-guided tor-pedoes, ADCAPs (Advanced Capability). The Russians always claimed the Kilo could take a hit and survive, but not from one of these. Hopefully *Columbia* would bring 12 of them home with her. Plus her eight Tomahawk missiles, the 1,400-mile killers, and the four Harpoon missiles with their active radar-homing warheads. One way and another, the 362-foot-long *Columbia* was not an ideal candidate with which to pick a fight.

Her defensive line was also formidable. She carried an arsenal of decoys, specifically designed to coax any incoming weapon well away from the submarine. On station *Columbia* would use a low-frequency passive towed-array, designed to pick up the very heart beat of an oncoming enemy. Commander Dunning's boat was one of the first of the Los Angeles-Class to be fitted with the new WLY-1 acoustic intercept and countermeasures system. State-of-the-art EHF communications were already in place. Special acoustic tile-cladding, designed to reduce her active-sonar target-signature, made her one of the stealthiest submarines ever built.

She could run underwater comfortably at more than 30 knots if necessary. And she could operate at depths of almost 1,500 feet below the surface. She was twice as fast as a Kilo, twice as big, and twice as lethal. The Russian outpointed her on only one count: the Kilo was silent under 5 knots on her electric motors. *Columbia*, the sleek hunter-killer, running indefinitely on her GE PWR S6G reactor, was quiet enough, but never totally silent. She had another major asset denied to the Russian: her superbly trained crew, with the best equipment in the world.

Her final asset was perhaps the most priceless of all. *Columbia* had Boomer Dunning. And he was, by all known standards, the best of the breed, a scrupulously careful dare-devil, if such a combination is possible. There was no part of that ship Boomer could not operate, or even repair. He was an expert in hydrology, engineering, electronics, weaponry, navigation, sonar, radar, communications and nuclear physics. It was often said that if *Columbia*'s sail ever fell off, the best man to send out to weld the plates back on would be the Commanding Officer himself. The mere presence of the big ocean-racing yachtsman from Cape Cod in the control center of *Columbia* gave everyone heightened confidence.

'Morning, Mike,' he said as he came aboard. 'We got this wreck ready to go?'

Lt. Commander Krause, a fellow New Englander from Vermont, was pleased the Commanding Officer was back. 'Hello, sir,' he said. 'Everything cool at SUBLANT?'

'Not too bad,' said Boomer. 'I'm back a little before I expected . . . didn't want to miss out on our trials tomorrow. We got a real big job ahead. I think we should have dinner together tonight, with Jerry Curran and Dave Wingate.'

'On board, sir?'

'I think so. As black operations go, this one's on the dark side.'

The lieutenant commander laughed, but he could see that the boss was concerned about their mission. Later that evening he would find out just how concerned, as Boomer steered the senior officers through the stormy seas which lay ahead of them.

The radical difference between this and the operation against K-4 and K-5 was now clear to all of them. They were not going out in search of a couple of armed, but still sitting, Peking ducks. This time they were going after a couple of well trained, highly dangerous dragons, who not only expected them, but would be searching for the Americans night and day. And who would not hesitate to open fire on them at the first opportunity. 'At 5–0 down, you kinda got it all to play for,' murmured Jerry Curran.

'And if we want to stay alive, we better make absolutely certain every member of this crew operates right at the top of his game,' said Boomer. 'We got a great ship, the best there is. It's a privilege to serve in her, for all of us. But this time, we're gonna have to earn that privilege the hard way.'

August 6. Late afternoon. Admiral Zhang Yushu picked up the secure internal telephone in his office at Xiamen. Admiral Zu Jicai, on the line from the Southern Fleet Headquarters in Zhanjiang, spoke slowly and deliberately. 'We have them, sir. Picked them up at 1425. 8.30 South, 115.50 East, up at the north end of the Lombok Strait. Must be hull number 794, departed Suao July 23rd. The ACINT located her making seven and a half knots southwesterly, submerged. She was right on time, sir, two weeks out, with three weeks to run. That will put her in Heard Island, or the McDonalds, or Kerguelen, 21 days from now. We assess she must be heading for one of those three places. Nowhere else fits her sailing pattern so well.'

'Thank you, Jicai. Leave it with me for a while, will you? I'd like to study the charts. I'll call you back at about 1830.'

The Chinese Commander-in-Chief walked across to his chart drawer and pulled out the big blue, white and buff-colored ocean map, compiled by the Royal Australian Navy. On the lower right side it showed the sprawling West Coast of Australia itself, then 600 miles northwest of the Great Sandy Desert it showed the Lombok Strait. Admiral Zhang traced his finger expertly southwest over the contours of the vast waters south of the strait, muttering to himself all the while. 'Right here, over the Java Trench in 10,000 feet of water . . . then over the Wharton Basin where it's close to 18,000 feet deep . . . on southwest . . . past the East Indiaman Ridge, where it's still 9,000 feet deep . . . then just press on southwest all the way to the islands . . . the *Hai Lung* makes 200 miles a day, the distance is – let's see – 4,400 miles . . . that puts her off the McDonalds 21 days from now. As the good Jicai said, right on time.'

And now the Admiral abandoned his charts and walked back to his desk where there awaited him a new volume of the *Antarctic Pilot*, the Royal Navy publication which charts the entire coast of the Antarctic and 'all islands southward of the usual route of vessels.'

He turned first to the great sloping plateau of the main McDonald Island, located at 53.03N, 72.35E. It was a weird-looking rock, three-quarters of a mile long and a quarter-mile wide, rising from 100 feet above sea level to 400, a great slab of granite at a skewed angle. Tall, stark, frozen, with no hiding place. 'If the Taiwanese are burrowed inside that rock making a hydrogen bomb, my name's Chiang Kai-shek,' growled Admiral Zhang.

And he turned the page immediately to the 10-mile-by-5-mile volcanic rock of Heard Island, with its huge circular mountain, 'Big Ben,' located at 53.06S, 73.31E. The Admiral did not think much of that as a site for a secret nuclear facility either. For a start the place was covered in permanent ice throughout the year, but worse, there were frequent reports that the 9,000-foot cone of Mawson's Peak was belching smoke. 'If I was about to make an atomic bomb,' he muttered, 'I would not do it in the foothills of a volcano which was constantly threatening to erupt.'

His sailor's eye, skimming through the reports compiled by the Royal Navy's hydrographers, also noted that landing anywhere on the steep and unforgiving Heard Island would be a nightmare, except in the calmest of weather. 'Forget about that place,' he told himself. 'That leaves only Kerguelen . . . and when I think about it, it *has* to be Kerguelen. The place is comparatively large, full of coves, fjords, landing sites, anchorages, steep-sided bays to lee of the worst weather, and a thousand places to hide. The *Pilot* even suggests German warships were in there during World War II.'

Admiral Zhang pondered his problem for a while, and then decided. 'You could search for a hundred years all over that jagged Kerguelen coastline, and you might never find what you were looking for. Unless . . . unless the factory you were after was being powered by the reactor of a nuclear submarine. Our own submarine might find that, but the new Kilo with the latest Russian sonar would be even more likely . . . I am certain of that.'

★

They took *Columbia*'s nuclear reactor critical at 0800 on the morning of August 7. The big dock-lights alongside had burned until the sun had risen out of the Atlantic. Deep in the engine room Lt. Commander Lee O'Brien was watching the power-level of the reactor come up to self-sustaining, as they gently bumped the rods out, until the nuclear power plant was ready to drive *Columbia*'s two mighty 35,000 h.p. turbines.

Lee O'Brien worked in the most threatening part of the ship. But he knew, like his number two, Chief Rick Ames, that outside the heavily shielded reactor room itself, there was less radiation than Boomer Dunning would have encountered on a stroll along the beach in Cotuit.

Shortly after 0800 they hit their first snag – an electronics fault in the automatic reactor shut-down control. It was not serious in itself, but the repair involved shutting down the reactor. Then replacing the defective board. Then testing it. Then re-initiating the whole reactor start-up process. Right from the beginning. *Columbia*'s sailing time of 1400 was shot.

Lee O'Brien looked calm, but those who knew him well were aware that the big Boston Irishman was on edge. He hated an equipment failure near the plant, even when it represented only the tiniest crack in their safety defenses, and could be swiftly dealt with. He hated telling the CO that *his* department had somehow let everyone down, that *his* equipment had failed. Because in his eyes that meant *he* had failed. It was this near-fanatical attention to detail, and zealous sense of responsibility, that made him one of the most trusted men in the ship.

Anyhow, the early afternoon departure was off. Lee O'Brien told the CO they should delay four hours, and clear New London at 1830. Boomer agreed entirely, and conserved his energy by going to the wardroom for a cup of coffee.

Except for the engineers back aft, the delay left the crew with little to do except wait. They would write further letters home, but since this operation was black, they would not be mailed by the Navy until the mission was either completed, aborted, or failed.

After lunch Boomer retired to his cabin for a half-hour. It was small and spartan, containing just his bunk, a few drawers, a small wardrobe, a desk and chair, and washing facilities which folded into the bulkhead. But it was the only private place in the entire ship, a miniature office with a bed really. The Commanding Officer was not a man for undue sentiment, as his wife knew all too well, and he had never before written a last-minute message to Jo. He had always considered that to be an action which might tempt providence, and he did not understand sailors who drafted out their wills in the hours before departure, but he knew many did so, and indeed some were certainly doing so right now.

Nonetheless he took a piece of writing paper and an envelope from his attaché case, and, with the utmost sadness, sat down and wrote in the brief terse sentences of his trade, the only language he knew:

My darling Jo.

If you are reading this, it means that our great love has ended the only way it ever could. We have always understood the realities of my career, and as you know I have always been prepared to die in the service of our country. I go to meet my Maker with a clear conscience, and my courage high.

I am not very good with words, but I want you to know that I spoke to Dad's lawyers today and that everything is in order for you and the girls. You have no worries. The house in Cotuit is yours, and the Trust is in place.

Just to say again, I love you. Think of me often, darling Jo. You were always on my mind.

Boomer.

He sealed the note into an envelope upon which he wrote in block capitals, 'TO BE DELIVERED TO MRS JO DUNNING ONLY IN THE EVENT OF MY DEATH.' He carefully signed it, 'Commander Cale Dunning, USS COLUMBIA.'

He then left the ship and walked across to the executive offices, and deposited the letter. The Navy clerk nodded and filed it. Boomer did not see the 19-year-old silently salute him as he strode out the door to take command of the US Navy's black ops submarine. It was just 1600.

Back on board he decided to speak to the crew on the internal broadcast system at 1730, one hour before departure. He sat and made a few notes, then briefly visited Lee O'Brien. The reactor was back on line and the secondary systems were in the final stages of warming through. No further problems.

At 1710, Lt. Commander Krause alerted the crew that the

Captain wished to speak to everyone before departure. At 1730 the deep baritone voice of Boomer Dunning ran through the ship.

'This is the Captain speaking. We are going on an interesting mission today. It begins now, and it will take us across the Atlantic into the GIUK Gap. Now, I know that most of you were with me earlier this year when we carried out a well executed operation against two submarines which had been judged by the President and the Pentagon to be potential enemies of the United States. As you know, we prefer to kill the archer rather than the arrow, which is why we struck hard and fast, before our opponents knew what had happened.

'This mission, which begins one hour from now, is going to be more difficult, and I will not pretend it is without danger. Because it most certainly is not. You have all been briefed as thoroughly as possible by your department chiefs, so you know how seriously our journey is regarded by those in the highest authority.

'I have supreme confidence in the abilities of every one of you. You are the best I have ever sailed with. But we have a difficult job, and I want every one of you to ensure throughout this voyage you perform to 110 percent of your capacity. Stay alert for every second of your watch. This ship is not operated just by its officers, it is operated by every last one of you. Everyone has a critical role to play, otherwise you wouldn't be here.

'Remember our lives are in our own hands. We have a fabulous ship, and we hold every advantage. Just let's make sure we are at our best. At the end of this we will be forever sworn to secrecy. But we'll each know what we did, and that our great nation has reason to be proud of us . . . if only they knew.

'But we'll know. And in the end that's what matters. Let's just make sure that every one of us can leave this ship in the late Fall and say to himself, "I sailed with *Columbia* on that vital mission . . . and whatever happens for the rest of my life, no one can ever take that away from me."

'We leave in under an hour. Let's get to it, and let's stay right at the very top of our game. God bless you all.'

Deep in the ship a few fists clenched. Right now Commander Dunning had 112 men prepared to follow him into hell, if necessary.

At 1829, there was just one line left holding *Columbia* to the pier. High on the bridge, in a light evening sou'westerly breeze,

Commander Dunning stood with his navigator, Lt. Wingate, and the officer of the deck, Lt. Abe Dickson. A few of the base staff were alongside on the jetty to watch her go. The Squadron Commander was there, as usual when one of his boats was leaving harbor. All submarine voyages exude a somewhat heightened pressure, because of the sheer nature of the beast, but the taut atmosphere surrounding *Columbia* was infectious. None of the onlookers knew anything about her mission, and there was an unspoken sense of secrecy as Commander Dunning ordered the colors shifted, and Lt. Dickson called out, 'Take in number one . . .'

It was more than 90 minutes to sunset, and the Stars and Stripes now bloomed suddenly above the bridge. The Captain nodded to the deck officer, who leaned forward and spoke calmly into the intercom down to the control center. '*All back one-third* . . .'

Deep in the engine room the giant turbines turned, and a quiet wash of turbulent water surged over the after part of the hull, which now swung outwards in reverse. The submarine slowed, stopped in the water, and then moved forward, as Boomer Dunning called, '*Ahead one-third* . . .' And *Columbia* moved through the first few yards of her long journey to the GIUK Gap.

A group of workmen out on the piers of the Electric Boat Division of General Dynamics, where *Columbia* had been built in 1994, waved cheerfully as the 7,000-tonner stood down the sunlit Thames River toward Long Island Sound; running fair down the channel on her way to put more than 100 foreign sailors in their graves. Nothing personal. A matter of duty.

'Ahead standard . . .' ordered Abe Dickson.

'Course zero-seven-nine,' the navigator advised. That meant east-nor'east . . . straight up to the Nantucket Shoals. At the 30-fathom curve, they'd dive. East of the islands, out of the weather.

All three officers remained on the bridge as *Columbia* steamed out at 16 knots, into the shallow waters which surround Block Island. The first part of the journey on the surface would be in broad daylight. By dark, they would be off Martha's Vineyard, well east and submerged. Lt. Wingate set a course which would leave the Shoals five miles off their port beam, at which point they would be leaving American waters, running at 20 knots dived, and using less power than if they were making 15 on the surface.

Boomer watched the water sliding up and over the blunt, curved bow. It flowed aft with a strange flatness, only to be parted by the sail, and then to cascade off into the roaring, swirling vortex which formed on either side of the hull. The Commanding Officer stared as he often did at the silent waters which created the submarine's bow-wave and fed the raging hell-holes right behind him.

They pushed on into the gentle swells of the northern reaches of Long Island Sound. No submarines are really happy on the surface, even in flat conditions like these, because they are designed to operate under the water. They are designed to hide . . . and to do their awesome business in stealth and seclusion.

As such, the submariner's idea of first-class travel is to be 300 feet under the surface, in a nuclear boat, cruising silently and smoothly through the deep, oblivious to gales and rough water; the only disturbance the soft humming of the domestic ventilation. Down there the temperature is constant, the food excellent. There is little chance of collision; even less of attack. Their ability to see beyond the hull is limited to what they can hear. But their range is immense, and their 'ears' are exquisitely tuned to the strange acoustic caverns of the oceans – far-distant sounds, echoing and repeating, rising and falling, betraying and confirming.

The ship's company were all pleased when the CO ordered *Columbia* to submerge and increase speed 20 miles southeast of Nantucket Island. For the crew, that was when the journey really began, when they set course to the east, for the southern slopes of the Grand Banks, where the shattered hull of the *Titanic* rests, two and a half miles below the surface.

The journey to the Faeroe Islands would take a week, with the American submarine running fast northeast across the deep underwater mountains of the Mid-Atlantic Ridge. Boomer had her steaming up the long deep plain in 10,000 feet of water above the Icelandic Basin on August 13. At 1700 local time on the afternoon of August 14, they came to periscope depth at eight degrees west, just north of the 60th parallel, southwest of the windswept little cluster of Danish islands. Boomer Dunning knew these chill, heartless Atlantic waters well, and he accessed the satellite to report his arrival on station, and confirm he would stay right here patrolling until he received further orders.

One week later in Norfolk, Virginia, at midday on August 22, the temperature inside the SUBLANT Black Ops Cell rose from moderate to blazing hot. Metaphorically, that is. The air conditioning was working fine. But Arnold Morgan had sounded an alarm direct from the White House, ordering everyone to stand by, and that he'd be arriving, by helicopter via Fort Meade, ASAP.

Right now the National Security Advisor was coming into his old office where Admiral George Morris had been checking a set of pictures just in from Big Bird. They showed an unusual development: the two Russian Kilos were clear of Murmansk and under way, on the surface, escorted by one frigate and three destroyers, one of which was the 9,000-ton guided-missile destroyer *Admiral Chabanenko*.

Also in attendance was a giant 21,000-ton Typhoon-Class strategic-missile submarine, also on the surface, plus the massive 23,500-ton Arktika-Class ice-breaker, the *Ural*, a three-shafted, nuclear-powered monster, famed for its ability to smash through ice eight feet thick at 3 knots by riding up on it and crushing it beneath its weight, bearing down on the granite-hard floes with a prow reinforced by solid steel.

For good measure the Russians had fielded a huge 35,000-ton Verezina-Class replenishment ship, presumably loaded with missiles, hardware, ammunition, stores, diesel fuel and its regular operational crew of 600 Russian seamen. This is Russia's vast traveling naval superstore, cruising the oceans with two or three billion dollars' worth of merchandise on board.

None of this was especially good news for the Americans. But the really diabolical news was that the satellite had picked up the nine-ship convoy making a steady 8 knots 100 miles due *east* of Pol'yarni.

One hour earlier the Fort Meade Director had muttered, '*Shit!*' and hit the button on his direct line to the NSA. Morgan took in the carefully relayed information that the convoy had turned right instead of left, and within seconds snapped, 'I'm on my way. Hold everything.'

And now he was here, and one glance at the pictures told him everything he needed to know. And he stood, silently berating himself for not having anticipated the problem in advance, unable to believe what he had missed.

He paced up and down the Fort Meade office as he had so many times before, finally cursing loudly what he called the 'most crass and unforgivable mistake of my career.'

'I cannot believe this,' he said. 'How *could* I have missed it?'

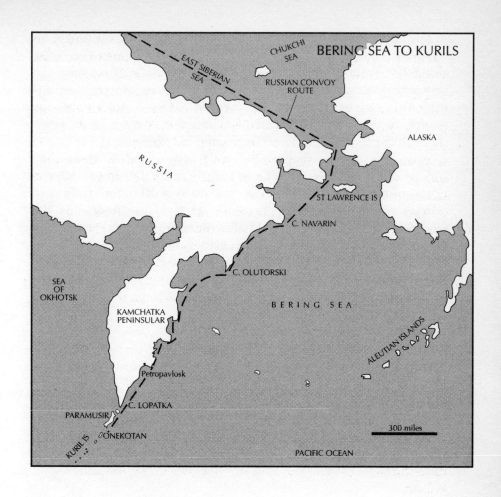

BERING SEA TO KURILS

CHUKCHI
SEA

RUSSIAN CONVOY
ROUTE

ALASKA

EAST SIBERIAN
SEA

RUSSIA

ST LAWRENCE IS

C. NAVARIN

SEA
OF
OKHOTSK

C. OLUTORSKI

BERING SEA

KAMCHATKA
PENINSULAR

ALEUTIAN ISLANDS

Petropavlosk

C. LOPATKA

PARAMUSIR

300 miles

KURIL IS

ONEKOTAN

PACIFIC OCEAN

But miss it he had. Admiral Vitaly Rankov had sent the two Kilos to China, under substantial escort, *the other way* . . . to the right, along the easterly route, inside the Arctic circle, following the northern Siberian coast, which is hard frozen in winter, but navigable in August with an ice-breaker. They would never go anywhere near the North Atlantic, and they would steam south through the Bering Strait into the Pacific in two weeks.

Patrolling the Faeroes, 1,200 miles away, the Commanding Officer of *Columbia* would wait in vain, because K-9 and K-10 were not coming. What's more, there was no way Boomer could turn northeast and give chase. The shallowness of the water and the closeness of the ice-edge would allow him a speed no greater than that of his target. And they already had upwards of 1,000 miles on him. He would never catch them up. Not even in an entire month. Right now he had two weeks max.

'That bastard Rankov,' rumbled Admiral Morgan. 'He's fucking well behind this. But I'm not beaten yet.'

CHAPTER TWELVE

Arnold Morgan left Fort Meade in a hurry, bearing with him the satellite photographs which showed he had been, temporarily, outwitted by Admiral Rankov. He headed straight to the helicopter pad and strapped himself into the big US Marines Super Cobra, which had been sequestered for his own personal use on this day.

The pilot had been ordered into the air from the Marines Air Station at Quantico, Virginia, and told to fly 25 miles straight up the Potomac into the White House grounds to pick up the President's National Security Advisor. It was a shade unorthodox, but no one who had ever been told, 'RIGHT NOW!' by Arnold Morgan ever quite erased the experience from his subconscious.

The Quantico station chief, responding to the hard word of the great man himself, had his only Ready-Duty helicopter up and flying inside nine minutes. And now the pilot was on the move again, for the third time that morning, lifting off from Fort Meade, while Admiral Morgan sat glowering behind him, alone in the 16-seater passenger area of the helicopter, muttering alternately, 'Step on it, willya?' and, 'Devious Russian bastard.' As usual on such ill-starred occasions, the Admiral gave the appearance of one who was about to declare war, right behind the 7.62 mm machine-guns which protruded from the Cobra.

They came clattering down into the Norfolk headquarters of the US Navy, where a staff car awaited their arrival. Arnold Morgan strode into the Black Ops Cell at SUBLANT at 1410 precisely. Admiral Dixon waited there already, attended by just his Flag Lieutenant. The CNO was expected any moment.

'We're in the crap right here,' said the NSA.

'I guessed as much by your phone call. What's happened?'

'K-9 and K-10 have sailed, under a four-ship escort, plus a big-missile submarine, an ice-breaker and a replenishment ship. They've made a break for it along the northern Siberian coast. Right now they're headed due east at 8 knots. They are not going anywhere near the North Atlantic, and *Columbia* cannot catch them. We're at least 1,200 miles behind, and as you well know, pursuit would be impossible up there in shallow waters, close to the ice-edge.'

'Damn,' said Admiral Dixon. 'That puts us right behind the power-curve.'

'Sure does. I checked out the possibility of sending *Columbia* the other way, via the Panama Canal and then north up the Pacific. But it would take three weeks minimum. I'm assessing the Kilos will be through the Bering Strait in 13 or 14 days . . . Here, take a look at these photographs. Satellite picked 'em up about 100 miles east of Murmansk.'

'Hmmm. There's the two Kilos on the surface. What's that? A goddamned Typhoon? Look at the size of that baby!'

'I've looked. It's a Typhoon okay. Still the biggest submarine ever built, right?'

'Christ, Arnie, that's no submarine escort. They'da used an Akula.'

'No. I agree. They must be making an inter-Fleet transfer from the Northern to the Pacific, and just held up the journey for a few days, so it could travel with the convoy.'

'And how about these surface warships? They're major escorts by any standard. What's the name of the big guy out in front?'

'That's the *Admiral Chabanenko*, 9,000-ton guided-missile destroyer.'

'How about these two? They look a lot the same.'

'Right. Two Udaloy Type Ones. We think the *Admiral Levchenko* and the *Admiral Kharlamov*. Similar in size, both with a hot ASW capability. All based in the Northern Fleet, going on a very special long journey.'

'And this one here, in rear?'

'Guided-missile frigate, the *Nepristupny*, 4,000-ton improved Krivak, probably their most effective small ASW ship class.'

'Jesus. And how about this fucking great thing out in front?'

'Giant ice-breaker, the *Ural*, can smash its way through just about anything.'

'Christ. They're not joking, are they? They really want those Kilos to reach Shanghai, wouldn't you say?'

'They sure do. But what really pisses me off is that I should have anticipated this. They often send convoys along the northeast passage at this time of year. And what a goddamned obvious ploy . . . it never crossed my mind they would do anything except run down the Atlantic with a big escort. I think I might be going soft. That bastard Rankov.'

Admiral Dixon smiled despite the apparent seriousness of the situation. He walked to the chart drawer and pulled up the big Royal Navy hydrographers' four-foot wide, blue, yellow and gray map of the entire Arctic region. He spread it wide on his sloping chart desk and measured the distance from Murmansk around to the Bering Strait – just less than 3,000 miles. 'If they make a couple of hundred miles a day at 8 knots it's going to take them exactly two weeks,' he said. 'And if *Columbia* set off now at flank speed she'd gain a lot of ground . . .' He paused and measured again. 'But not enough . . . because he'd have to run north to lay up with them across the Bear Island Trough . . . then the Russians, with that damned great ice-breaker, will angle even further north, to the edge of the pack-ice, passing the tip of this long island right here, what's it called? – Novaya Zemlya – then there into the Kara Sea . . . and, Christ! It gets really shallow in there . . . then they'll angle into Siberia to get into the easier shore-ice. Right there Boomer'd be in deep shit. There's no way he'd catch them – the goddamned water's only 150 feet deep up by the Severnayas, and if he was going fast he'd be leaving a big wake on the surface.'

'Looks damned narrow up there too.'

'Sure does. And up towards the northern ice-edge it'll be very difficult. You can't *see* the fucking stuff on sonar. And all the time the ice is grinding and snarling and fucking you about. If you put your periscope up, there's a good chance it'll get bent by a chunk of ice.

'See this, Arnie. Right after Severnaya it gets even more lousy – more shallow, and covered by ice. Right there, *Columbia* would be well behind the eight-ball, strapped for speed. More or less powerless, probably with no idea where the Kilos were, except from us, with the next choke point the far side of the Bering Strait.'

He was about to go on when the door swung open and the commanding figure of Admiral Joe Mulligan strode into the room. He took one look at the concerned faces of his two colleagues and said crisply, 'Okay, gentlemen. Lay it on me. Give me the bad news.'

Admiral Dixon outlined the situation, and the big ex-Trident captain moved over to the chart desk where the SUBLANT commander had already marked up significant points of depth and ice. He studied it carefully for all of 30 seconds, and then he said, 'You're right, I'm afraid. There's no way *Columbia* could run fast enough for long enough to catch them up there . . . that part of the ocean is a damned nightmare along the edge of the pack-ice – you can't see, you can't hear, and it's so shallow you can't run away if you get caught. Where are the Kilos now? Right here . . . yes. The situation is hopeless. Nearly.'

'Nearly, sir?' said the submarine Chief with exaggerated deference, knowing perfectly well what was coming.

'Yes . . . There is a way out of this . . . I think we might have to ask Commander Dunning and his team to make a trans-polar run, straight under the North Pole. Dive the boat in the Atlantic, and come out in the Pacific.'

The three men were silent for a moment, pondering the CNO's proposition. As ex-submariners they were well acquainted with the complexities of such a voyage. These trans-polar runs had been made by nuclear submarines in the past, but only rarely. And some had failed, stopped by the ice and shallow water in the northern approaches to the Bering Strait.

There is, of course, no land at the North Pole – nothing for a submarine to hit. The North Pole is not like the South Pole, which is located in the middle of a continent. The North Pole is surrounded by a vast floating ice-cap with an ocean beneath, 12,000 feet deep in some places, a lot less in others.

One of the original explorers had likened the picture to a 12-foot-high room. 'The ceiling is the base of the ice-cap; the floor, the ocean bed. Now imagine a matchstick suspended six inches from the ceiling – that's the nuclear submarine running dived right across the top of the world.'

Admiral Mulligan spoke again. 'We've done a lot of work up there over the years, much of it still based on the first polar transit underwater by a US nuclear boat more than 40 years ago – *Nautilus*, commanded by Andy Anderson. The trouble is these journeys need preparation, and *Columbia* has had none.'

'What's the timing factor?' asked Admiral Morgan.

'Lemme see . . . Boomer makes 20 knots all the way under the ice . . . across the north of Greenland, Iceland, and Alaska . . . could arrive at Point Barrow in northern Alaska in seven and a half days from right now. The Russians, who *cannot* make better than 10 knots on the surface, in those conditions, will get to the same place in about 11 days. Boomer will be waiting . . .'

'Brilliant,' rasped Admiral Morgan. 'We got 'em.'

'Yes. We got 'em, if Commander Dunning and his team feel they can make a trans-polar underwater run,' said Admiral Mulligan, grimly. 'And if the conditions are right in the Chukchi Sea. Still, if the Russians can run this little convoy through the ice, I guess we can too. Does Boomer have anyone on board with any experience?'

'He has some himself,' replied Admiral Dixon. 'He's worked up there under the ice . . . but more important his XO, Mike Krause, knows a lot about it. I'm not sure if he ever went right through, but Mike could have made a polar transit a few years ago.'

'But, hell, we don't even know if they have the right charts and books on board, do we?' asked Mulligan.

'I know,' replied Admiral Dixon. 'They haven't.'

'Beautiful,' said Admiral Morgan. 'You got a plan, John?'

'We get our skates on,' said Admiral Dixon. 'Our ice-skates, that is. I'll draft a signal, and we'll put it on the satellite. We'll probably have to make an air-drop with extra supplies, information and spares. Where do you think, sir? Somewhere up by Jan Mayen Island? That way Boomer won't have to hang around waiting.'

'Right. West of the island, I'd say,' replied the CNO. 'You better get moving on this, right now.'

August 22. Midnight local. 62.00N, 7.00W. The periscope of USS *Columbia* broke the surface of the rough, galeswept North Atlantic just southwest of Torshavn in the Faeroe Islands. Comms accessed the satellite, reported the submarine's position, and sucked off a message from SUBLANT.

Commander Dunning laconically ordered *Columbia* down into smoother waters once more, and waited for the print-out of SUBLANT's communication.

He was not, however, in any way prepared for what he was reading:

'*Assess K-9 and K-10 heading EAST along North Siberian coast in*

305

company with one Typhoon-Class on inter-Fleet transfer, four modern ASW escorts, one Arktika-Class ice-breaker, and a Fleet replenishment ship. Opportunities for attack by you in N. Siberian waters and Bering Strait considered minimal, and too dangerous.

'Proceed forthwith to deep water in Aleutian Basin via polar route. Report any special requirements for navigational advice, books, charts, spares, equipment ASAP, and in time for air-drop west of Jan Mayen by MPA a.m. 24th. Report position in time for drop.

'Latest ice reports Point Barrow area and Beaufort Sea will be passed to you within 24 hours, and as they become available.'

Boomer gulped. 'Under the Pole . . . Holy shit . . . MIKE! . . . get a look at this . . .'

Lt. Commander Krause read the message, his eyebrows rising as he did so. 'I've never been right through, sir,' he said. 'But I've been halfway and back twice, both times from the other end, up through the Bering Strait. In fact it's not that bad in the deep water, but there are a few awkward spots north of Point Barrow, where the bottom shelves right up, and you can get ice-pressure ridges coming down 120 feet below the surface. A couple of our submarines have been forced back over there . . . ran out of real estate where the downward ice-ridges almost hit the shoals on the bottom.'

'Shit,' said Boomer. 'Are you sure we're ready for this?'

'I guess we better be. That message from SUBLANT is an order, not a point for discussion.'

'Right. What do we need?'

'A couple more charts, and a couple of books, hopefully Commander Anderson's account of his journey in 1958, plus a couple of more recent patrol reports. Some of our guys found out a lot, the hard way. We'll also want additional upward-looking fathometer spares. Plus spares for the periscopes, which are apt to get knocked around in the overhead ice. Still, it's the right time of year. We might be all right . . . I'll round up our navigator and check out all the gear, then get a signal off to SUBLANT.'

Boomer studied the chart, estimated the distance northwest to the rocky Norwegian-owned island of Jan Mayen as 750 miles, and said: 'Tell 'em we'll be at 72 North 10 West for the drop-point, waiting at periscope depth. Make it a floating package with a dye-marker. We'll listen out on UHF channel 31, 30 hours from now.'

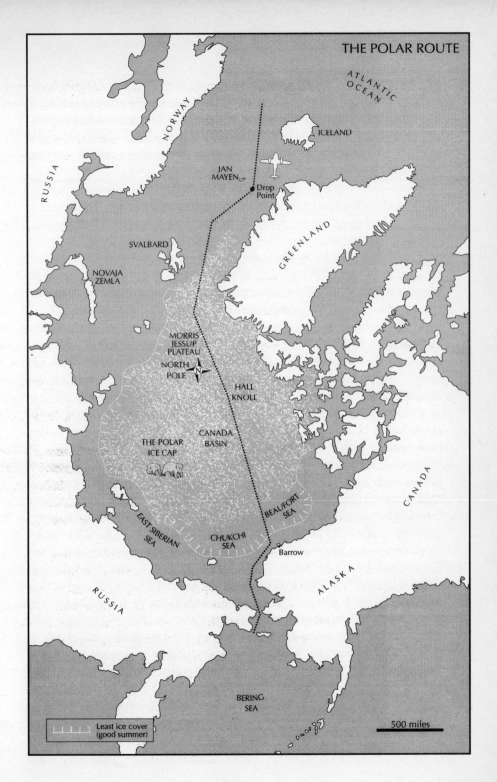

THE POLAR ROUTE

ATLANTIC
OCEAN

NORWAY

ICELAND

RUSSIA

JAN
MAYEN

Drop
Point

SVALBARD

GREENLAND

NOVAJA
ZEMLA

MORRIS
JESSUP
PLATEAU

NORTH
POLE

HALL
KNOLL

CANADA
BASIN

THE POLAR
ICE CAP

CANADA

BEAUFORT
SEA

EAST SIBERIAN
SEA

CHUKCHI
SEA

Barrow

ALASKA

RUSSIA

BERING
SEA

Least ice cover
(good summer)

500 miles

307

'Aye, sir.'

And with that, the long black hull of *Columbia* accelerated toward the deep Arctic waters which lead over the Icelandic Plateau, and on up toward the Eggvin Shoal. There, in difficult shelving water, the icy Maro Bank guards the western approaches to Jan Mayen, right on the edge of the winter pack-ice.

'Steer course three-five-five for 650 miles,' said Boomer. 'Speed 25. Depth 600.' He turned to Lt. Wingate and added, 'Right there we'll come right to zero-one-five for four hours and make that our pick-up spot.'

The Commander then called a navigation meeting with Lt. Commander Krause and Lt. Wingate one hour from now. And the time passed swiftly. *Columbia* came to periscope-depth to pass the rendezvous signal, and Boomer elected to stay there for 20 minutes pending a reply from SUBLANT. It arrived via the satellite almost immediately: '*Drop-point confirmed 72.00N, 10.00W. Floating package dye-marker. UHF 31. 0600 local August 24. MPA from US Naval Air Station Keflavik, Iceland, to make rendezvous. Call-sign BLUEBIRD ONE FIVE. Transmit UHF for homing 0550.*'

Columbia went deep again, and the three officers gathered in the navigation area, where the CO asked Lt. Wingate if he had a preliminary plan.

'Yessir. I suggest we head north in deep water, up between Greenland and Spitzbergen, and then enter the Arctic Ocean, under the pack-ice, through the Lena Trough . . . that's right here where the permanent ice-shelf begins. We'll be on course zero-three-five after the drop-point, with an adjustment after 200 miles to course zero-zero-zero. We wanna make that adjustment at the Greenland Fracture zone . . . right here, sir . . . over the Boreas Abyssal Plain. It's 15,000 feet deep there.'

'Yup, Dave. I gottit. Then you're plotting us running due north for another 700 miles, straight at the Pole?'

'Yessir. Right to here, where it says Morris Jessup Plateau. At that point the water is going to get suddenly appreciably more shallow. This is the 3,250-feet contour right here at the northern tip of the plateau. Our sounder will show it like an underwater cliff, shelving up from 10,000 feet to 3,250 in 20 miles. By then we will have curved around to three-one-zero, which will take us a couple of hundred miles south of the Pole itself.'

'Good call, Dave,' said Lt. Commander Krause. 'That way we'll avoid all that crap when the compasses go berserk and start spinning around. What do they call it? Longitude roulette?'

'Well, sir, I've never worked under the ice. But I know our gyros get real confused north of 87 degrees. Something to do with the Coriolis effect getting less as you reach the earth's spin axis. Anyway, if you reach the Pole, every direction is, obviously, south.'

'That's it. If you stand on the North Pole and take a few paces in any direction, you have to be heading south, towards Russia, Canada, the Atlantic, Pacific or wherever. Hard to know which. That's longitude roulette.'

'Yessir. We just gotta avoid violent changes of course, otherwise the gyros go ape. I got a book of words here which explains it. But in my view we're better to avoid the whole damn shemozzle, and stay south . . . right here, straight across Hall Knoll. Our entire journey from here to the Bering Strait is 4,000 miles, but we're only under the polar ice-cap for 1500 miles: three days at our speed. Not bad, right?'

'Good job, Dave,' said Boomer. 'I guess Hall Knoll is about our halfway point . . . and right here you've got a course change?'

'Yessir. A whole lot of small course changes, right past the Pole, will put us about south for a beeline on Point Barrow. We'll cross the Canada Basin in about a day and a half, and hope to come out from under the permanent ice on the coast of the Beaufort Sea, right opposite Point Barrow.'

'Right there we have the only really difficult area,' said Lt. Commander Krause, 'that last 120 miles in the Beaufort Sea. If it's been a warm summer there will be less than one-tenth ice-covering 100 miles north of Point Barrow. We'll still be in over 3,000 feet of water – and even the biggest pressure ridge in the overhead ice won't reach down more than 100 feet from the surface. So we're fine.

'*But* if it's been a cold summer we may get very open pack-ice, one-tenth cover, right down to Point Barrow itself, which means we'll have to stay submerged. Then, if the conditions below are simply appalling, we'll have to surface. I've been up there when it's been bad, damned great lumps of ice wallowing around all over the place, and thick fog. You can't see on the surface and it's too dangerous underneath.'

'I don't want to go on the surface at all, unless I can't help it,' said Boomer. 'Still, the ice-report from SUBLANT will tell us a lot about that before we start. And anyway, we can probably gut it out for a day or so; the ice should clear a few more miles to the southwest, and it is daylight all the time.'

Lt. Wingate, the only one of the three who had no experience working under the ice, wanted more information on the freshwater lakes which stud the Arctic ice-cap, especially in summer. They are known by the Russian word *polynya*, and any submarine trying to get a GPS fix, or to communicate while under the ice-cap, must find one – which can be quite bewildering because they vary in size from just a few feet across to quite large expanses of water, hundreds of yards across.

'How do you find them?' was the question on the navigator's mind. And the answer to that, according to Lt. Commander Krause, was, 'With the greatest difficulty.

'During a crossing like ours, which will be quite fast and stretch over three days, we would expect to see probably half a dozen,' he said. 'The only way to see them is by the light, which is much duller when it's filtered through several feet of pack-ice. But at the *polynya* the ice is very thin, and the light comes through brightly. Basically we are looking for a downward bright light in the wilderness directly above. We should be able to see it through the camera on the sail TV.'

'But say it's still a couple of feet thick,' said the navigator. 'How do we get through it?'

'We rise vertically and hit it with the sail . . . hard.'

'Will the ice break?'

'Sure. If it's thin enough, then we just pop up into an Arctic lake and take a look around. Get some fresh air.'

'How about if we misjudge it, and the ice is too thick?'

'That's inclined to be bad news. You kind of bounce off the ceiling a little, and hope to God you don't damage anything.'

'Jesus . . . that means you might damage the periscope or a mast, and you're still trapped.'

'We don't go up with any mast raised,' said Boomer. 'They are all safely lowered, but, yes, Dave, we are stuck below the ice-cap until we find thinner ice-cover – another *polynya* – and don't forget, we do have the upward fathometer which gives us some idea of the thickness.'

'Guess we're always looking for the bright spots, correct?'

Mike Krause smiled. 'That's us, Dave. Always looking for the bright spots.'

Meanwhile the Captain re-entered the conversation and mentioned that he had no intention of ramming any fucking overhead ice with anything, but that the entire crew should begin a 24-hour program during which they should check the ship over, searching for any source of any potential calamity. 'When you're trapped under the polar cap,' said Boomer, 'your real problems are apt to be avoidable – and by that I mean fire, radiation, steam leaks, planes-control etc. And, of course, a reactor-scram.

'The worst of these is probably a scram – a shut-down of the reactor. The tough part is restarting the damn thing, because right there you're on battery, which doesn't last long. There's just about enough juice for one try at rapid-recovery. But if the battery gets exhausted before you can get the reactor moving again, then you gotta run the generators to recharge – and for that we need air, the one item we don't have. Not without a *polynya*.'

'So we need to record the position of every one we pass?' said Lt. Wingate.

'Just that,' said the XO.

'And that's my dilemma,' said the CO. 'Do I leave the reactor scrammed, and run for the last *polynya* on battery. Or do I risk everything on one throw, using *all* of our battery power to restart the reactor. It's a tough one, if it happens. Because if I get it wrong, we're dead.'

'Shit!' said the navigator.

'But,' said Boomer, 'a far more likely occurrence is fire, or a major steam leak. That's when you really have to get into the fresh air. And right now we should get everyone activated, checking this baby from top to bottom for even the slightest possibility of that kind of trouble. Check, and double check.'

Columbia ran on northwards, arriving west of Jan Mayen in the small hours of the morning of August 24. Dave Wingate brought them to the drop-point, 72.00N, 10.00W at 0400, and the Captain ordered the ship to periscope depth to report their position to SUBLANT. The submarine then went deep again. She would begin transmitting at 0550 – 10 minutes before the US maritime patrol aircraft was scheduled to arrive with their package.

They returned to PD, raised the UHF aerial and transmitted on Channel 31, pausing every minute for 10 seconds to listen for the

MPA homing in on the signal. At 0558, they received a reply, suddenly from out of nowhere. '*This is Bluebird One-Five. Request yellow smoke.*'

Boomer ordered it instantly, and way out on the horizon the American aircraft came thundering in at 350 m.p.h., just 100 feet above the water, reducing the area over which its radio could be intercepted.

The navigator, sitting right next to the pilot, spotted the dense smoke now billowing off the surface of the water. 'Okay. Bluebird One-Five, *mark drop* . . . Now! Now! NOW! . . . *Columbia*, over.'

The big waterproof package, stuffed with everything the submarine had requested, hurtled through the air and crashed into the ocean right in the middle of the yellow smoke.

'*Bluebird, this is Blackbird. Thank you. Roger and out.*'

The MPA banked hard to starboard and climbed away to the south, back toward the US Icelandic base. The submarine surfaced gently, water cascading off the casing. The deck team were quickly up and out of the hatch, and they hooked the package adroitly. They were back below with the hatch shut inside two minutes. And once more Boomer Dunning took the black hunter-killer beneath the long dark swells of the North Atlantic.

They worked all through the day and for most of the night preparing their instruments for the 1,500-mile run beneath the polar ice-cap. After 200 miles on course zero-three-five they were in deep water at the northern end of the Greenland Fracture Zone, and right there Boomer Dunning ordered the critical course change which would see them head due north, into the Lena Trough.

'Conn – Captain . . . come left zero-zero-zero. Make your speed 25. Depth 600.'

Everyone felt the slight heel as *Columbia*, still running fast, altered course towards the pack-ice which covers the top of the world, swinging to the north toward the giant floes which would soon obliterate the light and seal the American submarine into the ice-cold water below.

The Greenland Sea grows deeper as it approaches the ice-pack, and as it does so, the ice becomes more frequent. Great chunks, some of them 50 feet across, lurk treacherously just beneath the surface, like jagged concrete blocks ready to smash the sail of any submarine which is running too shallow.

The crew of *Columbia* could sense the heightened tension among the officers as the big nuclear boat plowed ever northwards into ice which was becoming steadily more dense. At first the floes above appeared only occasionally on the TV screen, but five hours after the course-change, with the ship now within 50 miles of the cap, there were so many of these enormous, dark aquamarine hunks rushing by in the dim light above, it was almost impossible to find a gap through which the sky could be seen.

Boomer and Mike Krause found one, 30 miles short of the ice-cap, right on the 81 degree line. He ordered *Columbia* to periscope depth, very slowly, and she emerged into a field of loose ice, drifting in a light fog which hung over the water. The sun was completely obscured, visibility was less than 100 feet, and beneath the keel there was 15,000 feet of ocean.

They accessed the satellite and passed on their position, course and speed to SUBLANT. '*Package retrieved successfully.*' Then they sucked their messages off the satellite, the principal one being the ice-report about the far end of their polar journey, which dealt with conditions in the waters which lie south of the Canada Basin, beyond the permanent limit of the Arctic ice. Right here, opposite Point Barrow in Northern Alaska, *Columbia* would face a 125-mile run across the desperate, frozen wastes of the Beaufort Sea, before edging southwest into the equally dangerous Chukchi Sea.

The issue here is the quality of the summer. If it's warm, *Columbia* would run into clear water with ice-floes floating around occasionally. But if the summer should be bad, with serious heavy ice still there through July, *Columbia* would face an 80-mile journey across a half-frozen Beaufort, waters which would force her to stay dived; waters which shelve up treacherously: 10,000 feet . . . then 6,000 . . . then 3,000 . . . then 600 . . . then even less, as they reach the Beaufort Shelf, which protects the northern coastline of Alaska. This short stretch can be a submariner's horror story.

And the news was not good. Boomer could see Mike Krause and Dave Wingate going over the report. Both men were frowning, and the young navigator was using his dividers on the chart which dealt with the Pacific end of the Arctic.

Boomer too was anxious, because of the closeness of the big floes which surrounded the submarine right now. He ordered the ship dived again, and the planesman leveled her out at 600 feet. *Columbia* continued to head due north at high speed, running directly at the ice-cap, the millions of tons of snarling, frozen ocean which would imprison them for three days. The lives of every man in the submarine were entirely dependent upon the huge, sweetly running GE PWR S6G nuclear reactor.

With the ship settled on her course, Boomer joined his XO and requested the bad news from the ice-report. The Lieutenant Commander from Vermont was diffident, but somber. 'It's no use pretending, sir,' he said. 'Conditions in the Beaufort over the far edge are on the lousy side of average. Winter stayed too long this year, and the summer has hardly existed. The last 100 miles in towards Point Barrow are the problem. There's drifting pack-ice for the first 50 miles. And it's not much better for the next 20 or 30. As you well know, sir, that's when we run into the shoals. There's no way we can make reasonable speed on the surface, and we don't want to surface anyway . . . If we do, nevertheless, have to surface, will there be enough clear water for us to keep going?

'And right here there's only 200 feet . . . What we don't need is a big pressure ridge which will force us down to clear the sail from the ice, only to ground the hull on the bottom. Should keep it interesting.'

Boomer smiled, despite the clear and obvious problems which lay ahead. 'We'll just have to play it by ear, and hope to God things are a bit better when we finally arrive.'

'Aye, sir.'

At 2200 on August 24, just north of the 81st parallel, *Columbia* crossed the limit of the permanent ice-shelf northeast of Greenland. Six hundred feet under the surface, she passed across the unseen frontier which ends the North Atlantic, and entered the waters of the Arctic Ocean. When next she surfaced she would be in the Pacific Ocean, on the far side of the world.

Meanwhile, as midnight approached, *Columbia*'s quarry, the two Kilos bound for Shanghai, were in the middle of their nine-ship Russian convoy, almost 1,000 miles to the east, making 10 knots on the surface of the Barents Sea. At 2355 the Kilos were 42 miles northwest of the headland of the great jutting Russian island of Novaya Zemlya. Right now, as he headed due north in a dead straight line under the Pole, Boomer was already 250 miles *closer* to the Bering Strait, to which they were all headed. And the American was steaming forward at more than double the speed of the little Sino-Soviet convoy. If *Columbia*'s reactor stayed healthy, and the ice-cover allowed, the race would be no contest. Exactly as the Black Ops Cell in SUBLANT had forecast.

Commander Dunning went down to the maneuvering control room at 0030 to visit Lt. Commander Lee O'Brien. Boomer found the chief engineer on this watch himself, accompanied by his three-man team, including an electrician, and his chief mechanic, Earl Connard, who was at the reactor control panel. O'Brien was concentrating to catch any emergency at a split-second's notice; monitoring the power . . . power that sprang from the fission of atoms of uranium.

Lt. Commander O'Brien looked up when the Captain walked in. 'Hi, Sir,' he said cheerfully. 'We're chugging along pretty good right now. Tell the truth, she's never run better. Dead smooth. Nothing to report.'

'Good job, Lee,' said Boomer. 'We've got a ton of depth right here . . . no objection if we wind her up to 30 knots?'

'Nossir. That'll be fine. Sooner we get out of this frozen rat-trap the better, right?'

'That's my view, Lee. Come up and have a cup of coffee when you're off watch.'

Boomer went down two decks to the big bank of machinery which formed part of the ship's air-purification system. He found engineman Cy Burman at work with a wrench and spanner, making an adjustment to the CO_2 Scrubber. This is Navy jargon for the wide gray bank of purifiers which controls and keeps down the levels of carbon dioxide — a lethal, insidious gas which would wipe out the entire crew, if the air pressure inside the hull increased and more than four percent of CO_2 was permitted into the air supply. Boomer watched Cy working, and reflected that at this moment, as at all times, the man in command of this bank of machines held the lives of everyone in his hands. He stopped and chatted for a few moments, but sensed that the engineman was edgy.

'Not a major problem, Cy?' he asked.

'Nossir. Not even a problem. Just a small adjustment I'd like to make — no one's gonna even notice. But while we're down here, without much prospect of fresh air, I want this thing at maximum efficiency.'

Less than 100 miles into the pack, and the tightness throughout the ship was already obvious. Up in the Conn, the hub of the entire ship, he found the watch crew working quietly together, silently in the dimly lit room, checking *Columbia* held to her course and depth as she raced under the heavy ice.

From the other side of the compartment where the navigation systems were centered, Boomer could see the long trace of the fathometer, sounding regularly off the ocean floor, far, far below. The smooth line of the soundings was a comfort, providing no sense of the deep lonely echoes, bouncing back through ice-cold water which fell away to a thinly charted ocean-bottom, almost three miles below the keel. Soundings from the submarine made short work of the colossal depth.

The hunched figure of young Wingate could just be seen through the light of the operational area. And right beside him, Boomer could see the yeoman tending the ice-detector, waiting for a *polynya*, watching the stylus rapidly tracing the shape of the 40-foot-thick ice ceiling, which stretched with cruel and jagged indifference 480 feet above *Columbia's* sail.

Boomer walked over and joined them, stared at the swiftly moving stylus, and asked, 'How's it going?'

'Pretty regular, sir, at about 40 feet thick,' replied the yeoman. 'But about 15 miles back it suddenly went crazy, and drew a huge downward indent, like some kind of a stalactite . . . must have been nearly 100 feet deep into the water.'

'Pressure ridge,' said Boomer. 'We have to be really quick on those – not at this depth, because none of 'em are 600 feet deep, but they *can* stretch down 120 feet, and you really don't want to hit one of those sonsabitches. They not only look damned ugly, they're as hard as fucking concrete.'

Lt. Wingate spoke next. 'I've never been exactly certain what causes them, sir,' he said.

'Oh, just the pressure of the ice. You imagine two vast floes, millions and millions of tons, crushing into each other from different directions because of wind or current . . . well, it just forces the huge ridges downwards, and those ridges are our main enemy, all the way under the Pole until we reach the north coast of Alaska. When you see a big downward pattern on this little machine, we're coming up to one of them.'

'Yessir. By the way, do we expect to see icebergs?'

'Not really. Not up here. The pack-ice above us is too closely rammed together. If you go up in an aircraft above the cap, it looks like a kind of patchwork, a huge pattern, made up of hundreds of big floating jigsaw pieces, some of 'em miles across. They're crammed close, but not necessarily joined, not in one solid stretch. They're separate, and they're drifting and floating, grinding into each other, right up there over our heads. Icebergs are different – they're vast hunks which break off from the land ice-shelves, or even off the edge of the polar ice-pack, but you don't find 'em here because they can't break off and float. You may get 'em down towards the Bering Strait, lying deep, right where we're going.'

'Aye, sir.'

All through the bright northern night, *Columbia* ran due north up the Lena Trough in the dark, deep water. By 0700 Lt. Wingate had plotted them up over the Morris Jessup Plateau, one of the most famous of all the Arctic undersea beds, where the bottom comes sweeping upwards for almost a mile and a half, the depth changing steadily from 11,000 feet to only 3,500 feet, until the great underwater plateau provides its unmistakable landmark. Dave Wingate's fathometer worked on steadily as the echoes sounded off the relatively shallow bottom. And the trace was somehow more friendly.

Right there, above the Jessup heights, the navigator spoke to the Captain, and Boomer ordered a course change, one which would swing them at last away from their due north bearing. 'Conn – Captain . . . come left slow to three-three-zero, maintain speed 25, depth 600.' His words would steer *Columbia* on a course 200 miles south of the Pole, angling left to 270 across the 86th parallel, in water which would again run 10,000 feet deep, but which would avoid the unnecessary confusion of longitude roulette, and the risk of toppling compasses.

Boomer decided to run all day at 25 knots, and to begin searching for a *polynya* sometime after 2300. That way he could put *Columbia* on the surface around midnight in broad daylight, pass the PCS and take any signal update from SUBLANT. He went over to the navigation room to check their likely position at that time, and was pleased to see they would be right above Hall Knoll, well past the direct line of the North Pole and running very firmly south, instead of north.

He also decided to sleep for a few hours, and at 0800 he formally handed the ship over to his XO, whose forenoon watch was just beginning. The Captain had been up throughout the night, and slept soundly in his bunk for five hours, awakening in time for lunch, which he ordered specially: a bowl of minestrone soup, a rare sirloin steak, salad, and a mountain of french fries, which his wife would undoubtedly have confiscated at birth.

Boomer grinned privately at his brilliance in outwitting her, and sprinkled the fries liberally with salt, another item Jo would have whisked from his hands before as much as a grain hit the plate. Come to think of it, Jo would not have been crazy about the thick blue-cheese dressing which flowed across the salad. There were not many reasons why Boomer was ever glad to be separated from his wife, but right here, in the banquet spread before him, was one of them. It was a 15-minute respite from his devotion to her. Commander Dunning chewed luxuriously. Still grinning.

By 1530, at the halfway point between the Morris Jessup Plateau and Hall Knoll, Dave Wingate had plotted them at their closest point of approach to the North Pole, which lay more than 200 miles directly off their starboard beam. Right now the gyro-compasses were working perfectly as *Columbia* crossed the limit of her northern journey. At this point, 300 miles off their port beam, were the northern boundaries of the Queen Elizabeth Islands, the vast snowbound archipelago which sits atop the northernmost coastline of Canada. From here on, as they raced on toward the Bering Strait, *Columbia* would be running southward, 550 feet beneath the ice-pack.

The temperature inside the ship was a steady 71 degrees, everyone worked in shirtsleeves, and there were near-constant movies being shown in the crew's mess hall. Above them an Arctic storm might be raging, the ice-cap might be swept by gales, and the cold unbearable. But inside *Columbia*, cocooned against the unsurvivable conditions which surrounded them, the living was pleasant, if not easy. They lacked only one small comfort: the ability to surface at will. Every man knew they were imprisoned by deep pack-ice. That was the difference between this voyage and any other voyage. If their ship faltered, mechanically, in any way, *Columbia* could quickly become a tomb. Unless Boomer and Mike Krause could crash her through the gigantic granite-hard ceiling of ice which held her captive.

All through the afternoon they ran on, down to Hall Knoll, above ocean valleys 10,000 feet deep. They were in the middle of it now, way past any point of no return. If the reactor were to fail terminally, they could not even make it on the battery to the edge of the pack-ice, because the distances were simply too great. The crew were aware of the risks and of the horrendous consequences of disaster striking them, and they tried to conduct both their duties and their leisure time with especial normality. But the strain and tautness would not entirely evaporate. *Columbia* was quieter than usual. It was as if both she and her crew were traversing these silent, rarely traveled waters with a still, small voice inside them, warning over and over, 'Beware! Beware!'

From time to time, the upward sonar had revealed stretches of open water, and there were occasions when the moving ice-mass above was plainly breaking up, and some of the floes looked to be around 20 feet across, with small dark channels in between. But as the evening of August 25 wore on, the pack-ice seemed to tighten. Dave Wingate and Mike Krause had not seen sign of a *polynya* of any size for three hours.

The hour of 2300 came and went. The officer of the deck ordered a 5-knot reduction in speed, and the navigator's assistant went on special alert for the bright light of an Arctic lake to bloom above them. But for a further half-hour there was nothing. There was a light blue tint to the water now, which suggested the entire ice-layer was thinner, but that could be 10 feet thick, since *Columbia* had run for a long time under drifting chunks that went to 50 and 60 feet in depth.

They passed a pressure ridge which cleaved almost 100 feet down into the water, and right afterwards Boomer ordered the submarine to run at reduced speed nearer the surface . . . depth 250 feet and 15 knots. Forty-five minutes later, Lt. Commander Krause, now watching the TV monitor as well as the upward fathometer, spotted a narrow *polynya*, a bright clear light through the ice. He thought it was probably a couple of hundred yards long, but very narrow. 'That might do. MARK THE PLOT,' he called. 'But we have to take it real steady, and be ready to submerge real quick.'

Then he alerted the CO. 'We have a possible *polynya*, sir . . .'

Boomer arrived in the Conn and ordered, '*ALL STOP! Turning back, slowing down for a second look.*'

Columbia made a careful Williamson turn, and Boomer ordered the planesman to head upwards slowly to 150 feet. Boomer ordered the periscope up with 50 feet above the sail, and decided to take a good look around himself. What he did see was chilling. Columbia was nearly stationary just under a narrow inverted crevasse, with terrifying craggy stalactites of ice, 20 feet thick, jutting down towards her in almost every direction. If she ascended exactly vertically, she might make it unscathed. One deviation from the vertical, and she would crunch into the ice-pilings which guarded the *polynya*.

'Jesus Christ,' said Boomer. 'Flood her down NOW . . . We're outta here.'

Columbia returned to the safety of the deep and accelerated away. Midnight came, and still they watched for the chink of light which would allow her to surface. At 0106 Mike Krause saw it, a yawning bright light, which seemed to suggest a *polynya* with only thin ice on the surface. It was a long open channel in the ice, which was dark-blue in color and 100 feet wide.

Columbia slid right past, even though she was making less than 15 knots, and the helmsman made another Williamson to bring her back to the *polynya* as they slowed. It took 10 minutes to maneuver her right back under the *polynya*, 10 difficult minutes before Boomer Dunning commanded, 'All stop . . . rudder and planes amidships . . . check all masts fully lowered . . . we're going for a vertical ascent.'

Again the buoyancy was adjusted and very slowly the black ops submarine began to rise. Right now the XO had taken over the diving officer's stand, and the officer of the deck, Lt. Commander Abe Dickson, stood back ready to help and learn from Mike Krause.

Columbia kept rising. The XO called out the depth, and Boomer checked the TV monitor. He stared into it, and was again shocked by the amount of 20-foot ice lances jutting down towards him at the south end of the *polynya*. But they were not so close as on the previous occasion . . . and he called out for Mike Krause to keep the submarine slowly rising. What really concerned him was that he could not discern ripples on the surface water; the picture seemed hard and smooth. *Columbia* was going to have to bust through the ice. The question was, how thick was it?

Mike Krause took a look at the TV and said he thought it must be thin, the light seemed so bright. But there was no doubt, the *polynya* had a firm ice-crust to it, maybe five feet below the surface.

And then, despite their inching ascent, they hit the overhead ice with the most shuddering impact. They smashed it all right, but at what cost? *Columbia* shouldered her way out of the ocean as Boomer ordered the main ballast tanks blown, into a trackless twilight of a snowscape at exactly 0127. Blocks of flat ice from the base of the *polynya* slithered off her hull, sliding down and crashing back into the almost fresh water which now surrounded her, as they burst upwards into the air. Right now the sail ice-detector was nonoperational, and it had been so since they had slammed into the crust. The XO guessed they'd somehow clobbered the upward-looking fathometer when they had used the sail as a battering ram. 'Guess it was a bit thicker than we thought,' he growled. 'Christ knows what's the matter with this . . . but at least up here we can check it.'

Boomer ordered the main ballast tanks to full buoyancy before he led Abe Dickson up the ladder, through the two hatches and out into the Arctic daylight. The air was nothing less than frigid, and a light wind out of the north wafted across the American submarine with teeth like iced razor blades. Everything was white, flat and endless. The flowing lead, which ran out of the *polynya*, wandered for miles in a westerly direction, winding away between the floes. The light was not as bright as Boomer had anticipated, at least not so bright as it had seemed 150 feet below the ice-pack, but the dazzling white of the snow increased it, and Boomer could see for a long way.

Within moments, a team of technicians arrived topside to check over the upward fathometer, and it took them only a few minutes to ascertain the transducer had probably broken upon impact. There were two spares on board, which solved only part of the problem, because the repair would have to be carried out in extreme conditions. None of the men should work for more than 20 minutes in these temperatures, crouched on top of the sail, handling tools so cold they could stick to a mechanic's flesh.

They measured the temperature at 30 degrees below zero. They'd need a heat gun, blowing hot air, while they vulcanized the leads to make a watertight seal when they had completed the electrical joints. Boomer ordered everyone below to get fully kitted against the cold, and he was quite surprised to discover that he himself was shivering violently after only eight minutes outside. Even in his Arctic jacket, pants, hat and gloves.

They now raised the mast and accessed the satellite, calling in their position, and intentions for the next 24 hours. Then they collected their own signal, originated by SUBLANT, as it happened, just a half-hour before.

'*K-9 and K-10 still heading east in Kara Sea. In company with escort as previously stated. 260001AUG, position 78.00N, 90.00E, speed 10 knots on the surface. Heading for Strait of Vil Kitskogo south of Bolshevik Island. Good hunting.*'

Boomer took the message into the navigation area, where Lt. Wingate located the correct chart and placed a mark on the spot where the American satellite had recently photographed the Russian convoy. The navigator made a few measurements, and then said firmly: 'We're doing it, sir. I have us 480 miles closer to the Bering Strait . . . and once we're under way, moving much faster.'

Topside, the mechanics and the two electricians took turns in the freezing conditions to fit the new transducer. It should have taken about an hour, but it was taking more than double that time.

And all the while they worked, they could feel and hear a weather front coming in from the north. The wind was rising, but even more eerie was a dull roaring sound a few miles away. By 0300 they could actually see, far out on the horizon, a heaving wave in the ice, rumbling and cracking, slowly rolling toward them. The Captain was on the bridge when it first happened, and he turned his binoculars to the north to witness the Arctic phenomenon, where the wind was now whipping the snow off the top of the giant ice-wave as it ground its way toward *Columbia*.

'In one hour, that roll in the ice is gonna arrive here and crush this ship like a tin can,' snapped Boomer. 'How close to ready are the guys on the transducer?'

'FORTY MINUTES, SIR,' someone yelled. 'Two more waterproof seals.'

Boomer turned his glasses back to the north and tried to get a distance fix on the line of ice-slabs, rising up to 12 or 15 feet in the air in an upward pressure ridge, hundreds of yards long. All around *Columbia* there was nothing but endless flat ice-fields, and the jagged wall of rafted ice, way out, possibly two miles off their starboard beam, now fractured the smooth, level plain of the Arctic snowscape.

Boomer tried to lean forward on the edge of the bridge to steady the binoculars, to see if he could discern movement on the ridge to equate with the distant thunder of the floes. But the wind

322

seemed to whip between the glasses and his eyes, which were watering uncontrollably, the involuntary tears freezing hard on his cheeks within seconds.

But there was movement. He was sure of that. In the pale sunlight he could see the great chunks rise up, and then make a prolonged roll forward, forcing more ice upward and onward.

'Jesus Christ,' muttered the CO. 'This ice is on the move, but I sure as hell don't want to go back under – not with the ice-detector still up the chute. But we can't stay up here, because this *polynya*'s gonna start closing in on us real soon.'

He tried to work out how long they had, but even as he stood there, he could hear a rise in the noise level, a kind of high shrieking sound, punctuated by an almighty 'CRACK!' as a mile-long split suddenly appeared to port, and then, just as suddenly, closed again.

Boomer Dunning, after a lifetime at sea, had never seen anything quite so dangerous as the shifting deep floes which formed *Columbia*'s lethal harbor.

'What's the quickest time you can make those seals tight?' he called calmly to the chief electrician.

'Thirty minutes, sir . . . It's so cold . . . my fingers will hardly move . . . and I have to keep taking my gloves off . . . the working area's so small.'

'Okay, keep at it,' replied Boomer. But in his mind, he knew this was a race he might lose. And once more he turned to the north, to stare at the ponderously rolling wall of ice, rumbling always closer.

Mike Krause came on the bridge, his tall, slim frame lost in the bulk of his heavy-duty Arctic kit. He turned instinctively toward the rumble, raising his binoculars and gazing out at the moving wall. 'Christ,' he murmured. 'We don't wanna hang around in the path of that fucking lot for very long, sir.'

'You're right there,' replied the CO. 'But we don't want to go under without the ice-detector either. We're just slightly between the rock and the hard place right here.'

'How much longer to fix the transducer, sir?'

'Latest estimate was 30 minutes.'

'Christ, sir. That pressure ridge looks about ready to crush us in the next 10.'

'I've been trying to get an accurate fix. It's difficult . . . but one thing's for sure: that ridge looks a lot closer now than it did 15 minutes ago.'

'Yup. And I think the noise level is rising. It sounds higher . . . like a scream. Guess that must be from the floes grinding together. Can you imagine the forces behind that pressure, sir?'

'Can I ever. And I wonder where it starts from . . . how many miles away either the wind or the current is causing the wave to happen.'

Just then, the roar of the ice grew louder, and suddenly there were three explosions on the starboard side, as the five-foot-high walls of the *polynya* split apart, sucking water in and sending great slabs of ice cascading into the water around the submarine.

Deep inside the hull the noise level also rose, as the little icebergs, only 10 feet wide but as heavy as cast iron, banged against *Columbia*'s casing.

'Guys, we're gonna have to get outta here,' Boomer called to the electricians. 'How quick can you make it work?'

'Might be through in 15.'

The sound of the ice was growing so loud, he and Boomer were having to raise their voices to hear each other. The thunderous rumble now seemed replaced by a howl, like a rising wind or a penetrating screech, interrupted by a distinct crash and thump as the ice-blocks tumbled one on top of the other.

But much worse than the hellish din was the grinding of the harbor walls which were closing in on them. The 30-yard channel to starboard was now only about 10 yards wide, and it kept splitting, and edging closer.

Boomer reckoned they had 10 minutes, maximum. Mike Krause would have guessed five. And both men could see now the jagged shapes of the slabs, like an ice-age Stonehenge, rolling in from the right of the submarine, each massive slab landing with a staggering 'KERRRUMP.'

'Two minutes, sir . . . gimme two minutes. We're almost there . . . it might not last forever, but it'll work for a few days.'

Boomer held his nerve. He just said, 'Great job, guys,' and he gripped the edge of the bridge as a new landslide of ice crashed into the *polynya*, rising up in the water, scraping the hull of the black ops submarine, causing deafening noise inside. The entire ship vibrated and for the first time on this voyage men began to feel a chilling fear.

But still Boomer Dunning did not order the bridge cleared, and *Columbia* to dive. Two minutes more ticked by, and now the wall of the *polynya* was against the hull to starboard, pushing her back across the narrowing *polynya*. Topside they could hear nothing above the bedlam of the moving ice.

The chief electrician's cry of '*Repair complete, sir!*' was whipped away by the wind. The first time Boomer and the XO realized the new transducer was in place was when the five-man team began clambering down through the hatch, two of them with numb, frostbitten fingers.

The walls of the *polynya* were beginning to split asunder on the right as Boomer commanded, 'Clear the bridge.' He and Mike Krause dropped down the ladders behind the repair party. Hatches were shut behind the topside watchmen, and just before 0400 Boomer ordered the main vents open and buoyancy adjusted to help them down.

Columbia began to sink below the treacherous crush of the moving ice-cap, which would shortly render the *polynya* non-existent. The upward fathometer was working perfectly, and at 150 feet, Boomer put them on a new course: '*One-nine-zero . . . speed 25 . . . depth 600.*'

Before them stretched a long, slightly curving course, 800 miles right across the 10,000-feet-deep Canadian Basin. At a steady 25 knots, they would make it in 32 hours . . . 1130 on the morning of August 27. Whether or not they would be able to surface when they cleared the permanent ice limit and reached the waters of the Beaufort Sea was, at this stage, a matter for pure conjecture. The ice-report indicated no change, no comfort ahead. But what mattered that minute was their last-minute escape from the vise-like grip of the Arctic ice-cap. After that everything had to be better. A whole lot better.

Halfway along their course, 400 miles south of Hall Knoll, they would cross the 80th parallel. Boomer considered it unlikely they would find a spot to surface around here and anyway, he was nervous about time. He understood the critical requirement for *Columbia* to be neatly in position, awaiting the arrival of the Kilos. He was determined that he should have the element of surprise, the advantage of the stalker, setting his own ambush. He was not about to squander that by wasting valuable hours trying to batter his way through the goddamned ice-cap for a further update . . .

and anyway, in his opinion the die was cast. The Russians were making for the Bering Strait, as he was. He knew their course, he knew their maximum speed, and he knew their destination. But he was going to be there well in front.

Again he went into the navigation room, and pulled up the big chart which detailed all of the oceans which span the top of the earth. He measured and remeasured. Whichever way he cut it, when *Columbia* emerged from beneath the permanent ice, bang opposite Point Barrow, he was going to be 600 miles northeast of the strait. At that precise time, 1130 on the morning of August 27, the Kilos would be 1,200 miles northwest of the strait, in shallow, icy water approaching the Novosibirskiye Islands in the East Siberian Sea. Unless the conditions on his side of the Chukchi Sea were drastically worse, he was winning this race hands down. And there wasn't a damn thing the Russians could do about it.

The 32 hours passed swiftly, the watches came and went, Boomer ate french fries at every meal, and the fathometers kept working: one of them feeling, with its icy fingers, the contours of the far distant bottom; the upward ones sketching ceaselessly the irregular pattern of the ice ceiling above.

It stayed light all the way, and none of the pressure ridges stretched down more than 100 feet. Shortly after 1100 on August 27, *Columbia* entered the Beaufort Sea. Though you would not have known it. The ice-pack remained solid above the submarine, as Boomer held his course due south, and made directly for Point Barrow.

The first 50 miles were routine since the water was never less than 3,000 feet deep, but then the bottom began to shelve upward to meet them. Within two hours they were in under 500 feet. Boomer was not anxious to go any farther inshore, and 30 miles short of the Point he ordered a change of course. '*Come right to two-two-five . . . speed 12 . . . depth 200 . . .*'

They were approaching, he knew, the most dangerous parts of the journey, the notorious shallows of the eastern Chukchi Sea. And overhead there was still heavy drifting ice. They had even passed two deep pressure ridges in the past hour. What Boomer now dreaded most was the possibility of having to dodge both the ridges and possible icebergs, while staying clear of the sea-bed. In the long waters of the northwest Alaskan coast leading down to

Point Lay, it was possible to run into shallows of only 65 feet in depth, the surface laden with massive floating ice-floes.

A bad summer in the Chukchi is as bad as a grim winter off Greenland. The ice tends to break off from the shelves which pack along the coasts of both Alaska and Siberia, and then they drift south. Some of these floes can be two miles across, and they raft up, one climbing over the other, pushing the giant bottom hunk downwards, to a possible depth of maybe 70 feet, like deep-drafted icebergs, but virtually stationary. The Chukchi abounds with this kind of hazard, but it is rare in August, and Boomer Dunning cursed his luck that the ice forecasts were so bad.

They pushed on slowly along the coastline of Alaska, when suddenly the stylus on the upward fathometer jumped, sketching swiftly, and apparently recklessly, two giant downward shapes in the water. The yeoman watching the machine called for attention, and Lt. Commander Dickson and Mike Krause dead-heated in front of him.

'This right here is a pressure ridge,' said Krause slowly. 'Almost certainly rafted ice . . . but I'm damned if I can make this out . . .' He pointed at the next deep-drafted obstacle, jutting down with a jagged edge almost 120 feet from the surface. He studied it for fleeting seconds, and then hissed: 'Jesus Christ! It's a fucking iceberg . . . and God knows how wide it is.'

By now Boomer was also in there. 'Depth?' he questioned.

'Two hundred feet, sir. Sounding 60 below the keel.'

'We'll have to go deeper,' snapped the CO. *'Make your speed 3 knots . . . Take her down very slowly, no angle . . . Call out speed.'*

'Sir. Five knots . . . reducing.'

'Sounding . . . 50 feet, sir.'

'Three knots, sir.'

'Sounding 40 feet, sir.'

Ahead of them, in a matter of yards now, was the colossal blue-grey bulk of the iceberg, and the recording pen kept racing lower. Boomer ordered, 'ALL STOP!' He knew they were already committed to slide underneath, and hoped to God not to jam the submarine between the berg and the bottom. If they hit the iceberg the sail would probably be damaged. The worst scenario would be if they jammed irrevocably. Because death would come painfully and slowly, probably by starvation, while the reactor continued to provide endless fresh air, heat and water.

All four men watched the pens. No one spoke, and *Columbia* still went forward, now at less than a knot. There were less than 15 feet under the keel and the 7,000-tonner crawled forward, periscopes down, masts down, heads down, like a poacher sliding under a protective fence.

But this protective fence was almost 600 feet wide, and its base was uneven, and *Columbia's* sail was only three feet from the ceiling.

'Sounding 10 feet, sir.'

This was tight, but not as tight as it was going to be. Because the stylus was edging lower, showing a two-foot downward bulge at the base of the ice – not just an outcrop, but a long ridge. *Columbia* could not turn, or even swerve. She could only go astern to get out again. But she continued to crawl forward.

'Sounding five feet, sir,' called the yeoman calmly as they waited for the shuddering crunch of the sail against the iceberg's base, or the scrape of shale along their keel.

The 200 yards beneath the iceberg seemed like an eternity, but all at once the stylus took on a new life, and began to draw in a higher line. They edged up off the bottom, and now the line was a dramatic sweep into clear water as the berg slipped away astern. *Columbia* was through, clambering almost along the bottom, but through.

'*Make your speed 3 knots,*' said the Captain. 'Planesman, keep her level and plane up to 150 feet. We have water above . . .'

Three hours later, at 0530 on the morning of August 28, *Columbia* was clear of the heavy ice. There were still intermittent chunks floating around, but it was safe to go to PD in the bright dawn and access the satellite. The signal from SUBLANT was, by now, routine. The Kilos had been photographed a little over 1,000 miles northwest of the strait . . . still four days away. Boomer had all the time in the world to position himself for the attack.

He passed his PCS, informing the submarine chiefs in Norfolk, Virginia, he would swing south off Point Lay and make his way to the narrow radar-swept gap of the Bering Strait, which divides the USA and the old Soviet Union.

There was only 100 feet of water in here, and there was always ice drifting around, whatever the time of year. Boomer planned to run through the center at PD, then come west towards the Siberian coastline, but remaining in the outer limits of American waters, west of St Lawrence Island. Speed must be kept low in these shallow waters, and they would need to avoid the more rare, but still dangerous floes that sometimes littered the strait beneath the often choppy windswept surface.

With luck, he would have three or possibly four days to lay his ambush. And it had better be a good one. The Russians were not famously swift of thought, but they had thus far taken inordinate care of K-9 and K-10. And surely, if they believed the United States might attack again, they would be particularly wary south of the Bering Strait, where American waters run right into Russian waters, where a US nuclear boat could take out a couple of unsuspecting Kilos with comparative impunity. The difference was, K-9 and K-10 were not unsuspecting. They were armed, protected, and ready.

Commander Dunning knew that *Columbia* might be fired upon. And he knew his crew would have to operate right at the top line of their ability. And he thanked God for the one single paragraph contained in his orders, the paragraph which made him truly lethal.

The one signed by the Chief of Naval Operations himself. The one cleared personally by the President of the United States: 'In the event of a threatened attack on *Columbia*, any attack, by any foreign power, the Commanding Officer is empowered to use pre-emptive self-defense.'

Basically this meant he could fire first. Because to fire second might be too late.

CHAPTER THIRTEEN

*C*OLUMBIA RAN QUIETLY through the Bering Strait late on the afternoon of August 30, without detection. Boomer headed her toward the northwest headland of Gambell on St Lawrence Island, and slowed down in the broad waters where the Bering Sea begins to flow into the yawning Siberian Bay of Anadyrskij, a vast expanse of ocean, 200 miles across, north to south, and 150 miles deep to the west.

'If I thought for one moment they were going to make a run for it straight across the mouth of that bay,' thought Boomer, 'I'd nail 'em right here. But I don't think they're gonna do that. Because if I were them, I wouldn't either. I'd creep right around that big bay. I'd stay well inshore, hug the coastline, always within 12 miles of Russian soil. That way, I'd be forcing any enemy to break international law if they planned to hit me. I'd also be making it damned difficult for guys like us.'

In shallow water, Boomer continued dived, hidden hard in the lee of St Lawrence Island. Everyone was glad of the respite after the fast and dangerous run under the ice-cap, and the engineers used the time for light maintenance and routine checks. The torpedomen too stayed busy, for their part would be swift and deadly. One mistake from them and the entire exercise would have been in vain.

Columbia was many thousands of miles from home, and, as she was a black ops submarine, very few people knew her location. The CO wanted no mistakes, no hitches, and no carelessness. They accessed the satellite regularly and it obligingly provided them with precise daily positions of K-9 and K-10, and the small but powerful Russian armada which guarded them.

In the early evening of September 1, Big Bird photographed the Kilos, moving slowly through the ice-floes, still on the surface with the Typhoon and the escorts. They were west of Vrangelya Island which sits midway between the permanent ice-shelf and the endless frozen coastline of Siberia, bang on longitude 180 degrees. SUBLANT estimated they would cross latitude 70 degrees at about midnight on September 3 and come through the Bering Strait about 1400. Like Boomer they then expected all nine of the ships to swing hard to starboard into the Bay of Anadyrskij, staying close to the shore all the way.

Boomer pondered his position, and decided to head away to the southwest and select his spot further down the coastline. There were simply too many imponderables at the mouth of the bay; not least, which way would the Kilos go, and would they stay on the surface? He studied the charts with Mike Krause and, generally speaking, they were agreed on a position to set up their patrol: they would cross the bay, and then continue southwest for 230 miles, just short of the East Siberian headland of Ol'utorsky.

Boomer was sure this was the best place, about 30 miles northeast of the headland. 'If they're running inshore, we'll be waiting; if they swing suddenly offshore, the satellites will see them change course, and I can cornerflag to the south . . . where I'll still be waiting.'

All through September 2 the Kilos proceeded at 8 knots over the icy shoals of the southern Chukchi Sea. Moving carefully within the cover of the escorting destroyers, and behind the crushing weight of the giant ice-breaker, they crossed the Arctic Circle, and shortly afterwards turned hard right, rounding the great jutting square peninsula of northeast Siberia.

K-9 and K-10 entered the Bering Strait at midday on September 3, and changed course to two-two-five as they followed the Siberian coastline. But when Big Bird photographed the stretch of ocean where they should have been at 1900, local time, the pictures arrived in Fort Meade showing just the four escorts, the replenishment ship and the ice-breaker. There was no sign of the three submarines. Both Kilos and the Typhoon must have dived, somewhere west of St Lawrence Island, probably just on the Russian side of the dividing line.

It was 0430 in the morning on America's east coast, and the Fort Meade duty officer, Lt. John Harrison, looked at the satellite shots with considerable alarm. Losing both K-9 and K-10 at this stage of the game was, in his view, a three-alarmer. He stood helplessly, holding the telephone, willing Admiral Morris, just this once, to awaken and answer the damn thing. But he never did, not in the middle of the night, and he didn't now. Lt. Harrison handed over control of the busy 24-hour-a-day intelligence operation, and bolted for the door.

He arrived at the bedside of the deeply slumbering Director of National Security in four minutes, turned on every light and proceeded to shake the Admiral into life. As ever the boss growled his way towards consciousness with a mixture of indignation and wry good humor.

'This better be really important, Lieutenant,' he rasped. 'Really important, right?'

'Yessir.'

'Well, speak up, for Christ's sake. What the hell's going on?'

'According to the latest satellite pictures, sir, we just lost both K-9 and K-10. They've either dived, or made a bolt for it. Either way, sir, it's not perfect. The escorts are still there, but there's no sign of any submarines.'

'Jesus Christ! Gimme three minutes. Have the car right outside the door.'

By 0530 Admiral Arnold Morgan had joined Admiral Morris in Fort Meade and they were both staring at the satellite pictures. 'These escorts are still making some kind of pattern,' said the NSA. 'I suppose it is possible the submarines are still right in position . . . just running under the surface.'

'Yessir. That is possible. But it's kinda hard to make that assumption, just in case they have made a break for it. I was calculating just before you came. It's a little more than 4,000 miles from the Bering Strait down to Shanghai, where I presume they are headed. If they refueled the Kilos from that damned great tanker south of the Strait, they could make an 8-knot underwater run, and they'd be there in 19 days . . . they'd only have to snorkel a dozen times, and the chances of us catching them there, in that huge expanse of the Pacific which surrounds Japan . . . well, they are close to zero in my view.'

'Fuck it,' said Arnold Morgan.

And as dawn broke over the shimmering warm air of Chesapeake Bay, one solitary US Marine helicopter could be seen out over the Cape Charles lighthouse, clattering its way south, losing height as it swooped down toward the Norfolk Navy yards. It would land seven minutes after a similar helicopter, bearing the CNO in person, had come in from Washington. The time was 0715.

'Morning, Arnie,' said Admiral Joe Mulligan and Admiral Dixon in harmony. And the CNO added, 'I hear we're in deepest crap – again.'

'Well, deepest crap is certainly a possibility, though not yet a certainty,' replied Admiral Morgan. 'It's just that we can't see K-9 and K-10. But that doesn't mean the fuckers are not still there.'

'Can I see the pictures?'

'Sure. Take a look. If you follow the pattern you can see the escorts are still apparently on duty.'

'Right. Sure looks like it. Where's *Columbia* right now?'

'Latest satellite signal says Boomer was heading southwest. He correctly thought an attack at the mouth of the big bay was too complicated, and he is now on his way to a patrol position at 60.15 North, 171.30 East, about 30 miles northeast of Ol'utorsky. It's quite deep water fairly well inshore there. *Columbia*'s team is assessing the Russians will hug the coast, staying inside Russian waters.'

'He does of course need help from us,' said Admiral Dixon. 'Just in case he has to cornerflag it to the south if the convoy makes a run offshore. Personally I'm happy he's way south; gives us more options and more time. He was planning a fast run to Ol'utorsky and all being well he's there right now.'

'When do we get a new satellite fix?' asked the CNO.

'Not for another 18 hours,' replied Admiral Morgan. 'By which time the escorts should be 160 miles further on . . . either almost across the mouth of Anadyrskij Bay, or deep in it, right down at the western end.'

'I guess that next picture is critical,' said Joe Mulligan.

'Absolutely,' said John Dixon. 'I think if they are all down the bay, we should assume the submarines are still with them. If they are on their way down the coast, that makes it marginally less likely. However, if they are holding the escort pattern, that would still look to me as if the Kilos have not strayed far from Daddy. Particularly so if they are still making 9 knots . . . nice and comfortable for the brand-new submarines to snorkel.'

Admiral Morgan was thoughtful. 'Isn't it a bitch?' he wondered aloud. 'Everything we hate about that fucking little submarine, the sheer difficulty of finding it, is right here to haunt us. As soon as the little bastard dives. If ever there was a goddamned commercial to highlight the danger of that bastard in the Chinese Navy . . . goddamnit, we're looking at it right here.'

'I guess that's all true,' said Admiral Mulligan. 'Meanwhile, we better alert *Columbia* of the situation. Lay out the options as best we can, and advise them to try and keep some kind of a sonar watch not only on the coastline, but also out to the east, though I doubt he'll have much luck in those waters. The place is just too fucking big, right?'

'It is for one submarine, sir,' replied Admiral Dixon. 'Unless we can pick 'em up, and provide some hard facts.'

'Okay, gentlemen. I guess that's it. All we can do is keep watching and waiting.'

By 0400 on September 4, Boomer had sucked the bad news off the satellite. There was little he could do since he was now 400 miles southwest of the escort's last-known position, and no one yet knew which course they would make on this mammoth journey around the world to China.

The Commanding Officer of *Columbia* could only listen, and wait. And hope.

At 1900 that same day, the all-seeing space camera in Big Bird passed silently by, 20,000 miles above the lonely waters at the southeast corner of the Siberian Bay of Anadyrskij. The evening was clear, the quality of the pictures was excellent, and the content encouraging. Admirals George Morris and Arnold Morgan, sipping black coffee in Fort Meade at 0230, made their deductions from the photographs of the Russian ships.

Big Bird had snapped them right off Cape Navarin: the three destroyers, *Admiral Chabanenko*, *Admiral Levchenko* and *Admiral Kharlamov*, and the ASW frigate *Nepristupny*, in a crescent formation inside the 150-foot depth contour, against the shoreline. The ice-breaker *Ural* was out in front, and the giant replenishment ship brought up the rear. The key was that the convoy did not appear to have swung to the west around the bay, but had proceeded straight across, making some 210 miles in 24 hours, which meant they were still making less than 9 knots, which in turn meant that K-9 and K-10 were most probably still there. Dived and snorkeling, but there. Otherwise the convoy would have been making 15 knots or more for home, clear of the ice and the Kilos. Of the 21,000-

ton Typhoon, there was still no sign, which meant it had probably left to pursue its own special business.

'You little babies,' said Admiral Morgan. 'That speed's exactly right. Nine knots, 210 miles exactly. Those cunning pricks must have dived, just in case we were out there waiting for 'em. The other great news is the Typhoon seems to have beat it.'

George Morris packed up the pictures. Arnold Morgan decided to snatch three hours' sleep at his home in nearby Montpelier, and then track on down to Norfolk in the helicopter. His chauffeur Charlie would await him throughout the rest of the night until the Admiral and the package were delivered safely into the Marine helicopter, which waited on the Fort Meade pad.

The following day, the three admirals met again in the Black Ops Cell at SUBLANT. In the opinion of Admiral Dixon, the convoy would stay more or less in place all the way to Petropav-lovsk, the big Russian naval base which lies right on the northern Pacific, 700 miles southwest of Ol'utorsky, towards the end of the Kamchatka Peninsula. It was to this port Admiral Dixon had originally assessed the Typhoon might be going. But Big Bird had not seen it yet. Thus John Dixon now concluded it was on missile patrol in the Sea of Okhotsk.

'With that settled,' he said, 'we must have a reasonable chance. The water off Ol'utorsky comes up from 600 feet to the beach within 12 miles of the shore. That means *Columbia* can lie in wait outside of the limits of Russian waters, and fire from 14 miles out, straight inshore, straight at the Kilos.'

The three Admirals drafted their 'appreciation' of the situation accordingly, stressing that the Kilos were most certainly there, but that the Typhoon had almost certainly left. The signal concluded with the following sentence: '*Provided you are able to POSIDENT Kilos, you are free to attack at will.*'

Boomer, who now knew the time-frame of the satellite pass, ordered *Columbia* to periscope depth at 0430 on September 5. He sucked down the signal from SUBLANT, and then presented his own appreciation of the situation. He informed the Navy Chiefs he would like to receive one more fix from the satellite this evening, because that would probably have the Kilos at 60.40N, 173.30E, northeast of his patrol spot, 60 miles short of the headland. His signal required no further reply and *Columbia* slid swiftly back beneath the calm but chill Pacific waves. To wait.

He took up his position 14 miles due east of the Siberian shore, a mile outside the 600-foot depth line. Seven miles further inshore was the 150-foot line, and he fully expected the Russians to steam down here, just landward of that line, with the two big ships, the three destroyers and the frigate forming their crescent, presumably around the two submerged Kilos, six miles offshore. So far as he and Mike Krause could tell they had much in their favor. They had deep water to seaward, which would enable them to evade counter-attack if necessary. It would also allow them adequate sonar performance, even though they were looking 'uphill,' toward the noisier shoreline.

Boomer accessed the satellite at 2030, and received confirmation from SUBLANT that the convoy was proceeding as anticipated at the critical 9 knots. Big Bird photographed them at 1900, in position 60.40N, 173.30E, which put them a little more than 16 miles to his northeast right now.

Even as he lowered the mast, the sonar room, deep in the control center of *Columbia*, heard the first signals of their approach. The combat systems officer, Lt. Commander Jerry Curran, was in attendance, and his sonar chief mentioned that whatever was happening out there sounded a lot like World War III. Lt. Commander Curran himself was observing what was a most terrible racket, loud active sonar transmissions, massive cavitation, and many propellers, as the Russians came steaming into range.

'Captain – sonar . . . could you come in, sir?'

Boomer was there in seconds, and he too was temporarily mystified by the unearthly noise roaring through the water, and causing a complete white-out of the underwater picture. 'There's no pattern to it,' said the sonar chief. 'It's just chaotic, so loud and uneven it's obscuring all engine lines . . . just a total mess. We've got shaft rates and blade rates all over the place . . . can't make a lick of goddamned sense out of any of it.'

Lt. Commander Curran was thoughtful. The tall, bespectacled Connecticut native was a deep expert on these systems, and he had a Master's degree in electronics and computer sciences from Fordham. A world-class bridge player, he recognized a truly brutal finesse when he saw one. And the dizzying white lines on his screens represented exactly that. 'They know we're out here, and they're putting up a massive, deafening sound barrier between us and the Kilos,' he said slowly. 'Those destroyers' blades turn at 100

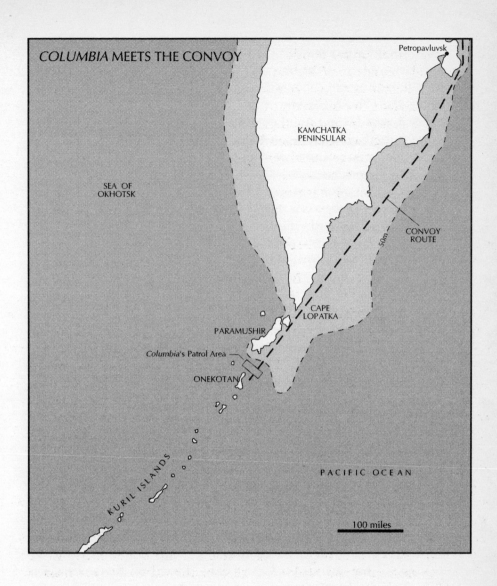

COLUMBIA MEETS THE CONVOY

Petropavluvsk

KAMCHATKA
PENINSULAR

SEA OF
OKHOTSK

CONVOY
ROUTE

50m

CAPE
LOPATKA

PARAMUSHIR

Columbia's Patrol Area

ONEKOTAN

PACIFIC OCEAN

KURIL ISLANDS

100 miles

revs a minute going forward, but we're not hearing blades going fast-forward . . . we're hearing 'em in reverse as well . . . making 60 revolutions the other way. That's what's causing the incredible cavitation. Those Russian ships' helmsmen are driving one propeller forward, and one in reverse . . . using a ton of gas – but they don't care, they've *got* a ton of gas.'

'If that's right, it sure works,' said the sonar chief. 'I never saw a wall of sound like this before.'

'That's just what it is,' said Boomer. 'A wall, starting with the ice-breaker which is still out in front, and running back in a four-ship curve to seaward with the replenishment ship bringing up the rear, seven miles from the lead ship. That's their formation . . . has been all the way down this coast. The Kilos are most probably behind that wall, maybe a mile inshore. We can't see them, and we sure as hell can't hear them. Basically, our weapons have absolutely no chance. We don't know *where* the targets are, we don't even know *whether* the targets are there at all . . . never mind getting a POSIDENT, and standing a chance of hitting it. And I'll tell you something else: if they've thought about us this carefully, they've got decoys towed behind all four of the escorts, helping with the noise.'

Columbia was patrolling right now six miles to seaward of the nearest Russian escort ship, which happened to be the frigate. 'We should assume they are all on active sonar,' said Lt. Commander Curran, 'which does mean we could be detected. If we come to PD, they could pick us up on radar . . . I assume they would attack us instantly if they either see or hear us.'

'Very likely. *Fuck it*,' snapped Boomer out loud, neither enjoying the reversal of roles, nor sharing his tumbling thoughts with his crew. 'It's supposed to be us hunting them, not the other way around . . . but the fact is I can't draw a bead on them. Isn't this an unholy bitch? And what the fuck am I going to do about it?

'OK, team, I'm gonna withdraw out into deep water for the moment. We can continue to head southwest, and we're never going to lose them with that racket going on . . . they can probably hear the bastards in Shanghai. But I need a little time to think some more.

'No sense hanging around here, that's for sure. We can't get off a shot, and we've got a reasonable chance of getting shot ourselves . . . Still, I want to go to PD very briefly, and take a look, see what's out there. For all we know the Kilos are on the surface. Then we're gone.'

Columbia angled her way slowly to PD, raising her periscope and ESM mast when she was ready. They both broke through long Pacific swells, and down below Boomer stared at the horizon to the west, where he could see, clearly, the two highest masts on the newest Type Two Udaloy destroyer, the *Admiral Chabanenko*, seven miles off his starboard bow. He could also see the two following destroyers, the Type Ones, but nothing further. The shape of the big two Palm Frond antennae spread stark above the *Chabanenko*'s bridge was unmistakable.

Almost immediately the urgent voice of the ESM mast operator was heard. '*Captain – ESM . . . I have at least eight different radars. You have danger-level racket on three of them . . . track 2405, 2406 and 2407.*'

Commander Dunning, like all submarine COs, reacted with an instant persecution complex, detesting the thought of being seen by the highly effective Russian radars. 'Down all masts,' he ordered. 'Five down . . . 300 feet . . . make your speed 8 knots . . . left standard rudder . . . steer one-eight-zero . . . I'm clearing the datum.'

Columbia angled down and away, and as she speeded up, headed east for deeper water. Boomer Dunning had seen enough: the powerful escort, the approximate shape of the wall which guarded the Kilos. Furthermore, the warning from the ESM operator meant that the American black ops submarine was very much expected.

052120SEPT. 60.40N, 173.30E. On board the 9,000-ton Russian destroyer Admiral Chabanenko. *Radar room, operator three:* 'Sir, I have a disappearing contact . . . three sweeps only . . . computer gives it automatic track number 0416.'

Officer of the Watch to Captain: 'Sir, we had a disappearing radar contact, three sweeps only . . . bearing one-five-five, range six miles off our port bow.'

Captain to Officer of the Watch: 'Possible US SSN, eh? No surprise. But also no danger. He can't hear the submarines, and he sure as hell can't see them. He's powerless, just as we planned. Even a crazy fucking

American cowboy would not shoot torpedoes at Russian surface warships in Russian waters. The submarines? He knows nothing!'

Columbia pressed on eastwards. Boomer accelerated as the depth increased, and then summoned Mike Krause to his tiny office to assist in drawing up a signal to SUBLANT. They waited for another hour, having put 25 miles between *Columbia* and the Russians, and then, at 2300, they came to periscope depth and transmitted the following:

SITUATION:
1. A) *Unable to attack. Russian convoy stays on 150-foot contour. Surface ships forming long protective barrier for Kilos, two to three miles to seaward.*
   B) *Intense and deliberate acoustic interference from surface ships prevents sonar detection of the Kilos. Therefore unable to make acoustic POSIDENT.*
   C) *Physical placement of escorts with active EMCON policy for sonar and radar denies me ability to get close enough for VISIDENT of Kilos snorkeling – if indeed they are there.*
   D) *Obviously reluctant to send in weapons on the off-chance of finding Kilos in difficult shallow waters inshore of the wall.*

INTENTIONS:
2. A) *To wait until convoy passes Petropavlovsk, to see if escort reduces.*
   B) *To set up ambush in deep water first opportunity. This should occur in position 49.90N, 154.54E between Onekotan and Paramusir, northern Kuril Islands, 300 miles south of Petropavlovsk. ETA 100800SEPT.'*

It was 0630 in Fort Meade when Boomer's signal was received. Admiral Morris and Arnold Morgan had waited all night, half expecting to be informed that *Columbia* had put both Kilos on the bottom of the Pacific right off Ol'utorsky. But not with any great degree of optimism. Both men understood this was a mission of extreme difficulty, and that Commander Dunning was operating under the most trying circumstances: attempting to lay an effective ambush, to hit two dived submarines, operating behind a big, highly capable escort, which was expecting just such an attack, and which would not hesitate to open fire, on or below the surface, with guns, torpedoes or depth charges.

Boomer's signal was frustrating, but highly professional. At least he was still operational. He was also unharmed and ready to attack at the first opportunity. Both men knew that if the *Columbia*'s CO pulled this one off, he would be placed automatically on the short-list of commanders due to be promoted to captain. Right here they were discussing instant promotion for a first-class submarine CO. Arnold Morgan would immediately demand that reward for the king of the black ops. And no one would argue.

Columbia returned to PD within a half-hour to receive the SUBLANT reply. And it was there, terse and unambiguous: '*Your para 2B) approved.*'

Admiral Zhang Yushu had vacated his summer home in the deep south, and was back with his family in his official residence in Beijing. Except that now, with the heightened tension caused by the impending arrival of the new Kilo-Class submarines, he was ensconced at the Chinese Navy Base in Shanghai, in conference with Vice-Admiral Yibo Yunsheng, the East Fleet Commander, who normally worked out of Fleet HQ in Ningbo, 100 miles south across the long seaway at the mouth of Hangchow Bay.

The two Admirals, who had worked so diligently with Russia's Admiral Rankov to ensure the safe delivery of the submarines, now sat within sight of victory. They had three Kilos safely home, they had lost five, probably to illegal American action, but there now seemed nothing to prevent the final two – Kilo 9 and Kilo 10 – from arriving in the great warship-building port of Shanghai.

If indeed that did happen, the Russians had agreed to apply all Chinese money given in part payment for the lost five to five new Kilos – a circumstance which both the C-in-C and his great friend Yibo Yunsheng were already anticipating with enormous relish. They always stated, with solemnity and concern, that the Kilos were a purely defensive measure, to keep the US Navy out of legal Chinese waters. What they never said was that the Kilos would facilitate within a few short months the military recapture of Taiwan, and the untold wealth that would bring to the nation; just as the re-annexing of Hong Kong and Macau had done.

The Paramount Ruler understood the motives of Zhang Yushu and his most senior trusted admirals, and he raised no voice against them. For they were all men, he knew, who essentially treated China's problems as their own. They were also men who would gladly have laid down their lives for the People's Republic. And such men were rare. The Paramount Ruler knew that, and would indulge their ambitions endlessly.

For the past two weeks, Admirals Zhang and Yibo had watched the signals being routed now through Russia's Pacific Fleet Communications Center in Vladivostok, via the satellite, on a direct link to Shanghai. Every 24 hours they heard only that the two Kilos, accompanied by the three destroyers, the frigate, the big missile submarine, the ice-breaker and the replenishment ship, were making smooth and steady progress along the icy northern route across the top of Siberia.

The C-in-C agreed that if the Americans were laying a trap, they would have done so in the GIUK Gap in the North Atlantic, as they had probably done for Kilo 4 and Kilo 5. He also agreed that the men in the Pentagon must have been furious when they saw the cunning of the Russian plan, to go east instead of west, and to protect the Kilos with such an impressive flotilla of naval power.

Each day, while the Russians and Admiral Yibo had grown more enchanted with their own brilliance, a feeling of disquiet began to cast a shadow over the street kid from the Xiamen waterfront, who had made it to the very top of the Chinese Navy. It was true, Zhang admitted, that the Americans must have been severely outwitted on this one, and yet . . . he knew about those terrible men in the Pentagon, he understood their ruthlessness, their determination, and their no-holds-barred attitude to military power. Of course he did. He was of the same breed. From another culture, another place. But nonetheless just like them.

In his hand he held the latest signal, transmitted from the destroyer *Admiral Chabanenko* at 2130, two hours ago, from somewhere off the eastern coast of Siberia. He kept reading the words over: '*052120SEPT. 60.40N, 173.30E. Short transient contact picked up on three sweeps radar. Six miles off our port bow. No data for firm classification. Did not reappear. Possible US SSN. No subsequent attack. No reason for additional defensive measures. Acoustic barrier well in place. US powerless, especially while we proceed in Russian waters.*'

No more. No less. But Admiral Zhang, alone among the Chinese High Command, did not like it. For a start he was uncertain whence any possible US submarine might have come. 'We probably left one behind in the North Atlantic,' he murmured. 'Then what might they have done? The Panama Canal route is too far . . . Maybe they sent one north from Pearl Harbor or even San Diego, but I'd be surprised . . . They would want their subversive actions kept quiet. Certainly not broadcast all around the Fleet. If there is a US nuclear tracking the Kilos, it's got to be the best they have. Which means we had better be very careful. I just don't like the tone of that Russian captain . . . too complacent . . . and when you're dealing with Americans you don't want to be complacent. Otherwise you might not live.'

He walked into the next office, where Admiral Yibo was working. He too had, of course, read the signal from the *Admiral Chabanenko*.

'Do you have any thoughts on that?' asked the C-in-C.

'I've been considering it. But it seems highly unlikely the Americans could have a nuclear boat tracking the Kilos down the coast of Siberia. Where would it have come from? Perhaps the West Coast?'

'I suppose it's possible. But it's a very long way.'

'Sir, I would say just this. If I was commanding the *Admiral Chabanenko*, I would be very careful indeed.'

'So would I, Yunsheng, my friend. So would I. However, our Russian colleagues seem to think the Americans would not dare to open fire on Russian surface ships in Russian waters. And they also seem very confident that the Americans can neither see nor hear the Kilos.'

'Thus far, they have been right.'

'Yes. But I think they may not have faced the fact that an American submarine has only just arrived, and may just be working out its plan of action.'

'The Russians think their sound barrier is foolproof. They think that to get at the Kilos, the US nuclear boat will have to hit at least two of the escorts – which they are plainly not going to do. Because that is piracy on a drastic scale, too reckless, and too public.'

'The problem is, Yunsheng, it's so difficult to understand how the American mind functions. It is so foreign to us. We both have our pride, our sense of face, but we think differently. In two hundred years we have never really come to grips with Western thinking, especially American thinking.'

'No, sir, but we are at least starting.'

'We are?'

'Yessir, right here in Shanghai at the University of Fudan there is a new degree course for students: The Study of American Thought. They have been recruiting professors from all over the world, professors of politics, journalism, the arts and the military. For the first time we are building the basis of a study course from real US newspapers and magazines, rather than from our own government's official line.'

'Now that sounds like progress. And really it's time. Every modern leader in recent Chinese history has always studied for some kind of a scientific degree, including myself . . . and you.'

'Yessir. Let's face it, advanced thinking on Western politics and the liberal arts has essentially been banned in this country for as long as anyone can remember.'

'I wonder how they are progressing over at Fudan? Think there might be a few top-grade students who could tell us what the Americans are going to do about the last two Kilos?'

Yunsheng laughed. 'Probably not, sir. Nonetheless, if I were commanding that big Russian destroyer, I would not drop my guard for one split second.'

'Neither, my friend, would I. In fact if I caught one sniff of a US nuclear submarine, I would sink it without hesitation.'

'If you could, sir. If you could.'

'Yes, Yunsheng. If I could.'

061100SEPT. 130 miles east of the Siberian coastline. Navigation center, USS *Columbia*, steaming southwest, deep, at 20 knots. Boomer Dunning, Mike Krause, Jerry Curran, and Dave Wingate stood huddled over charts.

'From the convoy's last-known position in Ol'utorsky,' said the XO, 'it's close to 1,000 miles all the way down the Pacific side of the Kamchatka Peninsula. The convoy will definitely get there on September 10th, probably in the afternoon. SUBLANT believes we already lost the Typhoon, and I expect to lose the ice-breaker and the replenishment ship, and probably a couple of the escorts when they reach Petropavlovsk sometime on September 8th.'

'Right,' said Boomer. 'But lemme just say this. If I was in command I'd keep those four escorts in place until we reached the Shanghai Roads, somewhere west of Nagasaki in the East China Sea.'

'Yessir. That's just because you know what you know. They don't know what you know. They don't even know we're here.'

'Don't they? I wouldn't be surprised if they got a sniff when we took a quick look around back at Ol'utorsky.'

'Possibly, sir. But even if they were sharp enough to catch us onscreen, they still might not have been sharp enough to interpret the "paint" as a marauding US nuclear submarine.'

'Maybe yes. Maybe no. But I'm here to tell you, if someone had taken out five of my brand-new submarines, I'd open fire on a fucking lobster if it waggled its claws at me.'

Lt. Wingate laughed at the Captain's choice of metaphor, as he usually did. But they all took the point. The Russians simply had to be on full battle alert. Unless they were crazy.

'Meanwhile we better familiarize ourselves with our patrol area . . .' Boomer had his dividers on the big navigation chart of the Kuril Islands, a sure sign that he meant business. 'Okay,' he said. 'Right here we have the end of the Kamchatka Peninsula, which tapers off to Point Lopatka, a couple hundred miles southwest of Petropavlovsk . . . these are pretty lonely waters. Then the islands, the Kurils, stretch in a near-straight line for 800 miles, right down to the big bay at the northeastern corner of Hokkaido, Japan's north island.

'According to this chart, the islands were occupied by the Soviet Union from 1945, heavily disputed of course by the Japanese, who claim the four nearest ones are owned by them. Which they would, wouldn't they?

'Anyway, we don't give a rat's ass about that end of the chain. We're concerned with this big bastard right up here in the north, by Point Lopatka. It's called Paramusir Island, and it's about 65 miles long. The next one to the south is Onekotan, which is about a quarter the size. The bit we care about is the seaway which separates them . . . it's about 40 miles across, and it will be the first time, since we've been on the case, that the Russian convoy has crossed a wide stretch of sea in deep water, without land off its starboard beam. At their speed of 9 knots, they will take four and a half hours to make their way from the southern point of Paramusir to the northern headland of Onekotan. Sometime during those four and a half hours, I intend to sink both Kilos.'

'How about the sound barrier, sir?' asked Lt. Wingate.

'It's going to be reduced, because some of the ships will probably peel off at Petropavlovsk. The rest will then have to form an all-around barrier instead of just the crescent along the seaward side. That could reduce the effectiveness of their sound barrier. It could also make the target area smaller. Plus, all of our systems will work better in deep open water. We'll set up our patrol right here.'

Boomer pointed with his ruler to a mark at 49.40N, 154.55E, in 600 feet of water. 'First time in the whole passage we've had it deep enough and clear enough. Gentlemen, trust me, this is good submarine hunting country. Right here we do have Russian international waters . . . but we'll be 14 miles offshore, just out of 'em.'

'Sir,' said the navigator, 'I've plotted our turn into the patrol area right here on the 50th parallel, exactly where it bisects 160 East.'

'Looks good, Dave,' said Boomer. 'But of course, there is one other question: which side of the Kurils do we think they will go? They could swing inside and steam all the way down the edge of the Sea of Okhotsk, which the Russians regard as a private inland sea of their own. Or they could stay outside and keep on running down the Pacific. It's possible they may feel safer on the inside, so we better be ready. Get the ship well into the seaway between the islands. We can always slide back outside if that's where they are. At least we have the elements of speed and surprise on our side.'

Back in Fort Meade, for the third night in a row, the satellite picture arrived at 0300 their time, and there were no surprises for Admiral Morgan or Admiral Dixon. Big Bird still showed all six escorts in their crescent formation, 200 miles further south from Ol'utorsky. Of the Kilos there was still no sign. But the surface ships were still making 9 knots, and there was no further sign of the Typhoon either.

'No news,' grunted Morgan. 'That's the best kind. There's no way the Russians are going to be dumb enough to use a 21,000-ton ballistic-missile submarine to protect a couple of export Kilos. If it's there, they would want us to know it was there, in order to deter us from shooting. They know good and well we might hit it by mistake if we open fire. Well, we can no longer see it, and we must thus assume the Typhoon is gone on the inter-Fleet transfer we first considered. Let's hit Boomer with this information. Then get the hell outta here.'

082030SEPT. Shanghai Naval Base. Admiral Zhang made his

346

nightly perusal of the communications from the Russian Pacific Fleet headquarters. Tonight he was informed that no further transient contacts had been observed by the lead destroyer, despite vigilant radar and sonar surveillance. The ice-breaker and the 35,000-ton replenishment ship had peeled off at Petropavlovsk, but the four surface escorts were still in place, and would continue to make their presence obvious to any enemy for the rest of the 3,200-mile journey to Shanghai. For the first time Admiral Zhang was given a solid ETA. 'We expect to berth in the port of Shanghai late afternoon on September 24.' A sharp frisson of excitement prickled the scalp of the Commander-in-Chief of the People's Liberation Army–Navy. It had been a long wait.

100200SEPT. 49.40N, 155.54E. *Columbia* patrolled silently, at 5 knots, 200 feet below the surface, deep in the seaway which separates the Siberian islands of Paramusir and Onekotan. Commander Dunning and his XO were in conference. The satellite signal from SUBLANT had confirmed, two evenings previously, the projected disappearance of the ice-breaker and the replenishment ship. The latest communication showed the four escorts still making 9 knots, still in their regular crescent formation, 'bulging' to the east, presumably to seaward of the Kilos.

This latest satellite picture, shot at 1900 the previous evening, showed the three Russian destroyers and the frigate steaming steadily southwest, 51.00N, 152.80E, 30 miles east of Point Lopatka, fifteen and a half hours from *Columbia*. Right now they were four hours up-range in the dark, and plainly staying east of the Kurils.

Boomer Dunning ordered the submarine once more to periscope depth, principally for a weather check, because at this moment he could not believe his luck. Conditions were set fair, with a brisk force-four breeze off the Sea of Okhotsk – just enough to whip up the waves a little; just enough to make it difficult for the opposition to see *Columbia*'s periscope. But not too choppy for the sonar conditions to deteriorate. 'Perfect,' said Boomer. 'Couldn't have hoped for better.'

'I think we ought to assume they'll change their formation when they get into deep open water south of Paramusir,' said Mike Krause.

'No doubt,' said Boomer. 'They'll probably make some kind of a

347

ring around the Kilos. Maybe one on each corner . . . that's when I might be able to get at 'em a little better. There will definitely be less noise blanking them out, so I ought to be able to fire a couple of weapons deep into the "square" between the escorts. We'll use the new guidance system for the search pattern – keep those babies under tight control – which ought to find the Kilos, if they're there.'

'They're there okay,' replied Lt. Commander Krause. 'That 9-knot speed they've held all the way from the Bering Strait confirms that. Unless they've been trying to fool us all along and the submarines split off way back. Either way, we'll know soon enough.'

100350SEPT. USS *Columbia*, patrolling 200 feet below the surface, holding her position 49.40N, 155.54E. Lt. Commander Mike Krause has the ship. The Captain is in the navigation area. The sonar officer, Lt. Bobby Ramsden, carefully monitoring the work of his team of sonar operators, turns suddenly to Lt. Commander Jerry Curran, standing behind him. 'We're getting something, sir. Bearing zero-three-zero . . . several ships . . . unusual amount of noise . . . allocated track 4063.'

'*Captain – sonar*,' Jerry Curran says into his microphone. 'We just picked 'em up. The Russians bear zero-three-zero . . . twenty miles plus. Could you come in, sir?'

Boomer enters the room quickly. 'Okay, Jerry, we ought to be able to see them on the infrared in what, say . . . 75 minutes from now?'

'Yessir.'

'Okay. Now, we're using the new guidance system, right? I'm going to fire two Mk 48s into the area between the four escorts. All the way in, we're gonna hold them at passive slow speed, under tight control. No automatic release if they get a contact. We're gonna guide 'em right past the lead destroyer, then on into the box. Then we put 'em on active search, still under control. No one releases anything until I say so. I gotta be sure we're not looking at a decoy.'

'No problems, sir. If we get a contact deep in the box, it's gotta be a Kilo, right?'

'Right. And we'll set a depth ceiling at 40 feet on each weapon. That way they cannot attack a surface target. They'll go for any submarine dived in the box, but they'll leave the escorts alone. If there are no submarines in the box, they'll just run out of gas and

348

sink to the bottom without exploding. Judging by the amount of noise the destroyers and frigates are making, they'll never detect a torpedo transmission . . . not with all that other junk to confuse 'em. They may just hear a hit I guess, but even the sound of that might get lost . . . by which time we'll be outta there.'

0505. '*Captain – sonar . . . seven miles, sir. The Russians now bear zero-two-five . . .*'

Commander Dunning ordered *Columbia* to PD, and, as the great black hull swept toward the surface, he raised the special search-periscope. Staring now at the dark skies in the north, he swung it round to zero-two-five, and waited for the infrared picture to come up. And for the second time in a week, the submarine CO from Cape Cod saw the great angled radar antennae of the 9,000-ton Russian destroyer *Admiral Chabanenko*. Just to the left he could see the identical antennae of one of the Udaloy Type Ones, which was now positioned about two miles off the *Chabanenko's* starboard beam.

'Looks like they could have formed a two-mile square,' he said to Mike Krause, standing beside him. The periscope was lowered after its five-second look, and the recording of its picture now showed on a screen. 'Here, Mike. Take a look . . .'

The executive officer stared at the picture. Then he said slowly, 'Yessir. That's exactly what it is. Should be able to see the antennae of the quarter escorts in 15 minutes.'

He predicted correctly. 'That must be the other Udaloy nearest us, sir,' he said, 'with the *Nepristupny* holding position on the north-west corner of the square. Right now the *Chabanenko* is six miles from us . . . it's just beginning to get light over there . . .'

Columbia, with no masts up now, remained at PD. Boomer and Mike Krause assessed the Russians would pass to the west, but Boomer wanted to be at least eight miles off track, and he ordered the submarine to change course. '*Come right zero-nine-zero . . . I'm opening the range a bit, then I'm turning back to attack.*'

Sixteen minutes later, at 0527, *Columbia* was in position and the Russian convoy was still 15 minutes away from the Americans' target area. The southeastern escort was bearing three-zero-zero, putting up the best sound barrier she could, with the other escorts' screws threshing away, their active sonars blasting loudly. The towed decoys, those stubby little bombs trailing behind the escorts, added their little bit to the general racket and the truly hopeless under-

349

water picture. From the sonar traces in *Columbia*, even the lowest frequencies appeared to be blanked out by the new acoustic jammers now generally available to those who cared to afford them.

In the opinion of the Russian commanders they were on the hog's back. Because, in addition to the acoustic barrier, they also had the radars of the three destroyers and the frigate sweeping over the empty seas. Two of their helicopters were up and patrolling the waters which surrounded the little convoy. Does any possible US submarine have a chance against these mass defensive measures? *Niet*, was the plain and obvious answer to that, not unless the attacker was prepared to take on the escorts first.

What they did not know was that Boomer Dunning, hidden just below the surface, did not require an underwater picture. He could see the two-mile square formed by the four escorts, and he was sure the Kilos were right in that square, if they were there at all. He would try to find them with his controlled search-and-kill wire-guided torpedoes, and then leave the weapons to finish the job. If the Kilos were not there, no harm would be done. Except to Arnold Morgan's already fraught nervous system.

Jerry Curran had briefed the team. The torpedomen were ready. The weapons-controllers were ready. All *Columbia*'s firing systems were go, as *Admiral Chabanenko* led the Russian convoy forward.

'*Captain – sonar . . . track 4063 bearing two-nine-five.*'

The weapons-control officer added, 'That puts the southeastern escort bearing two-nine-seven . . . range 10,600 . . . course two-two-five . . . speed eight . . . good firing solution.'

'STAND BY ONE . . .'

'One ready, sir . . .'

'Stand by . . . check bearing and fire.'

'UP PERISCOPE . . . bearing . . . MARK! . . . Range . . . MARK! . . . Down periscope.'

'Last bearing check . . .'

'Two-nine-six . . . SET.'

'SHOOT! . . . STAND BY TWO . . .'

'Track 4063 bears two-nine-three . . . SET.'

'SHOOT!'

In the sonar room they heard the metallic thuds of the weapons leaving the tubes, then near silence as the engines of the big, stealthy torpedoes powered them forward, aimed off, in order to stiletto into the box right behind the stern of *Admiral Chabanenko*.

Only the *faintest tremor* disturbed the smooth slow movement of *Columbia*.

'Both weapons under guidance, sir.'

'Arm the weapons . . .'

'Weapons armed, sir.'

The torpedo-guidance officer, standing next to the CO in the attack area, watched on the screens as the torpedoes moved menacingly through the water, their speed-setting slow, quiet and deep, sonars passive. Streaming out behind were the thin, super-tough electronic wires, along which would flow the commands into the computer brains behind the warhead.

The four-mile journey took nine minutes and 36 seconds, at which point the first torpedo got passive contact to port – and it was ready to attack.

Boomer snapped instantly, *'IGNORE THAT! It's Chabanenko's decoy . . . do NOT release the weapon. Switch to active search.'*

The guidance officer hesitated for a fraction of a second, then he steered it right past the lead destroyer, watching the torpedo cruise on into the box . . . searching . . . searching . . . searching for a submerged target across a long 1,000-yard swathe.

One minute later, it reported firm active contact close to port, and now it was transmitting its lethal short, sharp 'pings.'

'Weapon One release to auto-home,' ordered Boomer.

Columbia's Mk 48 swiftly adjusted course, accelerated to 45 knots, and locked on, with chilling indifference, to the black hull of K-9, which was moving southwest 200 feet below the surface at 9 knots, oblivious to the mortal danger which now threatened. The acoustic barrier which had made Boomer's task so difficult, now made detection of the tell-tale active 'pings' impossible for the Russian Captain. Neither he, nor the Chinese Commander who accompanied him, knew what hit them.

Boomer Dunning's torpedo smashed into the Kilo 120 feet from the bow, and exploded with deadly force. It blasted a four-foot hole in the pressure hull, a gaping wound which put the Kilo and her crew beyond any chance of survival. No one lived for more than a minute as the cruel waters of the North Pacific surged through the submarine, destroying her buoyancy, forcing her to the bottom.

Back in *Columbia* Boomer Dunning heard the unmistakable sharp bang as the Mk 48 hit home. But that was all. The roaring acoustic barrier of the Russian warships blotted out the loneliest sound any sonar operator ever hears: the endless tinkling noise of broken glass and metal which echoes back as a warship sinks to the bottom of the ocean. It was 0555, on the clear morning of September 10, just as the sun was beginning to cast the rose-colored fingers of dawn along the eastern horizon of the Pacific.

'That'll do,' said the CO of USS *Columbia*.

And now he turned his attention back to the second torpedo, also under tight control, and now well on its way across the box, almost one mile astern of *Admiral Chabanenko*. It too ran at a slow and deliberate pace, deep and quiet, crossing into the box almost halfway along the line between the two easterly escorts.

Boomer watched the guidance officer quietly drive the torpedo in towards the target area. He saw it pick up the frigate *Nepristupny*'s threshing screws to starboard, but did not have to warn against letting it loose this time. He ordered it switched to active search and 15 seconds later, it reported a new contact to port, which could only be a submarine. 'There he is,' rasped Boomer. 'Release to auto-home.'

'Contact 600 yards . . . closing . . .'

'MALFUNCTION, SIR . . . TORPEDO MALFUNCTION . . . LOST ACTIVE CONTACT.'

'TRY PASSIVE . . .'

'MALFUNCTION, SIR . . . Nothing coming back up the wire . . . it must have broken, sir.'

'*Stand by three . . .*'

'*Captain – sonar . . . I have underwater telephone on the bearing . . .*'

'Jesus, he must be talking to his fucking self!'

'Nossir. He's talking to someone else.'

'You got the interpreter down there?'

'Yessir. He's saying it's between two submarines . . . We're checking the call signs in the book right now, sir . . . They seem to be calling a third boat.'

'JESUS CHRIST!'

'Captain – sonar . . . the third boat is not answering. Call signs work out: from an export hull . . . and a Russian boat . . . trying to reach another export hull.'

A chill shot through Boomer Dunning's churning stomach. There could be but one answer. *The Typhoon was still there.* Unbelievably. Grotesquely, still there. And he, Commander Cale Dunning, had come within about 30 seconds of starting World

War III by accident. 'Jesus, Mary and Joseph,' said the CO of *Columbia*. '*STAND DOWN THREE TUBE . . . we will not, repeat NOT, be firing.*'

The picture in his mind was one of absolute clarity. He had assumed two Kilos were in the box, and he had hit one of them, and apparently gotten active contact on the other, just before he lost his second torpedo. Now the remaining Kilo was talking to the Typhoon, which had been there all the time, both of them trying to figure out what had happened to K-9 . . . the Kilo which was just about arriving at the bottom of the Pacific. With all hands.

There was little doubt as far as Boomer was concerned. If there was a Russian submarine in attendance, it was clearly the Typhoon. The issue now was, 'Can I risk firing again? Answer: NO. I have just been goddamned lucky not to have started World War III, by blowing up a Typhoon-Class Russian nuclear, which was built specifically to fire intercontinental ballistic missiles. I plainly cannot, knowingly, take that risk.

'I am already in the deepest possible crap. I had no POSIDENT of the Kilos. Acoustic or visual. Let's face it, I fired on the off-chance. Right here is where I back off, and throw myself on the mercy of SUBLANT.'

Boomer ordered *Columbia* deep and fast, to clear the datum and head east, away from the impending chaos. He handed the ship to Lt. Commander Krause, and retired to his cabin to prepare a signal to the Black Ops Intelligence Cell. It was, he knew, about 1300 in Norfolk, Virginia.

He wrote his signal carefully, wasting no words. When it was complete it read: '*Kilo Group attacked north of Onekotan. Unable to obtain fire-control solution on any submarines. Fired two Mk 48s into center of two-mile-square box formed by remaining four escorts. Torpedoes set for active-pattern search. One explosion heard. Subsequent telephone traffic, underwater call signs, strongly suggests one export hull sunk. Intercept also strongly suggests continued presence of Typhoon-Class submarine in the group. Do NOT intend further attack.* Mea culpa. Mea maxima culpa.'

Boomer ordered Columbia to periscope depth and accessed the satellite. He transmitted his signal at 0630, Eastern Daylight Time. At 0647 Admiral Arnold Morgan, the President's National Security Advisor, almost had a heart attack. At the time he was having a cup of coffee and a roast beef sandwich with the CNO, Joe Mulligan, in the Pentagon, and the craggy ex-Trident driver had calmly read it all out, verbatim, to the NSA.

'What the hell does he mean, *mea maxima culpa*? What kinda bullshit's that?'

'You ever been an altar-boy?' asked the staunchly Irish Catholic head of the US Navy.

'A *what*?'

'An altar-boy. You know, a kid who assists the priest during the Mass, rings the bells, lights the candles . . . holds the water during the consecration.'

'Hell no. In my part of Texas we played baseball on Sunday mornings. Mea catcher.'

'Arnie, I accept that my great office requires that I fraternize with those of a heathen persuasion, such as yourself. However, I think you should know the routine of a God-fearing family such as mine. Each Sunday at the foot of the altar, another boy and I placed our hands upon our breasts, and prayed: "*Mea culpa, mea culpa, mea maxima culpa* . . . I have sinned, I have sinned, I have greatly sinned." '

'You mean Boomer's admitting he overstepped the mark?'

'He sure is. And that's the mark of a fine officer. A man big enough for his rank. And not threatened by the admission of a mistake.'

'NOT THREATENED? I'll fucking threaten him. That boy's nothing short of a dumb-ass sonofabitch. What if he'd hit the fucking Typhoon? . . . Good morning, Mr President, we just had a bit of bad luck in the Pacific . . . one of our best submarine commanders blew up and sank a big Russian nuclear submarine in Russian waters by mistake. The nuclear cloud from its 20 intercontinental ballistic missiles is in the process of wiping out most of the Orient . . . ain't that a gas?'

Joe Mulligan chuckled at the brutal, exaggerated irony of Arnold Morgan's words. 'Steady, Arnie. In an operation like this, there's a ton of risk, every step of the way. Why don't we just think ourselves lucky? Boomer has removed one of the goddamned Kilos on a 33 percent chance of starting World War III. And he seems to have got away with it. That makes him a very lucky commander. But you need luck in the game we've asked him to play.'

'Right, Joe. We all need luck. Christ, I know that. But our signals to *Columbia* never stopped stressing the fact that he *must have*

POSIDENT. Therefore his actions were in direct contravention of his orders. He not only did not have POSIDENT, he had no fucking IDENT whatsoever, POS, near-POS, or *fuck-all* POS.'

Admiral Mulligan blew coffee down his nose, trying to stop laughing at the infuriated NSA. 'Come on, Arnie, if we send off a blast to *Columbia*, which others may see, humiliating their commanding officer, we will do nothing except hurt the morale of his ship.

'Just remember what Commander Dunning has done. He's actually sunk three of those Kilos. He's made a trans-polar run past the North Pole, and he's still operational. Undetected.'

'Don't gimme his fucking life story, for Christ's sake, Joe. I'm not talking about what he's done. Any good nuclear submarine officer would have done the same. Right here, I'm talking about what he *could have done*. Like started a goddamned world war. Nothing serious. Because he is, apparently, unable to obey a simple order. Like *get* POSIDENT. Nothing earth-shattering. Just routine sense. He's a dumbass sonofabitch.'

'What would you have said if his signal had claimed he did have POSIDENT on the Kilos?'

Admiral Morgan grappled for words, but for once in his life found none.

'Commander Dunning *could* have said that. And we would have been none the wiser. And if, as you are now implying, we give him a severe reprimand, he might also remind us that we kept *telling* him the Typhoon was gone . . . Oh, I know we can look at the small print and say we did not *quite* say that. But we did, and we advised him so several times. Let's face it . . . *none of us knew the Typhoon was still there*. Never even suspected it. In my view the Commander behaved in an exemplary way, and to tell the truth, I'd probably have done the same.'

'So would I, fuck it,' replied the NSA. 'But I'm still not prepared to listen to reason.'

Joe Mulligan laughed. 'Come on, old buddy. Fight the battle you're in. We got clean away with it. Beautiful, right? What'll we do now? Given that K-10 is still on the fucking loose?'

'Okay. I agree. You need not haul Boomer over the coals. But I do insist you make my thoughts clear to him. And I don't want him promoted. You can't have officers like that becoming captains. He's a fucking maniac.'

Admiral Mulligan grinned, and said, 'Yes, of course, Admiral. As much of a maniac as we were, in our youth. I wish to Christ we had a few more like him. But . . . down to business. Right here, we can't do much. It's no good hanging around and shadowing all the way to Shanghai. The Typhoon will now almost certainly stay as well.'

'Right. That bastard Rankov has been too clever for his own good. His stupid ships made too much noise. Boomer couldn't get a classification, but the Typhoon turned out to be no deterrent, because they failed to make it obvious that the sonofabitch was there. But I'll tell you one thing — it does show how determined they are to get the Kilos through to Shanghai.'

'As far as I'm concerned, the Kilo's split,' replied Joe Mulligan. 'That's what I would have done. Which means that right now we haven't got a chance of picking him up because the trail's gone cold. He's making a run for home. We're not going to get him . . . and I think we may as well send *Columbia* to Pearl for maintenance. It's only 3,000 miles from where he is now. It'll take him six days, and he can spend some time getting his ship into top shape. CINCPAC could use him to patrol with the new CVBG in the Arabian Sea in mid-October. But right now, I guess he and his crew could use a little R and R.'

'Okay, Joe. Let's do that. We'll just have to keep a weather eye out for K-10, as and when we can. Still, of the seven we went after, we got six, right? Not bad.'

The SUBLANT signal to Commander Dunning in *Columbia* was transmitted within the hour. *Columbia* sucked it off the satellite at 0900, local time, the next day, September 11. It read: '*Personal for Commander Dunning. Received your signal. Well done. Proceed to Pearl. Lack of POSIDENT: NSA assessment – D-A SOB . . . Mulligan.*'

Three hours later, running deep now, due south down the Northern Pacific, Boomer read the signal privately and ruefully. He had expected worse. They might even have relieved him of command. He had been instructed to get POSIDENT. But he was not the first front-line commanding officer to reflect upon how damned easy it is to sit in a Washington armchair, and how very much different things appear when you're actually out there, trying to attack, trying to keep your ship safe, trying to do the business of your higher command.

How typical, he thought, of the Navy to accept cheerfully the demise of the Kilo, and to intimate guarded approval of the attack.

And yet, as ever, to leave a commanding officer in no doubt that he will be held to account, should they consider he exceeded his orders.

'That's known, Admiral Mulligan, as having your cookies and eating them,' he murmured. And he wondered, quite seriously, whether he would ever gain the promotion to captain that was so important to him. How? With an apparent enemy like the mighty Admiral Morgan watching his every move. He also wondered, reflectively, how long it actually was since *anyone* had been brave enough to call him a dumb-ass sonofabitch, even in code, even from the other side of the world.

CHAPTER FOURTEEN

THE STAFF CAR drew up to the locked corner gate of the Garden of Yu the Mandarin, and the big man in the rear seat stepped out and strode forward. Two officials in Mao Zedong overalls hurriedly undid the locks, and the powerful, uniformed military officer marched into the near-deserted showpiece of Shanghai's waterfront. It was 11 a.m. and the gardens were not open again to the public until 2 p.m., but in China warlords have, traditionally, an entirely different set of rules.

The steel-tipped black shoes of the lone figure clicked on the concrete path as he passed the Hall for Gathering Grace, and he continued through the hedgerows to the long lake, striding towards the Tower of Ten Thousand Flowers. But there he slowed, and in a light September drizzle, he walked to the towering ornamental gingko tree which dominates this end of the gardens . . . and there he sheltered beneath the large fan-like leaves of the last species of a tree family which grew in Northern China 200 million years ago.

He stood in solitary fury under the branches, breathing deeply as if trying to control himself, somehow forcing himself not to commit murder. And he crashed his clenched right fist into the open palm of his left hand, and he hissed under his breath, 'If I could, I would blow the Pentagon to pieces . . . if I only could.' There were times when Admiral Zhang Yushu was the Orient's answer to Admiral Arnold Morgan. And right now he did not trust himself to fraternize with other human beings. Especially since he expected, imminently, a call from Moscow, from Admiral Vitaly Rankov, who he now believed was possibly the biggest fool in Russia.

The satellite message had been what he considered trite, explaining that there had been some sort of an accident off the southern end of the Kuril island of Paramusir, and that one of the two Kilos had disappeared. At the time it had been running at a depth of 200 feet in a protected two-mile square between three Russian destroyers and the ASW frigate *Nepristupny*. It had also been accompanied under the water by a 21,000-ton Typhoon-Class submarine, and was surrounded at all times by an acoustic barrier which would make its detection impossible by any enemy.

The Russians were mystified. Not one of the sonar rooms had detected the approach of a torpedo. And though three ships had reported a possible explosion in the immediate area of the box, none could be positive as to its cause. Suddenly the Kilo was not answering on the underwater telephone, and now, five hours later, the destroyers were combing the area, having summoned search-assistance from their base at Petropavlovsk. An oil slick and some wreckage had been found, but at this stage, given the iron-clad strength of the Russian escort, they suspected only an accident, possibly a massive battery explosion inside the submarine.

Admiral Zhang had never read anything in his entire life more complacent, more dull-witted, or less thoughtful. Or less likely to be accurate. When the signal had first come in, the Admiral had asked himself just one question: Would it have been obvious to a potential enemy that the Kilo was accompanied by a Russian Typhoon? The answer had been: No. The Typhoon was in attendance to deter an enemy, and had, in his view, failed. Even Rankov must now understand that it had failed because the Americans had not *known* it was there.

He had read the signal with incredulity, baffled at what he called, in white anger, the 'bone-headed intractability of the Slav peasant mind.' Alone in his office he had actually been physically affected by the depth of his outrage. He felt claustrophobic, hemmed in, when all he wanted to do was hurl something at the wall. Instead he had summoned the staff car and told the driver to arrange for the gates of the Yu Yuan to be opened for him, and then to take him there immediately.

Zhang loved lonely places. He would not have dreamed of spending time in the gardens when the teeming masses were in attendance, as they were between 8 a.m. and 10 a.m., and then again from 2 p.m. to 5 p.m. And now he walked around the wide gingko tree, repeating to himself, over and over, a jumble of cascading thoughts . . . 'Their obsession with secrecy . . . their sheer mind-blowing dumbness . . . all they had to do was *tell* the Americans the Typhoon was there, and this would never have happened. Because the Americans would never have dared to fire a torpedo with even a one-percent chance of hitting a Russian submarine carrying intercontinental ballistics, as the Typhoon certainly was . . . because that's what she's for . . . *and* she was in Russian waters.'

Admiral Zhang Yushu was in no doubt. The men in the Pentagon had blown the ninth Kilo apart, under the water . . . as they had blown apart Kilo 4 and Kilo 5 . . . as they had destroyed Kilo 6, and Kilo 7, and Kilo 8 in the canal. Whatever Moscow said, Zhang would not have bet a second-hand rickshaw on the arrival of Kilo 10 in the Port of Shanghai. He shook his head in exasperation, and he reflected in fury on the entire scene which had taken place in that wide distant seaway south of Paramusir. He could imagine, certainly, the roar of the cavitation, as the shafts and blades of the escorts thundered around, one ahead, one astern. He knew the active sonars would add to the din, and he knew also that such a racket would present serious problems to a marauding US SSN. Of course the American sonar team would have trouble obtaining any detection of the Kilo.

But there was another side to that coin. There were several other sides, as a matter of fact. And the most important of these was that the Americans were forever improving their underwater weapons. They had long been able to program torpedoes to search and destroy any target more than 40 feet below the surface, or 30 feet or 60 feet, whatever. Such a weapon would plainly miss the surface escorts and hit the submarine below.

Zhang knew also that the Russians would have been towing decoys off the stern of all four escort vessels, designed to seduce away *any* incoming torpedo. But he had also heard of a further tactical development in the USA – one which allowed the torpedo-guidance officer at the other end of the wire to force the underwater missile right on past the decoys, then allow it to search and lock on to a target beyond, all under strict control from the firing submarine.

This would even allow the torpedo, if necessary, to charge right through the box and then turn to race back in, for a second look, still searching for an underwater target using 'active' to home in on its helpless prey. In Zhang's view that had probably happened to Kilo 9. He was prepared to bow to advanced technology. What he could not bow to was the idiocy of running a thunderous sound barrier, 24 hours a day, in the full knowledge that it would probably deny you the precious detection of an incoming 'smart' missile.

What he also could not bow to was the Russians' truly numbing decision not to alert the Americans, or at least make it patently obvious, that if they opened fire, they had an excellent chance of slamming a torpedo into a cruising Russian Typhoon, and thus provide a *casus belli* for World War III.

In Zhang's view, *that* was the entire key to this terrible situation. And he gazed upward through the little clusters of newly sprouting gingko nuts – such a delicacy in China – and he thought of the wide Baltic faces of the Russian Navy personnel with whom he dealt . . . and he heard in his mind the sonorous, triumphal military music of their vast gray neighbors to the west . . . sounds so utterly crass and discordant to the Chinese ear. And he wondered, quite seriously, precisely which he hated more: the dull, unsubtle, flatly predictable mindset of the Russians, or the swaggering, high-tech outlaw-sweetness of the United States Navy.

He strolled over to the great Arbor with its views over the 200-yard-wide Huangpu River, and decided the answer to that was clearly defined. He had contempt in so many ways for the Russians, but the Americans he detested.

While his driver waited at the Fu Yu Street gate, the Commander-in-Chief of the Navy elected to walk his problems along the wide boulevard of the Bund, the road and its walkway which winds behind the sea-wall, following the great right-hand bend in the river on its way to the Yangtze Delta. He stopped occasionally, listening to the sounds of China's most prosperous and busiest seaport, with its docks which stretch for 35 miles along Shanghai's waterfront.

Zhang heard the lifelong familiar sound of horns and sirens blaring out over the water, and he watched the packed ferries vie for space with old flat-nosed steamers and freighters. And all the time, ancient sailing junks tacked against the tide, ducking between huge coal barges, and in the middle of it all there were local trading families, trying to maneuver their sampans, hauling on the big single oar, the *yuloh*.

The professional head of China's Navy shook his head at the ghastly lack of discipline, the gentle chaos of this quasi-commercial carnival taking place on the brown waters of the Huangpu. It was vibrant, but not entirely typical, because Shanghai also represented the very heart of the Chinese Navy. Here, in the massive shipyards of Jiangnan, Hudong and Huangpu, they built some of China's finest warships: the 4,000-ton Luhu-Class guided-missile destroyers, the 25 Jianghu-Class frigates, the guided-missile Luda-Class destroyers, one of which, the 3,670-ton *Nanjing*, had been home to Admiral Zhang for several years.

He could see her now if he closed his eyes: her stubby, sloping funnels, her sleek 433-foot-long hull, the state-of-the-art launcher for the anti-submarine mortars, positioned up on the bow, just for'ard of the main 130 mm gun. Captain Zhang could handle that ship all right, old Number 131. Such days they had been. And he imagined the 120 mortar rockets he used to carry. He would genuinely have given his life for the opportunity to fire those mortars right now, viciously into the waters somewhere east of the Kuril Islands, where he knew an American nuclear submarine ran silently and deep, waiting for a new chance to hit the surviving Kilo.

He cast his mind back to the early morning of September 5 when the message had come in from Vladivostock, relayed from the *Admiral Chabanenko* off the Siberian headland of Ol'utorsky: '*Short transient contact picked up on three sweeps radar. Six miles off our port bow . . . Possible US SSN.*' And he recalled too the imprudent smugness of the Russian captain: '*No reason for additional defensive measures. Acoustic barrier well in place. US powerless . . .*'

Yeah, right. Admiral Zhang walked grimly back along the Bund and into the gardens again, back to the huge gingko tree which to him seemed to embody the ancient soul of his land. He loved to stand in its shadow, and he did so whenever he came to Shanghai . . . just stood there, beneath a tree which had already lived for 400 years, and would live for 600 more – a tree whose natural heritage in his beloved country made the dinosaur look like an upstart.

His anger was abating now, and the rain had stopped, and he walked around the small lake to the Pavilion of the Nine Lions. He strolled on down the long east bank of the central lake, past the Tower of Elation, which did not reflect his mood. And he considered how he should deal with his masters. He could, he felt certain, buy time, if he could just obtain a private audience with the Paramount Ruler. Surely the old man would grant him that. But one thing would change the tide in his favor . . . if only, sometime in the next two weeks, Kilo number 10 would slide, unharmed, up to her berth in the port of Shanghai.

Wearily he walked back to the gates of the Gardens of Yu the Mandarin, and he stepped into the Navy staff car. Now he must prepare to face the inevitable inquisition that was taking root in the Chinese Government. It would end, inevitably, with him, Zhang, and his senior admirals trying to explain to civilians why a simple delivery of a few submarines, conducted in peacetime, mainly in the waters of their friends and allies the Russians, was proving to be so catastrophically difficult.

Admiral Vitaly Rankov, in full uniform, had been in the Kremlin for most of the night. Ever since the signal had come in from the Pacific Fleet at 0200 that one of the two Kilos, bound for China, was lost off the northern Kuril Islands. He had tried to stay calm, listened carefully to the reports of the captains of the Russian escort ships, and noted that they all were saying they could find no suspicion of foul play. But they would, wouldn't they?

They reported that no one had any hard evidence of an attack. The Americans *could not* have detected the Kilos on sonar, and, equally certainly, could not have seen them either. Certainly, *no one* could have attacked the Kilos. Unless an American submarine commanding officer had taken a reckless decision to blast a torpedo straight past the escort, somehow dodged the decoys, swerved past the world's biggest submarine, and crashed it into the Kilo. No, Admiral Rankov did not really understand that either.

The giant ex-Russian intelligence officer may not have been a submarine weapons expert; not quite such a scholar of naval warfare as his Chinese counterpart Admiral Zhang. But he knew the capabilities of the US weapons systems well enough.

Nevertheless, against all of the plain logic that stood before him, he *knew* whose hand was behind this. It was the same hand that had somehow smashed three submarines, two *Tolkach* barges, and a sizable length of the Belomorski Canal in one diabolical strike three months ago. It was the hand of Admiral Arnold Morgan. And not for the first time this year, Vitaly Rankov could, with an easy conscience, have throttled the pugnacious ex-US Navy intelligence chief.

Right now he would have loved to call the White House and remonstrate with Morgan, threaten him with everything: reprisals, the Court of Human Rights, the United Nations, humiliation in front of the world community. But he just could not face the inevitable mortification of a conversation with the stiletto-sharp Morgan, the awful, criminal-smooth tones of the Texan . . . *Hey, Vitaly . . . you gotta get your security beefed up . . . stuff happens.*

No. He just could not bear it. Instead he must placate the Chinese. And above all he must do everything in his power to ensure the last Kilo would arrive home to Shanghai. Despite all of the wicked efforts of the fugitive from justice who rejoiced in the title of the US President's National Security Advisor.

Columbia was 150 miles clear of the datum, moving swiftly south-southeast in 12,000 feet of water toward the Midway Islands. The submarine was still running sweetly, but Boomer had been driving men and machinery hard for over a month now, and he was happy to head for the excellent American submarine base at Pearl Harbor for R and R, rest and recreation, plus some overdue routine maintenance. Once there, they would shut down the reactor, replace supplies, load on stores, check working parts. But they'd do it all alongside, because *Columbia* would not require a bottom-scrape. The freezing waters in the Arctic do not support the warm-water crustaceans and weeds which always take root on the hull when a submarine is in warmer seas.

Columbia made a peaceful seven-day voyage down the Pacific, passing to the north of Midway, and staying north of the Hawaiian Ridge. Boomer left the island of Kauai to starboard, and then swung right down the Kauai Channel, past Barbers Point and along the rocky southern coast of Honolulu. They steamed into Pearl Harbor on September 17, exactly one week after dispatching K-9 into 600 feet of ocean off Paramusir.

The crew of the blacks ops submarine were glad to be in the bright sunlight of the island. They would be there for four weeks, while *Columbia* was re-stored and given her minor overhaul. Officers would catch up on paperwork, many of the crew would be at work assisting the Pearl Harbor engineers, and others would supervise the loading and logging of supplies. They would all be permitted ample time off to visit the island, and the unmarried ones looked forward eagerly to Honolulu's legendary nightspots.

Boomer telephoned Jo in Connecticut when he arrived, despite the appalling hour of the morning on the east coast of the United States, and broke the equally appalling news that *Columbia* might be required for a three-week patrol with the new carrier battle group arriving in the Arabian Sea in early December. However, this was by no means definite. Jo received the news of another Christmas shot to pieces with equanimity. She was just so relieved that her husband was safe.

He told her he was at Pearl Harbor for a while, and Jo ventured to ask him how the hell he got there. 'I thought you were somewhere in the Atlantic, not the Pacific,' she said.

'Sorry, sweetness, can't tell you that,' he replied breezily. 'Remember always, our business is classified . . .' He deepened his voice and added, 'My name's Dunning . . . Cale Dunning . . . double O six and three-quarters.'

171630SEPT. 34.00N, 142.00E. 150 miles off the east coast of Japan, in 30,000 feet of water, the Kilo-Class submarine, Russian-built but now under Chinese command, was making 9 knots 300 feet below the surface, running south on its battery.

Captain Kan Yu-fang, formerly commanding officer of China's new 8,000-ton nuclear Xia-Class (Type 093) submarine, was by now an expert operating the Russian diesel-electric which meant so much to his C-in-C. Captain Kan was the most senior officer in the Chinese Navy still serving on operational submarines. He had built a distinguished record in the notoriously difficult Xia, which had suffered endless and constant problems with its huge nuclear-warhead missiles, the CSS-NX-4s.

The Captain had finally left the program because it seemed so unlikely that China would ever have a perfect three-boat fleet of these SSBNs. And in any event, Admiral Zhang regarded Kan Yu-fang as the ideal man to command the next new Kilo during its most dangerous voyage. A native of Shanghai, the Captain was a disciplinarian of the old school. When Kilo 9 had vanished off Paramusir, it was he who had told the Russian officers still on board he was going to clear the datum, forget the escort, and move slowly off at a silent 5 knots, toward Shanghai, submerged. He instructed the Russian Lieutenant Commander on board to inform the Escort Group Commander what he was doing, and from there on Captain Kan ignored all other ships and signals, ordered a general decrease in speed for a day, and just crept away.

Thereafter they would make all speed to Shanghai. In a Western phrase, Captain Kan had decided to go for it.

He had no time, anyway, for unnecessary heroics. And he had no wish to seek out and engage a possible US nuclear boat. Because he knew there was but one achievement for which he would be profusely thanked by the C-in-C: the safe delivery of the tenth Kilo to Shanghai.

And now he was well on his way, seven days further south from Paramusir, and running free. For the first time in a long while he could take responsibility for his own actions. And he was going to deliver. He liked the new ship, which he thought handled well. And he especially liked its overall feel of steadfast reliability. Captain Kan expected to dock in Shanghai on the afternoon of September 23. And when he came up to snorkel east of the central Kurils on that first night, he accessed the satellite and informed the C-in-C of his intentions. Two hours later he went deep again and pressed on south with his torpedo tubes loaded, toward his beloved home city in his beloved China. Captain Kan was a very dangerous man.

Quite how dangerous was unknown to the Pentagon. But the 52-year-old Kan had been hand-picked for his command by Admiral Zhang himself, not merely because he was the most seasoned of China's front-line submarine commanders, but because of his background and his political 'pedigree.' Kan Yu-fang had been a Red Guard, one of Mao Zedong's teenage fanatics, back in the mid-1960s, when the Chairman had willfully and deliberately unleashed a bloody insurrection upon the Chinese populace. Kan was then, and still was, a zealot in the cause of a greater China. In 1966, at 15, he had led the First Brigade of the First Army Division of Shanghai's infamous Number Twenty Eight School. This was a fearsome group of 20 young Red Guards who made national news when they tortured three of their own teachers, blinding two, and caused two others to jump to their deaths from a sixth-floor window. Kan Yu-fang led what amounted to an armed street gang. He changed his name to 'Kan, the Personal Guard to Chairman Mao,' he carried a gun and a stock-whip, and he made nightly rampages through his poor local streets in the cause of the Cultural Revolution, searching for those he judged were enemies of the people – in Mao's phrase, 'capitalist-roaders' – which broadly meant anyone who was successful.

During the 12 months in which Mao gave power over adults to

the most violent elements of Chinese youth, Kan was responsible for so much torture of teachers and intellectuals he took over an entire theater in central Shanghai so that he and his colleagues could there routinely beat scholars, intellectuals and professors to within an inch of their lives. The suicide rate in his district approached alarming levels, because Kan always made the spouse and children watch the shocking torture of the other parent. It was said that his greatest joy was to enforce the 'jet-plane position' on women; he twisted their arms right back, up to their shoulder-blades, until they dislocated. It sometimes became necessary for his men to kick protesting husbands to death.

Kan made no allowances for women. He was, in a more modern phrase, gender-blind, and he never married.

When the vicious and hated regime of the teenage Red Guards came to a close, young Kan made a smooth and efficient change to the Rebel Red Guards, endlessly broadcasting in the streets, shouting Mao's thoughts: 'The savage tumult of one class over-throwing another.'

By the end of the 1960s his brutality had come to the notice of one of the cruelest women in the entire history of China, the former actress Jiang Qing, who had become Mao's wife. She made Kan one of the youngest leaders of her rampaging cabal, which roamed through the country destroying schools, universities and libraries, burning books, smashing windows and enforcing a reign of pure terror on the academic communities of China's great cities.

Madame Mao employed the young Kan for four years, at the end of which she personally granted him his wish to join the People's Liberation Army–Navy. As a kid born a block from the Shanghai waterfront, he made the most of the chance, quickly attaining officer rank. He was a tall, distant man, dark, smooth and friendless, but an efficient commander of a surface ship. Never popular, he was involved only once in scandal: he was suspected of cutting the throat of a Shanghai prostitute. The suspicions were, however, left unproven.

When Kan made the transfer to submarines his status improved rapidly. He became a fearless underwater commander, reputed to be the best weapons officer in the entire navy. However, a few senior commanders knew of his terrible past, and anyway most of his colleagues preferred to give him a wide berth.

Admiral Zhang had known all along that the bloodstained hands of this strange and emotionless killer were the precise hands he wanted at the helm of Kilo 9 or Kilo 10. Zhang had understood instinctively that, if the US Navy were hunting down the Chinese submarines, the task was being performed by a black ops nuclear boat. He had also known that the American commanding officer on such a mission would be a merciless opponent. Whoever that American might be, he would find a good match in Kan, who would shoot to kill at the slightest provocation. Such orders Admiral Zhang had no compunction about issuing – not in this instance. The new satellite message to Kilo 10, as it snorkeled briefly while heading for Shanghai, conveyed his views to the letter.

231730SEPT. In the Shanghai Naval Base, Admiral Zhang Yushu threw his arms around Captain Kan with delight as the Commanding Officer of Kilo 10 stepped ashore from the submarine which had journeyed the Siberian route from northern Russia. He instructed his staff to ensure the Russian liaison team who had accompanied the Chinese Captain halfway around the world be treated with immense honor, and that all six of them should dine with the senior Chinese officers and himself this evening.

Before that, however, he wished to debrief Captain Kan personally. But in the ensuing hour he learned little that he did not already know.

No, the submarines had never been aware of a pursuing US nuclear boat. Yes, the underwater acoustic barrier, which they had believed would keep them safe, did block out everything. No, they had no hard evidence of an attack. If the ninth Kilo had been hit by a torpedo it must have been brilliantly delivered. Yes, they had been almost a mile away at the time. Yes, their sonar room had reported an explosion at that time, but it was just impossible to come to any positive conclusion as to what had caused it, with all the tremendous noise around them. As indeed there had been since the Bering Strait.

Finally, Admiral Zhang asked the one question of his top submarine captain which would plague him for all of his days, 'Do you think it would have been better to make the Americans aware of the definite presence of the Typhoon, running south right between the two Kilos?'

'Yessir. Yes, I do. As a matter of fact, I thought they *were* aware.

You have surprised me greatly . . . I cannot believe no one knew the Typhoon was in attendance.'

On October 1, Admiral Zhang dispatched the new Kilo to the southern base of Canton, a 1,200-mile journey from Shanghai which would take six days, under the command of Captain Kan, now with an all-Chinese crew.

Thus on October 7, in the new submarine docks on the Pearl River, the Kilo came formally under the care of Vice-Admiral Zu Jicai, the Commander of the Southern Fleet. It was a dual purpose inter-Fleet transfer. Admiral Zhang simply believed that the business of the submarine was better conducted from Canton, because he might soon send it much farther south, to find out precisely where the Taiwanese were conducting their nuclear experiments. The actual recapture of the island of Taiwan would have to wait until he had negotiated a new deal for further Kilos from the Russians.

At 10.30 a.m. on October 14 a field officer in the Chinese Intelligence Service reported in from deep cover in Taiwan. He was speaking from an apparent safe house – but he was in a desperate hurry, and he would speak only to General Fang Wei in person.

His message was cryptic in the extreme. 'Professor Liao Lee of Taiwan National University has vanished suddenly, right in the middle of his most important course. Failed to show up after the Double 10th National Day vacation. Students mystified. Faculty silent.'

General Fang recalled the biannual June Conference vividly, and he hit the secure phone line to Admiral Zhang's nearby office in Naval Headquarters, Beijing. He reported the conversation verbatim, and requested information about the next departure of *Hai Lung* 793.

Admiral Zhang suggested the General come to his office instantly. And one hour later they had ascertained beyond doubt that the Dutch-built submarine had already left two days previously, on October 12. Both men were certain that the renowned nuclear physicist was on board. They were equally certain that something important had happened at the mysterious nuclear laboratory, wherever it was, in the cold south.

But Zhang thought he knew where, and he sent an immediate

signal to Admiral Zu Jicai in Canton. '*Order recently arrived Kilo, under the command of Captain Kan Yu-fang, to the southern Indian Ocean island of Kerguelen within 24 hours. Distance 8,500 miles. Re-fueling south of Lombok Strait. Briefing follows.*'

At 1100 local time – 12 hours later – still October 14, in the CIA headquarters at Langley, Virginia, the Far-East Chief, Frank Reidel, fielded a coded satellite message from Taipei. It had plainly originated from their priceless dock foreman in the submarine base at Suao, Carl Chimei.

It stated that he was almost certain he had recognized a civilian passenger boarding *Hai Lung* 793, at first light on the 12th, two days previously. He had just read a long article in a Taiwan National University brochure which carried two photographs of the man. Carl Chimei would swear the passenger was Taiwan's most eminent nuclear physicist, Professor Liao Lee.

Frank Reidel cast protocol to the winds, and opened up the ultra-secure line to the White House, straight through to Admiral Arnold Morgan.

'Morgan. Speak.'

'Frank Reidel here, sir.'

'Hi Frank, what's hot?'

'Our man in Taipei is certain he saw the most important nuclear scientist in Taiwan board one of the *Hai Lung* submarines, hull 793, at first light on October 12th, two days ago. It left almost immediately. As usual no one knows quite where.'

'Hey, Frank. That's good information. Real good. Keep it tight.' At which point he just slammed down the phone.

'Rude prick,' said the CIA man, grinning. But added to himself, 'some kind of an operator, that ignorant sonofabitch . . . and the worst part is, I almost like him.'

Admiral Morgan told his secretary to get Charlie right outside the door, and then to call Admiral Mulligan and tell him to 'sit still till I get there.'

An hour later, in the Pentagon, it took only a few minutes for the two Admirals to agree it was just about time they took a serious look at the activities of the Taiwanese on that goddamned island. 'Jesus Christ,' said Arnold Morgan. 'Those crazy pricks might be into germ warfare or something . . . they're so damned neurotic about the mainland Chinese.'

'More likely nuclear, especially with this hotshot professor on his way there in a goddamned submarine,' growled the CNO.

At 1237 Admiral Mulligan put a secure signal on the satellite to *Columbia* in Pearl Harbor. '*Personal for Commander Dunning: proceed with despatch to Kerguelen. Conduct thorough search of the island for duration two weeks.*

'*Aim: Find whereabouts clandestine Taiwanese operations. Remain undetected, repeat, undetected. COMSUBPAC informed of your continued operations under SUBLANT OPCON. Suspect either germ-warfare factory or nuclear-weapon fabrication in place. And/or potential government hide-out in event of Chinese occupation.*

'*Taiwan Hai Lung submarine hull 793 cleared Suao October 12. ETA Kerguelen November 18/19, most probably on re-supply task to Taiwanese facility. Your job is to find WHERE. Nothing else. ROE self-defense only — negative pre-emptive self-defense.*

'*When your aims are achieved, clear area immediately and report. Further action, in event your success, still under consideration.*'

151200OCT. China's newest Kilo-Class submarine left Canton and ran fair down the Pearl River for 50 miles, past the cities of Kowloon and Macau which stand on opposite banks, guarding this huge Chinese estuary. Beyond the myriad of tiny islands which litter the hectic expanse of the South China Sea, the Kilo dived and headed east, making 9 knots. It would take her three and a half days to clear the northern point of the Philippines, before turning south, bound for the distant Lombok Strait, and then Kerguelen. Captain Kan Yu-fang was in command.

151936OCT. USS *Columbia* headed out, down the long, historic waters of Pearl Harbor. On the bridge, wearing his dark blue jacket against the evening chill, Commander Boomer Dunning stood next to the navigator, Lt. Wingate, and his XO, Lt. Commander Krause. They had a long, long journey in front of them: 11,700 miles.

But the nuclear boat would run at about 550 miles a day, and they would be oblivious to the very worst the Southern Ocean could throw at them. The waters they would travel would be cold and deep, but calm, upwards of 300 feet below the surface. *Columbia* was in top condition; Lee O'Brien had the reactor running perfectly. And if he had not been in such bad shape with the

President's National Security Advisor, Boomer would have been at ease with the world.

That, however, was not the case. He knew that the NSA would not have instructed Admiral Mulligan to pass on that withering, coded judgment unless he had been absolutely furious. And Boomer felt somewhat defenseless about the whole incident. It was all true. He *could* have hit the fucking Typhoon. God, wouldn't that have been awful? Trust Morgan to comprehend, with slicing clarity, his, Boomer's, derelictions.

The incident was, manifestly, still in the minds of everyone concerned. There had even been a satellite signal from SUBLANT, 15 minutes before they left, informing the Commanding Officer personally that K-10 had cleared its berth in Canton, and was heading along the Pearl River. Destination unknown.

Boomer shivered, despite his jacket, as *Columbia* shook off the Hawaiian Islands, and pressed on down the Pacific. At 2030, he cleared the bridge with his two officers, and took the submarine down. And that was where she would stay, all the way down the east coast of Australia, around Tasmania, and along the Southern Ocean, to the frozen hell-hole of an island he had already visited once, under much more agreeable circumstances.

'God knows what I'll find,' he thought. 'I just better do exactly as they say, and no more. My career's probably shot anyway. And I may not make captain. I just don't really wanna return to New London as a civilian.'

The Chinese Intelligence Service pressured their field officers in Taipei for more and more information. It trickled through slowly to the office of General Fang Wei. By October 24 there was no room for any further doubt whatsoever . . . the Taiwanese were developing a nuclear capability and it was somewhere among the 300 islands which make up Kerguelen.

The General met Admiral Zhang at Naval Headquarters in Beijing that morning, and provided him with the latest information, some of which dealt with secret deliveries of heavily guarded containers from two of Taiwan's nuclear power stations to the submarine base. It was plainly uranium.

Zhang spent another two hours alone, studying the detailed chart of Kerguelen drawn under the supervision of the Royal Navy's hydrographer, Rear-Admiral Sir David Haslam. Then, at

1630, he drafted a signal for his friend and colleague Admiral Zu Jicai in the south. It ordered him to transmit to the Kilo the following message: '*Locate and destroy Taiwanese laboratory/factory on Kerguelen. Avoid southeast area near French weather station at Port-aux-Français (49.21N, 70.11E) on southern coast of Courbet Peninsula. West coast also unlikely, high coastal terrain and unprotected from prevailing Antarctic weather.*

'*Most likely area big bays to the northeast – Gulf of Choiseul, Rhodes Bay and Gulf of Baleiniers. Possible ex-French nuclear submarine reactor power source could assist detection. Use whatever means necessary to complete destruction of Taiwanese facility.*'

Columbia ran deep at about 20 knots all the way, except for her daily communications routine at periscope depth. By October 18 the Americans had covered 1,600 miles and were almost across the Central Pacific Basin. They passed the Fiji Islands on October 21, and three days later entered Australia's Tasman Sea. By noon on October 26 they were off Hobart, Tasmania, on latitude 45 degrees, south of the big hotel on Storm Bay where Boomer and Bill Baldridge had delivered *Yonder* on the last day of February.

Ahead of them were 3,500 miles of the Southern Ocean, which, in late October, were subject to wild swings in weather patterns, often culminating in raging gales and mountainous seas. All of which *Columbia* would, of course, treat with supreme indifference.

The black ops submarine ran swiftly westward on the Great Circle route toward Kerguelen. The atmosphere was carefree, as it had been ever since they burst clear of the Arctic pack-ice. Even the schemozzle off the Kurils had been treated by the crew with complete confidence. It was as if they had undergone the one great suppressed dread of the submariner – the fear of being trapped under the water. Everything else had to be better than that, even if it was not wonderful.

To most of them, a routine search of the desolate island ahead of them was kids' stuff. They were not going to shoot anyone; no one was going to shoot *Columbia*, and they could slide up to the surface whenever they wished. The weather might be godawful, but all weather is sublime compared to being trapped under the ice. Life in the nuclear hunter-killer was more relaxed than it had been at any time since they had left New London almost 12 weeks ago.

They had renewed their supply of videos at Pearl, everyone was tanned and fit, and Lt. Commander Curran, in partnership with Dave Wingate, was in the process of winning a long-running contract bridge tournament, in which all other contestants were like lambs to the slaughter. 'Jerry's got fucking X-ray eyes,' was the verdict of Lee O'Brien, the mathematician of the engine room, who found it incomprehensible that anyone could count the cards as they were played more accurately than he could.

The only other serious bridge player in the entire crew was Chief Spike Chapman, the highly trained ship's systems boss, who worked long hours at the console which controlled every mechanical and electrical function in the submarine, except for propulsion. He could count the cards and he could play well, but his regular partner, Lt. Commander Abe Dickson, tended to bid rashly, and, even as a guest in the wardroom, Chief Chapman was occasionally heard to sigh, 'Jesus Christ, Abe, sir . . . couldn't we play it safe . . . just once?' His barely controlled exasperation caused everyone to fall about laughing, as the deck officer set off up the mountain of seven trumps, too often to find that three would have been a more realistic contract.

The Commanding Officer was not a bridge player. Which was just as well because Boomer had been very self-absorbed throughout the journey, not really at all like his usual self. His closest officers in the crew were slightly baffled by this, but then none of them had read the cryptic views of Admiral Morgan.

But there was something more on the mind of Commander Dunning. And it was a feeling of general unease about the island of Kerguelen. He was the only man on board who had actually been there, and he was also the only man on board who had taken a serious interest in the long-running story of *Cuttyhunk*.

Boomer might not possess the mercurial guillotine mind of Arnold Morgan, or even Joe Mulligan, certainly not of Admiral Dunsmore. But the CO from Cape Cod was more than capable of executive command at a very high level. He was normally rock-solid in his judgments, and he never mislaid a truly salient fact. He liked to read books involving major court trials, and he was fond of announcing that all trials swing on one simple fact which is undeniable, utterly incriminating and is usually undisputed except for the spurious cry of all defenses, 'The evidence has been tampered with.'

With regard to the disappearance of *Cuttyhunk* there was just such a fact, and Boomer Dunning's selective memory had recorded it, word for word, from Freddie whatsisname, Goodwin's, articles: the last satellite message of Dick Elkins, the radio operator ... '*MAYDAY* ... *MAYDAY* ... *MAYDAY!* ... Cuttyhunk *49 South, 69* ... *UNDER ATTACK* ... *Japanese* ...'

So far as Boomer was concerned, this meant *Cuttyhunk* had most definitely come under attack, otherwise the radio operator would not have dreamed of sending such a highly charged communication. The fact that the signal had ended with such brick-wall finality was compounded, surely, by the equally undisputed fact that the entire ship's company, plus all of the scientists, plus even the ship itself, had at that point vanished.

In Boomer's mind it was obvious that the aforementioned Japanese were plainly Taiwanese, the group for whom he now searched. They had clearly attacked *Cuttyhunk*, with some fairly heavy-duty hardware. Their motive was equally conspicuous in Boomer's mind ... it must have been a simple fear of discovery, since the Woods Hole research ship posed no military threat.

If the Taiwanese were operating behind armed naval power, which did not hesitate to open fire on US citizens, and either sink or confiscate their ship, it was not beyond the realms of reason that they would open fire on *Columbia*. He already knew they had submarines in the area ... he and Bill Baldridge had seen one with their own eyes.

What further shore defenses the Taiwanese might have, Boomer did not know. But he took the view that this surveillance project must be conducted with unerring care. He had specific orders to shoot only in accordance with the normal international rights of self-defense, and to remain undetected. And he proposed to carry out these routine instructions to the letter.

However, the Commanding Officer of *Columbia* shared none of the general cheerfulness which was apparent in the rest of the crew. When they came within 100 miles of Kerguelen he proposed to change their mindset drastically. Until then he was perfectly happy for the videos to run, and for Abe Dickson to overbid his hand with reckless disregard for the conventions of the game ... a criticism Admiral Arnold Morgan all too obviously leveled at Boomer himself.

★

Fort Meade, Maryland, October 26. Admiral George Morris made his morning report by telephone to the NSA's office in the White House. His statement today was the same as it had been yesterday, and the day before. As it had been every day since October 15, when the satellite's photograph, shot at 1500 local time, had shown K-10 missing from its berth in Canton.

'Not a sign of the damned thing, sir. If it's been running at around 9 knots it could be nearly 2,500 miles out from base now. And it could have gone in any direction, back to the north or anywhere else. Beats the hell out of me.'

'And me, George. Of course it might just be circling Taiwan, or even on patrol up around South Korea . . . That's the whole trouble with the little bastard, you can't see it, and you sure as hell can't hear it at its low speed. Who knows? Anyway, lemme know if anything shows up. I don't like that little sonofabitch out there on the loose.'

Columbia cleared the Australian Antarctic Rise at 2100 on the night of November 2, and came steaming in toward Kerguelen, from the east, at 0100 on November 5. Seven hours later, 100 miles off the Courbet Peninsula, his submarine still running at 600 feet, the Commanding Officer addressed the ship's company over the public address system.

He said, 'This is the Captain speaking, and as you all know we will soon be approaching the island of Kerguelen. I have not wished thus far to spread alarm and despondency, and nor do I now. But I want to alert everyone to the idea that I do *not* regard this search-and-find operation as strictly routine, and without danger.

'I want all of you, if you will, to cast your minds back a couple of years to the disappearance of that Woods Hole oceanic research ship, which vanished with all hands. As some of you may know, it vanished right where we're going, around the island of Kerguelen.

'Some of you may have read the reports of the tragedy in which 29 people were apparently lost. If you did, you will also have read the reports of the last message from *Cuttyhunk* . . . the one in which the radio operator signaled "*Mayday!*" and then announced the ship under attack from the Japanese.

'Well, in my view that ship was most definitely attacked. And it may have been attacked by some foreign Navy patrol craft, which was here to protect the guys we're trying to locate. In short, that craft may also try to attack *us*, and we don't know if it is carrying any antisubmarine gear, depth charges, or mortars. But I'm telling you, if I was in charge of protecting something down here, in these narrow seaways, I sure as hell would be!'

That received a predictable burst of laughter. But the Captain continued, 'Let's face it, guys, no one is a match for us – we're the best, and we're in the best ship – but my orders are specific: we're here to search and locate and report. We're not here to attack anything.

'So let's just get our heads straight. We *might* be in dangerous waters, so we wanna stay right at peak form, keeping our eyes and ears open at all times. Let's conduct this search like the professionals I know we all are. And remember we are not here to attack, except in the event of a clear and obvious aggressive action against us . . . one which we judge to be "them or us." Because there is always only one answer to that: *not us*.'

Everyone liked that. And the CO concluded, 'That's it. Let's get to it. The search begins right now at 0800, first light. I intend to cruise in quietly, and do our business. Take nothing for granted. We don't know who or where our enemy may be. But we sure as hell wanna see him before he sees us. That's all.'

Columbia slipped through the cold dark waters beneath a howling Antarctic gale, and came to periscope depth nine miles off the high granite headland of Cape George, the southeastern tip of the island. With the wind out of the northwest, there was some lee further inshore, but not out here, and the US submarine wallowed around in the big swell with 30 feet between trough and crest.

'Can't see much in this,' growled Boomer. 'Who has the Conn? . . . Okay, remain at PD . . . continuous visual IR and ESM lookout. I'm gonna survey the south coastline. We'll probably have to go in closer to see anything. Bottom's about 300 feet here . . . watch the fathometer . . . don't go inside 200 feet and don't trust the chart – it's old, and probably suspect.'

They steamed on through the grim, gray day, and once more came to periscope depth. Now Boomer could see the towering, forbidding southeastern coastline of Kerguelen. The weather had improved and the sea was calmer in the lee, but the light was poor and the sky overcast. No rays of a rising sun had yet lit up the tormented granite cliffs of the great curved hook of Cape George.

Boomer, peering through the periscope, took a few seconds longer than usual, just to acclimatize himself to the sense of dejection he felt, staring at the sullen, hostile magnificence of this dreadful place. It was a feeling he had not encountered since last he stared at the rockface of Kerguelen nine months ago. And he remembered it well. He shuddered, and handed the periscope to the watch officer.

His basic plan was to move quietly westward along the southern coastline at periscope depth, while the weather held. They would run at about 5 knots, using passive sonar with a constant IR and ESM watch. At this latitude there would be only eight hours of suspect daylight, between 0800 and 1600, but Boomer would search all night, using his infrared, picking up not so much light as heat. And heat was probably his best chance.

He decided to spend 48 hours on the south coast, which was more than 70 miles long, then turn north up the forbidding 80-mile-long windward west coast, beyond Cape Bourbon.

The south yielded more or less what he thought it would. Nothing. Except the French met. station. And all through the two days and two nights, *Columbia* rolled and pitched through the water like a stranded whale in the mountainous seas. They broke more cups and plates in the wardroom than they had all year as the submarine struggled through conditions for which she was not best designed. Twice they lost trim and broached to the surface, and Boomer ordered them to 7 knots, which gave them better control.

Mike Krause noted that even the names of places were in tune with their mission: Cape Challenger, Savage Bay, plus a succession of deep fjords were guarded by heavy, heaving swells at the entrances, powerful enough, said Lt. Wingate, to capsize an oil tanker.

At the end of the second run along the south coast, Boomer considered the task well and truly completed. They had observed nothing of any interest, and the CO had not even seen a fjord or a bay through which he would care to navigate . . . the Bay of Swains, Larose Bay and the 12-mile-long fjord of Table Bay looked, to him, lethal. 'If the Taiwanese are hiding in one of those, they deserve their fucking atom bomb or whatever it is,' thought Boomer. 'Poor bastards'll never get out alive.'

At dawn on November 7, Boomer turned *Columbia* north off Cape Bourbon. In Mike Krause's opinion, the chart was showing one of the most terrible looking coastlines in the world, strewn with jagged islands upon which survival was out of the question: strewn with craggy uneven rocks, just above and below the surface; strewn no doubt with the skeletons of ships and their masters, who over the centuries had plain run out of luck in weather conditions which were usually frightful.

Up past the Île de l'Ouest they steamed, staring in awe at the snow-capped 2,200-foot Peak Philippe d'Orléans, which rises up over the western headland of the island, six miles from the mainland. Lt. Wingate informed the CO they should remain at least seven miles from the shore for the next 20 miles because of the treacherous rocky shoal which lies three miles off the entrance to the Baie de Bénodet and the Baie de l'Africain. Full of submerged rocks, its foul ground extends for over two miles.

As *Columbia* passed by, in a force-six westerly, leaving the shoal safely to starboard, Boomer could see through the periscope the huge swells become white breakers, driven shoreward before the wind, thundering into the shallow waters of the ridge, three miles offshore. 'Holy shit,' said the CO. 'What a place. You couldn't *hold* a surface ship in that water . . . you'd just get driven onto the rocks.'

So another day and another night passed in their slow, tortuous journey, searching for a place which could never be; a place inhabited by human beings, in a place where natural life was unthinkable, unless you were a seagull or a penguin. But the job had to be done. And Boomer, laboriously, doggedly, did it.

At the end of the light on November 8, they passed the Îles Nuageuses, the Cloudy Islands, right of the northwest point. But no shelter awaited them there, and Boomer turned away to starboard, to the deeper water up near the huge rock Captain Cook had named Bligh's Cap, after his sailing master. The Global Positioning System, as always, provided precision navigational data, and Boomer Dunning knew as well as anyone that without it, this entire search would have been nothing less than a nightmare.

Then, on a new, dark, galeswept morning, they headed southeast for Cap Aubert, just in case the Taiwanese had set up shop in a cave or a tunnel facing due north into the teeth of the weather.

By midday it was growing dark, and Boomer Dunning elicited a groan from Lt. Commander Dickson, manning the periscope, by

379

observing that he was probably the first man in history to be looking for a tunnel at the end of the light.

And with the weather building ominously to the northwest, they ran on past Cap d'Estaing for another five miles, swung wide around the shoals, and ducked down the 15-mile-long fjord of Baie de Recques, where the water was a couple of hundred feet deep, and relatively calm, sheltered from the weather.

The storm raged for the rest of the day, and all night, with great blizzards of snow and sleet slashing across the water. Tucked right in the lee of the north shore, *Columbia* hardly noticed it. The following morning, November 10, they emerged to a brighter day, and Boomer elected to make a 70-mile journey east-southeast right out beyond the kelp-beds, which extend to Cape Sandwich on the distant easterly limit of the island. From there he would drive slowly back, working around the islands of the Golfe des Baleiniers and Baie de Rhodes, before arriving close to Cox's Rock.

This was the landmark in his mind, a black sea-swept hunk of granite, which he and Bill Baldridge had been able to see, up at the seaward end of Gramont, when Bill had spotted the periscope. That was the only real signpost he had, and the latest communication from SUBLANT suggested the Taiwanese *Hai Lung* 793 might very well show up in these exact waters a week from now.

This would give him ample time to make a thorough search of the archipelago in the heart of Kerguelen, and get right back into position to observe the incoming Taiwanese by November 18. And of course, this time he would not need to see the Dutch-built submarine's periscope. The sonar system in *Columbia* would pick up the noise of hull 793 in a heartbeat. Or less.

And so, for almost a week, Boomer Dunning and his team groped around the windswept waterways to the northeast. They mostly stayed at PD, and spent much time avoiding kelp-beds and making sure they stayed clear of rocks. David Wingate seemed to be glued to his charts 24 hours a day. They crept back and forth down the Baie de Rhodes, traversed the short channel up to the mouth of the Baie de Londres. They circumnavigated Howe Island and Gramont, both ways. But they heard not a sound. The only good news was a satellite signal from SUBLANT which told the Commanding Officer to forget the Arabian Gulf and to return to New London at the conclusion of the Kerguelen patrol, on November 19. Christmas at home, thank God. And a unique circumnavigation of the world too. Though they could never claim it.

At dusk on a bright November 16, Boomer ordered them to a position two miles north of where he and Bill Baldridge had seen the periscope from the deck of *Yonder*, in the Gulf of Choiseul. If the *Hai Lung* should show up, they had a fair to middling chance of locating it, but from several points of view it was not an ideal position for a watchful submarine. The inner waters of this relatively narrow bay, surrounded by land from the north-northwest all the way south and back to the northeast, were a real headache for a sonar operator. So was the relatively shallow water – 600 feet max. – not to mention the constant threat of a rough sea.

Lt. Commander Krause did not like it. And Boomer felt very uneasy. That evening he and Jerry Curran spent much time discussing the problem, until finally the CO said bluntly, 'You know, Jerry, if that Dutch sonofabitch came sneaking through here at night, in a sea, we might never see her, and we might not even hear her. She could just go right by and we'd never know . . . there has to be a better way.'

'Sir, I know it's a pain in the ass, but I think we should get right out of here, 150 or so miles back out to the northeast, beyond the big shoal area where there's deeper, quieter, water and we can probably pick up an incoming snorkeling submarine as far out as the second convergence, 30 miles plus. It's hopeless right here, too noisy, too shallow and too confining. If we can get a decent distance offshore, in the open sea, the *Hai Lung* has much less chance of getting past us, if he's on a direct course from Bali, which of course he must be. And if he is snorkeling, which he is quite likely to be.'

'You're right, Jerry. We'll move our operational area right now. We'll be in good shape before midnight and we'll follow the Taiwan boat right in, soon as she goes by.

'*Make your speed 8 knots . . . steer zero-zero-zero. Abe, I want you to go on up here for 12 miles, then come right to zero-six-zero, out to the 650-foot line.*'

'Aye, sir.'

Columbia cleared Choiseul Bay at 2106, and headed back up the track northeast, back along the route they knew the *Hai Lung* must follow if the Taiwanese really were bound for the precise same spot where Boomer and Bill had observed the periscope the previous February.

The Americans reached their patrol area, just south of the 47th parallel at 72 degrees East, and waited, for a patient 24 hours. The trouble was, the *Hai Lung* did not show up, and they patrolled slowly all through November 17, the sonar men silently watching the screens, and listening.

That evening was scheduled to be their second-last in the Kerguelen area, and Boomer knew he would soon have to access the satellite, report their plan, and request permission to leave on November 20.

But, at 2224 on November 17, a charge of excitement shot through the ship. Boomer was in the navigation area when a sudden voice from the sonar room stopped him dead. It was the sonar officer, Lt. Bobby Ramsden. 'We're getting something, sir . . . slight rise in the background level . . . it's difficult to explain . . . but I don't believe it's weather.'

A few minutes went by, with Boomer now in the sonar room with Lt. Commander Curran. The young sonar lieutenant spoke again. 'Faint engine lines coming up. Relative 92. Alter to 135 to resolve ambiguity.'

Columbia slewed around. Ten minutes later, the bearing was resolved at zero-five-three. The 'waterfall' screen was now showing definite engine lines. The computer was flashing the information through its brain, comparing the lines to the bank of examples it carried. Jerry Curran was monitoring three screens simultaneously and when he spoke, a bolt of electrified emotion shot clean up Boomer Dunning's spine.

'Hell, sir, this is a Russian . . . the computer says right here we got the engines of a goddamned Kilo.'

'*The computer doesn't know its ass from its elbow,*' commented the Commanding Officer, softly. '*It's K-10.*'

'Might I ask with due respect how we know that, sir,' asked Lt. Commander Krause, who had just materialized, as he was prone to do at critical moments.

'You sure can,' said Boomer. 'Because that's the only one it could be . . . No other nation which owns a Kilo, except China, has the remotest interest in being anywhere near Kerguelen. If it did, Fort Meade would know.

'Besides ourselves, China is the only nation truly exercised by

Taiwanese activity. They own four Kilos now. And Fort Meade knows where three of them are: two in Zhanjiang, and one in Shanghai. The fourth, K-10, is missing, according to our latest satellite report. It left Canton on October 15, three days after the *Hai Lung*. But it was a bit nearer, and it's a bit faster . . . Trust me, Mike, the engine lines on that screen are the lines of K-10.' And then he grinned and added, 'The one that got away.'

'What now, sir?'

'We stay clear, watch him from a safe distance. He might know something we don't. But the *Hai Lung* is still our first objective.'

This was the first sign of life *Columbia* had encountered since passing a tramp steamer in the Tasman Sea three weeks previously. Every eye in the control center was focused on the computer screens.

Commander Dunning, who had watched and waited patiently for so many days, was standing next to the periscope, and he snapped out his first urgent command since the Kurils. '*Come left . . . three-five-zero . . . I wanna stay 10,000 yards off track.*'

'Three-five-zero, aye.'

Lt. Commander Curran spoke next. 'This, sir, looks like a little task for our new sonar-tracking system.'

'Oh yeah . . . the one where we blunder around disguised as a porpoise.'

Lt. Commander Curran laughed, like most people did, at the deep-water nightclub comedian turn of phrase of his CO. 'Yessir, that's the one . . . and I do understand your skepticism, but it'll work. I've seen the trials. We can ping the intruder on active sonar for as long as we wish, and he's never gonna know we're here.'

'Of course, if it doesn't work,' replied Boomer, 'we might be a bit too dead to know whether it worked or not.'

'Sir, it won't malfunction. It's just regular active sonar, but when it pings the Kilo'll think it's a porpoise singing, or a shrimp farting, or a whale copulating . . . we can vary the sound all the time. Honestly, this thing is one big miracle. It's designed for active tracking and it's perfect for us right now. Just so long as we don't use it too regularly or too often.'

Commander Dunning, accustomed to a lifelong belief that active sonar alerts your enemy, shook his head. 'I guess so, Jerry. But don't be wrong, for Christ's sake. Something tells me the Chinese in K-10 are likely to be trigger-happy, and I'd prefer them not to open fire right back down the beam of the singing fucking porpoise.'

'Yessir, I agree with that. But I'm very confident. We've been testing it for about three years. We can just ping 'em on active, enough to keep track, and they'll never know they're being watched.'

'Who bats first?' asked the Captain, drolly. 'The porpoise or the farting shrimp?'

'Sir, I thought we'd come to the plate with a blue whale waving his dick,' replied the Lieutenant Commander with mock seriousness.

'Excellent,' replied Boomer, with equal mock seriousness. 'Please proceed.'

Lt. Commander Krause, like everyone else within earshot, had been smiling at the highly charged, false-joke repartee of the Commanding Officer and his sonar officer. But now he spoke seriously to Boomer Dunning. 'Sir, has anyone given much thought to what precisely K-10 is doing down here?'

'Same as us, I guess,' said Boomer. 'Trying to find out what the Taiwanese are up to and where . . . if they don't already know.'

'You actually think the Chinese know where they are, sir?'

'No. Not really, Mike. But let me put it this way . . . Just think how we found out the little we know: a billion-to-one sighting of a periscope last February . . . the outlandish disappearance of *Cuttyhunk* . . . both kinda flukey, not real intelligence.

'Then we get some half-assed report of a hot-shot nuclear pro-fessor being seen in some remote submarine dockyard near Taipei, and Arnold Morgan puts two and two together and makes about a zillion. Except that he may very well be right. My point is that we have not tackled this project with any serious determination, and yet we have damned nearly walked right in the front door.

'Can you imagine how much *more* the Chinese must know? They have about a million spies in Taiwan for a start, and they watch every move that nation makes. If they don't know, pro-fessionally, more than we know accidentally I'd be amazed. And here comes their newest Kilo . . . you think it's a tour ship? Nossir, that baby is here on business . . . and I would not be in any way surprised if it had come to do our dirty work for us. What's more we're gonna let him.'

'*We're about 10,000 yards northwest of the Kilo's projected track. He's about eight miles out right now.*'

'Okay. Come right . . . zero-five-five. I intend to remain on a northeast–southwest patrol line, 10,000 yards clear.'

At a steady seven and a half knots the Kilo came on, driving forward under the command of Captain Kan Yu-fang, holding her on course two-three-seven.

An hour later, the Chinese submarine went by, at periscope depth, still snorkeling, her intake valve jutting starkly but unseen into the bright moonlight, which had, unusually, cast a cold path on the long, black ocean swells. Kan Yu-fang plainly suspected nothing.

The Americans followed for six miles, keeping way out, until the Kilo stopped snorkeling and settled into a lazy patrolling pattern at about 3 knots, as if on a racetrack.

'She seems to be just waiting, sir,' said Lt. Ramsden.

'If she is, she's waiting for the same thing we are,' said Boomer. 'Let's face it, the departure of the *Hai Lung* from Taiwan is just about public. We all knew that. The 11-week cycle, before she returns home, is also pretty public. If we know, without even trying much, she's due in Kerguelen sometime around November 18th – tomorrow – then I guess the Chinese know the same thing. And their view of the situation is more urgent than ours . . . if Taiwan is going to throw a nuclear weapon at someone, it's gonna be at them, not us.'

'You mean, sir,' said Lt. Ramsden thoughtfully, 'that the Kilo is waiting to follow the *Hai Lung* inshore, just like we are.'

'That's my reading,' replied the CO. 'How about you, Jerry? Mike?'

'You got my vote,' replied the sonar boss.

'And mine,' added the XO.

'Just make sure that whale-dick keeps working,' said Boomer. 'Don't wanna lose 'em. Don't wanna get caught either.'

The Kilo continued on her pattern, back and forth, all day. Lt. Commander Curran pinged them very occasionally, with various deep-ocean sounds, recognizable only as fish to the Chinese sonar operator. And all the while, Boomer Dunning's team kept an iron grip on the precise whereabouts of the Russian-built boat. The nature of the slow-motion chase meant *Columbia* had to avoid passive detection by the Kilo, yet give herself the best chance of

385

catching the approaching Taiwanese submarine. Jerry Curran's crafty kit was yet another of his trump cards.

Just as the daylight began to fade up on the surface, Bobby Ramsden called urgently from the main screen. It was 2148.

'Conn – sonar . . . I have something on the towed-array, sir. Just a faint mark on the trace . . .'

Columbia, for the second time in less than 24 hours, swung around, allowing the towed-array to reveal if the rise in level was to port or starboard. There were no surprises when Lt. Ramsden called again.

'Designated Track 27. Bearing zero-four-five. Probably engine lines . . . checking machinery profiles.'

There was total silence in the attack area, words being strictly unnecessary among these ultimate professionals, except from the sonar operator, whose fingers now flew over the computer keys.

'Conn – sonar . . . looks like the Dutch example we were given. No other profiles come anywhere near it.'

The atmosphere in *Columbia* moved from tense anticipation to careful, watchful determination. Not a phrase was uttered. In the time-honored mode of submarine warfare no one said anything, unless it was critical, like 'SHOOT.'

But *Columbia* was not authorized to shoot anything, and for more than an hour they watched silently as the *Hai Lung* moved closer, running through the water at 7 knots, snorkeling in the southern dark. She passed them 8,000 yards distant, and Lt. Commander Curran confirmed he had just hit the Kilo on active with a shrimp-fart and that they were in position to track and follow both the Kilo and the *Hai Lung*.

At 2305, Captain Kan began to speed up. He accelerated in behind the Taiwanese, some two miles astern, unaware that five miles off his own stern there was a US nuclear boat watching his every move. Only Boomer Dunning and his team were aware of the existence of all three submarines. The Taiwanese knew of only one, themselves. The Chinese knew of two.

But now the three were in some kind of manic strung-out convoy, and the leader, the *Hai Lung*, held course two-two-five, southwest, still making 7 knots, snorkeling. She was heading direct for Choiseul Bay. So were her pursuers. And they would run through these dark, turbulent seas throughout the night, with

Lt. Commander Curran occasionally pinging them with his fish-disguised active sonar. Just to keep their distance.

In the early evening, they crossed the wide, rough seaway at the head of the Gulf of Baleiniers and headed due west in 300 feet of water towards Choiseul. The *Hai Lung* was taking a more southern route towards Cox's Rock, but then the Taiwanese Captain was much more acquainted with the territory than either Captain Kan or Boomer Dunning. It was the precise direction of the periscope he and Bill Baldridge had spotted from the deck of *Yonder* back in February.

Now running at periscope depth, in the calmer water, the Taiwanese submarine crossed Choiseul Bay, and finally reached the estuary of Baie Blanche, with the Chinese Kilo still two miles astern.

Boomer too had closed in to three miles, inside the curved land-surrounded Kerguelen coastline. And the CO found himself thinking about the first time he had ever come here. And he thought too about his crew-mates on *Yonder*, and the fun they had all had in May when the droll Kansan rancher had married his Laura at last, in the presence of the President of the United States.

For no apparent reason he wished profoundly that Bill was here now, because he felt suddenly chilled, and alone, and he needed a friend, not a dozen colleagues. But he had only fleeting seconds for reflection. The *Hai Lung*, making 5 knots through the wide bay, was disappearing down Baie Blanche, chased by a boatload of malicious Chinese. At least Boomer thought they were malicious.

Boomer ordered *Columbia* to press on, to keep following the Kilo, now at a range of about two miles. None of the passive sonar worked very well inshore, but pursuit was simple, thanks to their brilliant active sonar.

He slotted in behind, and the *Hai Lung* continued its carefree journey at the head of the convoy, still making 5 knots, presumably carrying Professor Liao Lee all the way down Baie Blanche. It ran on for 10 miles, oblivious both of the Kilo and of the American nuclear boat which tracked the two of them. Boomer took one look through the periscope on the gentle left-hand bend at Saint Lanne, and was not spotted by the Taiwanese lookout post, up on the heights of Pointe Bras, which guards the entrance to Baie du Repos.

The *Hai Lung* was holding a course to the right-hand side of the mile-wide deep-water channel, and Boomer was not surprised when the Kilo headed resolutely after her, down the Baie du Repos. He took another fast look through the periscope, as he came under Pointe Bras, and again the Taiwanese lookouts were unable to spot him . . . as they had spotted *Cuttyhunk*.

Eight miles down the ever-narrowing dead-end fjord, with a freezing south wind whipping the snow off the peak of Mount Richards and pawing the water out in front of *Columbia*, the *Hai Lung* suddenly stopped snorkeling and went silent. Boomer cursed under his breath, and raised the periscope, just as the Taiwanese *Sea Tiger* burst out of the water, now only three miles distant, and continued her journey on the surface.

The Kilo appeared to stop but remained dived at the entrance to the last narrow three-mile section of the fjord. Boomer stayed two miles north of the Kilo, but he could still see right down the length of the channel.

He decided to risk another furtive look, always aware he might just be observed. And out in front he could actually see the *Hai Lung* heading off to the right. He could also see two old rusting gray buoys, spaced about 400 feet apart off the rocky western lee shore. And the sonar chief was reporting the unmistakable signature of a pressurized water reactor at power . . . and it was echoing down the fjord.

He guessed it was coming from right between the two buoys, moored to which, under the water, there *had* to be a nuclear submarine. Certainly nonoperational as a warship, but nevertheless doing a pretty good job.

'That's their power source,' muttered the Commander. 'Where's the goddamned factory, or whatever it is?' And then he could see in the distance the *Hai Lung* slowing almost to a complete stop, drifting in toward the shore. From where Boomer watched, it looked like a potential collision with the cliff. But very slowly, and without any sign of panic, the submarine just vanished, slipping behind what Boomer realized must be some kind of overhang, or steel curtain. He stared at the high granite cliffs which lined the shore, and called out for a depth check.

'*Three hundred and sixty feet, sir.*'

'That's what we came for, guys,' said Commander Dunning. 'Right over there, right-hand bank . . . one mile on the chart from the end of Baie du Repos.' Boomer pronounced it to rhyme with 'rip-off.' 'Good job. Let's get the hell outta here, real careful, real slow and back the way we came to Choiseul.'

Columbia headed once more for the big bay at the head of the Kerguelen fjords, leaving the Kilo to do its worst. It was 1915 and still fairly bright, but windy along the surface of the water as they approached the mouth of Baie Blanche. Boomer proposed to hold here for an hour, and then head out into clear seas, to access the satellite and send an immediate signal to SUBLANT that he had located the Taiwanese factory, at 49.65N, 69.20E, at the far end of the Baie du Repos. He proposed also to inform headquarters that he had observed the *Hai Lung* docking right there, and that the facility was being powered by a nuclear reactor moored out in the bay. Furthermore there was a Russian-built Granay-Type Kilo patrolling in nearly 400 feet of water close to the factory.

Boomer put *Columbia* into a holding pattern, and assessed that, once in position, it would take the Chinese boat about five minutes to accomplish its plain and obvious task.

As educated guesses go, that one was not bad. At 1955, Columbia's sonar room picked up a succession of almighty explosions as the Kilo sent in a barrage of torpedoes, splitting asunder the rock in which the Taiwanese factory was built, obliterating the facility, the *Hai Lung* and the still-active French nuclear-powered Rubis-Class submarine in a 10-minute underwater bombardment.

What the American sonar men could not know was that the Kilo had surfaced immediately afterwards, and fired six successive SA-N-8 SAM missiles from the launcher at the top of the fin. From point-blank range. Straight through the steel curtain which had obscured the factory for so long. All of the weapons and launchers had been provided by the Russians.

On board *Columbia* the sonar operators were incredulous at the length of time the Chinese Captain spent blasting away at the cliff. The Americans would have required no more than a minute. But Captain Kan was not just a driven man – he was a fanatic, with a psychopathic edge to his mind. He enjoyed killing, and the instinct had been suppressed for too long.

Now, with every thundering explosion, he struck a blow on behalf of his late mentor Madame Mao, and of his Commander-in-Chief, against the traitorous Taiwanese and their American allies. Every hit was one back for the Kilos the Chinese had lost. Every echo was an echo from the rising military dragon of the People's

389

Liberation Army–Navy. Kan smiled the uneasy, slightly crazed smile of the psychotic as his missiles wiped out every last possibility of life in Taiwan's secret nuclear plant.

'Shit,' growled Boomer Dunning. 'These crazy bastards really mean it. Guess that's *sayonara* Taiwan . . . back to the drawing board, right?'

'What now, sir?' asked Lt. Commander Krause. 'You wanna head back to open water, update the signal to SUBLANT? I got a draft right here. We sure found what they were looking for.'

'Yes, Mike . . . now I want to get out of these enclosed waters because, if I'm not mistaken, the Kilo is going to be coming right out of here in less than a couple of hours. Don't wanna get caught with our shorts down. Specially in the mood that fucking Chinaman's in!'

Columbia turned away, below the surface of the calm, now dark waters. There was moonlight again tonight and through the periscope Boomer could see the shape of Pointe Pringle and Cap Féron, with the huge black granite cliffs between them. They increased speed to 8 knots and Boomer ordered the watch officer to make a holding point between Îles Leygues and Cap D'Estaing.

It had been a long day for the crew and especially the officers, few of whom had enjoyed much of a break since the late *Hai Lung* first came sneaking into range the previous evening.

But Boomer did not feel sociable. He delayed sending his signal, and sat alone in his cabin and sipped coffee, and wished to hell his Kansan buddy Bill had been there. He just felt once more that he would have liked a chat with a friend. But that was not a luxury to which he had access. Instead he took out the signal sent to him by the CNO, and he stared again at the coded zinger from the NSA. 'Well, I sure know what he thinks of me right now,' he muttered.

The clock ticked on. At 2140 he was still pondering the draft signal to SUBLANT. *Columbia* ran her familiar slow racetrack pattern, awaiting a decision from the Commanding Officer.

At 2200, Boomer was back in the control center, just as the sonar operator picked up the Kilo, running due north now, at 8 knots, snorkeling away from the scene of its crime, bound for the nearest open water, and eventually Canton.

'Captain – Conn . . . Kilo bears one-eight-zero, sir. Gotta be heading toward . . . range six miles. She snorkels now, sir. Good contact on ghoster. I'm opening off-track to the northwest. Track 28.'

'Captain, aye.'

Boomer ran his hands through his hair, and returned briefly to his cabin. Four minutes later he went back to the control center. He hesitated for a few seconds.

Then he took his entire career in his hands and snapped: '*I intend to sink the Kilo as soon as she's clear of the shoal water. Estimate one hour. Ready one and two tubes . . . 48 ADCAP.*'

Lt. Commander Curran, the combat systems officer, never blinked, and he strode back into the sonar room.

Deep in the ship the torpedomen now prepared two weapons, as ordered.

Fifteen minutes went by and the sonar room called: '*Track 28 bearing one-seven-eight, sir. Range six miles.*'

Down in the torpedo bay, weapons were now loaded into both number one and number two tubes, in case of a malfunction. The guidance officer was at the screen murmuring into his pencil-slim microphone, and Jerry Curran watched the sonar, with Bobby Ramsden and the Chief. It seemed everyone was on duty right now. Lt. Commander Krause had the Conn, as the CO concentrated on the task which might very well see him court-martialed.

The time inched by, and the black hull of the Chinese Kilo pressed on through the water, running south of the American nuclear trouble-shooter. The *Columbia* sonar team checked her approach, calling out the details, softly now, in the high-tension calm that grips a submarine before an attack.

Boomer Dunning glanced again at the screen, then he ordered: '*STAND BY ONE . . . Stand by to fire by sonar.*'

'*Bearing one-two-zero . . . range 5,000 yards . . . computer set.*'

'*SHOOT!*' ordered Commander Dunning, and everyone in the area heard the thud as the heavyweight Mk 48 swept away. The faintest shiver ran through the submarine as the torpedo set off.

'Weapon under guidance, sir.'

Boomer Dunning ordered the weapon armed, and another minute passed. The only sounds were the occasional quiet order, or comment, and *Columbia* seemed to hold her breath. There was just the hum of the air in the ventilation, and outside the hull the only sound was at the approximate level of a computer or word processor.

Fifteen hundred yards away the Mk 48 was searching passively as it ran fast through the water at 30 knots.

Now, eight minutes after firing, the torpedo picked up the Kilo and switched to active homing, as it was released by *Columbia*. The Mk 48 accelerated, and came ripping through the water straight at Captain Kan's submarine. Kan was an experienced commanding officer, but his ship was full of elation, the crew's guard was temporarily down, and he himself was still giggling nervously at what he had done. Some of his officers were concerned at his demeanor; he and they were in no way prepared for an attack. K–10 was at periscope depth and the Mk 48 was only 300 yards away when a cry came out of the sonar room: *'TORPEDO... TORPEDO... TORPEDO... RED ONE SEVEN FIVE... ACTIVE TRANSMISSIONS... INTERVAL 500 YARDS... BEARING STEADY...'*

Too close and too late. The pressure hull of the Kilo split as the big American torpedo blasted its way into her port quarter. The Kilo-Class was known to be able to absorb a pretty good hit, but not one from a weapon like this. Boomer Dunning's wickedly aimed Mk 48 blew a gaping six-foot hole in K-10 at exactly 1921 on the evening of November 18. Captain Kan died still grinning at his own brilliant malevolence. There were no survivors and no direct witnesses. No one aboard lived longer than 30 seconds after impact.

The entire crew were either drowned or slammed to pieces against machinery by the onrushing water, which roared through the compartments, crushing bulkheads one by one as the vessel went down. The submarine, upon which the far-distant Admiral Zhang Yushu had staked so much, sank slowly to the floor of the southern Indian Ocean, in 2,000 feet of freezing water. No one would ever quite know where she rested. Or indeed what had happened to her. Though there would be those in Moscow and Beijing who might make educated guesses.

A half-hour later, Commander Dunning sat down to write his signal yet again. He kept it short: *'Russian-built Kilo arrived Kerguelen 172224NOV. Hai Lung arrived 182148NOV. Believe Kilo destroyed Taiwan factory we located 49.65N, 69.20E one mile from dead-end Baie du Repos. In accordance with my original orders, issued 011200AUG04, I sank K-10 at 2221 on 19 Nov, off northern Kerguelen – Commander Cale Dunning, USS Columbia.'*

It was 1350 in SUBLANT when Boomer's signal arrived. Admirals Mulligan and Dixon were in a meeting awaiting news from Kerguelen. And they contacted Arnold Morgan immediately, requesting assistance in drafting the response.

Columbia's Commanding Officer read the reply at 2315 local: '*Not a bad shot . . . for a D-A SOB. Morgan.*'

The message was addressed to him, direct from the office of the President's National Security Advisor in the White House. It contained the one phrase Boomer thought was lost to him forever: '*Personal to Captain Cale Dunning, Commanding Officer USS Columbia.*'

EPILOGUE

Front page lead story, *Cape Cod Times*, November 25, 2004:

Port-aux-Français, Kerguelen. November 24. The mystery of the vanished Woods Hole research ship, *Cuttyhunk*, was finally cleared up here last night when six of the missing scientists were rescued by meteorologists at this remote French weather station.

The group, attempting to walk across the 90-mile-long Antarctic island, were picked up by helicopter on the shore of the Baie de la Marne, after their radio transmissions were received by one of the station's 14 electronic masts.

They had been missing for 23 months, and are believed to be the only survivors of the 29-strong expedition, which is thought to have come under attack on December 17, 2002, at the entrance to one of the island's northwestern fjords.

Last night none of the group was prepared to give an interview, save to confirm that *Cuttyhunk* is still floating, damaged by gunfire but moored in deep water in a sheltered cove at the end of the Baie du Repos at the northern end of the island. One of them stated the research ship had been their prison.

Staff at the weather station last night confirmed the names of the six scientists: Professor Henry Townsend, Dr Roger Deakins, Arnold Barry, William Coburg, Anne Dempster, and Dr Kate Goodwin.

Tonight, the *Times*' syndicated columnist Frederick J. Goodwin, a cousin of one of the rescued scientists, is flying to the US base at Diego Garcia in the Indian Ocean, to join a Navy frigate going south to evacuate the group from the almost inaccessible island. Mr Goodwin, who has campaigned for many months to instigate a further search on Kerguelen, has been granted exclusive rights to talk to the scientists.

Their amazing story will be transmitted from the frigate to the *Cape Cod Times* and will begin in these pages next week.

AFTERWORD

By Admiral Sir John Woodward

Kilo Class is Patrick Robinson's second novel and once more I acted as his technical advisor on navy matters. As with *Nimitz Class*, I was operating on the inner edges of an imaginative plot, which contained a core of valid reality.

The events which unfold in this book may at first seem difficult to understand. By that, I mean why should the United States have taken such extreme action against the Russians, and the Chinese, merely to prevent the delivery of seven submarines?

At first sight, it might seem reckless overreaction. But upon close examination, it becomes less violent, more logical. China *has* ordered this small fleet of Kilo-Class submarines, brand new, directly from the Russians. It is plain enough what they want them for – primarily to block the Taiwan Strait, to deny the customary rights of passage through an international strait. The issue is simple: China believes the Strait is NOT international, that Taiwan is nothing but an offshore part of China. Therefore the waters which separate them are purely Chinese.

The Pentagon is well aware that ten Kilo-Class submarines would permit the Chinese to keep at least four on patrol continously. And the United States, which has occasionally passed carrier battle groups through the Strait, particularly when China has been seen to make threatening moves in the area, would be extremely wary of this. In my view, no US CVBG would venture into the Strait, in the clear face of a submarine threat, merely to make a political point. Just in case a big carrier should meet a similar fate to that of the *Thomas Jefferson*.

There is a xenophobia about China, and its rulers. They have a large but ill-equipped Navy, essentially a coastal Navy, which operates almost exclusively in the waters off the extensive Eastern shoreline, almost from the Inner Mongolian border to the South China Sea. But China's ambitions are no secret. They seek wealth and status, power and equality with the West. And they seek to end Taiwan's present independence and return it to Greater China.

It ought not to be forgotten that when Chiang Kai-shek left the mainland for Taiwan, he dispatched 14 trainloads of magnificent artefacts and historic documents containing almost the entire dynastic heritage of China. Which is, broadly, why the great museum in Taipei is reputed to be the finest in the world.

Chinese determination to bring Taiwain back into the fold ought not to be underestimated. The order for the Kilos was, in my view, one of the first significant moves towards one of their ultimate goals.

First, they would close the Strait to international passage. Then, as the submarine force built up in size, experience, confidence and reputation, extend their patrol areas further offshore, at once threatening the approaches to the island of Taiwan.

These patrol areas would ultimately extend up to 500 miles offshore, wherever shallower waters favored the Kilos. Such a presence would greatly restrict US naval protection for the Taiwanese, for whom an unavoidable sense of isolation would set in. Remember, submarines are best at sinking surface ships; the lesson of the *Thomas Jefferson* ought not to be ignored. The Kilo that nailed her, did not stalk the carrier. It was just lying in wait, hardly moving, virtually silent, an explosive hole in the water.

With just four of these little Russian diesels on continuous patrol, China could swiftly show the Taiwan Strait no longer offered safe passage, in international waters. The Strait would actually become a no-go area. And clearing them out would be a long and very costly military operation, even if political considerations allowed it. With a few more Kilos in place, Taiwan's days as an independent nation could be numbered.

The United States has enormous financial interests in the island, which has, in the last 30 years, turned itself into one of the world's major trading centers. I believe the United States would take very strongly against any threat to that trade. In *Kilo Class*, the United States is prepared to do just that. And I doubt Patrick Robinson and I are all that wide of the mark.

Once on patrol, the Kilo is the devil's own job to find and kill, even with the amazing air, surface and sub-surface assets of the US Navy. Simple logic will dictate that the Kilos are better caught and destroyed when they are far from home, before they are operationally ready, before they can be delivered. Russia is presently refusing even to discuss putting a ban on the sale of major warships to China, or anywhere else for that matter. In the winter of 1997, they delivered a third Kilo to Iran, under a Russian flag, escorted by a Russian warship, as accurately forecast in *Nimitz Class*.

I also noticed that on page 94 of the 1997–98 edition of *Jane's Fighting Ships*, the bible of the world's navies, the Russians are actually running a two-page color spread advertizing their top export warship – beneath the headline: '*KILO-CLASS SUBMARINE* – the only soundless creature in the sea.' They then provide the St Petersburg address, phone, fax and E-mail for RUBIN, their central design bureau for marine engineering.

The West must give serious thought to this new aggressive marketing of the updated version of the old Soviet diesel-electric boat, and also to the new relationship between China and Russia. Because the men from Beijing are already Moscow's biggest customers for new-build submarines.

I believe that *Kilo Class* is uncomfortably close to reality in its assessment of the intentions of all three of the big players. China wants Taiwan. Russia is desperate for cash and will sell a Kilo-Class boat to anyone with $300 million. The US cannot tolerate a serious threat to the continued independence of Taiwan. Speculation as to who will do what, is the theme of this book.

Patrick has turned that theme into another page-turning thriller. The book is wracked with tension, and punctuated by spectacular adventures, as Admiral Morgan's men go to work in a variety of deep lonely waters. Far up in the North Atlantic, under the polar ice-cap, off the frozen coastline of Siberia, even in the great lakes of central Russia north of the Volga. And, finally, around the frozen, barren island of Kerguelen, a place so remote, so rarely visited, it might not be inaccurate to describe it as the end of the world.

If you enjoyed *Nimitz Class*, I believe you will love this book. Patrick Robinson, who helped me turn my own biography into a bestseller, has again written of complex matters in an easy, compelling style which can be understood by anyone . . . and should be read by everyone.

Sandy Woodward, 1997